P9-DDU-870

WHEN SHADOWS FALL

Also by New York Times *bestselling author*
J.T. Ellison

EDGE OF BLACK
A DEEPER DARKNESS
WHERE ALL THE DEAD LIE
SO CLOSE THE HAND OF DEATH
THE IMMORTALS
THE COLD ROOM
JUDAS KISS
14
ALL THE PRETTY GIRLS

Look for J.T. Ellison's next novel
available soon from Harlequin MIRA

WHEN SHADOWS FALL

J.T. ELLISON

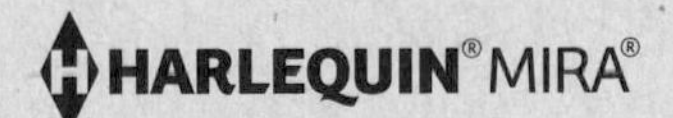

Recycling programs for this product may not exist in your area.

ISBN-13: 978-0-7783-1604-6

WHEN SHADOWS FALL

For questions and comments about the quality of this book please contact us at CustomerService@Harlequin.com

Printed in U.S.A.

First printing: March 2014
10 9 8 7 6 5 4 3 2 1

For my mom, who asked every day if the words were any good.

And for my dad, who assured me they were.

And, as always, for Randy

PROLOGUE

SOMEONE IS FOLLOWING ME.

I hear the footsteps coming closer, quiet on the thick, wet leaves of the forest floor. I duck behind a white pine tree, then realize it's big enough to hold my weight and scramble upward, hands pulling me into the branches, where I cling to the trunk like a monkey, praying they haven't seen me. The steps stop, but the forest isn't tricked; the birds are silent as the grave, the squirrels frozen in their perches. They know evil has come to their world.

My breath is too loud; sweat is prickling on my brow. I see the blood then, on my hands—his blood—and swallow hard against the sudden spike of nausea.

He is gone. He is gone, and now I am alone.

Tears drip down my face, fall off my chin. I swipe my jaw against my shoulder so they don't splatter onto the leaves below and draw attention to my hiding place.

A starling bursts from the brush fifteen feet to my left, and startles me. I nearly fall out of the tree but hang on. Even my fingers know the danger of letting go.

This dance, inextricably tying us together, is entering its final moments.

They have come for me. I will not let them take me alive.

FRIDAY

"A human being is only breath and shadow."
—Sophocles

"You are a human being, and so you must honor thy mother; she is the life of all things, the soul of your breath, your stars, your moon, the bringer of air, the guide of the tides. I am your mother, your breath, your sight and your feelings. Honor not me, but what I can be for you."
—Curtis Lott

CHAPTER 1

Georgetown University School of Medicine
Washington, D.C.

DR. SAMANTHA OWENS STARED OUT THE WINDOW OF HER OFFICE, ADMIRING THE view she'd be enjoying for the next several years. Trees. Lots and lots of trees. The Georgetown University campus was landscaped to perfection, bringing the joys of wildlife and green space to their urban oasis. Maples and willow oaks, zelkovas and ginkgo, viburnum and holly, and more she had no names for. In truth, this deep into the warm, wet D.C. summer, everything was so green it made her eyes hurt. It was all so bloody alive.

And so different from her anonymous, stainless-steel office in Nashville. A welcome change. A change she'd openly pursued, sure to the core she no longer wanted to work in law enforcement. The idea of keeping herself separate from the hurt and fear and messiness of the real world appealed to her.

Her new reality: she was the head of the bourgeoning forensic pathology department at Georgetown University Medical School. Her first classes would start the following week, though students were already on campus doing their orientations. And now that she was here, the sense of adventure and excitement were gone.

Looking out at the tree-lined campus, she couldn't help wondering, yet again, if she'd made a mistake. The freedom she'd hoped for, planned on, felt like a noose around her neck. Even though she was calling the shots, she was increasingly feeling trapped. So many people were counting on her. She'd developed the forensic program, made a commitment to the university, even signed a contract. She was stuck.

No longer a medical examiner, no longer a part of organized law enforcement. She was a teacher, with two class sections of doctors who wanted to help solve crimes. Students who seemed so young, teenagers, almost, though many were in their twenties, and even thirties. Untouched by tragedy; unknowing of the world's painful embrace.

They'd learn soon enough, especially with her at the helm. She'd seen more than most in her career, especially during her tenure as the Chief Medical Examiner for the State of Tennessee. Her job was to teach them everything she knew so they could stride out into the world in pursuit of justice.

The way she used to do.

Sam turned from the window to her desk, a thick slab of oak polished to a high gleam, and casually straightened the stack of papers in her out-box. Her OCD was under strict rein, especially in front of all these new people, but there was no need for things to be messy.

She should be eager for this new life to begin. She honestly had been, until a few weeks ago, when her friend John Baldwin, from the FBI's Behavioral Analysis Unit, sat her down and threw a bomb into her world. Sent her spinning, unsure of all the choices she'd made over the past few months.

He'd come to town for a case two weeks earlier, taken her

out for lunch and, before the food arrived, got straight to business.

"I wish you'd talked to me before you made this drastic change."

"It's the best thing for me. I don't want to be out there anymore, Baldwin. I paid my dues, with more than I care to remember."

"Which is why I'm here. We want you to join the FBI."

She choked on the water the server had set down. "Excuse me?"

"You heard me. We need your mind."

She laughed. "I'm a medical examiner, Baldwin, or I was. Not a field agent. For starters, I hate guns."

"I know. That's not a problem. You'd be an official consultant, mostly with me and my team, but with other parts of the Bureau, too, depending on the cases. You'd need to go through some training at the Academy in Quantico, to make it all official, but you'll be able to work on cases again. Sam, you can't tell me you don't miss it."

"I don't. Not at all."

"You're lying to yourself."

Watching the students wander the campus, Sam wondered if he was right. Did she belong here? Innocent faces glued to smartphones, earbuds firmly embedded in ears, an insouciant walk; these kids didn't seem to have a care in the world. What if she wasn't cool enough for them?

"Right. There's the thing to worry about. Being cool."

She settled at the desk and opened her laptop. Debated putting in her own earbuds; decided she was being silly. She knew her lesson plan cold, but giving it one more look wouldn't hurt; she hated using notes. Regardless of the doubt she was feeling, she was here to engage these young doctors, intrigue them, but also allow them a glimpse into the real world of forensic pathology. Not the exciting, tumultuous world they saw on television, but the bloody, messy, heart-wrenching process of dissection, both of bodies and of lives. To show them the hardest truth of all: the dead have no secrets.

But the living do.

Forget the notes. Maybe she'd just read for a bit, settle into her office. Adjust to the sights and sounds of her new life.

She was deep into an article on forensic ballistics when a soft knock pulled her from her review. She looked up to see Xander in her doorway, a grin on his face.

"Hey," he said.

Her stomach flipped, as it always did when he caught her unawares. A biological response to an emotion none truly understood. An emotion she was grateful for, because she knew the depth of it had saved her from sinking into the deepest abyss.

Alexander Whitfield. Known to his parents and family as Moonbeam, or Xander Moon. A true misnomer for a tough former army ranger. And Xander was still a ranger through and through: intense, alert, always combing the background for unseen threats. Romantic, and a fatalist. Just like her.

He was a different man now than the one she'd met several months before. More open, more forgiving. Happier. They'd settled into a version of domestic bliss, splitting their time between her Georgetown town house and his cabin in the backwoods of the Savage River Forest.

He'd separated from the army the previous year after the terrible cover-up of a friendly fire incident that had killed one of his best friends. He'd run to the woods, disengaged from the world and would have stayed there, lost and alone, if it weren't for Sam. Two broken souls, made whole by their joining.

Xander wasn't fully ready to reenter the world, but he was coming back, a bit at a time. Though he'd done his best to hide it, she knew he was happy she had turned down Baldwin's job offer.

"Hey," she said. "What are you doing here?"

"I thought I'd bring you lunch. I know how you can lose yourself in your work. What is it today? Blood spatter?"

"It's eerie how you do that." She turned the laptop around

and showed him the article. "I was just starting the section on backspatter."

He didn't pale, but his lips tightened together in a grim line. He'd spent most of his life behind the trigger; he was more than familiar with the concept.

Sam glanced at the screen, saw the full-color image of a man at the wrong end of a shotgun and slammed the laptop closed. "Sorry. What's this about lunch?"

Xander's dark hair flopped onto his forehead. "You're not one of those M.E.s who can eat a tuna sandwich standing over a corpse, are you?"

"Highly unethical behavior, tuna eating. I'd stick with cookies or crackers myself. The crumbs are easier to brush away."

He laughed, deep from his belly, which made her smile. She loved his laugh.

"I wouldn't kick you out of bed for eating crackers." He glanced over his shoulder at the open office door. "Maybe we should inaugurate your office."

He kissed her, long and lingering, and she was damn close to saying *lock the door* when another knock sounded, this one accompanied by a high-pitched throat clearing. They jumped apart like teenagers caught making out on a porch, and Sam smoothed her shirt down—good grief, one of her buttons was undone; how had he managed that?—before turning to see who'd so rudely interrupted them.

It was one of her new T.A.s, Stephanie Wilhelm, a slight blonde with a sharp sense of humor to match her highly unorthodox look—today a black Metallica concert T-shirt under a black men's pin-striped jacket and dark jeans tucked into leather combat boots. Sam liked the girl. Her independence among the clones had landed her the coveted T.A. position in the first place.

"Forgive me, Dr. Owens, but this letter arrived for you. It's marked urgent. I thought I should bring it to you right away."

Her words were directed to Sam, but her eyes were locked on Xander, who was sitting on the edge of Sam's desk, arms crossed on his broad chest, vibrating in amusement as he watched her fumble with her button.

"Thank you, Stephanie. I appreciate it."

"If you need anything else…" She dropped off, winked lasciviously.

"Out," Sam said, and Stephanie left with a grin.

"I'm hot for teacher," Xander said, and Sam swatted him with the letter.

"Quit it. The last thing I need is a reputation for looseness among my students." She sat on the desk next to him and opened the letter. Thick strokes of black ink, the words slanted to the right. A man's handwriting.

She read the first line, felt the breath leave her body. "Uh-oh."

Xander caught her tone. "What's wrong?"

She scanned the rest of the letter. "You need to hear this." She read it aloud, vaguely noticed her voice was shaking.

"Dear Dr. Owens,
If you are reading this letter, I am dead. I would be most grateful if you would solve my murder. I know how determined you are, and talented. If anyone can figure out this mess, it's you.

I've compiled a list of suspects for you to look at, and set aside some money to cover your expenses. I fear your life may be in danger once they find I've contacted you, so I urge you to take every precaution.
Yours,
Timothy R. Savage"

"Let me see that." Xander took the letter from her, barely touching the corner between his thumb and forefinger. Sam watched his face as he read it, saw the darkness draw over him like a shroud.

"Who the hell is Timothy Savage?"

"I have no idea. But it's a pretty sick joke. Who would do such a thing?"

"I don't know. John Baldwin, maybe? Trying to draw you into a case against your will?"

She opened her mouth to deny the possibility, but stopped herself. She'd known Baldwin for many years. He was engaged to her best friend. He was a good man, a no-nonsense cop in addition to being a talented profiler. He wouldn't resort to manipulation. Would he?

"No. It's not him."

Xander shrugged. "Where's the envelope?"

In her surprise, she'd dropped it on the floor. She pulled a tissue from the box on her desk and picked it up, careful not to directly touch any part of it. Ridiculous, she'd already gotten her prints all over it, so had Stephanie and countless others, but she had to treat it as evidence now.

"Return address is Lynchburg, Virginia," she said. "Let me plug it into my laptop, see if it's real."

He read the information to her, and she entered it into Google. The name Timothy Savage popped up, along with a map of his address, and a death notice from the local Lynchburg paper.

"Oh, no. Xander, Timothy Savage really is dead."

Xander breathed hard out his nose. "Then Sam, honey, you better call Fletcher. This might not be a joke, after all."

CHAPTER 2

Kenilworth Aquatic Gardens
Anacostia
Washington, D.C.

D.C. HOMICIDE DETECTIVE DARREN FLETCHER WAS KNEE-DEEP IN MARSH WATER, standing over the body of a male Caucasian, approximately twenty to twenty-four years of age, who didn't appear to have a mark on him. But he was dead, without a doubt, staked to a small canoe dock ten feet offshore, bobbing in the gentle tidal flow of the Anacostia River. Fletcher stared at the boy—he really was too young to be called anything else—and thought of his own son, only a few years younger, and promised to be a better father. He'd lost count of how many times he'd stood over deceased young men and made the same fervent prayer.

He slapped at a mosquito, brought his hand away from his neck with a smear of blood on his palm.

Murder. It came in all forms.

But this, who would kill a man this way? Tying him to a

stake in a river, leaving him to drown? Had the killer watched as the tide slowly rose, waiting to see the results of his handiwork? Watched the terror of his victim, the dawning knowledge that death was coming for him? The boy's eyes were open, caked in mud, as if he'd looked at someone in his last moment. The water had spilled over his head, then receded, leaving its filthy, choking mark.

Fletcher shook off a chill, glanced around for cameras and saw none.

Lonnie Hart, his longtime partner, came down the path to the water. He gave a sharp, clear whistle.

Fletcher's head snapped up. "What's the matter?"

Lonnie waved for him to come back onto dry land. He headed off, not unhappy to have to get out of the marshy water. It smelled, fecund and ripe, and the body's bloated rawness wasn't helping.

When he got closer, Hart said, "We're in luck. Another five feet out and it would belong to us, but you're standing on federal land. I called the Fibbies, told them to get their pretty little behinds over here. National park, it's their jurisdiction. We'll let them take over."

"Thank God for small mercies, eh, Lonnie?" And to the body: "Sorry, dude. Red ties are coming. They'll treat you right."

He squished up the bank, climbed out of the muck. Hart stuck out a hand and helped tow him onto the small wooden dock. Once on dry land, he shook like a dog, spraying droplets of water on Hart, who punched him on the shoulder and nearly toppled him back into the river.

"Ugh. Come on, man. That's gross."

Fletcher grinned at him, then stripped off his socks and wadded them up, stowed them in the pocket of his gym shorts and slid his dry loafers back on his feet. It was a stroke of luck his gym bag was still in the car, sheer laziness on his part not taking it into the house after his workout last night. He hardly wanted to ruin his good pants getting into the nasty water.

"Not sure if I'm happy about this being a Fed case. Haven't seen one of the strange ones lately. I could have used a challenge."

"Fletch, you've seen enough weird for two lifetimes."

"True that."

He cast a last look toward the boy, shrugged and started back up the hill into the park. There were two patrol officers guarding the scene, both sweating in the steamy August heat, plus several others milling about, waiting for Fletcher and Hart to tell them what was what. It might rain this afternoon, a welcome storm to cool things off for the evening, but now the air was still, hot and sticky, and Fletch was thankful he wasn't in uniform.

Hart grabbed the logbook and signed out of the scene. Fletcher followed suit, then said, "Heads up, kids. The Feds will be coming. Once they're here, you can release the scene to them."

The patrols nodded miserably, the lights from their patrol cars flashing red-and-blue streaks across their faces.

He ignored the rest of the masses, went to his car and stripped off his gym shorts. Splashed some warm water from a bottle in his console across his skin and wiped his legs down with a dirty towel. Got back into his lightweight summer slacks. He debated about the shorts, just trashing them, but ended up wringing them out and stowing them with the socks in the trunk of his vehicle.

Fletcher heard a woman calling his name, hurriedly buttoned his fly. No privacy left in the world, especially for a cop.

He turned and saw Lisa Schumann, a crime reporter from *The Washington Post* who was too pretty for her own good, and not afraid to use that to her advantage, making a beeline across the gardens toward him, determined as a bull facing a red cape.

He stifled a groan. Hart took one look at her and peeled off, back toward the patrols.

"Ass," Fletcher said after him, then squared his shoulders to meet Schumann, who looked as fresh and frisky as ever despite the heat. He didn't know how she managed; all of his people looked like puddles.

"Detective Fletcher, can I get a statement?"

Fletch shook his head. "You'll have to talk to the Feds, Schumann. This one's not ours."

Her eyes were practically glowing. "Come on. Give me a little something. I won't attribute it."

"Yeah. Nice try."

"Fletcher." Her voice dropped an octave, and she shifted so he could see she wasn't wearing a bra under her white button-down. She licked her lips and cocked her head to the side like a puppy. "I heard it was gruesome. If you'd just let me get a peek, I could be convinced to let you buy me dinner."

He resisted pulling his best Scottish accent and saying, *Keep looking at my crotch like that, you man-eater, and it will gruesome more,* and shrugged instead.

"Is it true that she's staked to the dock naked?"

"I don't know what you've heard, but the victim is male, and he is not staked to the dock naked. Sorry, but I've got to run. You take care."

"Oh." She actually sounded disappointed, and then her fervent grin returned. The audacity of youth and ambition. She flipped a page in her notebook and stared at him expectantly, her water-blue eyes locked on his. He could see the thoughts scrolling by on her face. Naughty thoughts. She was going to get herself in trouble one of these days, telegraphing like that.

"So, see ya," he said, and deliberately jangled his keys.

"Oh," she said again, this time truly surprised. She dropped the notebook to her waist. "Yeah. Call me if you hear anything, okay, Fletch? Thanks."

He watched her cross to the patrols, which sent Hart scurrying back to him. He didn't like Lisa Schumann at all, not after she'd attributed a deep background quote to Hart in the paper. Not smart. Never screw your sources. Hart wouldn't get within twenty feet of her now, and Fletch had to admit, he wasn't keen on giving the girl any information, either. He had plenty of reporters he could trust, and an oversexed coed with a byline wasn't one of them.

"Did you hear what she said?" Fletch asked.

"No, too busy humming the theme to *Jaws.* What's the scoop?"

"She flat-out propositioned me."

Hart's eyebrows rose. "Well, you're a handsome lad, and she's pretty, if you can get past the bubble gum. Why not? A weeklong course of penicillin would clear things up quick."

Fletcher snorted. "Penicillin and a million dollars. I wouldn't get near her with your—"

"Hey, now. Overtime for everyone."

"Ever the optimist."

Fletcher's cell phone rang. "That's Sam. Hang on a sec." He put the phone to his ear. "What up, buttercup?"

She laughed, and a tiny piece of him, the piece he'd shoved away into the darkest corners of his heart, constricted. He really liked that laugh, and liked to be the one who brought it forth. She laughed more and more lately; she was very different from the hard, closed-off woman he'd first met in the spring. She'd come back to life, it seemed, and Fletcher liked to think he had something to do with that.

"Heya," Sam said. "You got a minute?"

"You know me, I'm just standing around with my, um, twiddling my thumbs."

She laughed again, deeper this time. But he heard the strain in her voice; she was putting up a good front. He immediately went on alert. "What's the matter, Doc?"

"I received a letter from a man who claims to have been murdered. He wants me to look into his death."

"Creepy. You think it's for real, or someone pulling your chain?"

She sighed. "It may be real, Fletch. There's definitely a man with the same name who's recently dead. I found an obituary for him. Matches the return address on the envelope. Out of Lynchburg."

"Are you at home?"

"No, at my office in Georgetown. The letter came here."

"Good. If it had come to your house, we might be dealing with a nut job."

"We might be, anyway." Her voice was soft, the voice of a woman who shouldn't have to deal with these kinds of things.

Sam, you're gaining quite a reputation. He stopped himself from saying it aloud; she knew that, and didn't need to hear it from him.

"I'll be there in fifteen minutes. Hang tight."

"Thank you, Fletch."

He hung up and looked at Hart. "I'm gonna take a ride. I'll call Armstrong from the car, tell him what we found down here. Have fun with the Feds."

CHAPTER 3

Georgetown University School of Medicine
Washington, D.C.

SAM HUNG UP THE PHONE. "FLETCH IS ON HIS WAY," SHE SAID.

"Good," Xander said. "There's no sense in you becoming involved with this. Even though the letter was sent to you, this is a job for law enforcement. Shall we eat something before he comes? I did bring you a tuna sandwich."

A job for law enforcement. Which she most decidedly was not. She had to admit, the casual reference stung.

Stop it, Sam. You made your bed.

"Considering what seems to happen anytime Fletcher comes around? Yes, let's eat something now, in case he bundles me off to give an official statement and I never come back."

They settled in to their lunch. She took a bite of the sandwich, realized she wasn't hungry anymore. Her eyes drifted to the letter—she couldn't help herself. It was disconcerting to have a stranger say he knew her determination. Yes, she'd managed to land herself in the papers on more than one occasion, being quoted regarding a case, and recently, the whole incident with the Metro terrorist, but the familiar tone of Savage's missive freaked her out.

Not to mention the warning accompanying the request. *I fear your life may be in danger....*

Why her? Why did these bizarre situations keep finding her? Was it some sort of psychic retribution for getting on with her life? Karma, pissed off and wanting her pound of flesh?

You've already taken everything from me. What more do you need?

She glanced at Xander, who was staring out her windows with a look of private joy on his face. The view clearly pleased him; he loved anything to do with nature, the outdoors. She took advantage of his distraction to admire his dark eyes and dark hair, broad shoulders, capable hands. A man who could build a cabin with just an ax and his time, shoot a deer and skin it for dinner and love her in the darkness—she put down the sandwich and cleared her throat, suddenly both embarrassed and exceptionally turned on.

She loved the man. There was no question. He'd asked her to marry him, and she'd managed to put him off, citing the fact that he was under the painful influence of a gunshot wound and thought he might die.

But Xander wasn't a man who would wait for long. What he wanted, he got. And for some odd reason, he'd decided he wanted her. Problem was, just the idea of marriage, after what she'd been through, was enough to make her lace up her running shoes and take off for parts unknown. But this was Xander. He was different. Everything was different now.

Quick as a rabbit in the brush, he turned to her. "Are you eyeing me, or coveting my sandwich?"

She dropped her gaze and smiled. "Eyeing your sandwich, coveting you."

His voice was husky. "How late are you planning to work today?"

"I could be convinced to knock off early."

His eyes locked on hers, the sandwich forgotten. "What shall I do to convince you?"

A throat cleared. "Would you two get a room, already?"

Fletcher was standing in her doorway, half-exasperated and half-amused.

Sam got up and gave him a hug. "Hey, Fletch. Thanks for coming over."

"No worries. You saved me from a nasty crime scene. I left Hart there, waiting for the feds to show. What's this about a letter?"

Xander shook Fletcher's hand and handed him the letter. "Thanks for coming. Here it is."

Sam watched Fletcher read the letter, a couple of times if his eye movements were to be trusted, and when he finished, he set it gently on her desk as if it might explode.

"Weird, huh? Do you think it's for real?" she asked.

Fletcher frowned, making a deep groove between his eyebrows. "Threatening is more like it. Who the hell is this Savage character?"

"Here's the obituary, it was in the *Lynchburg News and Advance,* the local paper." She handed him a printed sheet of paper. "It's not comprehensive at all."

Fletcher read the obit aloud. "*Timothy R. Savage, 45, resident of Lynchburg, died Tuesday. A memorial service will be scheduled later in the month. In lieu of flowers, please direct donations to the Wounded Warrior Project, a cause near and dear to Timothy's heart.* You're right, there's not much to go on. It doesn't say how he died, either."

"We thought it best to let you handle this," Xander said.

Fletcher shot him a look. "Gee, thanks."

"Better you than me, friend. Or Sam."

Fletcher stared at him for a moment, eyes narrowed. "I'll take the letter to the lab. It's probably a hoax. I wouldn't worry about it."

"Not worry about it?" Sam said. "You're joking, right?"

Fletcher folded the letter and placed it back in the envelope. "Sam, you're going to get this kind of attention for a while. Your name was plastered all over the papers and the web after your stunt in Colorado, so of course, some crazies are going to come out of the woodwork. Let me look into it, and I'll let you know. Okay?"

She watched him for clues that there might be more going on here, something he might be hiding from her. Both Fletcher and Xander had a default overprotective mode toward her that could sometimes be stifling. But she didn't see any ripplings below the surface.

"Fine," she said finally. "You want to come over for dinner Friday?"

"What are you making?"

"Lasagna. Lots of it. Bring Andrea. We'll open some wine and catch up."

Fletch smiled. "Assuming my week isn't shot to hell, and she's actually in town, will do. I'll call you when I know something about this, all right? In the meantime, enjoy your new gig. I like the digs. Very professorial."

"You should see the classrooms."

"Yeah, think I'll pass. I can head down to the morgue any time of day for that particular brand of excitement."

Sam hugged him again. He nodded at Xander and left, and the tension left with him.

Sam waited until she was sure Fletch was out of earshot. "I wish you wouldn't poke at him, Xander."

He mocked surprise. "What? Me? I didn't do a thing."

She rolled her eyes. "Please. And now that he's back to D.C. Homicide and off the Joint Terrorism Task Force, he and Andrea Bianco have started dating. Sort of. I think they're a good match."

"Doesn't mean he won't be making eyes at you anymore."

"Quit grumbling. Fletcher does not make eyes at me, Xander. He's a friend. A good one. I don't have a lot of people I trust in my life—he's up there. Okay?"

He kissed her, softly, and ran his thumb across her lip. "Okay. Listen, I have to run. I'll see you back at the town house, okay? I thought we could head to the cabin early tomorrow morning, get some fresh air over the weekend, before classes start. Sound good?"

It did. Nestled in the Savage River Forest, his cabin was more than an escape. It was nirvana.

"Thor must be homesick," Sam said. The gorgeous German shepherd seemed content, but he was used to running the hills and chasing squirrels, something severely lacking from her renovated Georgetown town house where they'd set up base camp. The look on Xander's face made her wonder if he, too, was missing his undomesticated life on the mountain.

"Better missing home than missing Daddy. He's fine, he's a tough dog. I'll take him for a run along the canal this afternoon. That will cheer him up."

"See you at six, then."

When he left, Sam waited until she saw him striding across the quad toward the city. She admired the view for a moment, then went to her laptop and looked up the name Timothy Savage again. She glanced at her watch—2:00 p.m. She knew she needed to leave it alone, let Fletcher handle things, but maybe a quick phone call wouldn't hurt.

She had a friend who was an assistant M.E. in the Virginia Office of the Chief Medical Examiner. If there was anything interesting to hear about how Timothy Savage died, Dr. Meg Foreman would be all over it.

CHAPTER 4

MEG FOREMAN ANSWERED HER PHONE ON THE FIRST RING.

"Sam Owens, as I live and breathe. How the hell are you? How long's it been, three years?"

"Too long, that's for sure. I'm good, Meg. Working in D.C. now, running the new Forensic Pathology department at Georgetown."

"You left Nashville? I can't believe it. How'd you convince Simon to move?"

Sam stopped short. Meg didn't know. The huge, oppressive weight of sorrow smashed her in the chest, taking her breath away. As she struggled for air, her mind scrambled to think how long it had been since she and Meg had talked—yes, it had been three years ago, at the annual conference for forensic pathologists.

Before.

She reached for the bottle of Purell in her purse without even thinking about it, poured out a huge dollop and started rubbing her hands together. The old words marched through her head, at once comforting and embarrassing. *One Mississippi, two Mississippi, three Mississippi. Simon, Matthew, Madeline.*

Stupid, stupid, stupid. Serves you right for sticking your nose in where it doesn't belong.

"Sam? Are you still there? Is everything all right?"

Sam stared at her hands, cleared her throat. "Meg, I'm sorry. I thought you knew. Simon passed away. With…with the twins. Two years ago. The flood, in Nashville—"

How she'd managed to get those words out, she didn't know. It wasn't something she generally discussed with people. *Hi, my name is Sam, and a random act of God made me a childless widow.*

Meg reacted immediately, her voice overwhelmingly sad. "Oh, my God, Sam. I didn't know. I am so sorry."

"Of course you didn't. Don't apologize. How would you know? I haven't exactly advertised it. Took me a while to accept it myself."

"And have you accepted it? Are you coping? Sleeping, eating? Seeing a therapist?" It was the clinical voice of a doctor overlaid with the kindness of a friend. Sam blurted out the truth before she could think not to.

"It's… Well, things aren't okay, but they're better. This isn't something you ever get over, not really. Work helps. Moving away helped, too. There are no daily reminders anymore. And I've met someone. He keeps me going."

There was an awkward silence, then Meg said, "That's good, Sam. Is there anything I can do to help?"

Sam's voice was stronger now. The past couldn't be undone. It was something she'd only recently come to terms with.

"Here's how you can help me, Meg. You can tell me if you've handled a case recently. Timothy Savage, out of Lynchburg. Obit said he died on Tuesday, but there wasn't any indication how."

Meg sounded relieved. For people who lived with death, day in and day out, medical examiners weren't the best with handling grief. "The name's not ringing a bell, he wasn't one of mine this week. Let me look in our database."

Sam heard her typing.

A few moments later, Meg said, "No, nothing here. It doesn't look like we autopsied him."

"You're sure?"

"I am. Definitely. It must have been a natural death. You may have better luck with the funeral home who buried him."

"Thanks, Meg. I appreciate it."

"No problem. Listen, Sam—" She broke off, then said, "Will you be at the conference this year? We can have dinner. Or better yet, we can skip dinner and I can get you drunk."

Sam smiled, remembering why she liked Meg Foreman. "I may. Let me look into it, and I'll let you know."

"Either way, you're close to Richmond now. If you aren't coming to the conference, let me come up there. We can have lunch, catch up."

"I'd like that," Sam said. She reeled off her new contact information and hung up, setting the phone softly in the cradle.

Jesus.

She stashed the Purell back in her bag, feeling guilty. It had been a while since she'd been caught off guard like that. It wasn't like Simon and the twins were ever far from her mind—she'd fled Nashville to get away from the loneliness she felt, the strange dislocation of losing everything and still waking up every morning, air filling her lungs, even when she was sure she'd never take a breath again. Their memory was what held her back from Xander, from giving all of herself to him. He knew it, understood it deeply, more than anyone else in her life, but at some point, she had to let go and move on.

Yet every time she thought she was there, ready to take a step forward, something like this happened and shot her right back to the person she was for so long after they died—lost, and so very empty. Too empty even to cry.

She slapped her hand on the desk. She needed a drink. Or something. She knew herself well enough; she would be useless the rest of the day. And she hated herself for her weakness.

She packed up her Birkin bag and headed out. The house was only a ten-minute walk, ten minutes that would allow her to wrestle her demons back into their box. Maybe instead of pouring a Scotch, she'd go for a run with Xander and Thor, try to sweat the sorrow out of her. A healthier response. It showed her she wasn't lost, not all the way.

And then she'd begin again, as she had done so many times before. Handling grief was almost like quitting smoking, or drinking. You do well for so long, then suddenly you slip, and indulge. And in the cold light of morning, you have to start counting the days all over again.

She stepped out into the glorious sunshine, trying to ignore the words that rolled through her mind in time with her steps. The words she used in succor, dampening the horror of her wounds.

One Mississippi, two Mississippi, three Mississippi, four.

CHAPTER 5

XANDER HAD ALREADY TAKEN OFF WITH THOR FOR PARTS UNKNOWN WHEN SHE arrived home.

Disappointed, Sam poured herself a finger of Laphroaig, added two ice cubes and went out onto the covered patio that edged the backyard. The previous owners of her town house had redone the place, removing any feature that could be mistaken for traditional and replacing it with modern to the extreme. Everything was sleek and stark, stainless steel, marble, glass—if she were in an unforgiving mood, impersonal—but it suited her new life. Outside, they'd landscaped with fervor as well, putting in a small Japanese garden, which bordered a lap pool with an automatic current, so they could swim in place and still get a workout. The pool was hidden from the neighbors with a large screen of bamboo, and concealed from the street by a tall wooden fence. The illusion of privacy in the heart of the city.

Suddenly hot, Sam set the Scotch on the edge of the pool, shimmied out of her clothes and slid naked into the water.

The sweat and grime and craziness of the day washed clean, she set out at a languorous pace, breaststroking the length of the water. The endless current drove her crazy, so she rarely turned it on; it felt like she was expending so much effort, yet never really going anywhere. Xander loved it, put his head down and swam and swam.

Timothy Savage swam with her. A natural death; no autopsy needed. So why would the man write to Sam and ask her to investigate his murder?

The pool was out of the direct sunlight now, and she got chilled. She ducked her head under, swiped her hands along her face to get her hair slicked back then stepped dripping from the water.

She jumped when she saw Xander sitting by the edge of the pool. He'd snuck outside, silent as a cat.

"I like the view."

Their eyes locked, and she gestured toward the water. "Are you interested in a swim?"

He shook his head and started toward her. She held her breath. The way that man moved, sinuous and graceful, the unconscious warrior in him always alert and ready, drove her wild. He had his shirt off after two steps, his shorts a heartbeat later, and then their skin touched and he put his mouth on hers. She was shocked by his warmth. He was hot, so hot, his skin overheated from his run, slightly sweaty and damp, and his mouth was hotter still, ravenous for her.

He was much bigger than she was; she could just reach her arms around his body. She pulled him closer, and closer still, until he picked her up as if she weighed no more than a leaf, and her legs wrapped around his waist. He went to his knees and bent her backward into the grass, and she wanted him, wanted him so badly. She didn't care that people were walking down the street five feet away, on the other side of her fence. She wanted him now.

He knew it, but held back, his hand running the channel down from her throat, between her breasts, over her stomach and down between her legs. He stroked her, and it didn't take long. He knew exactly what she liked, and had her at the edge within seconds. He kissed her again, long and sweet, and laughed quietly when she whispered, "Now, please. Oh, God, Xander. Now."

Oblivion. She bit his shoulder to keep from crying out. He lost himself moments later, arms wrapped tight around her, a hand in her hair, shaking, tense in silence.

The grass was soft under her back, and the shouts and beeps of the Georgetown traffic became loud again. A mockingbird scolded them from the pear tree. Xander was giggling slightly, trying to hold it together. He always laughed after, some bottomless well of joy unleashed, and it made her laugh, too.

Sam put a finger across his lips and hushed him. "You cackle like that, everyone will know exactly what we're doing back here."

"I don't care. Let's do it again." He reached for her just as Thor came bounding through the back door and launched himself into the pool. His splash drenched them both, and this time Xander couldn't stop laughing. He grabbed Sam in his arms and rolled them both right into the pool.

It was dark when the message came.

They were in the kitchen, finishing off a light dinner—prosciutto and melon, fresh buffalo mozzarella, sweet basil torn from the small herb garden out back, a loaf of crusty bread. They might have had too much to drink; there was maybe an inch of wine left in the bottle. Thor was snoozing on his green plaid flannel bed. It was a normal night, a happy night.

The knock at the door made Thor leap to his feet and go tearing into the hall. He was too well disciplined to bark, but stood at attention, yellow eyes fixed on the door. Xander tensed. He didn't like unscheduled visits.

"Don't answer it."

"Don't be silly." Sam snapped a dish towel at him and went to answer the door.

The man on the step was gray. Gray hair, gray suit, gray skin, gray shoes. Probably gray eyes, but it was hard to tell in the dim light of the streetlamps. He was small, his eyes were even with Sam's and his hands shook slightly, a distinct resting tremor Sam immediately identified with Parkinson's disease.

Thor growled, deep in the back of his throat, and Sam instinctively took a step back.

The gray man didn't move.

"Can I help you?"

"Dr. Owens? Dr. Samantha Owens?"

"Who's asking?" Xander stepped next to Sam, one hand on Thor's ruff, the other hidden out of sight, tucked behind his right thigh. Sam knew it held a SIG Sauer, the gun he kept stashed in the small drawer in the foyer desk.

The man was apparently used to causing alarm when he knocked on doors. He took one look at Xander and Thor, smiled and held out a white business card. "Rolph Benedict, with Benedict, Picker, Green and Thompson, out of Lynchburg. I represent the estate of Timothy Savage. Ah, you are familiar with his name, I see. Good. May I come in?"

A lawyer.

"It's late, Mr. Benedict. You couldn't have called ahead?"

The little man shook his head. "I apologize, sir. My cell phone died on the drive up. I would have been here earlier, but I took a wrong turn, managed to hit 66 going out of town instead of into the city."

His tone didn't sound very apologetic, but Sam shot a look at Xander, who sighed and made a show of putting the gun in the waistband of his jeans before he stepped away from the door. A rumble of thunder sounded in the distance.

"I suppose you better come in," Sam said to Benedict. "Can I get you something to drink?"

CHAPTER 6

SAM FIXED BENEDICT A CUP OF TEA, SERVED IT TO HIM AT THE DINING ROOM TABLE. Allowing him to settle into one of the comfortable leather chairs in the living room felt too welcoming, too personal. This was a business call, and the lawyer didn't seem to mind her treating it as such. The table was a round of thick glass surrounded by six Eames chairs in white ash. Beautiful, functional, comfortable enough.

Once settled, Benedict set out a pad, a Montblanc fountain pen and a document backed by blue paper. He took a sip of his tea, gave Sam a nod of thanks. Understanding the challenges of Parkinson's, she'd given him the mug with the biggest circumference and handle, and hadn't filled it all the way. He managed well, though soon enough he'd have trouble. Without aggressive treatment, resting tremors didn't improve, only steadily worsened, and it was probably too late for him already. His age, the advance of the disease: he didn't have much time left.

Xander was through with the niceties. "What's this about, Mr. Benedict?"

"I'm not sure we've met, Mr.…" He trailed off expectantly.

Xander cleared his throat. "Whitfield."

"Ah. Mr. Whitfield. Thank you. Now. Mr. Savage hired my firm last week to prepare a trust to handle his estate." He turned to Sam, eyes shrewd and assessing. "He named you as executor, Dr. Owens, and left you a respectable amount of money."

"What? Me? Why? I don't even know him."

"Be that as it may, he insisted. He said you'd understand why, when the time came. I must admit, the situation is curious, but understandable. Many people wish to clear up loose ends before they, well, leave this life on their own terms."

"Is that even legal, putting a stranger in charge of your estate?" Sam asked.

"It certainly is. And better a named stranger than a faceless government drone whose only interest is taking as much as possible for Uncle Sammy." His lips moved into an approximation of a grin.

Sam felt a chill run down her spine. This dead stranger, this lawyer on the edge of the grave, this whole situation—it was too much. Xander picked up on her discomfort, reached a hand to her under the table. She squeezed it, then stood and murmured, "I'll be right back. I need a sweater."

Sam picked up her favorite cashmere pashmina from the living room couch and wrapped it around her shoulders. Feeling much less exposed, she marched back into the dining room in time to hear Xander say, "I think you need to explain yourself, Mr. Benedict, and quickly. Who exactly is Timothy Savage?"

Benedict ran a shaky finger along the rim of his mug. "You are aware, of course, of the circumstances surrounding Mr. Savage's death?"

"Enlighten us."

"Oh. You really don't know." Benedict's voice took on a classic Southern ghoulishness, horror and delight coupled in a high-pitched whisper. He leaned forward as he said, "He killed himself. With a very nasty chemical agent he cooked up in his kitchen. Detergent suicide, is what they call it. Very big in Japan."

Benedict's earlier words hit Sam then. *Left this life on his own terms.* "But Mr. Savage was—"

Xander put a hand on her knee and stopped her. "A suicide. And he retained you last week to draw up a will, and named Dr. Owens as executrix. May I ask, who is the beneficiary? Does he have an heir?"

Another gummy grin from the ghoul.

"There are several people named in the will, but he's left the bulk of the estate to a Mr. Henry Matcliff." He was silent for a moment. "Unfortunately, Mr. Matcliff is proving difficult to locate. We wanted to alert you to the situation, and locate the primary beneficiary before contacting the rest of the heirs. We were hoping you would know where he is."

This was getting ridiculous, and Sam wasn't in the mood. The letter this morning had upset her terribly, and now this? No. She wasn't going to let this go on a moment longer.

"I'd never heard of Mr. Savage until this morning. And I have no idea who this Matcliff character is. I'm sorry, Mr. Benedict, but I respectfully decline the offer of handling Mr. Savage's estate. I trust your practice will do right by him." She stood, and Benedict stood also in reflex, a look of shock on his face.

"But Dr. Owens, you're the only one Mr. Savage trusted to handle things for him."

"I said no, and I meant it. It's late. I believe it's time for you to go."

"But—"

Xander stood and took three steps toward the front door. Benedict gathered up his things and followed. Once in the foyer, he said, "There's more. You need to know he's asked for you to do an autopsy on his body."

Sam felt another chill down her back despite the pashmina. "What?"

"I'm afraid he was very specific. He clearly thought all of this through. He wanted you to be involved, Dr. Owens. He's begging for your help…from the grave."

She shook her head. "Stop trying to manipulate me. I don't want anything to do with this."

Benedict nodded grimly. "I understand you don't want the responsibility, and there will be forms you'll need to sign, declining the executor role. I will have them drawn up and sent to you. If you're absolutely sure, that is."

"I'm sure. You can send them to my office. And next time, Mr. Benedict, please be sure to call first. I could have saved you a long trip today."

He hesitated, hands shaking silently, then shrugged and said, "I can't force you to do something you don't want to do, Dr. Owens, though I hope, once the shock has passed, you'll reconsider. Perhaps we can speak again in the morning."

"Perhaps not."

Undeterred, Benedict said, "In the meantime, there is one last detail. Mr. Savage wanted you to have this."

He dug in his pocket and dropped a small silver key into her hand. "He said you'd know what to do with it."

Sam tried to hand it back. "I'm sorry. I don't want to be involved at all."

Benedict ignored her, tipped a finger to his forehead in a goodbye salute then walked down the stairs and disappeared around the corner onto P Street.

Xander closed the door and watched Sam, clearly upset, stalk into the dining room and begin clearing the cups away. He didn't like this, not one bit. For a stranger to seek her out was one thing, but to get her involved in a legal predicament, to write letters claiming she was in danger because he was contacting her and now this, leaving her holding the bag with his estate inside? If Timothy Savage weren't already dead, Xander would have killed him himself.

He thought back to Savage's letter. He said he'd compiled a list of people who could have murdered him. Who were these people? And why, if it was clearly a suicide, did Savage try to rope Sam into his world with the claim of murder?

There was something rotten in Denmark. Without a doubt.

The crash of broken china came from the kitchen. He hurried in to see Sam with a finger in her mouth, cursing under her breath.

"You okay?"

She shook her head. "Broke a cup and sliced my finger. It's nothing, just an ouchy."

She went pale as she said the words, and he knew it was a phrase she'd used with her kids. They slipped out, these motherly incantations, when she was highly upset, or drunk. This was the former—any pleasant tipsiness from the wine at dinner was long gone after the lawyer's disconcerting visit.

"Let me see." He went to her, pulled her into his arms. She was right; it was just a scratch, no worse than a paper cut. The bleeding had all but stopped. He brought her hand to his lips and kissed the wound. "Better?"

Her shoulders began to shake. He thought there might be tears, but she was laughing quietly. She was back, pulled from the edge by his touch. She nodded.

"I'm fine. If you'd offered to kiss my boo-boo, I would have smacked your bum."

"I might have enjoyed that. Seriously, are you okay?"

She kissed him, quick and hard, then pulled away and shut off the lights. She turned toward the stairs, let the wrap fall to the floor. "No, I'm not. Help me forget, Xander."

And he did.

CHAPTER 7

SAM'S CELL PHONE RANG AT 10:30 P.M. FLETCHER. SHE EXTRICATED HERSELF FROM Xander's sleeping form to answer the call. There was still something weird about being naked with Xander and talking to Fletcher. She grabbed the blue cotton button-down Xander had been wearing earlier, snuggled into it and went into the bathroom so she wouldn't wake him, though she'd learned that as light as he slept, only an actual emergency would rouse him. Years of military training. She wished she could follow suit.

She shut the bathroom door, anyway. "Hey. You have news?"

Fletcher sounded tired, a certain weariness in his tone she understood completely. "Yeah. Did I wake you? I know you go to bed early."

Some nights earlier than others.

"No, I'm awake. You don't sound like you're getting any beauty sleep, though."

He laughed. "You know how it is. Things are popping, multiple cases, lots of craziness. Listen, I got a call back from the Lynchburg police. They say the dude, Timothy Savage, was a suicide. Took them a day to clear the air enough to retrieve the body. Detergent suicide isn't deadly only for the victim, but for anyone else who might inhale it, accidentally or otherwise. It's not a pretty death."

"I know. Hydrogen sulfide gas is quite lethal. I assume asphyxiation was the cause of death?"

"I don't know. They didn't post him. It's a small town, just a coroner on hand. They sent the chemicals in for testing, but he didn't see the need for an autopsy. Apparently it was quite clear what had happened. There were warning signs on the windows, and a note, the whole shebang."

"Lazy of them. All they needed to do was send the body to Richmond. Where is Mr. Savage now?"

"In the cooler at the mortician's place."

"Damn. Damn, damn, damn." She leaned against the sink, caught a glimpse of herself in the mirror. Her dark hair was wild, sticking up all over, and her lips were swollen. She smoothed her hair down, thinking hard. Why had Timothy Savage drawn her into his mess?

"Sam? You still there?"

"Yes. My turn for show-and-tell. I had an interesting visitor tonight. Creepy lawyer from Lynchburg. Apparently Savage named me executrix of his estate, and demanded I do an autopsy on him. He left me a key, too, though I have no idea to what. This is getting weirder and weirder, Fletch."

"Are you going to do it?" He sounded intrigued.

"No. No way. This is a job for the police, not me. I'll recommend his body be sent to the OCME in Richmond, and ask my friend Meg Foreman to handle the case personally. But that's as far as I go. I already declined the legal aspect. I just want to prep for my classes and get the semester under way."

"Don't kid a kidder, Sam. You're totally on the hook."

She looked herself in the eye. Spoke to the woman in the mirror, as much as to Fletcher. "I most certainly am not."

"Yeah, you are. Sleep on it. If you still don't want to be involved in the morning, I'll back off. But if you're in, I'll go with you down to Lynchburg. It won't kill you to post the dude."

Permission granted, ma'am.

She did have several days before the semester officially began and she'd have to be at the university full-time.

Don't be an idiot, Sam. This isn't your problem. Don't allow yourself to be drawn into someone else's intrigue.

But something was eating at her. Something that made her say, "Fletcher, do you really think there's a case here? More than a loony coming out of the woodwork?"

"Honestly? I don't know, but it's pretty clear someone wants *you* involved in this case. Which is why I'm coming along if you decide to go. Cover your back. Just in case."

"Just in case. Great. I'll think on it, Fletch."

"Good. Call me first thing, let me know."

"Night."

She dropped her cell into the pocket of Xander's shirt and went back to their bedroom. He was still out cold. She wasn't tired anymore. Her head was aching, a residual effect from the wine at dinner, and more. She was gritting her teeth. Her shoulders were tense and her hands balled into fists.

Why are you fighting this so hard?

She took a few breaths, slowly let herself relax and went downstairs in the dark. The rain had never come, the storm scooting off to the east without a drop, and the moon was shining brightly, reflecting off the glass and metal as it bounced through the house. Without turning on a light, she collected her cashmere throw from the base of the stairs and tossed it over her shoulders. In the small butler's pantry they used as a bar, she poured a finger of Laphroaig and went into the living room. Thor raised his head from his bed, saw his mistress wasn't in harm's way and went back to sleep with a sigh.

She had to be honest with herself. Her natural inclination

was to hightail it down to Lynchburg and post Timothy Savage. She *was* fighting it, fighting it hard, but the investigator in her was overruling the new, calm, Zen, *I'm a teacher now.* She *wanted* to see what was behind all the craziness today.

She didn't want the bother of being the executor of Savage's estate; that was something better left to the courts. But giving the body a once-over, how could it hurt? Detergent suicide was becoming more and more common, though she'd only seen the abstracts written in the medical journals. Having firsthand knowledge would do nothing but enhance her repertoire.

With Fletcher there to pave the way with the local authorities, she figured she could be in and out in fewer than twenty-four hours. Technically, she should have the body transferred to the OCME in Richmond, but if there was an appropriate facility in Lynchburg she could handle it herself. Hydrogen sulfide gas meant they'd have to take some precautions, but so long as the body was washed and the room well ventilated, no special biological hazard precautions would be necessary.

Fletcher was right, damn the man. She was on the hook.

"When are you going to Lynchburg?"

Sam jumped and gave out a little scream. "Xander, you scared me. Can't you clump down the stairs like a normal man? I've had cats that make more noise on the stairs than you."

He grinned, his teeth flashing white in the moonlight. "Sorry, babe. I'll try to sound more like an elephant next time." He sat on the couch next to her, took her hand in his easily. He didn't seem worried, or concerned, just curious. Thor started to rise, but Xander gestured for him to stay put.

"I thought you were asleep."

"You were thinking so loud it woke me up. Want to talk about it?"

She traced the edge of his finger. "Fletcher wants to go to

Lynchburg with me, thinks I should go ahead and post Savage's body."

"I think you should, too."

Her head whipped up. He was smiling at her, a lopsided grin.

"What?"

"Oh, hon. It's a mystery, and you love a good mystery. It's going to eat at you until you do it, so why not go? Take a couple of days, drive south with your pet cop."

She narrowed her eyes at him.

"Teasing. Seriously, I think you should go for it. You're ready for your classes. This will occupy all your brain matter until you figure it out."

"I don't know what the school will say. I'm supposed to be available in case any students need prep prior to the semester's start."

"They'll be fine."

They would. She was looking for excuses now, and she was all out of them. Only one thing left to do, and that was go. "All right. Fine. I'll go post his body. But that's it. Why don't you come with me?"

"And do what? Watch while you cut the dude open?" He shook his head, tucked a piece of hair behind her ear. "I love you, honey, but not that much. Thor and I will hang out on the mountain, get our forest fix, do some fishing and wait for you to come home to us."

There was a note of melancholy in his tone, and Sam wondered if the city, her lifestyle, was getting to him. *Of course it is, silly. He's making a huge sacrifice to be with you. The least you can do is let him get away and reset.* "Two days. Give me two days, and I'll meet you at the cabin. Deal?"

He kissed her softly, briefly. "Deal. Now. Before you run off to Southern parts unknown, I have something for you."

Sam couldn't stop the smile. "A present?"

"Yep. Shut your eyes."

She did, heard him rustling around, then he came back and she felt the couch sink under his weight.

"Okay. Open 'em."

She could swear she felt her heart stop, just for a moment, then adrenaline poured through her system and it took off at Thoroughbred pace. There was a small robin's-egg-blue box in his hand, with a familiar white ribbon tied in a lovely bow. Tiffany.

Oh, God. She looked up to see Xander smiling widely at her obvious discomfort.

"It's not what you think. Well, not exactly. Open it."

She was possessed by an irrational thought—run. Run, now, out the door, and don't look back. But she took a breath and unwrapped the box.

Inside was an incredibly delicate band of diamonds set in platinum, so small, so perfectly tiny and exquisite they were nearly diaphanous. She couldn't help herself; the words came out before she could think.

"Oh, Xander, it's beautiful."

"It reminds me of you. Strong, unbreakable, but fine and delicate and made of stars." He took it from the box and picked up her right hand. "I know you aren't ready to take a bigger step, so I had this made for your right hand. If you're ever ready, we can move it to the left. But for now, I wanted you to have something of mine. Something of me. Something to remind you of us when you're away from me."

He put the ring on her finger, then brought it to his mouth and kissed it. She was speechless. The panic was gone, replaced by a warm, gentle pulsing in her chest that signaled happiness, safety. A feeling she hadn't had in a very long time. Tears hit the edges of her eyes and she used her left hand to wipe them away, then touched her wet fingers to his lips. "I love it. And I love you."

He was quiet for a minute. “I know you do, hon. I know.” He sighed. “Just promise me you won’t take too long.”

They didn’t see the face in the window, watching them hug, and kiss, and touch. They only had eyes for each other.

CHAPTER 8

DARKNESS NEVER ENDS, EVEN IN THE DAYLIGHT. THIS IS SOMETHING I LEARNED when I was a child, locked away in a dark, dank room, with spiders and centipedes for companions, and the occasional rustle of a mouse, or a rat, or a snake that slipped in through the grate after its prey. I had a tattered blue blanket I assume belonged to some other child kept in the hole, which I used alternately as a pillow and a cover. There was a chipped sippy cup I could use to catch rainwater when it dripped through the ceiling. The floor was dirt, and there was a bucket in the corner. Once a day, there would be footsteps, closer and closer until they stopped. The small window in the steel door would open, and something edible would be shoved through. Bread. Cheese. Once in a glorious while, an apple. And on the special days, the days I was briefly, brutally visited, after—if I'd been good—I was given an orange.

I hate oranges.

I hate the dark.

And spiders and rats and snakes and mice and everything that reminds me of those days.

Everything but him.

I've often wondered how many children came before me. I don't want to know how many came after. He told me, when we left, I couldn't ever look back. Not to the time before, nor to my time there. Looking back would make me unhappy, and it was best to never, ever think about those dark days again. We would make a new life. A life looking forward. A life free from shadows, from pain and humiliation and sharp things in the night.

I did my best.

I always did my best.

Even before, on the special days, when they came for me, blindfolded me, walked me one hundred and fifteen steps to the cold place. They told me I was special. That I was beautiful. Perfect. And when they were inside me, tearing me open, squeezing the breath out of me with their weight hard on my flat chest, they said unspeakable words, words I shudder to remember. Words children shouldn't know. Instructions children shouldn't get.

Don't look back. Don't look back.

Every step I take, deeper into the forest, the bad words come to me. I stop, stand against a tree, take a deep breath. Conjure his face, his kind, loving face. But now the vision is marred, his skin pale and waxy, his tongue sticking out of his mouth, the emptiness of his bulging eyes, the blood on his body. I will never see him smile again, never hear him read to me, or do flash cards at dinner, or watch fireflies as they gather in the twilight.

Or chase away the nightmares.

The truth can't help me now. I crumple to the ground, sobbing so hard my body shakes. The forest screams at me, cicadas and birds and crickets and bats in an alarming cacophony;

the trees shriek and stamp their feet, waving their arms, trying to catch the wind. Leaves rain down on me, dead and yellow, and I hear them coming.

Oh, God, they're coming. And there's nowhere left for me to hide.

SATURDAY

"To think of shadows is a serious thing."
—Victor Hugo

"Let not your heart be concerned with death,
for the three corners of our life are at hand.
Birth, life, death: this is the only cycle that matters.
Death is the great equalizer. Whether your life is
one year or one hundred years, you will be
resurrected in me, and we shall all live forever
when the shadows at last fall."
—Curtis Lott

CHAPTER 9

Georgetown

SAM WOKE EARLY TO THE SUN STREAMING IN THE BEDROOM WINDOWS. XANDER was gone, a note on the bed saying he was out for a quick run. She remembered last night in a sudden rush and stared down at her right hand. The delicate diamonds flashed in the morning sunlight, and she smiled. Clever and romantic, Xander's ring, as she was already thinking of it, anchored her to this life more than any emotion she'd had since Simon and the twins died.

The thought of them hurt, but she let it in, breathed through it, touched her new ring. She whispered, "Forgive me, my loves."

Sam jumped in the shower, then dressed in flax-colored linen Bermuda shorts, leather loafers and a cream cotton tank top with a matching cashmere sweater, packed a large black-and-tan Longchamps bag, pulled her damp hair off her face with a headband. She brought the bag downstairs and called Fletcher.

He didn't even say hello. "Morning, sunshine. You ready? We can be down there before lunch if we take off soon."

Sam said, "You didn't even know I was going to call."

"Well, a little bird might have mentioned you were planning a trip south."

"Xander? He called you?"

"Texted. He knew you'd want to get on the road early. I'm on my way to your place now. Think you could scrounge me up some breakfast?"

"Don't you ever grocery shop, Fletch?"

"Sure I do. Sometimes. Well, maybe not, really. Just coffee is fine, if food is too much trouble."

"Yes, Fletcher, cooking for you is always a bother. I'll see you shortly."

He was laughing when he hung up.

She went into the kitchen and hurriedly put together omelets and bacon, enough for three. She was assembling the last plate when she heard the men in the hallway, Xander's deep voice answering a question from Fletcher's tenor. She shook her head. Sometimes she wondered who was running her life. It certainly didn't feel as if she was.

She shot Xander a look when he came in, and he smiled merrily at her. Fletcher tossed her a salute and without a word, the two men tucked in to the food. Sam brought a pot of coffee to the table and joined them. Thor drank water noisily from his bowl in the corner, not wanting to be left out of the moment. He came and sat next to Xander's left leg, hoping for a bit of omelet. Xander was strict with Thor's diet, but Sam saw him hand a piece of bacon to the dog under the table.

Sam toyed with a mushroom and watched the two men. So different, these two. Xander was dark-haired and dark-eyed, bigger, more heavily muscled. Fletcher was lighter in every way, square-jawed, brown eyes bordering on hazel, with brown hair. Both smart. Both honest and kind, and caring. Maybe a little too caring. Something about the morning suddenly felt wrong. What were they up to?

They both stopped eating and turned to her expectantly.

"What?" she asked.

"You're staring," Xander said.

"The way you do when you're about to make a pronouncement," Fletcher added.

She shook her head. "No pronouncements. Just wondering what this is all about. It's like you both want me involved in this case."

Fletcher shot Xander a glance, then cleared his throat. "It's an intriguing case, and you're damn good at what you do. And the man did ask for you personally."

"But?"

"No but. That's all."

Xander set down his fork and said, "That's not fair. *But,* when you're occupied, you're happier."

Ah. There it was. The truth, at last. She didn't know whether to laugh or smack him on the hand with her fork.

"And I've been malingering too long? A few days left before school starts, and I'll drive the two of you crazy in the meantime if I don't have my hands into something?"

Neither responded. For the first time, she noticed Xander wasn't drenched in sweat, though he was dressed in his running clothes.

Sam lost her appetite, pushed her plate away. "You didn't go for a run, did you?"

He watched her, eyes suddenly serious. He looked over at Fletcher, who shrugged slightly. The air in the kitchen grew tense. Xander sighed a little. "No. I didn't go for a run."

Her heart sped up. "And Fletcher just happened to be on his way over when I called. What's wrong? What are you keeping from me?"

It was Fletcher who said the words that made her stomach turn.

"Rolph Benedict was found dead in his hotel room early this morning."

CHAPTER 10

SAM'S FIRST REACTION WAS SHOCK. THE SECOND WAS FURY. "WHAT THE HELL? I can't believe you didn't tell me right away. How did Benedict die?"

"We don't know yet. Dr. Nocek will do the post this morning, see what's up," Fletcher said.

"I should stay. I should be there. I can help Amado—"

Xander touched her lightly on the arm. "No, you shouldn't. Let Fletcher take you to Lynchburg. You've been drawn into this against your will, but now it's time to take care of business. Do what Timothy Savage asked of you. Find out what's happening."

She crossed her arms, let the anger course through her. "And what exactly are you planning to do?"

"Keep an eye on things."

She knew what he meant. He'd be covering her back, as he'd done before. Out of sight, and, hopefully, out of harm's way.

As if he'd read her mind, he smiled at her. It took him from dangerous to innocent, and she couldn't help smiling back. He nodded. "They won't know I'm there. Promise."

She searched his eyes, but saw only determination. She squared her shoulders. "You do anything stupid, and I'll be very upset with you."

"I can take care of myself, hon. It's you I'm worried about. Savage warned you this was going to be dangerous, and two people involved in this case are already dead. Watch your step, okay?"

"You need to stop. There's no reason to worry about me. I'm a big girl. I can handle this." She turned to Fletcher. "Finish your breakfast, and let's go."

Fletcher stood, rolling his eyes. "Finally. Thought you'd never ask." He turned to Xander. "I've got her back. You, keep in touch, all right? Regular check-ins, every four hours. Read me?"

Xander snapped a precise salute. "Loud and clear, sir."

The drive to Lynchburg was a beautiful three hours through rolling green hills and black-fenced horse country, and Fletcher had been silent since they left Georgetown. That was fine with Sam. The morning's subterfuge worried her. She should have been told about the murder immediately, and instead the men she loved wanted to coddle and protect her.

Maybe they don't know you've changed, Sam. Maybe you haven't given them a reason to think you're strong enough to handle this.

She was the first to admit she'd been a basket case when she came to D.C. Crippled by grief and an obsessive compulsive need to wash her hands, she'd been a weak caricature of her true self. She'd lost two years giving in to the psychological horrors of losing her family.

But in the months since she moved, she'd gotten strong again. Determined, as Timothy Savage pointed out. She'd finally forgiven herself for the hardest realization of all—she was still the same person she was before they'd died.

Changed, certainly. But it was still *her* inside her skin, and that realization drove her away from forgiving herself and moving forward with her life. Until now.

Baldwin had recognized this, and reached out with an opportunity to let her get her world back on track. She wished Xander and Fletcher had realized it, too.

Fletcher turned on the stereo. "Will a little bit of tuneage bother you?"

"Of course not."

He hit Play and a song started, one she recognized.

"Hey, that's Jason and the Scorchers," she said. "They're a Nashville band. How'd you find them?"

"They played the 9:30 Club a while back. I bought a couple CDs off them. It's good stuff."

"I didn't know this was your bag. I always pegged you for a hard rock guy. Led Zeppelin and Pink Floyd."

"I'm alternative all the way. And rockabilly cowpunk *is* hard rock. Listen to those guitars."

Jason belted out a John Denver ballad, "Take Me Home, Country Roads." Sam hummed along, but Fletcher sang the words, and she was shocked to realize he had a fabulous voice. When the song was over, she applauded. "I never knew you could sing."

"We've never been on a road trip together where it seemed appropriate. I did my stint as front man during college. Chicks dug the guitar."

"Aren't you full of surprises today. You play guitar, too?"

"Used to. I gave it up when Felicia and I got married. She wasn't thrilled with the cop hours to start with—to add the band's touring on top, even if it was only weekends, was too much for her. I still noodle around when I get time."

"You're really good. Why'd you choose being a cop over taking the show on the road?"

"Tad. He was sick a lot when he was a baby, and I needed the steady paycheck."

She heard a small, unuttered sigh in that sentence, and it made her sad for him. Fletcher sacrificed a lot for the people he loved; she'd seen it firsthand. Though maybe she was more sensitive to it. Coming from Nashville, a town where everyone had a dream, she knew how hard it was to accept reality, buckle down and work for the man instead of following your heart.

She'd lost herself in thoughts of home, was tapping her fingers on the laptop balanced on her knees in time to the music, when Fletcher startled her with "Nice ring."

Sam glanced over at him. He had his sunglasses on, gold aviator frames, and his hand dangled over the top of the steering wheel. He looked so much like a cop she nearly laughed. But he wasn't smiling.

She took a deep breath. "Xander gave it to me. Last night, actually."

"It's pretty."

"Yes, it is." She was quiet for a moment. "It doesn't mean anything. Not really. It's not like we're engaged or anything."

"You should be."

Her head rocked back. He saw her surprise, and this time, he did smile.

"I have to admit I was a bit surprised when he texted, said to take you to Lynchburg or else this would drive you nuts," he said.

"I don't know why he thought that. I was perfectly fine letting things lie."

Fletcher scoffed. "This is me you're talking to, sunshine. You don't have to lie. I don't think you do with him, either. I'm just saying, he's a good man. He loves you. He doesn't want to change you, and trust me, that's rare."

She thought about his words. Having this conversation with Fletcher was utterly bizarre, but she sensed he wanted to have it. They'd been dancing around it for months. She knew Fletcher had feelings for her. She simply never acknowledged them. It was too much to deal with—she'd had two years of grief and numbness, and suddenly, three months ago, in the course of a single week, she'd lost another man she used to love and, while investigating his death, found Fletcher and Xander. Two wonderful men who were both good for her, in their own ways.

Two loves lost. And two found. But only one made her heart sing.

By his words, she realized something had subtly changed between her and Fletcher. Everything she'd hoped for—namely, his friendship—was matter-of-factly being offered on a plate. But there were things that couldn't be left unspoken. Not anymore.

She said quietly, "Would you want to change me, Fletch?"

He glanced at her briefly, smiled. "Naw. I like you the way you are. Though you'd drive me mad with all your nagging. 'Don't you ever grocery shop, Fletch?'" He did a credible impression of her, and she punched him in the shoulder, laughing.

"Damn, woman. Don't hit so hard, I might drive off the road and take out some cows." He gestured toward the field to his left. "Friggin' nature. Who'd want to live out here in the boonies like this? Not enough concrete for my taste."

"You're prevaricating."

"Your big words, too. Annoys the crap out of me. You're a walking thesaurus." He shot her another smile. "I'm not gonna lie, Sam. You're something special. When you came along, things started looking up. But I'd drive you nuts."

"You already do." She grinned at him.

"Ditto." He went quiet for a moment. "You'd be crazy to let things go south with Xander, is all."

He was absolutely right. "I know. I know he's a good man, and I love him. I never thought it would happen again for me."

"So marry him already."

"Good grief, Fletch, I've only known him for three months."

"You're a grown-up. You know what you need. He seems to fit the bill. You've been happy lately. Happier than I've ever seen you."

"You don't know me that well, Fletch. But yes, he makes me happy."

"So why not marry the dude?"

She blurted out the words. "To be honest, I'm afraid he wants kids. And that's not something I'm ever willing to do."

"Ah. That's what this is all about." He paused a moment. "Just the thought of it makes you panic, huh?"

"What?" she asked, then realized she was opening and closing the lid of her laptop unconsciously. She slammed it closed. "Yeah. You could say that."

"Have you told him? That you don't want to have kids?"

"No."

"Do it, Sam. Have a conversation, like we're doing. Tell the man, and get on with your life. He'll accept you no matter what. I suspect he already knows the cost of loving you, and is more than willing to pay it."

The cost. My God, is that how people see me? There's a cost to being with me?

"Hey. Did I say something wrong?"

She shook her head, fiddled with the edge of the laptop. "No. Not at all. You're fine. It's me. So what's with this new attitude? You've never been Xander's biggest fan before."

"I'm feeling like a change is in the air. Something good's coming, for all of us." He smiled again, and Sam realized she'd never seen him quite this content before.

"Darren Fletcher, what is up with you today? Are you in love?"

"What? Me? Hell, no. Definitely not. Lust, maybe. Andi's fun, for an uptight bureaucrat. It's a good setup—when she has time, she calls me. When I have time, I call her. It's casual."

"You're practically friends with benefits."

He grinned. "She ain't asking for a drawer, so that's good. Naw, I just like playing hooky. I haven't in a while. Even with all the green in the fields and blue in the sky, it's nice to get away from my desk."

"I'm touched you've taken the time to come play with me."

"Someone has to keep you on the straight and narrow."

Sam touched his arm. "I'm glad. And thank you for the advice."

He looked as though he wanted to say more, but settled for "Welcome."

Her cell rang. Saved by the bell. "Oh, good, there's Amado. Let's see how Benedict died."

CHAPTER 11

DR. AMADO NOCEK HAD THE QUIET INTONATION OF A GRAVE MAN, COUPLED WITH a slightly Italianate European accent. Some found him strange; he was serenely brilliant, very tall and much too thin, slightly stooped over, the physique of a praying mantis. The unkind called him Lurch, or the Fly, but Sam had liked him from the moment they met, recognizing a fellow scientific soul. He was a widower, too, and once, when he'd noticed she was having a panic attack during one of their meetings, he'd put his bony hand on her shoulder and said, "It doesn't get better, but it will hurt less, in time."

At that moment, she hadn't believed him. Now she realized he was right.

She put him on the speaker.

"Good morning, my friend. How are things in the OCME?"

"Insanity. But Samantha, my dear, your voice always cheers me. Detective Fletcher told you about our guest, Mr. Benedict?"

"He did. Fletch is on the phone with us now. What are your findings?"

"Oh, they have not told you already? Manual strangulation. He was garroted. The implement was still wrapped around his throat. It took very little time to subdue him. He was not a large man, and terribly ill. His brain presented with clear alpha-synuclein lesions, idiopathic to advanced Parkinson's."

"That's right. He had several physical characteristics of the disease, as well."

"Whoever killed him was much taller. The angle on the garrote went upward at nearly forty-five degrees. It was a small wire attached to two wooden dowels, like a miniature jump rope. Nothing remarkable about the device outside of the reality of it. We do not see professional garroting very often here."

"Professional?"

"Yes. There were no hesitation marks, no adjustments. This was an experienced killer."

"Could Benedict have been sitting when he was attacked?"

"Based on the crime scene reconstruction, he was attacked while in the shower. Mr. Benedict measured only sixty-eight inches, so it is safe to assume the killer is at least over seventy-four inches tall, if not more."

"Let me get a feel for this. How tall are you, Amado?"

"I believe I was seventy-seven inches at my last physical."

"So you're six-four, and Benedict is five-eight. Yes, it makes sense. It would have to be someone quite big to cause that up-angle. There was no indication the killer stood on something? The edge of the tub, perhaps?"

"Not from the current facts of the investigation, no. The man was in a handicap-friendly room, with a roll-in shower, no bathing tub. I suppose it was too difficult for him to step up over the ledge. The commode is too far away from the shower to make that scenario feasible."

"All right. When you're all finished, would you mind emailing me your final report?"

"Not at all, my dear. I know I do not have to remind you to be very careful."

"I have Fletcher. I'll be fine. I'll see you when I get back. We're overdue for dinner."

"It would be my great pleasure. Until then."

He hung up, and Sam turned to Fletcher. "Garroting? More you're keeping from me?"

"I didn't know. Pro hit, sounds like."

"Agreed. This is trouble, Fletch. We need to be on alert."

"Here's what I don't get. Why you? Why did Timothy Savage ask for you specifically?"

"I don't know, and it freaks me out. I'm worried we're walking into a trap, and without more information, I have no idea what it might be."

"We're only an hour from Lynchburg. We're going to find out soon enough."

Sam opened her laptop, started pulling every ounce of information she could find about Timothy Savage and Rolph Benedict. After twenty minutes of searching, Savage was still a mystery, a complete blank. But there was plenty of material about Benedict.

"Fletch, listen to this. Benedict's story is bizarre. He won a big case a decade ago, defending the daughter of a family friend accused of murdering her boyfriend. Remember this one? Her name was Gillian Martin."

"Gillian Martin? Oh, wait, yeah. All the evidence said she was guilty as hell, but her lawyer managed to convince the jury the girl was simply on the wrong end of a massive frame-up."

"Her lawyer was Rolph Benedict. The real killer was never caught, and Benedict retired from criminal defense work and joined the firm he mentioned last night as a partner, doing estate and contract law."

"Big change."

"It is," Sam said. "What would drive a successful criminal attorney to make such a drastic about-face right after winning the biggest case of his career? Granted, he'd been sick. Perhaps the rigors of trial law became too much. Parkinson's isn't an easy disease to manage. He could have decided a more sedate lifestyle was in order, and contract law fit the bill."

"Could have. I remember the case, though. The boyfriend was stabbed, shot and his throat slit, but it was all circumstantial evidence—they didn't have her prints on the weapons, DNA, nothing. During the trial, Gillian Martin did all sorts of strange things, laughing at inappropriate times, crying, claiming she didn't remember anything. She was on the stand for days. If the prosecutors had gone for a simple second-degree murder charge, the jury would have bought it, but this was a death penalty case. They overreached, and she walked."

"A big score for a small-town lawyer, right?"

"It is. Interesting."

Sam couldn't help wondering if it were something more. Bigger. It felt wrong, all wrong.

Lynchburg was composed of seven hills, a Southern city nestled on the banks of the James River with a stunning view of the Blue Ridge Mountains. It held the honor of being the only Southern city not captured by Union troops during the Civil War—known across many parts of the South as the Great Unpleasantness. It was a college town, with multiple universities ranging from Jerry Falwell's Liberty University to Randolph College, formerly Randolph-Macon Woman's College. When Sam was in high school and looking at colleges, a friend who attended Randy-Mac, as she called it, told her with great glee that Falwell supposedly called the students there "the intellectual whores on the hill."

"At least he recognized we're smart," she'd said.

Lynchburg's criminal element focused on burglaries and rapes, assaults and drugs, with the very occasional murder thrown in for good measure. It was a quiet town, full of students and bars and the gentility of the Old South. The sun was shining as they drove across the John Lynch Memorial Bridge into the city.

"Police headquarters are on Court Street. Our contact there is June Davidson. He's a lifer detective, born and raised here in Lynchburg. Seemed smart enough when we talked, but we'll see," Fletcher said.

Five minutes later, they pulled in to the police station and Fletcher glanced at his watch. "Made it in two hours and forty-five minutes. Not bad."

"When's Xander supposed to check in?"

He tossed his sunglasses on the dash. "Noon. Let's go talk to Detective Davidson."

The inside of Lynchburg's cop shop was generic, with wanted posters lining the walls, a receptionist behind a wall of glass and a big sign with the letters LPD in blue under a red arch, with the words *Leadership, Professionalism, Dedication* below and an incongruous sign underneath it that read *Find us on Facebook and Twitter.*

It was at once so strange yet so familiar it made Sam long for Nashville. How many years had she spent walking into the Criminal Justice Center in Nashville, coming to find Taylor or another homicide detective to relay findings on a case? This felt like home, even though it wasn't, and she had to push the thought away— *Why did you leave this behind? This is your passion, your love. You spent your life learning how to do this. What are you thinking?*

Maybe Fletcher and Xander were right. Maybe she simply needed to be here, for more than Timothy Savage's sake.

Fletcher walked up to the receptionist. "We've got an appointment with June Davidson. Detective Darren Fletcher and Dr. Samantha Owens."

The woman sported a small blond beehive and cat's-eye glasses, a retro throwback to another era, though she couldn't have been more than twenty. Sam caught the edge of a tattoo under her collar. Times, they do change.

The girl, whose name tag read F. Gary, nodded. "June's been waiting for you. I'm Flo. If you need anything, let me know." She had a soft and gentle Southern accent, the *g*'s barely dropped. She pointed at a small table behind them, against the north wall. "The coffee's probably gone cold, but there's a microwave in the back. Pour yourself a cup and June'll hook you up. I'll let him know you're here."

Sam and Fletcher poured coffee into paper cups and doctored them. By the time Fletch had finished adding three sugars to his, the door opened to their right and a tall blond-haired man in his midforties blocked the light. He wasn't just tall, he was at least six foot four and built like a linebacker, though there wasn't an ounce of fat on him. His tan linen suit fit well, the white button-down shirt underneath open at the collar. Sam couldn't help recalling the conversation she'd had with Amado earlier. They were looking for a man about this height as Benedict's killer.

She saw Fletcher look the man up and down and slightly raise an eyebrow. He'd had the same thought.

The man looked at her strangely, as if he were trying to place her face, then shrugged slightly. "Detective Fletcher? Dr. Owens? I'm June Davidson. Come on back. We'll talk in my office. You need to heat that up?"

Sam took a sip, it wasn't bad. "We're fine, thanks."

Davidson's accent was similar to Flo's, Southern without being overwhelming, rounded vowels and soft consonants, and his manner unhurried. This was a man who knew slow and steady won the race, and after several months of Washington hustle and bustle, Sam felt immediately at home.

He led them down an anonymous linoleum hallway to the end, took an immediate right into a bullpen full of detectives and uniformed officers, and eyes followed them.

Davidson ushered them into his office, which had a large window overlooking the city, and the James River beyond.

He raised his voice a bit so it carried across the bullpen. "We just had a briefing on the Benedict murder. Everyone knows why you're here. Forgive me if I say it aloud, but there's some concern. We do know how to do our jobs." He kicked his door shut with a cowboy boot and grinned at them. His front teeth overlapped a bit, making him charming rather than handsome. His blue eyes crinkled when he smiled, and lines etched into his cheeks. Sam figured he spent a great deal of time with a grin on his face.

He gestured toward the bullpen. "At least, most of those yahoos think so. Now me, I'm all about cooperation. So tell me, what can I do to help?"

CHAPTER 12

Lynchburg Police Department
Lynchburg, Virginia

FLETCHER KICKED THINGS OFF. "TIMOTHY SAVAGE. WHAT CAN YOU TELL US ABOUT him?"

"Other than the fool could have gotten my officers killed with his stupid stunt?"

Davidson pulled a file folder from his drawer and put it on the desk in front of Fletcher, draped his jacket on the back of his chair. "Detergent suicide. It's worse than running up on a meth lab without your gear. At least he had the presence of mind to warn us so we didn't blunder into the scene and lose men."

"What do you mean, he warned you?" Sam asked.

"Look at the pics. I have them arranged chronologically." Fletcher opened the file and scooted his chair closer to Sam's so she could see the crime scene photos.

Savage had died in a small cabin surrounded by forest. There were a few shots of the cabin from afar, then close-ups of the windows and doors. Large white signs with hand-drawn biohazard symbols were taped in the two front windows, and the front door had a note on it with the words:

HYDROGEN SULFIDE
SUICIDE
POISON GAS
DO NOT OPEN
DANGER!!!
1 BREATH CAN KILL YOU

Sam raised an eyebrow. “You’d have to have a pretty high concentration to die from a single breath, something like seven hundred seventy parts per liter, but this stuff is toxic. Even a small concentration will cause all sorts of respiratory problems. What did he use?”

“Muriatic acid and lime sulfur. Bought it at the gardening center down the road from his place. More than enough to do the job. We had to get HAZMAT involved to come in and clear the place so my coroner could retrieve the body. Took a day to make it safe enough to get anyone near without a mask.”

“Who found him?”

Davidson’s brows pulled together. “Anonymous 911 call from a pay phone in front of a 7-Eleven on Rivermont. No working cameras there, so we couldn’t get a shot of the person who called. I can play you the tape, it’s quick. Male voice states the address, and requests police response to a dead body. That’s it.”

“Have you dealt with many of these before?”

“Not many, but it’s getting more and more common. Usually they do it in a car, in an out-of-the-way parking lot where they won’t be discovered and disturbed. You seeing this in D.C., too?”

Fletcher shook his head. “I’ve heard of it but haven’t worked one. They still like the traditional means up north. Guns, pills, hangings."

"Well, some of these rural kids get pretty hopeless. This is a guaranteed death, without a lot of mess, and it's cheap, and fast. The ingredients are readily available and mostly unregulated, too. They can do it with dandruff shampoo and toilet cleaner if they're desperate enough. As long as there's an acid and a sulfur, they're in business."

"But Timothy Savage used industrial-strength elements for his concoction?"

"That's right. He wasn't messing around. At least he warned us."

Fletcher flipped through a couple more pictures and stopped. "Is this his suicide note?"

"It is. We found it right next to the body."

Fletcher pulled a plastic sheet protector from the file and handed it to Sam. Inside was a handwritten note. She read it aloud quickly.

"'I am sorry for all the trouble I've caused. This is best for everyone. Goodbye. T.S.'"

She set the letter down on the desk. "Fletch, the handwriting matches."

"Handwriting matches what?" Davidson asked, suddenly wary.

Fletcher removed a folded sheet of paper from his jacket pocket. "This is a photocopy of a letter Dr. Owens received yesterday. Before she was called upon by Mr. Benedict regarding Savage's will."

Davidson read the letter, frowning the whole time. "May I keep this?"

"By all means. I have the original in D.C."

"I don't get it," Davidson said. "Why would Savage kill himself but send a letter to Dr. Owens claiming to be murdered?"

"There's more," Fletcher said, and filled him in about Benedict, the will and the lawyer's subsequent murder. Sam noticed he left out mentioning the angle of the garrote.

Davidson rubbed a meaty hand across his face. "Let me get this straight. Not only did he send you this letter, he made you executor of his estate, meager though it may be? And then Rolph Benedict is murdered after delivering the message? I don't like this. I don't like it at all. We better get in touch with Rolph's partners, see what's up."

Sam finished flipping through the crime scene photos and a two-dimensional crime scene drawing. From what she could see, the Lynchburg P.D. had been thorough and careful. "Just so you know, the will stipulated I perform a secondary autopsy on Mr. Savage. I know he wasn't sent to Richmond for posting, so he must still be here in town. I'd like to arrange it as soon as possible."

Davidson stared at her for a heartbeat, then paled and grabbed the phone. He dialed a number from memory and breathed an audible sigh of relief when the call was answered.

"Roy? It's June. You haven't put Savage's body through the furnace yet, have you? Oh, thank the Lord. All stop, right now. Yes. We'll be down shortly. Bye."

He turned to Sam. "Lady, you have the Devil's own luck. Savage's body was set to be cremated this morning. Roy came in late and hadn't gotten to it yet. We caught him just in time—Savage is already in the retort, ready to go."

"Who is giving the instructions regarding the body? Who decided he should be cremated?" Sam asked.

"Well, that's where all this gets a little hinky. No one claimed the body— Savage is a loner, doesn't have any family nearby to speak of. The orders came from Benedict's law office. They're footing the bill."

Fletcher spoke up. "Cremation directly countermands the deceased's request for an autopsy by Dr. Owens. What the hell, Davidson? What sort of law offices are these?"

"Well-respected ones. I honestly have no idea what's going on here. No one mentioned the man had a will."

Sam asked, "Does he have any family? Someone must have placed the obituary."

"Honestly, Dr. Owens, that obituary is a bit of a mystery to me. Savage isn't from around here. He showed up with his son a decade ago, kept to himself, homeschooled his boy, didn't get into any sort of trouble. The boy's name was Henry, if I remember correctly. I think he went to Randolph College, but we haven't been able to locate him."

"Henry Matcliff?" Sam asked. "Benedict told me he's the primary heir to the estate, but they hadn't had any luck finding him."

"Matcliff? Never heard the name. Far as I knew, it was Henry Savage."

"It seems very odd that Henry wouldn't claim his father's body and have a burial, or a memorial service. Is there bad blood between them?" Fletcher asked.

Davidson shook his head. "I don't know. Like I said, this was so clearly a suicide we treated it as such." He stood up. "We better get on over to the law firm, see what they have to say for themselves. Then we can get you together with Mr. Savage, face-to-face."

Sam shook her head. "I want to do the autopsy first. Without the facts, nothing else matters."

"What more do you need? The man killed himself and roped you into his scheme."

"You'd be amazed at the facts you miss without a proper autopsy," she replied. "I must admit, I'm a bit surprised it wasn't done in the first place."

The note of admonition was clear to Davidson, who bristled. "Hey, now, I can only do what I can do. Coroner ruled it a suicide, looked the body over and there was no indication of foul play."

Sam shrugged. “Thankfully, it’s not too late. Take me to Mr. Savage’s body, please, and let’s get things under way. Then we can talk to the lawyers.”

CHAPTER 13

Lynchburg, Virginia

SAM LOVED THE SOUTH.

The Hoyle Funeral Home and Crematorium was housed in an antebellum mansion worthy of its own sound stage in Hollywood as a depiction of Tara. Huge Corinthian columns soared in front of three stories of pristine white clapboard, black shutters, a wraparound porch and a red double front door, its true purpose masked by the picture-perfect facade of a luxurious bed-and-breakfast. The main doors opened into a magnificent foyer with a small, awkwardly placed reception stand, currently empty. The counter had a small bell, like in a hotel, and Sam smacked it lightly with her palm. Moments later, a small man scurried into the foyer.

Roy Hoyle of the eponymously named crematorium was a mouse of a man with a mop of unnaturally black hair that was slightly crooked on his scalp, and thin, pale hands that hardly seemed capable of the duties they were called upon to perform on a daily basis. He shook Sam's hand and she could barely feel his fingers in hers. She saw Fletcher flinch when the action was repeated, and cautiously wipe his hand on his trousers.

While the man himself might have been a mouse, his setup roared like a lion. When Davidson told him why they were there, he quickly gave them a tour of the facilities. His embalming suite was tidy and boasted the latest materials, all polished to a high shine, and the attached crematorium was immaculate. He even had a small but separate autopsy suite, designed specifically for independent pathologists who were called in to perform private and secondary autopsies for families.

Sam felt bad for her earlier uncharitable assessment—a mouse he might be, but a professional, cautious and meticulous one. Exactly what she needed to get to the truth about Timothy Savage.

After a bit of small talk, Hoyle led her to Savage's body, which had been prepared for cremation. When Davidson had said all stop, Hoyle took him seriously—everything was as it had been a few minutes prior, but the heat to the retort had been turned off. Savage was ensconced in a cardboard box, waiting on the automated belt. It seemed he wasn't the only customer of the day; there were a few other boxes lined up behind his.

Hoyle showed her the environs shyly. He had a soft voice she strained to hear, and didn't make much eye contact. "Dr. Owens, if you need an assistant, I can provide that service for you. My sister, Regina, has been well trained, she worked for a time in Richmond at the Office of the Chief Medical Examiner."

"Why not you, Mr. Hoyle?"

He blushed. "It's not my forte, ma'am. I'm in charge of the crematorium, and I do the final work for the funerals. Everyone wants their loved one to look pretty, and I'm a good hand with the makeup and hairstyling. My grandmother taught me.

Regina does the embalming and autopsy work. Shall I call her? She can be here in a few minutes."

"Yes, thank you, Mr. Hoyle. And if we can move Mr. Savage to the autopsy suite, I can get started with the external exam."

Fletcher said, "I'll help."

Hoyle shook his head. "Thank you, but I've got it. We have a pulley system that moves the bodies around. Let me just call Regina, and I'll get the body moved for you."

Regina promised to come straightaway, and Hoyle got Sam situated.

A few minutes later, an automated cart on wheels arrived in the autopsy suite with the cardboard coffin.

"Handy contraption," Sam said.

He smiled shyly. "It is. We have the only crematory outside of the big cities that can handle bodies over three hundred pounds. My grandfather designed the pulleys. My father added the automation. They practically move the bodies themselves."

Davidson called to Fletcher, "Hey, you need to see this." He gestured to an outer room.

Fletcher looked at Sam. "You okay?"

"Sure thing. Go ahead. I'm not going anywhere."

He left, and a pretty young woman with the same slight build as her brother appeared in the door to the suite. Roy's face lit up. "Ah, here's Regina."

"Hi, Roy." His sister came and gave his arm a squeeze, then turned to Sam with a sense of awe. "You're Dr. Owens. I've heard so much about you. I've read all your papers. It's a real honor to have a chance to work with you, ma'am."

Goodness. She felt her face getting red; she wasn't used to this kind of adulation.

"Hi, Regina. Call me Sam. You ready to get to work?"

"I am. Are you strong? Savage isn't a little guy."

"I can handle myself if you can."

"Let's do it, then."

Roy excused himself, and the two women wrestled the body from the cardboard coffin.

Savage definitely wasn't little. Sam's measurements said seventy-two inches, and the scale showed him at two hundred pounds. He was fully dressed in a black turtleneck and jeans.

"Is this how he came in?" Sam asked.

"This is how we got him," Regina said. "We did the usual radiographs to make sure he didn't have any devices or replacement joints, but the orders were to cremate him clothed."

"Is that usual?"

"Sure. Put Grandma in her favorite blue dress before the cremation, that sort of thing."

"Who dressed him, do you know?"

"No idea."

"Okay. You have the radiographs?"

"I do." She put them up on the light board, and Sam looked them over. She saw nothing of great significance, only a previous tibia fracture, well healed.

"Let's get his clothes off. I can't believe they redressed him after they examined him," she said.

"From what I've been told, there was no real examination at all. You have a clean slate."

Sam looked at Regina. "What? I knew there wasn't an internal exam, but nothing external, either?"

"Not that I know of. It was a clear case of suicide, they told us, and warned us to be careful with the body because of the hydrogen sulfide. It's the only reason we haven't sent him through the retort yet—we wanted to give the chemicals time to dissipate."

Sam shook her head, partly annoyed and partly glad. When they said no post, she'd assumed they were talking about an internal exam. What sort of fool wouldn't do any external exam on a dead body? Someone was trying to get Timothy Savage out of the way, and fast.

Once his clothes were off, Sam started on a cursory check of the body. She stopped at the neck. There were bruises around his throat. Her first instinct was strangulation, but she thought about the method of his suicide, the hydrogen sulfide, and the reaction he might have had to suddenly being unable to breathe. People sometimes brought their own hands to their throat as if they could claw an airway open from the outside. It was suspicious, but not entirely unheard of. Sam looked closely at his eyes and under the edge of his upper lip, saw the red pinpricks of petechial hemorrhage. That was to be expected in the case of asphyxiation.

He'd also bitten his tongue, a deep black wound caused by his incisors. The injury would have bled profusely, and she had seen no evidence of blood on his clothes or his body. She tucked that fact away, but felt the hair rise on the back of her neck. Someone had cleaned up Mr. Savage, after all. The police? Or someone else?

"Take a vitreous fluid, would you, Regina?"

"Sure." She expertly drew the fluid from his eye with a syringe as Sam finished the rest of the external exam. "Let's flip him."

They manhandled the body so it was facedown, and Sam gasped. The upper part of Savage's back was covered in tattoos. Spirals and triangles and stars, what seemed to be a type of Celtic love knot. No faces, no names, just strange symbols, arranged in what looked to be a repeating pattern.

"Take a photograph please, Regina."

The girl hopped up on the autopsy table and motioned for Sam to hand her the camera. She snapped off a few shots. "Pretty."

"You think?"

"Absolutely. Here, look at the shot from above. They're arranged in a triskele. Do you know what that is?"

"Never heard of it." She looked at the photos and could see

now what Regina was talking about—the multiple symbols formed a clear pattern of three interlocked spirals.

"A triskele is Celtic, and it's ancient. It was a pagan symbol, the power of three—maid, mother, crone or land, sea, sky. Any triad, really, but once Christianity came into the land, it morphed into a trinity symbol. Father, Son and Holy Spirit."

"How do you know this?"

She smiled, and Sam was reminded of a pixie. "I studied Comparative Religion and the Classics at Randolph College. I was considering entering a convent for a while, then decided I could be of better service to my Lord by helping discover what causes death. I'm considering pathology, but med school is so very expensive."

It was a strange way to phrase it, what causes death, instead of the more common forensic phrase, cause of death. But Sam didn't pursue it. She looked at Savage's back again.

"It must have taken years to get all of these tattoos," she said. "Did you know Savage, Regina? Or his son, Henry? Where he went to church, or anything else about him?"

"No, I didn't. Then again, Lynchburg's a bigger town than you might think."

"I was told Henry went to Randolph College, too."

"Really? Must have been after I left. I graduated the last year it was all women. I'm still stunned they went coed on us."

"Too much to hope for, I guess, leaving the school single-sex. Let's flip him and get moving."

Sam put her hands on his shoulders. As they maneuvered the body onto its back, she felt something hard and crusty under her fingers.

She carefully brushed back his hair and saw a trail of something silvery by the man's ear. "Hold up a sec, I want to collect this. Can you hand me a DNA swab?"

"What is it?"

"Tears. I think. It makes sense. His eyes would be burning from the chemicals. Just want to be sure we catch everything."

She collected the sample, then they washed the body and got down to the internal exam. Sam added a second set of gloves, pleased Regina had the Marigolds she preferred, put on an eye shield and double-masked herself in case of any leftover gases from Savage's lungs. She wasn't too concerned, though. It had been long enough that most of the gas would have dissipated, and they were in a well-ventilated room. Just in case, she made sure Regina had taken the same precautions, then hefted the scalpel in her right hand and glanced at the girl. "Would you like to do the cut?"

"Oh, no, Dr. Owens. I'd like to watch you do it, if you don't mind. I can probably learn a thing or two from your technique."

Sam laughed to herself a little—her technique was rusty as hell, considering—but placed the tip of the scalpel into the flesh just below the clavicle and swept the knife downward decisively. The tough skin parted, the yellow subcutaneous fat along the edges thicker than she would have anticipated for a man in such good shape. She sliced down the other side, meeting the cut just above his groin, and stepped back to allow any gases to escape. After a few moments, she set to the task of autopsy. The rib shears made quick work of the breastplate, making little crunching noises that echoed in the quiet space, and when Regina lifted it out of place, Sam's first view of the lungs brought her to a halt again.

They were perfect.

She was looking at the lungs of a healthy man, in his prime, who'd clearly never smoked or lived in an industrial, polluted area. Nor did they show any sign of irritation, or inflammation. No frothy blood, no edema.

"Son of a bitch." The words were muffled behind her mask.

"What is it?"

Sam looked up at Regina. "Timothy Savage did not die from hydrogen sulfide poisoning."

CHAPTER 14

SAM TOOK HER TIME GOING THROUGH THE REST OF THE POST. SAVAGE'S BODY HAD a tale to tell, and she was listening.

His heart was normal size for a man of his age, with a nominal buildup of cholesterol plaque. The lungs: both upper and lower lobes, when dissected, proved to be clear of any indication of a chemical irritant. Liver, kidneys, stomach, intestinal tract, all were normal. He hadn't had a recent meal before his death, though she found traces of blood he must have swallowed antemortem, and he was in decent shape.

In the examination of his throat, she found what she was looking for. Timothy Savage's trachea had clearly been crushed. He'd been strangled, just as the bruising foretold, but by the very strong hands of another, with a towel or something soft to minimize the surface bruising. Sam had seen this sort of neck injury often, in accidental autoerotic deaths, but this was clearly murder—in those cases, the padded ropes or other devices were left in place. And in this case, the killer had been facing his victim.

With that knowledge in mind, she stepped back, looked at the body from a slightly different perspective. There was some slight internal bruising just below Savage's lower ribs. Someone had put a knee on the man's chest to hold him down. They'd very purposefully strangled the man, then set about making his death appear to be suicide.

Sam felt both vindicated and frightened. Savage had been correct. He had been murdered. And now she was into his case up to her eyeballs, and there was no going back.

She went through the final steps of the post. His brain was the last piece of the puzzle, and when they got his skull open, even that showed nothing irregular, just the typical undulating coils of gray matter, perhaps slightly looser than they would have been if he were younger.

Two things were bothering her. First, that Savage himself had known he was in mortal danger and had written to her directly instead of going to the police. It made her distrust June Davidson, someone she needed on her side. And two, that the law firm representing Savage's estate had ordered him cremated without a proper autopsy. Three things, if she counted Benedict's murder.

As she washed up and watched Regina craft beautiful stitches to close the Y-incision, Sam decided there and then to bring all the blood and tissue samples she'd taken back to D.C. for analysis. She didn't trust anyone in Lynchburg, not now.

Used to sending samples out for analysis, Regina produced a small cooler that housed everything perfectly. She didn't raise an eyebrow when Sam said, "I'll drop these directly at the lab so you don't have to make a special trip."

"Should we go ahead with the cremation now?"

"If you have the room, why don't you hold on to him for another day? I'll call you tomorrow and release the body."

"Sure thing, Dr. Owens. Thank you, so much, for allowing me to assist. It was fascinating watching you work."

"You have a great touch. Remember the trick I showed you about how to cut the lung tissue so you can always identify it if you need to revisit your samples."

"Triangles for upper, squares for lower. Got it."

"If you do decide to go to med school for pathology, let me know. I'd be delighted to write a recommendation. I'm teaching at Georgetown now, so if you need a hand, don't hesitate."

Regina smiled widely. "Thank you so much. Do you have a card? So I can keep in touch?"

Sam gave her one of her new Georgetown University cards, then excused herself, went back upstairs into the grand foyer and called Fletcher. He answered, sounding slightly out of breath.

"Where are you? I'm finished, and waiting for you on the porch. We need to talk."

"We had a looky-loo hanging around. Davidson and I chased him. Guy got away, he's fast as a greyhound, but I got a good look at him. Five-eight, Caucasian, blondish hair, red-and-white baseball cap. Lock the doors and I'll be back in five minutes."

Sam didn't hesitate. She wasn't in the mood to take chances. She went inside, threw the bolt and realized how ridiculous her actions were. The place was huge, with multiple entrances. She rang the bell, and after a few moments, Regina appeared.

"Dr. Owens, you're still here. Is everything okay?"

"Is this the only entrance?"

"No, there are the back doors to the veranda and the garages downstairs, of course, where we do intake. Why?"

"Detective Fletcher and Detective Davidson are chasing a suspect. They want us safely inside with all the doors locked."

Regina responded immediately. "Follow me. The veranda doors are kept bolted, but the garage door is always open during business hours."

They hustled down the stairs. Sam's hand was beginning to

go numb from carrying the weight of the cooler. She wasn't about to let it go, though. They passed the autopsy suite and the embalming room, and entered a long hallway that led to darkness. Sam followed Regina closely lest she get lost in the labyrinth. After a minute, they stepped into a cavernous space Sam recognized from her own facility in Nashville. There were two industrial garage doors side by side, and a decent-sized body cooler.

As they entered the room, the lights went on with a hum. Sam relaxed a bit. The overheads were on motion sensors. No one was in here.

Regina slapped the button and the large doors began to drop. There was an entrance door between the two; she hurried over to it and threw the dead bolt.

"There," she said with a grim smile. "We're all secure."

Sam patted her on the back. "You seem like you've done this before."

"Oh, we have to run drills all the time. And up in Richmond, well, they don't mess around. We're expected to know the emergency precautions for any situation. Now, since you're stuck here for a bit, would you like a cup of tea or coffee? Or something stronger?"

"Tea would be fabulous."

They started back toward the stairs, down the long, dark hallway. As they turned the corner, Sam saw the door to the autopsy suite was open. Regina noticed it at the same time, and flattened back against the wall, an arm held out in front of Sam in protection. They stared at each other, both listening. Sam could have sworn she heard a noise coming from the autopsy suite.

She pointed to the suite and Regina shook her head, admonishing her to stay put. But Sam knew they had to check, see what was happening. She edged forward, slowly, one step at a time. There, she heard the noise again. It was quiet, barely audible keening. Grief. A breathy little sob.

What in the world?

She stepped firmer now, and miscalculated a corner. The cooler clanged against the wall, and there was a flash of movement. Someone burst from the room, ran into them both. Sam was shoved against the wall and knocked down, Regina collapsed beside her. Footsteps rang out as the person rushed away. Sam recovered quickly, ran down the hall after him. She turned the corner into the garage just in time to see a red-and-white baseball cap disappear out the door.

CHAPTER 15

SAM RAN TO THE DOOR AND CAREFULLY DUCKED HER HEAD OUTSIDE, BUT ALL SHE saw was an expanse of green lawn and a curving asphalt drive. Whoever had just been in the autopsy suite was gone.

Fast as a greyhound was an understatement.

She used a tissue from her pocket to relock the door, careful not to wipe away any possible fingerprints, then hurried back to Regina, who was collecting herself up off the floor. Her eyes weren't totally focused on Sam.

"Are you okay?"

"I think I hit my head. Sorry. Did he get away?"

"He's gone. Let me see." Sam expertly ran her hands through Regina's hair, feeling for the lump. She found it in the front, near her temple. She gave the girl a quick neurological exam, but she was focusing better.

"You're going to have a headache, and you've got a little concussion. You might even sport a black eye tomorrow. Keep a close watch on yourself for the rest of the day. If your headache gets worse, go to the hospital immediately, okay?"

"Yeah. I'm fine. Just went down awkwardly. Hit my head on the edge of the cooler, of all things."

"We'd best check the body. Whoever that was wanted something from Savage."

They got Regina back to standing and entered the autopsy suite. The body was undisturbed.

Sam looked around the room but saw nothing out of place. "Regina, before he ran out of here, did you hear crying?"

"I thought I did. That is so weird. I've seen some odd things, but we've never had a break-in like this. Nothing taken, nothing disturbed. No harm, no foul. Oh, shoot. I better go check on Roy. He was supposed to be working on Mrs. Edmunds this afternoon."

Sam collected the cooler, which had been knocked over when Regina fell on it, and checked inside. Everything was still in its place. Regina led them down the opposite hallway to the embalming room.

Roy was inside, earbuds in, studiously brushing a dead woman's long silver hair. He didn't hear them come in. Regina smiled, then signaled to Sam to back away.

Once in the hallway, she said, "If he'd been disturbed, he wouldn't be so calm. He's a nervous sort, my brother. Scared of his own shadow. But so good at his job. You need someone caring at this stage, and he's a love. Come on. Let's get back upstairs." The girl's natural exuberance showed itself. "I'm sure you want to call your cop friend, let him know we had a visitor."

Sam called Fletch's phone, but he didn't answer. Moments later, they heard the doorbell ring.

"Ah, there they are," Sam said.

They went to the foyer and Regina unlocked the front door. The men came in, both breathing heavily and sweating.

Regina took Davidson to the autopsy suite to show him what happened, leaving Sam and Fletcher alone. She handed him a bottle of water from her bag. He gulped greedily while she explained what had transpired, and Fletcher's brows drew closer together.

"What happened earlier?" Sam asked.

"June caught a flash of the baseball cap, called out for him to stop, but he took off at a sprint. We got after him, but he ducked into the woods and disappeared. Poof, gone. He must have circled back and come in through the garage doors. Nothing's missing?"

Sam shook her head. "Not that we can see. Fletch, he was standing over the body, and it sounded like he was crying. Do you think this could be the son, Henry Matcliff? The glimpse I had, he looked young."

"Maybe. Xander checked in—he's going into the woods to see if he can spot the man for us. Keep that under your hat for now." His voice dropped, and she had to lean forward to hear him. "I don't trust Davidson, not yet. I don't think he's told us everything about Savage. Something odd's going on here."

"No kidding."

Before they could analyze things further, Davidson returned with Regina.

"We better get over to the law firm. I'll send an officer out here to keep an eye on things until we get Savage's wishes cleared up. Regina will keep watch, won't you, honey?"

Regina rolled her eyes at the endearment, clearly offended, but nodded. She pointedly ignored Davidson, but shook Sam's hand, and Fletcher's. "Thanks for everything, Dr. Owens. I'll see you around. You need anything, just call."

She waited for them to leave, and Sam clearly heard the bolt thrown on the front door. Good. At least someone wasn't going to take any chances.

The law offices of Benedict, Picker, Green and Thompson were on Rivermont Avenue, only a ten-minute drive from

Hoyle's. They were in a redbrick two-story Victorian dollhouse, complete with white trim and turrets, which, they soon found out, housed the firm's library of law books.

They were met in the reception area by an older gentleman with white hair and a rotund stomach. He wore a gray summer-weight wool suit, his tie a florid green slash across his belly.

"Good, you're here at last." He turned to Sam and Fletcher. "I'm McKendry Picker. You can call me Mac. We're all just sick about Rolph. What more can you tell us about his death? I need to let his wife know the details, and his kids, they're flying in from around the country to be with their mother, and this is all just so heartbreaking. We knew he wasn't going to last long with the disease and all, but to die like this, murdered, so far away from home, it's just—" He burst into tears.

Sam's first instinct was to comfort him, but Fletcher cleared his throat and imperceptibly shook his head at her, so she stood her ground.

Davidson was the one who laid a hand on the older man's shoulder. "Mac, shh, it's okay, man. I know how hard this is for everyone. Where are Tony and Stacey?"

Picker got himself together, sniffling and wiping his eyes with an embroidered handkerchief. "They're in Las Vegas. A deposition for a client. They'll fly back as soon as they're finished, should be in this evening." He turned to Sam and Fletcher and cleared his throat, the tears still sparkling on his cheeks.

"I'm so sorry to lose control like that. Saying it aloud made it so real. Rolph and I have been friends for forty years. I'm going to miss him dreadfully."

Fletch bowed his head and said softly, "We understand, sir. Is there someplace we can sit and chat for a bit?"

"Of course. We have pastries and coffee waiting in the conference room. Follow me, please."

Sam noticed the man's stride was slightly off, as if he were wearing a knee brace, or had twisted his ankle. When they got into the conference room, which was gorgeous—dark wood and gleaming floor-to-ceiling glass windows overlooking an extravagant all-white flower garden—Sam asked him about it as they settled around the table.

"Korea, I'm afraid. Lost the leg. I was shipped over toward the end, when I was only seventeen, though Uncle Sam didn't know that. I was green as a sapling, and stepped on a mine the first day I was there. Blew it right off. I was lucky, they saved my knee, and prosthetics have come so far since I first began wearing them. And I'm blessed with excellent insurance."

"I'm so sorry," Sam said. "You seem to manage beautifully."

"Years of practice. And don't be sorry. Government paid for everything, from my leg through to my schooling. I wouldn't have gotten into law without the push. Everything happens for a reason, Dr. Owens. Even losing a leg in a stupid accident, or the untimely death of a friend. Now please, tell me what's happening. Why was my best friend murdered?"

CHAPTER 16

FLETCHER LET JUNE DAVIDSON DO THE TALKING, AND WATCHED THE ARRAY OF emotions parade across Mac Picker's face as he heard the story.

"Let me get this straight. Savage hired Rolph to put together a will, and named Dr. Owens here executor? That's very odd, very odd indeed. When you called and told me the details, I checked our database. We don't have a record of Savage being a client. There's nothing to indicate he and Rolph ever even met."

"Did Benedict have a history of doing pro bono work?" Fletcher asked.

"Well, sure. We all do our part to help out indigents, and other cases where it would be to our benefit to be involved for a nominal fee. And there's always the chance Rolph was helping out on his own time, not on behalf of the firm. But I'm sorry, there's nothing here, nothing at all."

"Did Mr. Benedict have a paralegal? Someone who may have helped him draft the will?" Davidson asked.

"We do have paralegals, but they're absolutely one hundred

percent bound by the law and our internal policies to put everything into the system as it comes in. It's procedure. We may look like a small Southern operation, but we've got a state-of-the-art legal electronic filing system. We've been electronic for about five years now, and everything, *everything,* goes through our database directly into the judiciary. It's mandatory.

"Now the only outsiders are some interns who come in a few times a week, students from around town who are taking prelaw and want to experience the real deal. But they don't have access to the databases. The interns are more for show, if you'll forgive the admission. It makes them feel like they're learning, and the school gives them class credit for their time spent here. The firm gets the cachet of having the top students in the area fight to work for us. But we don't let them actually do anything."

Fletcher picked up an iced cinnamon roll, took a casual bite. He used the remains to point at Picker. "So you're saying Benedict must have done his work for Savage off-book?"

Picker's face reddened. "I suppose that's exactly what I'm saying, though the way you put it, it sounds quite sordid."

Davidson stepped in, hands up. "Mac, relax. We believe you. But we're gonna need Rolph's computer from his office, and his date book. I know you understand."

Picker's shoulders squared, and his chin rose. "And you certainly understand I'll need to see your warrant. That computer contains highly confidential material, and we can't just allow it to parade out of here. I've looked on it myself, and there's no sign of any files under the name Savage."

"Come on. You're gonna make me go to Judge Hessian? You really want him breathing down your neck? My God, Mac, that can be construed as tampering with evidence, and you know it."

"No, I don't. I'm sorry, I need that warrant first. And, June, don't threaten me. It's not polite. Your father wouldn't appreciate it, and I don't, either."

Fletcher was enjoying this exchange. Despite his misgivings, he thought Davidson was probably all right, once you got past the big-town-cop, small-town-cop posturing, but he wasn't above taking pleasure in seeing someone get a spanking. He glanced over at Sam to see if she was amused, too, and saw she wasn't paying attention anymore, but was staring at her phone screen. While Davidson and Picker went at each other, he nudged her knee and raised an eyebrow. She handed him the phone.

The text was from Xander.

At Savage's place. You and Fletch need to get out here. Now. No locals.

Sam took the phone back, and Fletcher stood.

"Gentlemen, I hate to interrupt this fascinating discourse, but while you hash this out, Dr. Owens and I should really get the samples from Savage's autopsy to the lab. Detective Davidson, would you mind calling me when you're done here? We can meet up after you've served the warrant."

Both men gaped at him, but Davidson recovered quickly. "Sure. No problem. Might take an hour or so. We'll have to pull Judge Hessian off the links. He has a standing tee time once court lets out for the day. You'll be on your cell?"

"I will."

"Lab's down the street, toward the river. Just go back the way we came in. You can't miss it. I'll see you there once we get things settled. Mac here will do the right thing as soon as Old Hessian gets wind of this. Won't you, Mac?"

Picker glared at the younger man and said nothing.

Fletcher shook hands with Picker, and he and Sam left the room. He heard Davidson saying, "Now, listen, you old fool, you know we have every right to see Rolph's computer." His voice drifted off, and Fletcher waited until they were outside to say, "Bunch of BS going on in there. Thanks for getting us out. They're going to argue for hours, and I don't feel like waiting around."

"Picker's hiding something," Sam said.

"I know. Maybe he'll be more open with Davidson once we're out of here. You have an address for Savage?"

"Yeah. We need to head back north on Highway 29, then take the first exit east toward Farmville. His cabin is just outside the city limits."

"You're a regular cartographer."

That made her laugh, and he was glad, because the worried dent left her forehead. "Maps are my secret love. No, Xander sent another text with the instructions. He says to watch for a large oak tree with a split trunk. That's the entrance to the drive. I hope he's okay."

"He's fine. He'd have sent an SOS if he was in danger. Sounds to me like he found something interesting and didn't want to share it with Davidson until we had a chance to look it over."

Sam nodded. "I'm sure you're right. We have to get these samples to D.C. as soon as we can. They'll be okay in the cooler for twelve hours or so—they're packed well—but that's it. I don't trust anyone down here to handle them properly. I took a DNA swab from Savage's neck and ear. I'm hoping we'll have something belonging to the killer. He held him down, a knee in his stomach, and strangled him face-to-face. It takes a lot of hate to watch someone die like that. I'm hoping he was talking while he did it, and some saliva got onto Savage's face."

"You're good at this."

"Too much experience."

He drove in silence for a few minutes, thinking to himself,

That's why Savage wanted you. He knew you'd be able to suss things out. Then Sam said, "There, that's the road we need."

"You sure?"

"I'm sure. Turn."

The road looked more like a donkey track, thin ruts in the dirt wending into a deep, dark forest, and Fletcher's Caprice didn't have the best clearance for off-roading, but he listened, going cautiously so he didn't bottom out.

"Whitfield has his Jeep, I take it?"

"I'm sure he does. He doesn't like to drive my BMW. Makes him feel icky, he says." She laughed. "His parents really did a number on him when it comes to anything that could be construed as capitalistic."

"BMWs are only for capitalists, I take it?"

"Yep. The road to his cabin isn't much better than this, and washes out in heavy rains, so he's got the Jeep jacked up a bit. I'm sure it was no problem. Come on, Grandma, put your foot in it. It evens out in a hundred feet."

"Grandma my ass," he muttered, but she was right, the road did get better once they got away from the highway. He supposed Savage kept it a mess to discourage visitors. It was effective.

Another mile into the woods, Savage's cabin appeared. It wasn't much to speak of. Fletcher had seen hunting shacks with more space, but he supposed only one person didn't need too much room. If the kid was grown and gone, and it was only Savage, it would be enough.

"Where's Xander's Jeep?" Sam asked.

Fletcher didn't see it, but he assumed Whitfield was smart enough to have it out of the way. He was right; as he pulled the Caprice to a stop, Whitfield appeared next to them, almost as if he'd walked right out of a tree.

"God, I hate it when he does that."

"Me, too," Sam said. "It's like he's part of the forest. He does it up on the mountain all the time. He and Thor can disappear in plain sight. It's spooky."

She got out of the car and went to him, and gave him a quick kiss. Nothing overt, nothing sloppy, only a peck, and even after everything Fletcher had said on the way to Lynchburg, he still felt a twist in his gut when he saw the way she looked at him.

Let it go, man. She ain't ever gonna be yours.

Better friends than nothing, that was for sure. He'd probably lose her, anyway, get himself into his familiar routine, once the novelty wore off.

Keep telling yourself that, Fletch. You might even start to believe it.

He stepped from the car and his cell rang. He looked down to see Hart was calling. "Hold on a sec. Gotta take this."

Hart's voice was tight and anxious. "Where the hell are you, hoss? I went by your place to bring you a study lunch and it was buttoned up tight."

"South. Lynchburg. I'm helping Sam out on a case. Why, what's up?"

"We have a missing kid. Ten-year-old girl named Rachel Stevens. Disappeared from Connecticut Avenue, near the zoo. Parents reported her missing an hour ago, and the cops who came to take the report found a note. Probable kidnapping. AMBER Alert just went up. We need you back here, right now."

"Who snatched her?"

"No idea. Parents are married. It doesn't look custodial. Armstrong's liaising with the FBI. It's task force city, all hands on deck."

"Shit."

"As in it's hitting the fan, yes. So get your sweet booty back to D.C., will ya?"

Fletch looked at his watch. It was 2:00 p.m. "I'll be back by 7:00. Tell Armstrong."

"This is going to be over by 5:00. Hurry up."

He hung up and Fletcher stowed his phone.

Sam had been listening. "What's wrong?"

"A little girl named Rachel Stevens has gone missing. I gotta get back to D.C."

Sam frowned. "That's awful. Well, I know all the players now, and the hard part's over. You can go back up. Xander can keep an eye on me. You can take the samples to Amado, and he can begin the tests. It gives us half a day's head start. And we'll come back up tonight."

Leaving Sam in the lion's den with all the lies flying around went against his better judgment, but he didn't see that he had a choice. She was right, the bulk of the work had been done. Now it was up to the evidence to lead them to an answer.

Whitfield was studying him with those dark, unreadable eyes. "You're cool with this?"

He nodded. "No worries, man. I can take care of her. But you're going to want to see this before you go."

CHAPTER 17

SAM FOLLOWED XANDER AND FLETCHER TO THE ENTRANCE OF SAVAGE'S CABIN. THE hand-drawn biohazard signs were still stuck in the windows, but the warning sign had been removed from the front door. She crossed herself as she entered the dimness, in case Timothy Savage was still hanging around. She didn't want to bring him home with her. It was a habit she had when visiting crime scenes. Both men looked at her queerly, but she smiled and nodded them inside.

Savage lived small. And off the grid, from the looks of it. Xander walked them through the house—living room, workable kitchen, two small bedrooms and a bathroom with a shower, no tub. The walls were rough-hewn wood, and undecorated, the beds little more than cots. There was a stone fireplace in the living room with three rows of neatly stacked logs running up the wall to the ceiling. The refrigerator was sized for an apartment and held an assortment of glass juice jars, unbound fruits and vegetables, all going rotten. There was a small pantry, with oatmeal, almonds, seeds, dried fruit and three different kinds of beans, and what looked like homemade granola. Sam thought back to the autopsy—the healthy heart and lungs, the muscle tone—she'd bet her life Timothy Savage was a vegan.

"I wonder if he lived here full-time?" Sam asked.

Xander nodded. "I think so, though it is rather sparse, even for a mountain man. There's a garden out back. He grew his own vegetables. Used newspapers as mulch, there's a tidy little stack on the porch. There's also a smoking shed, but no sign of any meat. This isn't the interesting part, though. Follow me."

He went back into the living room and walked straight to the wall where, in a normal house, there would be a television set. He waved his hands, said, "Abracadabra," and pushed on the center of the wall.

The latch was on a well-oiled spring connected to a damper. It allowed a three-foot-square piece of wall to fall open slowly, giving way to a sturdy and serviceable desk. Inside the cubbyhole, there was a small laptop computer and a wireless router, neither plugged in, and a whole series of pictures, maps, articles and photographs tacked to a corkboard that took up the entire wall inside the small space. When Sam's eyes adjusted to the gloom, she realized she was looking at herself.

She gasped. "Oh, my God. What is this?"

Fletcher spoke through his teeth. "It's a shrine."

She shot him a look, saw he was holding back. Fletcher did not like being in the dark, and Savage's mystery was getting darker and darker.

Xander used a pencil to poke through the detritus. "Looks like a log. Of all the cases Sam's worked, and everything she's published. Cases from Nashville—you worked a couple of serials down there, and they were big news. The photos are from the internet, none of them were actually taken and developed. Except this one."

He pointed to the center of the wall, where Sam was seen in

profile, walking in Georgetown. Fear coursed through her as she recognized the landscape behind her. "That's on our street."

Xander glanced at her. "It is."

"How can you be so calm about this?" Her breath began to hitch, and she started rubbing her hands together.

Fletcher touched her arm. "Hey. Chill. Nothing's going to happen to you. Dude's dead and gone."

"Don't tell me to chill, Darren." She couldn't help her tone, bitter and angry, and suddenly she was falling, losing control, and she didn't care if they saw—this man had been stalking her, and now he was dead, and his lawyer was dead, which meant she was probably next. And she was damn tired of having to be on her guard all the time. She thought she'd left that part of her world back in Nashville. In the top story of a house in Belle Meade, with her blood spilling out onto the floor, the twist of the knife in her gut.

She dimly realized Xander had his arms around her, was shushing her like she was a small child having a nightmare, which she was. The rational part of her mind said, *It's PTSD, you're having a flashback, you're okay, you're safe,* and the irrational part was screaming, *No, no, no, no, no! Not again, not now, not when everything is finally starting to be all right.*

Xander was crooning to her in a singsong voice, "Come on, honey, breathe for me. You're okay. You're fine. We're here. Nothing bad's gonna happen to you." To Fletcher he said, "Shit. If I'd known it would spark an attack, I'd never have brought her out here."

"It's disturbing as hell, Whitfield. What did you expect, she'd go skipping out happy as a clam knowing some dead guy was stalking her? What were you thinking?"

She heard them snapping at each other, realized she could hear again, and see. Air moved into her lungs. She slumped down to her knees on the floor, eyes closed, focused on their voices. *Here, and now. You're in Virginia, in Lynchburg, not in Nashville. You're safe.*

She opened her eyes to see Xander's face an inch from her own. She started and jerked back, then laughed shakily. "I'm okay. Sorry. I'm so sorry."

He wrapped his arms around her and buried his head in her shoulder. "I didn't think. Fletcher's right, I shouldn't have brought you here."

She glanced up at Fletcher, who should have had his *told-you-so* face on, but his was etched with concern.

"You okay, sunshine?"

She nodded. *Crap.* She hadn't had a full-blown panic attack in months. Her heart was still raw from pumping so hard her chest actually hurt. Her vision was fully back now. She'd gone totally blind for a minute, and that scared her as much as the breathless feeling of overwhelming doom she'd just experienced.

Stupid amygdala. If she could have it replaced, she would.

She got to her feet. Xander held tight to her hand. She took a deep breath and said, "I'm fine. Really. So, what are we going to do about this?"

Fletcher said, "We can worry about that another time."

"Seriously, I'm okay. What does all this mean?"

Fletcher shrugged. "Honestly? I think it's time we got out of here. Let Davidson come in and take over, or hand it to the Feds. Though how he missed this, I don't know. But I think it's best you leave Lynchburg now. Just in case."

She looked around the tiny cabin. *Who were you? Why me? What in the world drew you to me?* "You're right, Fletch. The man's dead. It's not like he can hurt me."

Xander had been poking around the pictures while they talked, moving them aside carefully with the pencil. He said, "Take a look at this."

Sam didn't want to, but she did. Behind the pinned-up detritus of her life, there was a safe built into the wall. "What's in there?"

Fletcher shrugged. "The better question is, how do we get in?"

Xander glanced back over his shoulder at Sam. They said the words at the same time.

"The key."

"What key?"

Sam said, "Benedict gave me a key before he left. He said Savage told him I'd know what to do with it. Xander, do you have it?" But he was already fitting the small silver key into the slot. With a small creak, the safe unlocked.

Inside was a tan envelope, legal size, and a white letter-sized envelope with *Dr. Samantha Owens* printed in careful letters. She recognized Savage's handwriting.

Xander opened the bigger envelope. "Ah, good. A copy of Savage's will. We'll take this with us." He looked at Sam. "Fletcher told me the law office where Benedict worked was claiming there was no file on Savage in their system. Looks like Savage was suspicious of them, as well, and wasn't taking chances."

"What's in the other envelope?"

They heard Thor begin to bark, a warning that someone was coming.

"Shit," Fletcher said. "Get that wall back up where it's supposed to be." He took the will and the letter and stashed them both down his pants, snug against his back, and dropped his shirt down over them. He pulled his Glock and stepped in front of Sam, to the door.

Xander put the wall back into place and went to stand next to Fletcher. He didn't have a weapon, but he didn't need one. He could handle things with his bare hands, if he had to.

The warning barks ceased. The nose of an LPD patrol car eased into the lane in front of the house and stopped. June Davidson got out, gun drawn, his head swiveling back and forth between Fletcher's car and the cabin.

"Detective Fletcher? Dr. Owens? You in there? Everything okay? We got a report about a prowler out here in the woods. Thought it might be the guy who showed up at Hoyle's."

Fletcher relaxed a bit, gave Xander a warning look, but didn't drop his gun hand. He went to the door, called out, "It's just us."

Davidson didn't put his gun away. "What in the world are you doing out here? I thought you were headed to the lab."

"We were, but Dr. Owens decided she wanted to see the scene, and I knew you were busy. We've had a chance to look it over, and she's comfortable with her findings."

Davidson was moving closer slowly. Xander pulled Sam back away from the door.

Fletcher stepped out and raised his hands, a friendly gesture except for the Glock in his right palm. "Slow down, there, fella. You put yours away, I'll put mine away."

Davidson smiled. "I don't think so. You go first."

"Come on, man. This is ridiculous. Put your fucking weapon down."

"I don't believe I like your tone."

Xander started edging Sam toward the back of the house. He whispered, "We can go out the back, through the garden."

Sotto voce, she replied, "I'm not leaving Fletch."

"He knows what he's doing. Come on, damn it, or I'll pick you up and carry you out."

He started to pull on her arm, and he was too strong; she had no choice but to follow. They'd just reached the back door when she heard Fletcher scream, "Stop!" and the bullets started to fly.

CHAPTER 18

A BULLET WHIZZES PAST MY HEAD LIKE A SUPERCHARGED BUMBLEBEE AND STRIKES the elm tree to my right, scattering bark and wood chips. The birds shoot into the air and I duck instinctively, ripping the hat off my head, cursing myself for forgetting it. It was clearly the target. I toss it away. It hangs on a bush and spins lazily.

I am not a fan of guns. I know how to use them, all kinds, from sniper rifles to shotguns, semiautomatic pistols to six-shooters. And I know how well they work, as a deterrent, or to bring down dinner. But when they're pointed at human flesh, something rises in me and I feel the urge to scream. So much hatred, so many deaths that could be prevented. Wars and school shootings and suicides and gangs. It hurts me.

Then again, everything hurts me.

Before the bullets, the forest was quiet. In mourning, as if it knows my loss, feels it along with me. It normally shelters me, hides me from the bad people. I know it like the back of my hands and they don't. Yesterday, I think it was yesterday, or the day before—they're all running together now—they got caught up in the limbs and bogs and finally, finally, gave up.

I retreat deeper into the woods, back toward the river, knowing they can't follow long. So I can grieve properly, in private, without them breathing down my neck. Revisit my memories, my life, with all its twists and turns and hurts.

More bullets fly, but they're high and back to the right, away from me. Toward the chalky cliff, where they'll assume I've retreated. No one in their right mind would go up, instead of down toward the road and escape.

I don't stop to wonder who is shooting at me. It doesn't matter. It used to be us against the world, and now it is only me. Me, and no one else. I have no allies. No friends. No family. No one even knows I still exist.

Five minutes of rough terrain, my legs burn and throb, but I'm on the high ground now, approaching the edge of a steep cliff where I've been sleeping, looking down toward the cabin. They've defiled it. I will never feel safe there again.

The gunshots are over now. The forest is returning to normal. The birds resettle in the high meadow, chirping madly; the deer creep from their thickets. I push onward, higher and higher, to the one place I know I'll be okay. Closer to heaven. Closer to him.

I don't see the branch coming. When it hits me, with the force of a baseball bat, I go down in a heap. Blood pools in my mouth, two molars on the backside are loose, I've bitten my tongue. My nose is broken; I can feel blood spurting from the wound.

"Where do you think you're going?"

Every ounce of my being panics. That voice. The voice I've been running from for so long, thrashing and screaming in the night to get away from, is here. It's over. It is all over.

I roll to my hands and knees, still stunned, scrambling backward. My heart pounds so hard it drowns out my thrashing. I can't speak, my tongue is swollen and in the way. Bloody saliva spills down my chin and mingles with the forest floor. I am afraid to look up, knowing what I will see.

"Where have you been, little one? I've been looking for you for such a long time."

The voice laughs, and my blood freezes. I can't be taken. Not again. Never again.

I inch toward the edge of the cliff. It is my only hope. I hear the water rushing; the waterfall is less than twenty feet away.

"Just where do you think you're going?"

I have one chance here, one chance to get away. I look up, and there is sudden recognition in the blue eyes facing me, but it's too late. I leap off the edge, tumble backward into the air. The free fall is sickeningly long. These may be my last moments, so I shut my eyes and allow the air to buffet me as I drop steadily, toward the water.

Death or freedom. There are no other choices for me now.

CHAPTER 19

1987
McLean, Virginia

IT WAS HOT FOR JUNE. WORKING CONSTRUCTION WAS SUPPOSED TO BE A STRESS reliever, a good way to get a tan, make some money and learn a trade. His father always said learning a trade will be your greatest asset later in life. Work with your hands. Figure out how to build things. You won't regret it.

His best friend, his only friend, really, was lifeguarding at the local country club. Adrian tried to apply with him so they could spend this last summer of high school together before they became seniors and their world changed forever. But the club was adamant; they only hired the children of members. So Adrian's choice was a summer of mowing lawns or building houses. He didn't have the temperament to be a waiter. He chose houses.

He liked seeing something created, liked knowing it was going to stand for years to come. After a day's work, there was discernible progress. Foundations were poured. Wall frames went up. Trusses were laid, roof beams installed, and shingles and drywall; then suddenly they were finished and on to the next house.

His foreman was a dick, but who liked their boss? Frank was a heavily muscled jarhead who chewed gum like a cow, mouth open, the elastic wad of tasteless Juicy Fruit snapping back and forth like cement in a mixer, and barked orders while sitting on his ass, watching everyone else work. He'd slide in when the heavy stuff was going on, take all the credit. Adrian knew to keep his mouth shut, and take his lumps along with the next guy. The pay was decent, he got to be outside all day and if Frank needed a favor, he usually came to Adrian first, the youngest, least experienced member of the crew.

Adrian was no dummy. He knew how to work being in someone's debt.

The first day, when Frank sent him to the 7-Eleven for cigarettes and a twelve-pack of Budweiser, he wasn't carded. The bored man working the counter never gave him a glance, never questioned him about his age, just rang up the beer and smokes and tossed them in a bag. Adrian saw an opportunity. He was already big, six-four and two-twenty at the tender age of sixteen, a year younger than the rest of the kids in his class. His build worked to his favor when he decided to pick up his own party accoutrements. He and Doug would take the nasty cheap beer he bought to the top floor of the parking deck of the Bennigan's restaurant in Tyson's Corner, where the servers hung out after their shift. They'd share the beer and get hammered with them. The servers were mostly freshman and sophomores at George Mason University and Northern Virginia Community College, older and more sophisticated and certainly felt it wasn't cool to befriend high schoolers. But they tolerated the younger boys because they could score the beer.

He'd party hearty, then drive home, weaving along the back

roads, pass out for a few hours before he had to get up at dawn to drive his beat-up pickup over to the build site. A couple of hours in the sun sweated out his hangover, and by noon, when they were all a sweaty, nasty mess and Frank sent him for lunch, Adrian would go willingly, grateful to let the breeze from the open truck windows cool him off as he drove toward town.

He didn't have a care in the world until the day Frank approached him for a favor. Adrian was up on the roof, straddling a beam, nailing together the edges of the truss they'd just laid. The *pa-pap* of the air gun slamming nails into the wood was rhythmic and smooth. He had a bad hangover, but he'd found if he timed the pressurized blast to coincide with his heartbeats, it was more like a drum tattoo and much less offensive to his aching head—*bump, hiss, da-bump, hiss, da-bump, hiss, da-bump.*

He was annoyed when a shadow loomed over him, interrupting his rhythm. He shielded his eyes and looked up. Frank, actually up on the roof, sunglasses on, bald head covered in a red bandanna, sweat streaming down his cheeks, looking like he had at least three sticks of gum wedged into his cheek.

"Kid. I need you after work. Meet me here at 10:00 p.m. Leave your truck at 7-Eleven."

"I have plans."

"Yeah, you do, dick weed. With me. Don't be late, or I'll fuck you up."

"What are we doing?"

"Do I pay you to ask questions?" He leaned over, the gum wad going full speed, little flecks of spit launching from his mouth onto Adrian.

Adrian wiped his face and shook his head. "No, sir."

"Good. 10:00 p.m. Don't be late."

After work, Adrian showered, drank a beer with Doug, made an excuse about not feeling good, dropped his truck at 7-Eleven as instructed. He smoked a cigarette on the corner of Spring Hill and Old Dominion, then walked to the building site. He tried not to be curious about what Frank wanted with him after dark. Tried to be cool.

The half-built houses looked different at night. There was a sliver of moon, a thin half crescent giving off a feeble light. Frank was sitting on a pylon, waiting for him. He was edgy, jumpy, his thick hands clenching in and out of fists.

"Finally. Thought you might pussy out on me."

"You told me to come, so here I am. What are we doing?"

"In a few minutes, a car's gonna drive up with a dude in it who owes me some money. I need to get a point across. You ever been in a fight?"

Adrian snickered. He'd been in plenty of fights, especially when he was younger. The collective pack, finding their appropriate places. Even as he got bigger, boys liked to test him, to see what he was capable of. He liked fighting, but he kept that under wraps, because his dad went ballistic every time he came home with a busted lip or a black eye.

"Good. If I ask you to hit him, do it. No hesitation, just pop him one. If I decide I want to pump him up myself, you hold him. Got it?"

"Why do you need me for this?"

Frank looked at him like he was an absolute idiot. "You see anyone else on the crew your size? Size matters, kid. Don't let the girls tell you different." He guffawed and spit out his wad of gum, tossed it in the bushes. Adrian wanted to tell him not to, that birds would eat it and get sick, like when they ate wedding rice and their bellies blew up, but he held his tongue. Something was weird about Frank tonight. He didn't want the negative attention focused on him. And he kind of liked being singled out to back up his boss in a fight.

Frank flexed his shoulders and cracked his knuckles. "Besides, I'm betting you can keep a secret. Am I right?"

Adrian didn't see the harm in telling the truth. "Yeah."

"Good. This is just between you and me. There's a twenty in it for you if it goes well."

And that's how, ten minutes later, he found himself with his arms wrapped around a strange man's neck, holding him in an unbreakable half nelson, as Frank tuned him up. The punches weren't easy; Frank's fists were like anvils, diving into the man's soft flesh like a baker punching down dough.

Adrian held on for dear life, and was embarrassed to realize he had a raging hard-on. He was holding this struggling man from behind, and every bump and groan and cry and flinch made him harder and harder until he didn't think he could bear it. The punches were landing with regular thuds, and the man was trying to cry out, trying to fight, to do something, but he was struggling less and less, and Adrian didn't want to let him go, didn't want to stop squeezing. It felt so good. He didn't know why he was so angry, so full of righteous fury. The man in his arms was so much smaller he couldn't even fight back anymore. Adrian squeezed, realizing dimly he'd pulled the man off the ground. His feet were in the air, kicking wildly and Adrian forced his forearm tighter against the man's throat.

"Jesus, kid, stop. Let him go. You're killing him. Adrian, you little shit, stop it!"

He heard the words in a fog, like the buzzing, annoying whine of a mosquito. He realized he was breathing hard, had actually climaxed in his jeans. Frank was pulling on his arm now, trying to release the man from Adrian's death grip.

Adrian finally released his arms and stepped back, and the man dropped to the ground with a thud, gasping and wheezing for breath.

"What the fuck was that? Are you insane? I said hold him, not kill him. Idiot."

Frank took one look at Adrian's face and reared back. He fell on his ass, eyes wild, grabbed a piece of rebar and held it out in front of him. Adrian took a step toward his boss and laughed, a sound he'd never heard out of his mouth, high-pitched and crazy. He had no idea where it came from; he found nothing funny about the situation.

Frank shouted, "Get the fuck outta here. Don't come back. You hear me?"

Adrian stopped. Frank was scared of him. Of him!

"Frank, it's fine. I'm sorry."

Frank waved the rebar. "No, it's not fine. You're gone. You get me? You're fucking nuts. I shoulda known it. Too quiet, watching everyone, doing everything you're told. Fucking freak."

Time stopped. Adrian didn't know what happened, what came over him, just that it was blackness and rage. He snatched the piece of rebar from Frank's hand and brought it down on his head once, twice, three times. The wet splats told him to stop, but he couldn't. He was riding high again, the pure energy of fury driving his arms up and down.

When he came back to himself, neither of the men were moving anymore, and Adrian was panting, covered in blood and sweat and tears.

His first and only thought was for himself. He'd just killed two men. He was going to go to jail. Forever. No one would let him see the light of day again. His breath hitched and he started to cry. What had he done? What had come over him? What had just happened? He began turning in circles, frantic, trying to decide what to do, when a voice spoke to him, quiet, calm, gentle.

That won't happen. Look where you are. You know they're pouring the foundation for Lot 8 tomorrow. You're okay. You can cover this up.

Without hesitating, he dragged the two bodies forty feet to the edge of the foundation on Lot 8. He rolled them over the edge, then grabbed a shovel, jumped down and dug as if his life depended on it.

It took him an hour to get them in place, dirt two feet deep over them, leaves and branches laid down around the site just as they'd been before. He shoveled off the blood-soaked dirt into the bushes, scattering it around, found a half-empty bottle of Gatorade and washed his hands, then, realizing it wasn't going to be enough, stripped off his shirt and pants and buried them, too.

All the while, the voice spoke, telling him what to do next.

There was nothing he could do about the man's car, but where it was parked was safe enough, off the beaten path behind the 7-Eleven. By the time anyone connected it with the build site, the cement would be dry. Frank's behemoth truck was nowhere to be seen, so he didn't worry about it.

He snuck back to his own piece-of-crap truck and drove home, showered then went out to the truck and wiped it down. Bleach. Scrub. He made sure there was nothing, *nothing,* that could tie him to the two men. Showered again, thankful as hell his dad was out.

There. He was safe.

Surprising himself, he slept soundly. He woke the next morning, certain the police would be standing in his bedroom, but his room was empty. He went into the kitchen, and there was just his dad, home early, looking vacantly at *The Washington Post,* a half-eaten apple cruller and a cold cup of coffee at his elbow.

Adrian choked down some eggs, went to the site, stood around with the rest of the crew waiting for Frank to show, then getting to work when he didn't. He stayed on the roof while the cement was poured at Lot 8, keeping a hawk's eye on the proceedings.

It went off without a hitch.

When the police finally came around asking about Frank, he shrugged along with the rest of the men. And then there was nothing. He was off the hook.

Adrian thought back to that night all the time, analyzing, wondering, trying to figure it all out.

It took a few weeks before it hit him, an insight so frightening it took his breath away, a terrible, awful, wonderful truth. The universe opened, a giant black maw, and the blackness of the sky suddenly had texture, depth, feeling. It caressed his skin and licked softly at his neck.

He'd liked the feeling of the man struggling, because he'd liked the power he felt, being bigger and stronger and holding a stranger's life in his hands. As for what happened after, when he lost control, well, that was simply the situation. Frank had pushed him over the edge. Right?

Maybe. Maybe not. Adrian wasn't going to lie to himself. The more he thought about the power he'd felt in those brief moments, the more excited he got. He'd liked it, more than a lot. He'd liked it so much that for the rest of the summer, all he could think of was trying it again.

CHAPTER 20

Lynchburg, Virginia

SAM WAS FACEDOWN ON THE CABIN FLOOR WITH ALL OF XANDER'S WEIGHT ON her. The sound of gunshots grew intermittent and farther away until the shooting stopped completely.

"Let me up, Xander. We're safe."

With a sigh, he finally relented. She brushed herself off. She'd skinned a knee when he'd dived on top of her and forced her to the floor. At first she'd thought Davidson was shooting at Fletcher, but the shouting told her the two were united, running off after a suspect. She was very relieved and dabbed the blood off her knee with a tissue.

"Do you know who they were shooting at?" she asked.

"All I saw was a flash of red—I think it was the same person we were talking about earlier. Someone else wants info on Timothy Savage." He touched the abraded skin gently. "Did I do that? I'm sorry."

She kissed him quickly. "It's okay. You're allowed to go all caveman on me when guns are going off. It's in the job description."

He smiled, then cocked his head and turned toward the front door. "They're coming back."

Fletcher and Davidson appeared on the tiny front porch of the cabin, both sweating and out of breath.

Fletcher's face was thunderous. "We missed him. And I'm getting damn sick of this ghost following us around."

Davidson nodded. "It's the same guy who was lurking around the funeral home. I'm going to bring in some officers and a couple of dogs, go after him before it gets dark. That's twice today he's run from me. There won't be a third."

"Well, don't kill him," Sam said. "He may be the elusive son and heir to Savage's estate. I doubt us murdering his kid was part of Savage's game plan. Maybe the boy knows his dad was murdered and he's being extra careful, sneaking around in case we're the killers."

"Or he's our suspect." Davidson wiped his broad forehead with the tail of his white shirt. "Our dogs will tree him, not bite him. We'll have a nice talk and get to the bottom of this. I don't know why he's hanging around, but he's going to get *himself* killed if he doesn't stop bumbling around our crime scenes. Speaking of which—"

He looked at Sam, distrust written all over his face. "I went to the lab and you never showed. Why not, who's this and why don't you just tell me what y'all are doing out here and quit playing games with me?"

Fletcher said, "Whoa, man. One at a time. You show me yours and I'll show you mine, get it?"

Davidson crossed his arms and didn't say a word.

"Okay. We're here because Sam wanted to see what Savage's 'estate' looked like. Now you share. What happened with Mac Picker?"

"All right. Mac let me look at the files. He's not lying. There's no reference to Timothy Savage in their system. Why didn't you go to the lab like you were supposed to?"

"We got lost. Why did you assume we'd be out here at the crime scene?"

"One of my officers saw you driving out of town. You took the exit for Savage's place, so I used my noggin and extrapolated that maybe you'd come on out here. What aren't you telling me?"

Fletcher shrugged. "Nothing. You've got it all."

Davidson stretched his arms up over his head, cracked his neck and sighed. "This is my town, my jurisdiction. Without my help, you aren't going to get anywhere." The two men glared at each other. Without moving, Davidson gestured to Sam and Xander. "And you've brought two civilians along on a murder case. I'm out of patience, Detective. Who the hell is this?"

Xander squared his shoulders. "Sergeant Alexander Whitfield, U.S. Army, retired. Let's just say I'm here in a consultative position."

Davidson took a deep breath and blew it out hard, clearly exasperated. Sam noticed he'd put his fingers on his Glock.

Xander cleared his throat.

Fletcher shot him a look, then put his hands up in the air. "Fine. Fine. Here's the deal. Something hinky is going on down here. We're taking the samples back to D.C. to be run in an independent lab. If you've got a problem with that, then let me hear it now."

Davidson scratched his neck. "This is what you're hiding behind? I'm fine with that. I want to work with you, not against you, and solve this case. *If*—and the lady says it's so, so I'll amend that to *since*—Savage was murdered, we have an open homicide on a case everyone here thought was cut-and-dried. I agree with you, this whole thing with Picker is not right. So you wanna give me the rest, or do you wanna keep wasting my time?"

The enemy of my enemy is my friend.

They brought him inside and showed him the shrine. He rocked back on his heels "Shit. How'd we miss this?"

"I assume your people were afraid of the gas and didn't look thoroughly," Sam said.

Davidson rolled his eyes. "You think? It was a rhetorical question, *Doctor.*"

To hell with cooperation. "Don't be snarky, Detective. Your people never even bothered to remove the victim's sweater—it doesn't take a pathologist to see the bruises around his neck. You didn't think it strange he was wearing a turtleneck in August?"

"Don't get feisty with me. Savage was a strange dude. We couldn't get within thirty feet of him for the first day. I didn't make the call not to autopsy the guy—and I admit, in retrospect, that was a big miss for all of us. So thank you for coming down here and showing us country bumpkins what idiots we are."

Sam was a patient woman. She really was. But she'd about had it with Detective June Davidson.

"Listen, *Detective,* I'm the one he was obsessed with. Now the man's dead, murdered, an event he was clearly aware was coming, and prepared for. Which tells me he knew his murderer. And you knew Mr. Savage. As you said, this is *your* town. Why don't you tell us what's happening instead of hiding behind the country bumpkin crap?"

She heard Xander say, "Sam," but ignored him and pressed on. "I've had some seriously bad things happen in my life recently, Detective, and some odd ones, as well. I've never seen anything this convoluted. So if you're through being facetious, why don't you do your job? Timothy Savage was murdered. Why don't you find out why?"

She turned on her heel and walked toward the door. "I'm going back to D.C."

Davidson called out to her, "Wait. Dr. Owens, wait. Please."

She stopped, turned around and crossed her arms on her chest. She avoided Xander's and Fletcher's eyes, knew both of them were fighting to keep a straight face and not pummel Davidson, or her.

He continued. "I'm sorry. You're right. This is a bizarre circumstance, and you've been pulled into this against your will. You did a hell of a job this morning with Savage's body. I'll tell you everything I know, everything Picker told me. I can't guarantee you'll like it, and it's thin, but maybe it will help us get to the bottom of this. But we have to work together. I've just had a suicide turn into a murder and I don't know why. Okay?"

"I thought you said Picker didn't know anything," Sam said.

"No, I said there was nothing in their system. Picker's secretary claims a man who fits Savage's description came in two weeks ago, asking for Benedict. They had a private meeting, lasted about two hours, and then Savage left. The meeting was scrubbed from the system, the log of visitors for the day doesn't show Savage's name. They have a camera on the front door, though, and there's footage of him coming in. He looks calm and sane and certainly not afraid for his life."

"Where's Benedict's secretary?"

"Denver. At a cousin's wedding."

"Convenient timing." Sam was quiet for a moment. "Savage didn't die from inhaling the hydrogen sulfide. He was strangled, there's not a doubt in my mind. Do you think it's possible he arranged for his own murder?"

Davidson said, "Maybe. Hell, anything's possible, but there's one problem with that theory. Who killed Rolph Benedict?"

"Someone who was trying to stop the will from being executed," Xander said. "If any trace of Savage has been scrubbed from the law offices, if they have no record of the will being filed, and Benedict, the only lawyer who knew about it, is dead, then it simply doesn't exist anymore, right?"

Davidson nodded. "If it wasn't filed with the court, no, it doesn't. Legally, at least. It was never filed in their automated system, and the notary in their office swears up and down she's never seen anything with Savage's name on it. I sure would have liked to see that will."

Fletcher looked at Sam, who nodded once. He removed the papers from his waistband. "Then it's a good thing I have a copy here."

CHAPTER 21

THEY GATHERED AROUND TIMOTHY SAVAGE'S TINY KITCHEN TABLE TO READ HIS WILL.

Sam hadn't seen the details when Benedict showed up on her doorstep, hadn't paid enough attention. If she'd only listened, maybe Benedict wouldn't be dead.

Then again, if she had listened, she might have made herself an easy target. Whoever killed Benedict could have lain in wait for him at his hotel, assuming he would go there first since it was so late in the day. Or, worse, tailed him all the way from Lynchburg. Had the killer followed Benedict to Sam's house and seen him summarily booted out the door? Benedict hadn't been inside for more than fifteen minutes; time enough to share information, but not enough for too many details. Hopefully the killer didn't think Sam had anything to do with this intrigue. And if he did…

Best not to go down that road.

Fletcher read through the will's introductory paragraph and revocation, then started listing the heirs. "Henry Matcliff is the primary heir. He's been left nearly one hundred thousand dollars, but there are several more names on the list, each due to receive one thousand dollars. June, tell me if any of them sound familiar. Curtis Lott, Arthur Scarron, Rob Thurber, Anne Carter, Frederick McDonald and Adrian Zamyatin."

Davidson frowned. "Two names are familiar. Arthur Scarron is dead, that much I know. He was an oil guy in Texas, his wife's from Lynchburg. He was a doctor for a long time, plastic surgery or O.B. or something. From what I remember, he got bored remaking housewives and went to work for his family's company, Scarron Oil and Gas. Ellie Scarron—that's his wife—she moved back when he passed last year. He had a heart attack."

"Why would Timothy Savage leave a dead man, who sounds like he was rather wealthy, a thousand dollars?"

"I don't know. We can go talk to Ellie, though, see if she knows anything about all this. The other one, Fred McDonald, I'm gonna have to do some checking, but the name rings a bell."

Fletcher glanced at his watch and cursed softly. "I have to get back to D.C. We'll have to do it another time. Maybe I can come back down tomorrow."

Sam said, "We'll go with him, Fletch. You go handle the Stevens kidnapping. Amado will be waiting for the samples, anyway."

"Stevens. Rachel Stevens?" Davidson asked. "I saw the AMBER Alert. She's a cute little thing. Your case?"

"Apparently it is now," Fletcher said.

"Good luck with it."

"Thanks. Excuse us a minute, would you?"

"Sure. I need to get the dogs out here, anyway, start looking for the idiot in the red ball cap who keeps showing up." Davidson stepped out onto the porch and Fletcher shut the front door behind him.

"Listen to me, both of you. Don't trust that man with anything you think is vital to this case. He's not telling us everything he knows."

Sam nodded. "I agree. We'll be careful."

"I'm going to take the will and the letter with me."

"Can I read it first?"

His lips seamed together. "It's evidence."

"It has my name on it."

He pulled the letter from his jacket pocket. "Here you go."

She nodded, used a flat pair of scissors from her purse to slit the lip open and extracted a piece of paper carefully. She unfolded it and read quickly, relief quickly flooding through her. "It's the same as the one he sent to my office. A duplicate. Nothing new. I have to say, this man certainly seemed to think it was important to have backups of his wishes, didn't he?" She folded the letter and started to put it back in the envelope, then realized there was something written on the back.

"What's this?" The word was small, and faint, as if it had been written in pencil and erased. A word they weren't meant to see. Sam brought the letter closer, letting the late afternoon sunlight play on the page.

"It's a name. Lauren. And something else. I can't make it out. It's like he wrote it, then erased it. It's barely an indentation."

She held it up to the light. "I think it says 'Look out for Lauren.'"

"Who the hell is Lauren?"

Sam met his eyes. "I have no idea."

"Shit. I'm sorry, guys, but I gotta go." Fletcher turned to Xander. "You'll be back tonight?"

"Late, yes. Don't worry, man. I've got her."

"I'll run the name, see if anything pops. Keep in touch." Fletcher nodded once, then went out the front door. Sam heard some low words. His car engine turned over and he drove away, the gravel crunching under his tires. Thor barked once in farewell, and the forest grew quiet.

Davidson was waiting for them on the porch.

"Ready? You want to ride with me?"

Xander shook his head. "We'll follow you."

"Suit yourself. It's about a thirty-minute ride. We're heading toward the city, then south a piece. Stay close so I don't lose you."

He got behind the wheel, and before he put on his sunglasses, Sam saw him stare angrily toward the hills.

Whoever was nosing around the case, she had the distinct impression Davidson knew exactly where to find him.

CHAPTER 22

THE ROAD OUT OF LYNCHBURG FOLLOWED A PATH THE LOCALS CALLED DOO-DOO Highway, an odiferous few minutes past the waste treatment plant. The temperature had risen, waves of heat dancing up from the asphalt, and the miasma bled in through the Jeep's doors. Thor whined once, and Sam simply took a huge gasp of breath and plugged her nose.

Xander started to laugh. "You look rather miserable."

"And why aren't you?"

"I am, but I've smelled worse."

"I have, too. No reason to be heroic about it."

They topped the hill. "It's safe now. You can breathe."

She dragged in a lungful of air. It was sticky and hot, but it didn't stink. "Not sure I'm in love with central Virginia in the summer."

"It's better down by the river. There's a breeze."

Davidson flashed his brake lights twice to get their attention, then turned off the road into an unmarked drive. He started a series of switchback turns that led up the side of a mountain.

"Where is this guy going?" Xander asked.

"Well, if the Scarrons are as rich as he says, they'll have put the house on easily defensible land. Right?"

"Never start a land war in Asia, or Lynchburg?" he asked with a wry smile.

"Something like that. I'm assuming we're dealing with seriously old money. Scarron Oil's been around awhile."

"It's his wife's place, though. Her family might not be rich."

"If it's the person I'm thinking about, her maiden name is Dawson, and she's richer than dirt," Sam said.

"You know her?"

"Know of her. There was a *Town & Country* profile on her a while back. She's younger than her husband by about two decades. Trophy wife."

"Are you going to mention this to Davidson?"

"What, that I read an article on her years ago? It's hardly worth mentioning. She's a designer, interiors and textiles. Has her own line of fabrics. They're a bit like Brunschwig & Fils. Too busy and bright for me, you know how simple I like things. So family money, husband's money and her own very successful business. Yes, Ellie Dawson Scarron is filthy rich. I'd be watching out for a moat."

That got another laugh out of him, and she relaxed against the seat, let the breeze move her hair off her face. Thor put his head on her shoulder and she stroked his ears. They could be out for a Sunday drive instead of barreling headlong into a murder investigation.

Ellie Scarron did not live in a castle with a moat. But the place was indecently large, ornate, a magnificent modern straight out of the school of Frank Lloyd Wright. The house was a series of rectangular boxes nestled into the side of the mountain with lots of glass, and a massive double front door that looked as though it was made from the trunk of a redwood.

Xander pulled the Jeep into the curved drive and shifted into neutral. “Funny. The old money’s in the modern palace and the funeral home is in Tara.”

Davidson waved for them to join him. Sam didn’t move, just stared at the house. After a moment, she put her hand on the door handle. “Come on. Let’s get this over with and get back to D.C.”

Xander immediately went on alert. “What’s wrong?”

“I don’t know. This place doesn’t feel right.”

She didn’t want to tell him she smelled blood, and fear, and more. Evil. Something wrong, and wicked. It was ridiculous. She was just being jumpy. They were off the beaten path with a cop neither of them trusted, and she was missing Fletcher. Xander wasn’t carrying, not on his person, at least that she could see. His concealed carry permit didn’t extend to Virginia, but she knew he had weapons in the Jeep. He’d never go anywhere without them.

She glanced over at him. He was watching her, tensed, hands curving around an invisible M-4.

She smiled. “It’s okay. I’m being spooky. Let’s go.”

He was darkly silent, but gestured for her to go ahead of him. They joined Davidson on the glazed cement, and together the three of them climbed the fifteen steps to the doors.

Sam cast a discreet glance behind them, just in case someone, or something, was there. She saw nothing but the rolling Blue Ridge Mountains, hazy and mysterious, butted up against the green farm fields. The effect was beautiful, a study in contrasts: the ephemeral mountains against the tangible land. She imagined the sunsets up here must be spectacular.

Davidson rang a bell, and waited. Nothing. He jabbed the button again, and they heard the singsong bells, not a traditional ding-dong, but a deeper sound, like the gong of a church bell. Hell, it probably was. Sam hadn’t seen a bell tower when they drove up, but these people probably had their very own Quasimodo in the backyard, swinging from a rope.

Davidson was knocking on the door now, loudly, and the bangs from the bold brass lion-faced knocker echoed through the house. He shielded his eyes and looked in through the thin strip of decorative glass running the length of the ten-foot door. There was a matching one on the left, and Xander leaned in to do the same.

Davidson stood back. "This is strange. I called her on my way over to let her know we were coming to talk to her. She sounded upbeat, offered to make us some lemonade. I can see through to the garage behind the house. Her car's parked out there. She's here, or she was ten minutes ago."

Sam didn't hesitate. "Exigent circumstances. We have to go in."

"I can't break into her house."

"You can, and you will. Something is terribly wrong, and you know it as well as I do."

"Let me just call her again. Hang on." He pulled out his cell phone.

Sam could hear the phone ring inside the house. Once, twice, three times.

Davidson frowned and hung up. "Let me get on the horn, get some more folks out here."

"While you're wasting time, I'm going in."

Davidson put a meaty hand on her shoulder. "I can't let you do that, Dr. Owens."

"Then charge me with breaking and entering."

She ignored his curse and put her hand on the oversize doorknob. It twisted easily in her fingers. "See, it's unlocked." She turned the knob and the door clicked open. It swung in silently. The house was quiet, too quiet.

"Mrs. Scarron? Are you home?"

Nothing.

Davidson was clearly struggling with his conscience. Sam rolled her eyes and entered the house, Xander on her heels.

She hadn't been imagining it. The meaty scent of copper hung in the air like a fog.

Blood.

CHAPTER 23

FIVE STEPS LED DOWN TO A SUNKEN LIVING ROOM. SAM SAW ELLIE SCARRON twisted on the floor, a pool of burgundy under her head.

Davidson yelled, "Jesus, don't touch her. Get back up here and don't touch anything. This is a crime scene."

She ignored Davidson, rushed down the stairs and knelt by the woman. Scarron's eyes were open, unseeing, staring upward. Sam avoided the carotid; there was a thin loop of wire around the woman's neck, cutting deep into the flesh. Instead she picked up Scarron's limp wrist. Her body hadn't begun to cool into inertness yet; the killer hadn't been gone long.

She was about to release the wrist when she felt a tiny bit of pressure, the weakest bump against her fingers. A pulse, thready and indistinct. Sam launched herself into CPR, hands intertwined, pushing hard on the woman's chest.

"She's alive, she's alive! Get an ambulance out here. Xander, come here and stabilize her neck for me. She can't breathe. We need to clear an airway for her."

The men jumped into action. They were both professionals, able to handle an emergency situation without second-guessing or arguing.

Sam took one look at the damaged tissue around the victim's neck and knew there was no safe way to intubate her. As Sam got her heart beating in a more regular rhythm, blood began to slowly pulse from the wound in her neck. Sam felt around the wire and pressed her fingers into the base of the woman's throat, then nodded to herself. There. She could do it.

Xander knelt by the woman's head, grabbed it with both hands. He'd been on enough battlefields to recognize what Sam was about to do.

"You're going to trache her?"

"I have to. Keep her head still, tell her she'll be okay. Put pressure on her carotid, not enough to knock her out, but keep that blood flow down. She's tachycardic. Watch her pulse. I'll be right back."

Sam rushed toward the kitchen, grabbed a paring knife from a block on the counter and looked around for something to use as an airway. A straw, a pen, something, anything hollow.

Come on, come on, come on. You're running out of time.

There. The plants on the windowsill had decorative glass watering bulbs inserted into their soil. She snatched one, cleanly cracked it against the edge of the stainless-steel sink. The head broke off with a clatter. She turned on the hot water and allowed it run through the tube. Thoughts of infection raced through her mind, but there was no time to properly sterilize the glass. She took off back for the living room, skidded to a stop by the butler's pantry and its crystal decanters. She pulled the stopper out of the closest and doused the glass rod in spirits. It smelled like a very good single malt, which was heartening: it was pure alcohol. She brought the decanter with her.

The preparations hadn't taken more than a minute. Back on her knees next to Ellie Scarron, she noted the woman's skin beginning to blue. *Hurry, Sam, hurry.* She would save her, damn it. The woman had been lying on the floor bleeding out while Davidson screwed around outside.

She had one brief dark thought. At least June Davidson hadn't tried to kill Scarron himself, but he'd had plenty of time to call someone to get out here and take care of things.

She splashed the Scotch on the woman's exposed throat, then expertly pushed the knife through the skin at the base of her very small laryngeal prominence, going hard through the surprisingly tough cricothyroid membrane and into the trachea. The woman didn't move, didn't wince.

"Come on, Ellie. Stay with me. I've got you. You can't die on me. I won't let you." As she talked, Sam used her finger to hold the opening apart, then gingerly placed the tube in the trachea. She pulled the skin together tight against the base of the tube, blew into it a few times, used the other to feel for a pulse and waited for the air to begin moving into Ellie Scarron's lungs.

Sam heard a slight whistle, realized her own eyes were closed. She opened them in time to see Ellie close hers, not in death, but in a deep unconsciousness.

Xander whispered, "You did it."

Sam blew out a breath of relief. "She's alive for now. Davidson, we need to get her transferred to the hospital quickly. They'll need to do a proper tracheostomy and get this wire out of her neck."

Davidson said, "They're two minutes out. Damn, woman, that was impressive. You brought her back from the grave."

She had. Ellie's pulse was bumping along merrily now that she wasn't hypoxic anymore, and the color was coming back to her face.

Davidson squatted down next to them. "When will she be able to talk, to tell us what happened?"

Sam shook her head. "It's too early to tell. She may never regain consciousness. There may be permanent damage to her vocal box. The wire is cutting through the skin there. I was careful as I could be, but I wasn't gentle. It could have made things worse."

"You were amazing. She's lucky you were here. Whoever tried to kill her couldn't have been more than five minutes ahead of us. Thank God we decided to head up here." He patted her awkwardly on the shoulder, then went up the stairs to the foyer.

Sam met Xander's eyes. He was still holding Ellie's head straight so the field tracheostomy wouldn't dislodge. She spoke quietly so Davidson wouldn't hear.

"Whoever tried to kill her used the same M.O. as Benedict's killer."

He nodded. "Clearly someone is trying to make sure we don't find out about Savage's world. They're killing off everyone who's had anything to do with him."

"Worse than that. You see what's happening, right? They're killing off people connected to the will. Keep your hands on her. I'll be right back." Sam stood and went to Davidson, who was waiting by the front door for the ambulance. She could hear the thin wail of the siren coming from the base of the mountain.

She looked at her hands and realized she was covered in blood. Davidson looked down at her, and silently handed her his handkerchief.

She wiped her hands on it, watching the white stain red.

His voice was shaky and she realized he was fighting back tears. Her estimation of him went up a few notches. He swiped at his eyes.

"I'm getting pissed off now. Ellie is a good friend of mine. What the hell is going on around here?"

Sam resisted the urge to touch his arm, to comfort him. He was clearly upset, his chest rising and falling quickly as he struggled to maintain control. Maybe she'd misjudged him. Maybe he was a good man, a solid, trustworthy man. Maybe her own issues were clouding her judgment. He hadn't done anything wrong. He'd only been delaying them, pushing them off the trail, reluctantly allowing them to be a part of the investigation. A small-town cop not wanting to be manhandled by the system, or a methodical one who didn't jump to conclusions?

Or was this about her? Had she been so twisted by the events of the past few years in Nashville that she saw the bad in people immediately, instead of the good? Her inherent distrust of mankind, driven by years opposite the working end of a scalpel, trying to figure out why people did such horrible things to one another?

"I don't know. We need to be cautious, and you need to find out who tried to kill Ellie Scarron. The attacker had to know we were headed here, and scrambled to murder her before we arrived. My God, another minute or two of us standing around dithering about whether she was home or not and he would have succeeded. Who did you tell? Who knew we were coming here?"

He held himself so still she wondered if he'd heard her. He finally dragged in a breath and sighed. "I made three calls on the way up here. One to Ellie herself, to tell her we were fifteen minutes out, one to a friend in the service to check out your boyfriend there and one to Mac Picker, to check what time his partners were coming back tonight."

"Picker. All roads seem to lead to Benedict's law offices, don't they?"

His voice was cold and hard. "They certainly do."

The ambulance lumbered over the crest of the hill and pulled to a stop in front of the house. Two EMTs spilled out, began gathering their gear. Sam shouted to them, "I had to do an emergency trache on Mrs. Scarron. You'll need to stabilize the surgical field, too. It's a little messy."

One of the EMTs raised a hand in acknowledgment. Sam

went inside, got a thumbs-up from Xander, who was helping the EMTs, had a glance at her patient, who continued to cling to life, if barely, then went into the kitchen to wash the blood from her hands.

CHAPTER 24

Metropolitan Police
Criminal Investigative Division–Homicide Section
Washington, D.C.

CAPTAIN ARMSTRONG STOOD AT THE FRONT OF THE ROOM WITH TWO FBI AGENTS—a man and a woman. They both were fit but looked drawn and gray, which told Fletcher more than he wanted. The woman was young, pretty, athletic, her dark hair drawn back in a ponytail, and she was frowning at a BlackBerry. The man, forties, blond hair high and tight and horn-rimmed glasses that made him look like a teacher instead of an agent, conversed quietly with Armstrong.

Fletcher slipped into his chair at 6:15 p.m., out of breath from his two-and-a-half-hour tear through the Virginia countryside and the mad dash across town to the run-down morgue that housed the OCME. He'd found Nocek and dropped off the cooler with the samples from Savage's autopsy, then rushed downtown to Metro headquarters.

He ignored the looks from the rest of the team. They'd been a little cold to him since he returned a few weeks ago, not understanding why he'd thrown away a chance to work full-time on the JTTF—the Joint Terrorism Task Force. They'd kill for it.

Let them have it. He was better suited to this. Death and mayhem one-on-one, not for a higher cause, but for personal gain. He understood it. He'd lived it for so long, he flat-out got it.

Armstrong shot him a look. "Glad you could join us, Detective Fletcher. Are you up to speed?"

Fletch nodded. He wasn't, all he knew was what he'd learned from the news in his car and Hart's texts, but he wasn't about to admit that. "Let's begin our evening update. The child has been missing for seven hours now. There have been no sightings, and damn few calls about this little girl. We're working the media angle hard. The tip line is going out on the local news right now, so expect this all to change. The FBI's child endangerment team is lead on the case—this is Special Agent Rob Thurber and Special Agent Jordan Blake. They'll take it from here."

The lights dimmed, and a picture flashed up on the screen, a three-foot-high shot of a beautiful little girl, hair a pale red, eyes blue as the sky. She was smiling, missing her two front teeth, and seemed so damn happy, and so alive, Fletcher could barely stand to look at her. The thought of those eyes staring unseeing toward the heavens made him swallow, hard. She looked vaguely familiar, but she was a kid—they all looked alike at that age, still pudding-faced and round, before their bones started pushing out of the skin to form their permanent features and identities.

Blake nodded at Armstrong. Fletcher watched her move toward the mike as though she'd done this a hundred times. She was pretty young to be putting off the *been there, done that* attitude. But she cleared her throat before she started to speak and wiped an invisible hair back from her face, a tiny self-conscious gesture, and Fletcher realized he was wrong. She was scared to death. It made him root for her.

"Thanks, Captain. We appreciate all your help here. As you know, Rachel was last seen by the main zoo entrance on Connecticut Avenue. Her nanny was talking with another nanny, and swears she only took her eyes off her for a second. We've done a background check on the Stevenses' nanny. She's Guatemalan, here legally, and so far, everything she says checks out. She seems to be a cautious and concerned player, not a suspect.

"There are cameras galore in the area, but a sweep has turned up nothing. Metro canvass is still ongoing, but they haven't drummed up any leads, either. Whoever did this was very careful, and managed to keep off-video. We're set up on the family's home phone and cells in case a ransom demand comes in, and my team has started deconstructing the Stevenses' lives to see why someone might want to take their little girl. Because this seems like a professional snatch, we'd like to think there will be a ransom demand."

Fletcher put up a hand. "A professional snatch? Agent Blake, what do the parents do?"

She nodded at him in appreciation. "Mr. Stevens works for an aerospace company in Bethesda, Lockheed Martin, and Mrs. Stevens is a legal attaché to the State Department. She is currently out of the country, and is expected back late tonight. They both have high-level security clearances and work with classified materials."

Agent Blake's demeanor, the mother's job at the State Department, the idea of a professional kidnapping... It sounded to him as though Mrs. Stevens might be working for more than the State Department, maybe was a CIA asset. They were thick as flies around town lately, it seemed. Which upped all this to the next level. If this wasn't a sicko after a little girl, but a terrorist trying to make a point, they could be dealing with a whole new level of crazy.

Agent Blake continued the briefing, running through the protocols her team had in place. Fletcher listened with half an ear. Snatching a little girl off a busy street in the middle of the day was quite a feat. There had to be more than one person involved. He knew the area where she'd gone missing. It was heavily populated, busy, two Metro stops nearby, lots of foot traffic and vehicle traffic. The National Zoo hosted daily field trips; there were busloads of excited kids running around. Add in the usual contingent of people wandering the streets and he could see why they chose the zoo to snatch her from. It was busy and crowded, and in all the confusion, a single kid could disappear easily.

What a couple of days. The eyes of the dead boy from yesterday crept into his thoughts, and he looked at the notepad in front of him to realize he'd drawn that crime scene, captured the boy's empty, horrified look quite well.

"Fletcher? Yo, earth to Fletch?"

Hart was poking him in the ribs with a pencil.

"Stop it, you jerk."

Hart pointed toward the front of the room, where their boss, Captain Armstrong, stood frowning at them, hands on his hips in exasperation.

Fletcher raised an apologetic brow. He ripped off the page and balled it up. "Sir?"

"Fletcher, I need you to run point with Agent Blake. If you're through with your nap, that is." The homicide detectives tittered, and the FBI agents had the audacity to look amused.

Fletch gave them a lazy smile. *Go ahead, laugh it up. You'll regret it later.* "No, sir. I'm fine. No problem."

"Good. Come on, people. Let's get our asses in gear and head out. Find this girl. We don't need another hit this year."

Another hit. They all knew what he meant. D.C. had been

under siege from terror attempts and drug wars for the past few months, and it was wearing on everyone. You could only keep your people on high alert for so long before things began falling through the cracks. It was one of the reasons Fletcher begged off the JTTF. The pressure there was obscene.

They all got to their feet. Armstrong called out, "Fletch, my office, please," and there was a round of boos and hisses. Fletch flipped his colleagues the bird and went to his boss's glass-walled office.

"Shut the door," Armstrong snapped.

He did. "Sorry about that, Cap. I've had a lot going on."

"I know. What were you doing in Lynchburg?"

"Chasing a dead end, I think. Dr. Owens received a letter from a dead man asking for her to investigate his murder. I wanted to be sure nothing went south. She posted the guy, sent some lab work up with me. I don't see it going too far." He hoped.

Armstrong sat behind the desk and smoothed his fingers across his mustache. "All right. This kid who drowned yesterday? They've got a preliminary ID. Name's Oscar Rivera. Catholic University, good kid. No known connections to anything that should have gotten him killed. FBI sent over the news, but they're handling the case. They think it might be related to another couple of murders they're working on. We're off the hook there."

"I figured it was part of something bigger. That was way too creepy to be an accident."

"They're thinking it's drug cartel related, but with a sweet kid like Rivera, I don't know. It doesn't fit."

"Saw the wrong thing at the wrong time, maybe."

"Maybe." Armstrong went quiet, then leaned back in his chair and stroked his mustache. What hair he didn't have on his dark, shiny head was more than accounted for on his lip. "Fletch, are you still with us?"

"What do you mean, sir?"

"You know exactly what I mean. You had a taste of how the other half lives during your sojourn at the JTTF. Is working homicide going to be enough for you?"

"I wouldn't have asked for the transfer back if I wasn't sure I wanted to be here."

"I know you wanted out before you left. You've made it clear you plan to put in your twenty and move to greener pastures. And that anniversary is going to be here sooner than you think. But if you want to stay, Fletch, stick around a few more years, I'd like to put you up for lieutenant. And God help me, I want to give you your own squad."

Armstrong's jaw was set, as if he knew what Fletch would say, since he'd said it so many times before. *No way, sir. I can't even think about it, sir. I want out as soon as my date comes, sir.*

Lieutenant. His own squad. Autonomy.

Fletcher surprised them both by saying, "I appreciate the opportunity, sir. So long as Hart gets to be my lead detective, I'm in."

Armstrong's face split in a smile, a rare enough occurrence it felt like the sun breaking through after a month of clouds. "Good man. I'm glad to hear it. Now, get out there and help the FBI find Rachel Stevens."

Fletcher went back to his office with a spring in his step. He'd made the decision in a split second, and he knew it was the right one. When Armstrong said *Lieutenant* he'd actually felt a click of *yes, this is the right thing to do.*

It meant more work, more hours, more responsibility, but for some reason, he wanted it. He wanted it bad.

He dialed Andrea Bianco, head of the D.C. JTTF. They'd met while Fletcher was attached there for a case, and had been very casually hanging out. He didn't want to call it dating. He liked her, maybe even a lot, but Fletcher wasn't exactly the settling-down type. He'd done that once to disastrous results, and vowed never to take things to the next level again.

Of course, he'd have been willing to make that particular sacrifice for Sam Owens, but he knew, deep down, he would have ended up hurting her, and she him.

Andrea answered in a rush of "Hi, how are you I'm running out the door is it important or can it wait," the words smashed together, breathless and excited, and he said, "Yeah, sure, but—" and she said, "Okay, great," and hung up without saying goodbye.

So much for that.

She had a seriously heavy duty job, with responsibilities he couldn't be paid enough in the world to handle. He didn't want it. Being at JTTF was a straight line into cardiac arrest.

Maybe he'd catch her later, but he was going to be tied up, too. No matter. This was the reason he didn't want to be tied down, ever again. Dating other cops was hard, but the only way a romance worked in this field was with someone who understood the hours, the devotion, the insanity and the horror.

He plopped down at his desk and pulled up his email. Nothing from Lynchburg. *Damn it.*

Hart knocked on the door.

"Hey, princess, ready to go chat with the looker from the FBI? Hey, why do you look all googly-eyed and happy? Did Armstrong suck—"

"And that's enough out of you, young man. I just agreed to take over your lowly ass. You're looking at your new homicide LT. And my first administrative move is to promote you, if you'll take my spot as lead."

Hart grinned, the muscles in his neck flexing. "Hell, man, that's great news. You deserve it. I deserve the bump, too. When is this blessed occasion taking place?"

"Next round of promotions, so next week, maybe." He stood, clapped Hart on the back. "Come on, let's go hook up with the FBI folks and find this kid. I remember the chick's name. What's the dude's again?"

"Rob Thurber. He's a lifer, been there for twenty years. He—"

"Rob Thurber? God, that name sounds so familiar. Where did I see it?"

And then it hit him. The will. Savage's bloody will. Rob Thurber was the name of one of the beneficiaries.

CHAPTER 25

Bethesda, Maryland

FLETCHER AND HART FOLLOWED THE FBI AGENTS TO THE STEVENS HOUSE OUT IN Bethesda. On the drive over, Fletcher made a couple of calls, used his contacts to get a background on Rob Thurber. He didn't want to go into the conversation about his relationship with Timothy Savage totally blind.

Thurber was, by all accounts, a straight shooter. Dedicated to the cause, he'd been an agent for twenty-five years, applied early, right out of school, and had served in several capacities within the organization. He was part of the Behavioral Analysis Unit tasked to the child endangerment team. He was their profiler, the one who looked at the victims and told you what sort of person would be interested in lifting them from their lives.

He'd asked a couple of quick questions about Jordan Blake, as well—she, too, was a lifer, though she was twenty years younger than Thurber and just getting her feet wet. But she had a track record of solves, a knack for finding missing kids, so she was running the show.

They seemed like solid people. So what was Thurber's connection to Savage?

Nothing to do but ask the man face-to-face.

He debated calling Sam, telling her he'd found a possible heir, but decided to wait until he talked to Thurber himself, determine if it was a fluke or a coincidence, or if he was the real deal.

Fletcher didn't believe in coincidence.

And the backdrop of this missing kid was sure to keep things interesting. Fletcher knew the odds weren't good for Rachel Stevens, and he felt immediately guilty for thinking it. The longer she was missing, the bigger the chance she was gone forever. This was a noncustodial kidnapping, the worst possible scenarios at play. It would break his heart, if he let it. He couldn't afford to. He had to stay detached, stay focused. If he let himself think about what might actually be happening to the little girl, he wouldn't be worth a flip. He had to do his best to find her before the worst happened.

They took a final turn into a small, neat neighborhood. The Stevens home was a modest two-story brick house with a professionally landscaped and maintained yard on a cul-de-sac. There was a lot of activity on the street: neighbors taking cover in the shade of large, leafy trees, children at play signs at the intersections. This was a good area of town, perfect for young families, and normally untouched by a tragedy of this magnitude.

There was a chalk drawing on the asphalt in front of the house—a big pink heart with the words *We Love You, Rachel* underneath. A few teddy bears and batches of flowers were leaning against the black wrought-iron mailbox post, forlorn on the ground, and the neighbors who weren't already gathering peeked out from behind their curtains every time they heard a car.

Fletcher saw a satellite truck make the turn behind them. The media were here, too. Great. Let the cacophony begin.

He put the Caprice in Park. "You ready for this?"

Hart nodded. "Better go in before the gauntlet arrives. The minute the 6:00 p.m. broadcast goes live, this place will be overrun with newsies and the tips are going to start flowing in."

They followed the agents up the front walk. Before Thurber had a chance to knock, a dark-haired man with a long nose and thin, round silver wire glasses opened the door. His eyes and the tip of his nose were red, but he seemed to be holding it together. At the sight of the agents, his expression changed—hope and dread spilling across his face, etching so deeply into the lines of his skin he seemed like a detailed painting instead of a real person.

His voice shook. "Is there news?"

Agent Blake shook her head. "Not yet, sir. May we come in?"

Stevens's expression fell. He sniffed once, then melted back away from the entrance, and the four cops trooped in. He shut the door behind them and gestured to the living room.

While the house looked tranquil on the outside, inside it was humming with activity and was packed with people: agents running wiretaps, a grandmotherly looking woman who was crying quietly—Fletcher recognized her as the nanny—a couple of teenagers. They all looked up expectantly, then realized these were simply interlopers—there was no news—and went back to their business.

Stevens brought them to a small den off the more formal living room, a library and office space. There were two comfortable sofas facing each other, and a desk at the head. He sat on the edge of the desk, and everyone else arranged themselves on the sofas.

"What's happening?" Stevens asked.

Special Agent Blake took the lead. "Sir, this is Detective Darren Fletcher, and Detective Lonnie Hart, both with D.C. Metro. They're going to be helping with the investigation. I'm sorry to say we don't have anything new. The tip line should be out now, and I know you want to get the reward under way. Like I mentioned, we don't want to go with that just yet. Let's give it a day and see where we are."

Stevens was wild-eyed, a man trying very hard not to tip over the edge. "Give it a day. A day? What you're really saying is you think she's gone. You think my little girl is gone." He got up and started to pace. "What are you doing to find her? Why are you all here, in the house? Why aren't you out on the street, looking? I need to get out there. I need to go look for her. I can't wait around here anymore."

He started out of the room and Jordan captured his arm. "Sir, Mr. Stevens, I know this is difficult. You're doing great. We are doing everything possible to find your little girl. Please, don't give up hope. The more we look into this, the more it looks like a professional kidnapping, not just a random event."

He stopped cold. "Why do you say that? What in the world makes you think a pro took Rachel?"

"Both the cleanness of the snatch and the nature of your work, sir, and your wife's. You're both cleared for Top Secret classified materials. Your wife's position at the State Department is quite sensitive. The kidnapper managed to disappear Rachel in the middle of a busy city street with no one the wiser. It's not like she wandered off the beaten path, and vanished. She was taken. There one minute, gone the next, as your nanny stated. It's risky to take a child in the middle of a crowd like that, so whoever did it knew what they were doing. They'd most likely been following the family's routines for days, getting a sense of how things work."

The cords in Stevens's neck stood out; he was about to completely blow. "So you're saying there are professional kidnappers out there, roaming the streets, just waiting for us to turn away so they can snatch our kids? I don't buy that for a second."

Fletcher's phone rang, buzzing discreetly in his pocket, and he stood, moved away from the fight about to break out between the Feebs and the dad. He felt terrible for Stevens, totally got it. What parents would want to stand back and wait when their kid was missing? At least he didn't get the sense Stevens was involved. His outraged demeanor, his fear and upset, was genuine.

Fletcher answered quietly when he noticed the number was Nocek's personal line. "What's up, Doc?"

"Detective, we have had a most unusual discovery in the samples Dr. Owens sent from Lynchburg. A DNA match in the missing persons database."

Fletcher's heart gave a double thump. Awesome. A hit, right off the bat. And fast, too. That meant it was a high-profile case, just waiting in the system for a match. "A match to whom? Are we looking at our killer?"

"It is possible, but I am not certain," Nocek said. "The match is to a missing child from seventeen years ago. Do you remember the case of a young girl named Kaylie Rousch?"

"Kaylie Rousch? Kaylie Rousch." But as he said the name, it clicked. "Wait a minute. I do remember the case. She's the one who got off the bus after school and flat-out disappeared. No sign of her, nothing. No suspects, no sightings, no ransom demands. It was on the news for weeks. Man, I had just joined the force. I was still in training. And then they found her body a year later, just the skeleton. So there must be some mistake. Kaylie Rousch is dead."

"I do not believe we have made a mistake. The child, she's a woman now, is very much alive. I have taken the liberty of sending the file I have, meager though it is, to your email account. I would suggest you speak to the FBI agents who are working on the Stevens girl case. They may be able to flesh out more information."

"Son of a bitch. Where was the DNA collected from?"

"According to Dr. Owens's evidence log, it was collected from the victim's neck and ear. The composition of the sample is from a tear duct. If I were to hazard a guess, I would say Kaylie Rousch was leaning over the victim, crying."

Fletch was trying to wrap his head around the information. "Okay, you've got the DNA, and it's a match to the Rousch cold case. Let me get this straight. You are one hundred percent convinced this is fresh DNA, as in the girl was there at the scene in Lynchburg?"

"This is exactly what I am saying."

Fletcher took that in, tuned back in to the conversation with Stevens. They were getting nowhere, but he watched Thurber with a fresh eye. There was little doubt in his mind the FBI agent would be familiar with the Rousch case, and if he was, there was also a good chance he was the same Rob Thurber who was mentioned in Timothy Savage's will. What were the odds? And was it possible the two cases—three now—were connected?

"This is interesting news, Doc. Just one question. If Kaylie Rousch is alive, whose body did they find and bury?"

CHAPTER 26

Lynchburg, Virginia

IT FELT LIKE HOURS SINCE SAM HAD WATCHED THE AMBULANCE PEEL AWAY FROM the Scarron house, Ellie Scarron inside, still unconscious but alive. The sun was threatening to set, plunging them all into darkness. Davidson had a crew of crime scene techs combing the premises, pushing hard to find anything they could before it got dark, looking for any clue to their attacker. Sam had her adrenal glands back under control, but they started pumping again when she thought about this faceless killer, big and brutal and merciless, and several steps ahead of her.

And steps behind. This man had been shadowing her for two days, murdering the peripheral contacts she made. It was starting to piss her off. And if she was being honest with herself, she was scared, too.

She sat on the steps, looked down on the bloody living room floor and tried to decide what to do. The professionals were on Scarron's attempted murder, and now Savage's murder, as well. Davidson had transformed from a sleepy, somewhat uncooperative Southern cop to a hard-as-nails detective, ordering everyone around and doing a good job of running the show. She was comfortable that he could handle things from here. She had another job to do.

Xander sat down beside her. He leaned in close and in his unerring way, said, "What do you want to do? Get out of here and go back to D.C., forget you were ever involved?"

Sam took his hand. "I wish I *could* forget. We're in this now, in it deep. Our next step is to find the rest of the names in Savage's will, and warn them. Let Davidson handle the criminal investigation. I'm going to honor Savage's wishes and track down his people, especially his son, Henry Matcliff. He may be our killer, he may be an innocent, but either way, we need to find him."

"I'm with you."

"Good. First thing, my iPad's out of juice, and we need to get to a computer." She looked around at the scene, where there were two dozen people stomping around. "And I don't want them on my back while I do it."

"Leave it to me, my lady. Did you see the cameras?"

"No, where?"

He pointed up, to the corners of the room. She stared for a few moments, unseeing, then caught the very cleverly hidden cameras. There were false ceilings in the corner, angled to look like the exposed wooden beams of the rest of the room. The cameras were nestled inside their virtually invisible boxes, recording everything that happened in the house.

"They're all over the place. The control room is downstairs, in the basement. We can use the computer there," Xander said.

Sam whistled. "And maybe find a killer, too. Isn't anyone from the Lynchburg Police looking at the tapes?"

"I showed the cameras to Davidson. They gathered the tapes

up about twenty minutes ago. We should have the room to ourselves. Let's go."

They went quietly to the staircase. Xander led the way, spiraling down into the basement. It was beautifully finished, just like the rest of the house, the walls a golden stucco that reflected the setting sun through floor-to-ceiling retractable glass doors. It was a lovely indoor-outdoor space, and Sam couldn't help stopping on the stairs and admiring the view. She'd been right. The sunsets up on this mountain were stunning. She hoped Ellie Scarron would have a chance to see one again.

The golden orb finally slipped below the horizon and the sky lit up, pinks and purples and blues spreading over the misty mountains.

"Red sky at night, sailor's delight," Xander said.

It was a private joke between them; they got to see some pretty spectacular sunsets from Xander's cabin, too.

"Where's Thor?"

"In the car, being a very patient young dog. We'll have to spring him soon. It's too hot for him to sit still much longer. He needs to drink and eat and run for a bit."

"This won't take long. I just want to do a Google search on these names, see if anything comes up."

Her phone started to buzz. "It's Fletcher. Finally." She pressed the button.

"What's happening there? Has the missing girl been found?"

"No, she hasn't, but boy, do I have some news for you. You sitting down?"

She sat in the desk chair, put him on speaker. "I am now. What is it?"

"The DNA you collected off Savage's body is a match to a cold case from seventeen years ago. Little girl named Kaylie Rousch. Do you remember the case?"

"Not off the top of my head."

"Kaylie Rousch went missing from her bus stop, and they

found a skeleton a year later, out in Ryder, Virginia. Kaylie Rousch is dead. Or so we've thought for the past sixteen years."

"Jeez."

"Yeah. The DNA was composed of tears. She was crying over him, according to Dr. Nocek."

Sam leaned back in the chair, thinking about the specimen she'd taken from Savage's neck. "He's sure? The composition and trajectory certainly indicated tears, but I thought they were Savage's. Wow. That's rather amazing."

"It's pretty wild, I'll give you that. This all gets more interesting. I just pulled Kaylie Rousch's file. She bears a strong resemblance to this little girl we're missing today—Rachel Stevens. And the FBI agent on both cases? His name is Rob Thurber. And I'm looking right at him."

Sam felt a zing of recognition. "Thurber, that's one of the names in Savage's will. Have you told him?"

"No, not yet. I thought we should touch base before I did anything."

"Well, I have some news for you, too." She told him about Ellie Scarron's very close call. She could hear his mind whirling.

"Son of a bitch. Get out of there, Sam. I want you back up in D.C. where I can keep an eye on you. This is clearly bigger than just Savage's death. We're going to sit down with the FBI and hash this out."

"I want to look at the rest of the heirs first. If we can find them, we need to warn them. Someone is trying to silence them. The lawyer is dead, and the wife of an heir is clinging to life. Savage knew this was coming. He knew they were going to kill him, and the rest of these people. We need to find the others and talk to them right away. Find out who is behind this."

"Sam, that's my job. I'm the law enforcement officer here, and I say get your sweet little ass into Whitfield's Jeep and back here, right away. You get me?"

"Fletch—"

He cut her off, his voice cold and hard. "Don't. I'm dead serious, Samantha. I don't want you prancing around down there with a killer on the loose. Whitfield, can you hear me?"

Xander grabbed Sam's hand, pulled her to her feet. "We're already gone, Fletcher. We'll see you in D.C. in a few hours."

"Good. You call me every half hour until you're back here, and come directly to my office in Homicide. Do not pass go. Do not collect two hundred dollars. Am I clear?"

"Yes, you're clear," Sam said. "We're on our way. Watch your back, all right?"

"It's not my back I'm worried about, sunshine."

No kidding. She ended the call.

Xander started towing her out the basement door. Sam said, "We need to let Davidson know we're leaving."

"No, we don't. If he's a part of this, we can't take that chance."

"Xander, come on. You saw how he worked the scene. He's not part of this. I'm sure."

"I'm not." He clamped his lips together in a way she recognized. There was no more talking to be done; he'd made his decision. Arrogant caveman. She didn't like being ordered around like this, but she wasn't stupid. She wanted to get as far away from Lynchburg as possible.

The Jeep was parked on the side of the house. Thor let out a happy yip when he saw them. They bundled into the Jeep and Xander took off.

They didn't see June Davidson standing on the steps to Ellie Scarron's house, watching them drive off into the night. When the taillights disappeared down the mountain, he sent a text on his cell phone, let out a soft sigh and went back inside.

CHAPTER 27

Bethesda, Maryland

KEVIN STEVENS WAS CRUMPLED ON THE FLOOR IN THE CORNER OF HIS OFFICE, weeping, when Fletcher finished his call. Jordan Blake was kneeling next to him, a hand on his shoulder, trying to console him. He had no idea what had been said, didn't want to know. He signaled to Hart, and caught Thurber's eye. The two men moved toward him, and he led them through the house to the back garden. Once outside, he turned to Thurber.

"Do you recall the name Kaylie Rousch?"

He nodded, clearly startled. "Yes, I do. Of course. It was my first big missing child case. Terrible, too, especially when we found her body. It was the cleanest kidnapping I've ever seen. There were no clues, no threads to follow. We did everything right, kept the story in the news for weeks, did ground and aerial searches. The body was buried in a really deep grave—whoever was responsible did a good job of covering their tracks." He frowned. "That's a closed case. Why do you bring it up?"

"Kaylie Rousch's DNA was found on a body in Lynchburg today. On a murder victim named Timothy Savage."

Thurber touched his forehead as if the news had brought on a headache, then straightened. His voice was stony, prepared, careful. "What *kind* of DNA?"

"Looks to be tears, actually."

Thurber's face went from wary to confused to delighted. Fletcher watched the array of emotions, recognizing the stages himself. A case solved, a case broken wide-open—either feeling was nirvana, even if the resolution brought terror and pain.

Thurber's face fell just as quickly as it had lit up. "There's no way that's right. We found her body. It was identified with DNA."

"Well, either someone made a mistake today or someone made a mistake back then. Which do you think is the more likely scenario?"

"Honestly? I think—" He stopped. "All right. I'll play. But who was the child we found, if it wasn't Kaylie Rousch? Because trust me, I was there when we pulled what was left of her body from the earth, and there was only one little girl who was missing from the area who matched her description."

"I don't know the answer to that. We have another problem. We have reason to believe Rousch was the one behind Timothy Savage's murder."

Thurber got quiet, his dark eyes watchful. "What gives you that impression?"

"The man had been strangled. The woman's DNA was on his face. You do the math. And this story gets weirder. Savage wrote a letter to a friend of mine, Dr. Samantha Owens—"

"I know of Dr. Owens. She's from Nashville, is a friend of a friend here at the Bureau. She was involved in the case of the Pretender, that freak serial killer who had acolytes across the country reenacting the famous serial killers—Son of Sam, the Zodiac and the Boston Strangler. She was kidnapped and injured, if I recall correctly."

"That's her. She's a professor at Georgetown Med School now. Savage wrote her and asked her to solve his murder, and to autopsy his body. She's in Lynchburg. She posted him this morning, and that's where we found the Rousch girl's DNA. Do you know a man named Rolph Benedict, or a woman named Ellie Scarron?"

"I know them both. Of them, at least. Benedict represented Gillian Martin, the murderer who went free. And Ellie Scarron is famous in her own right, married to Arthur Scarron, the oil magnate. Before he died, of course. Why? Are they involved in this?"

Fletcher ran a hand across his forehead. "Benedict was murdered last night here in D.C., and someone tried to kill Mrs. Scarron this afternoon. Both were garroted. And Timothy Savage left you a thousand dollars in his will."

Thurber's voice grew louder. He was losing patience. "What kind of game is this, Detective Fletcher? I have no idea who that man is."

"It's not a game. It's very serious. People are dying, and if you ask me, it's got something to do with Kaylie Rousch. And I think she's tied to your current case."

"Rachel Stevens?"

"We can't rule it out."

Thurber shook his head. "I can't believe I'm hearing her name now, after all this time. That case haunted me. Still does. And now you're saying we got it wrong?" He stretched his shoulders, as if he'd come to some sort of decision. "I take it you're asking for my help? We—Agent Blake and I—we can't be deviated from this case. As much as I'd like to sideline back to Rousch, our primary goal must be recovering Rachel Stevens. We'll have to get another team in to deal with this. We're gonna have to get that body exhumed, too. Jesus, her parents. The mother was a piece of work. Someone will have to talk to them. And—"

"Hold on. Before you slough this off on someone else, tell me something. Why would a man connected to Kaylie Rousch leave you a thousand dollars? You sure you've never heard of Timothy Savage?"

"I've never heard of him before now. I have no connection to him." But something sparked in Thurber's eyes, something like recognition, and Fletcher leaned closer.

"What is it?"

"It just hit me. Do you recall what Kaylie Rousch looked like when she was abducted?"

"Light red hair, blue eyes. The old photos I've seen show a slight resemblance to Rachel Stevens. I'm telling you, there's a thread here. We need to follow it."

Thurber gazed into the woods that backed the Stevens house. A muscle twitched in his jaw. "I don't know what's going on," he said darkly. "But I don't like this at all."

Fletcher's phone dinged with a new text. It was from Sam, telling him she'd emailed him Savage's autopsy photos. Thurber turned to go into the house, but Fletcher stopped him.

"Do me a favor, take a quick look at these. It's from Savage's autopsy this afternoon." He handed Thurber his phone and opened the email. The first shot was a full facial profile of the dead man. Thurber took one look and dropped the phone on the concrete patio, shattering the screen.

"What the hell, man?" Fletcher bent down and grabbed the damaged phone and stood to see Thurber's face was white as milk, and he was swaying like he was about to faint. "What's wrong? You look like you've seen a ghost."

"Because I have," Thurber said. "Jesus, let me see the picture again."

Fletcher handed him the cracked phone, his heart starting a drumbeat tattoo.

Thurber stared at the photo, eyes wide with disbelief. "I can't believe it."

"So you do know Timothy Savage, after all."

Thurber looked up, his blue eyes blank. His voice was ragged. "That's not Timothy Savage. That's Special Agent Douglas Matcliff. He was my partner. On the Kaylie Rousch case. He's been missing for over ten years."

CHAPTER 28

I AM NOT DEAD, WHICH IS SURPRISING, CONSIDERING. I'M SORE AND BRUISED. MY head is full of cottony water and my ears won't pop. A shoulder feels scraped raw. But I am alive.

I hide until nightfall, in case he braves the waterfall and tracks me downstream.

The bank of the river is muddy and dank, but overgrown. Things crawl from the muck, their feathery touches tracing over my body, but I lie perfectly still, knowing the slightest movement could mean my last breath.

After what seems like hours crouched in the mud, I feel certain I am safe. For the time being. I travel downriver, careful to keep to the rushes in case they are looking for me, but once again, they will assume I am dead. Who could have lived through that fall?

It is a miracle. I am a miracle. Still walking, still talking. Still sane, after all these years.

My painfully empty stomach finally drives me away from my hiding place. I am thirsty and hungry and covered in mosquito bites and leeches. The sun sinks away into the tall grasses and the river comes alive, fish rising to the surface to snatch their dinner from the eddy pools, the moon bringing her favorite creatures to life. An owl hoots three times, and I shiver. Three hoots means death is coming.

With Adrian on my trail, I know she is right.

Three miles downstream now, and the river banks sharply to the left. I know it is time to reenter the world. There is a trailer park a few miles inland. I find clothes hanging on a line that look like they will fit me. It is not the first time I've helped myself to some clothes, nor will it be the last. It happens when you have nothing, and until I can get to D.C., to the woman I was told could help, who I can trust, I won't be rolling in cash.

I tear off my muddy, torn jeans and waterlogged shirt, use a towel to wipe the dirt from my body and hair, slip into a too-small red T-shirt with *Munich* printed on it in raised white lettering, pull on a pair of fatigue green cargo pants. I leave my clothes behind in recompense—the woman who lives here might be a firm hand with a needle and can tidy up the mess I've made of mine. I can't give up my boots, but they're meant for hard times. I slip them back on my feet; they are old friends, worn but broken in, my favorites.

I've spent years trying to make them believe I am dead and gone, lost into the wilds, but now that he has seen me in the flesh, nine long years after I made my escape, all hope is lost. He will be hunting me, won't quit until he sees my lifeless body into the ground. It may not be today, or next week, or next month, but he will not stop. Unless I stop him.

You will ask why I did not return to my family when I found my freedom. To tell them the child they buried was not their own.

You are right to ask. It makes little sense to someone who has not experienced the horrors I have. It is shame, prideful shame, that keeps me from them. To look Mother in the eye and admit how sullied I am, to see the confirmation of all she believed about me come to fruition? To see Father cringe when he looks at me, wincing at the thought of what I have endured? To have them whisper about me in the night? They were not kind people to start with. Oh, does this surprise you? It is hard to imagine having anything but pity for people who lose their children. But I will tell you the truth. This happens to good parents, and to bad.

I chose not to return, not to let them know I still lived. Hate me if you will. But I know my family, and I know that the idea of an angel child, sitting on a branch in some heavenly tree gazing down at them adoringly, fits their narrative much, much better than the rotten, tainted thing they would see me as if they knew the whole truth.

I breathe deeply, tie off the belt at the waist of the khakis. Shirt: too small. Pants: too large. Boots: just right. Goldilocks strikes again.

Yes, I hear the bitterness in my tone, too. This is what the thought of those people does to me. All of them. The ones who were supposed to care for me, and the ones who hurt me.

Love.

It comes in all forms.

The only real parent I've known lies dead in a stainless-steel drawer, unable to protect me any longer.

I march toward the road, toward the town, toward an uncertain life.

He trusted her. I must, as well.

CHAPTER 29

1989
McLean, Virginia

HE DISCOVERED EDEN BY ACCIDENT. OR, AS CURTIS LOVED TO SAY, EDEN DISCOVERED him.

Adrian was in love with his newfound power. He loved killing. Loved it so much that a year after the incident at the construction site in McLean, he'd already taken four more lives. He was very careful, had been preying on the homeless who wandered the dark night streets of D.C. Off the Key Bridge into Georgetown, under the Whitehurst Freeway, there was a parking lot across from a bar called Chadwicks. D.C.'s homeless crowded in the back of the lot, near the river, away from the streetlights, under the shadow of the bridge. They had a full-blown camp, and Adrian found he could move among them without too much trouble, passing out blankets and water, magazines and candy bars and greasy fast food bags. They liked him all right. He liked himself, too. He was becoming a regular philanthropist.

His knew his size was an issue; he stuck out and was easily remembered, but there was nothing he could do about that. Better to be their friend. There was less chance of them turning on him if he was found out. He was very careful no one would match the sweet high schooler who brought them some much-needed things out of the goodness of his own heart with the vicious killer dropping bodies in the Potomac.

Even when the police came calling to do a welfare check and talked to everyone about the rise in homeless deaths, he played it perfectly. He'd gone up to one of the cops who'd been eyeing him and asked if he was safe being down here. The cop had shrugged and said, "You're a big kid, but best be careful, just in case."

A big kid.

Yes, he was.

Life was good. During the day, he was an average senior, making decent enough grades to stay off the radar, hanging with Doug in Georgetown, even venturing on a few dates. He doubled with Doug to the Homecoming dance, managed to get through having his cock sucked in the parking lot behind the school by a stoned blonde with a nose ring who wanted him to call her Candy, though her real name was something like Elizabeth. What he wanted to do was put his hands around her neck and squeeze the life out of her perfect body, but he restrained himself. Doug wouldn't have approved if he'd dragged his date back to the dance dead. And his only real friend's approval meant the world to him.

The days were long, and boring, and uneventful. But after midnight, he became his true self. He almost felt as if he was becoming a vampire, feeding on the blood of his victims, becoming strong and capable. Of course, he hated blood. It was messy, and too easily transferred between people. He'd tried stabbing and cutting, but it didn't give him the same rush. Looking into someone's eyes as they realized what was happening didn't do it for him, especially the resignation he'd seen from some of the homeless, who almost seemed grateful to him for ending their suffering.

No, it was the struggle he craved. The spastic, panicky movements of arms and legs, the chest heaving, hands ripping at his forearms, feet kicking his shins. The struggle was his thing, what he sought.

He'd had his final growth spurt; at his school physical, the doctor had measured him at six foot six and suggested he go out for football. He was seventeen, huge and strong, and not afraid of anything. He had to keep up appearances, being his usual quiet, deferential self. But inside he was on fire. Inside, he was a god.

Under cover of his advanced biology class, he spent some time in the library learning about the process of dying. They said when the heart stops, the brain has two to three minutes of continued activity while the body shuts itself down, so he was always careful to speak to his victims afterward. To thank them for their sacrifice. To assure them their death had not been in vain. He'd always been a polite boy; there was no reason to devolve into a raving maniac at the end the way he'd done with Frank and the nameless defaulter. He felt bad sometimes for Frank, but he never felt sorry for the other man. Neither a borrower nor a lender be, dude.

It was late April toward the end of his senior year when he discovered the garrote.

He read about it in a book—one of his dad's spy thrillers—and decided it might be worth a try. It seemed...elegant. Sophisticated. Grown-up. Sheer brute force had gotten him by until now. If he was going to continue on this path, he needed something a little more seemly.

He knew using a device was more dangerous than his own

hands, so he was careful when he bought the materials—borrowing Doug's car to drive to Bethesda to buy the wire from a hardware store, getting a child's jump rope at a sports store in Falls Church. He fashioned the garrote, admired his work, then tested it out on one of his old stuffed teddy bears, shoved away in the corner of his closet, forgotten and unloved.

One good twist and the bear's head was sliced clean off.

Smiling, on top of the world, he went to his favorite testing grounds under the Whitehurst Freeway for the first attempt. He chose a young guy with a brain full of cats—he'd be strong, but no one was going to miss him. He'd already been talking about moving south, to warmer climes, and the other homeless wanted him gone. Even the forgotten didn't like being around crazy.

Adrian followed him out of the lot, down to the river and waited until the guy finished taking a leak to jump him.

The garrote worked perfectly. He was able to relax the pressure a few times, let him start to breathe again, which was ideal. Before, if he'd let his arms go slack, his prey could slip out, run away. No more. He took his time. It was fifteen minutes of sheer, heady bliss. When it was over, satiated and happy, he slid the body into the water in a good solid current, knowing it would be days before it was found.

This newfound toy consumed all of Adrian's thoughts. He was edgy, and distracted, always on the lookout for the next neck to wrap his wire around. His grades started to slip—who could do homework when you held life in your very hands? His dad was questioning his comings and goings. Even Doug started drifting away. He had become obsessed with going into the marines to impress Candy Elizabeth, who'd smartly moved her oral attentions to a boy who didn't make her feel like a lamb about to go to the slaughter. He still hung out with Adrian, but there was an invisible wedge between them. As if

Doug sensed the strength of the man below the surface, and couldn't reconcile that person with his old friend.

Alone, Adrian became the night. He couldn't help himself. He was going down the rat hole, his stack of bodies growing. But the perfect kill eluded him. His pursuit became more and more frantic. Toward the end of May, even the homeless shut him out, realizing something wasn't quite right about the big blond-haired kid who'd been hanging around a lot more lately.

Discouraged, he was sitting on a bench on the National Mall, watching the flags surrounding the Washington Monument flip and snap in the breeze, when she walked by.

The one.

Not the next one, but the one who was going to be his perfect kill. He'd take her down, then lie back for a while. Take the summer off. He needed to get himself back under some semblance of control.

He didn't hesitate. He stood and followed, watching how her ass moved beneath the thin cotton of her skirt, her slender ankles shifting and moving in worn espadrilles, the muscles in her thighs tightening and lengthening with each step. She was young, an intern on the Hill, maybe. A dangerous victim. He felt the familiar tingle in his groin. He felt the blood rushing through his veins, and knew he was powerless to stop things now.

It was twilight, the sun fighting to hang on in the west, and he decided to take her right there in the middle of the Mall, with all the people around. The softball teams finishing their games and settling in with a beer or three, the congressional staffers walking down to the Metro, the tourists soaking in the last bit of the city before night set in. He could do it. He could grab her and pull her into the sculpture garden by the Hirschhorn Museum. No one would be there now, after museum hours, and he knew the lone camera that watched over the gardens was placed at the entrance. He would go over the wall to the downward path, yank her right over the edge.

His pulse raced, and his breath came short. He stalked her, waiting for the moment she'd be his.

In the shadow of the gardens, where no one could see them, he took three swift steps, pulled her behind the wall and wrapped the wire around her delicate white throat.

She was light and graceful in his arms, and in his frenzy of adrenaline, he'd pulled the garrote too tight. She didn't fight, didn't struggle. She went limp.

Caught off guard, he relaxed his grip.

And a voice commanded, "Let her go, Adrian."

Startled, he gasped and dropped the girl in a heap on the ground. She lay unmoving, and he searched for the owner of the voice, legs poised to sprint him away from the scene.

A woman of unsurpassed beauty stepped out of the shadows.

In the space of a heartbeat, she stared into his eyes, and he was mesmerized. Frozen. Her eyes were green, the color of moss, and wide-open. There was no fear. She wasn't afraid of him at all. Her reaction confused him. He didn't know what to do.

He wondered then if she was an angel. If something had happened to him, and he'd died.

But the birds were chirping, and he could hear the shouts and traffic. He was not dead. The calm was an illusion.

The only sane thing for him to do was to pounce on her, swing the silver wire around her neck, bunch his fists and turn her away, hard and fast, yanking the twin dowels close. She'd witnessed him attack a woman. She could put him behind bars forever.

He took a step toward her, but something told him to stop. He waited a heartbeat while she approached him. She took the garrote from his hands and smiled. Then she leaned toward him, breath warm and soft, like a ripe peach, and kissed him.

Her lips were soft and gentle, her tongue slick. She kissed him for what felt like a very long time, the unmoving girl at their feet, and then she pulled back and squeezed his hand, those moss-green eyes locked on his.

Her voice was like honey when she finally spoke again.

"My name is Curtis Lott. I've been watching you for a very long time."

CHAPTER 30

Federal Bureau of Investigation
Washington, D.C.

THE BRUTISH, DIRTY CREAM CONCRETE EDIFICE OF THE HOOVER BUILDING GAVE THE first clue to its coming demise. The FBI was planning to move its headquarters away from the crumbling building that had housed and protected them since 1975, but for the time being, the bureaucratic machine was moving at a glacial pace, and Headquarters remained on Pennsylvania Avenue.

The spacious marble lobby was significantly more impressive. A very subdued young agent was waiting for Sam and Xander when they arrived. He got them signed in, through the metal detectors and in the elevator for the quick ride up three floors, then led them through the winding halls into an empty conference room. With a nod toward the water and coffee service on the table by the window, he left them alone.

Xander wasn't talking to Sam. It had taken her an hour on the road to convince him to take her back to D.C. instead of bundling her off to his cabin in the Maryland mountains and hiding her in his closet. They'd gone round and round—he could keep her safe; she would be protected. She didn't need protecting; she was a big girl who'd faced much worse. He'd mumbled something about her falling into trouble headfirst, which got on her last nerve, and they'd been inches from having a knock-down, drag-out, hurt-each-other-with-nonretractable-words fight when Fletcher called and interrupted. They'd retreated to their corners, glaring at each other while she'd answered the call.

"You need to head directly to FBI Headquarters. We're going to be debriefed on Timothy Savage and the Kaylie Rousch case."

That's all he'd tell her over the phone, and she spent the second hour of the drive in awkward silence, feeling the hollowness of her victory over Xander's objections, and fretting about what was going on. Xander hadn't done anything more than grunt noncommittally since the George Washington Bridge, and she felt it was important to fix things.

But before she had a chance, the doors to the conference room opened and people started streaming in. Fletcher entered first, and he introduced them to Agent Rob Thurber and Agent Jordan Blake. They all shook hands, Thurber quick and hard, Blake no less intense but softer. She was a pretty girl, probably ten years Sam's junior, brown hair pulled back in a high ponytail, very focused. Thurber was older and struck Sam as a bit uptight. They complemented each other, yin and yang.

Last through the door was a man Sam knew well, tall and intense, with black hair and the greenest eyes she'd ever seen. Supervisory Special Agent Dr. John Baldwin, head of the FBI's elite Behavioral Analysis Unit II team, and her best friend's fiancé. The man who'd recently implored her to come work for the FBI.

He looked completely whipped, his hair standing on end, his

clothes rumpled. But his smile was genuine. "Sorry I'm late. Hope I didn't hold you up. Hi, Sam."

She ignored the pointed look from Xander, rushed across the room to hug him. He hadn't shaved and his beard scratched her cheek when he leaned down to hug her back.

"Baldwin! What are you doing here? Is Taylor with you?"

"No, Taylor's back in Nashville. As to why I'm here—it's a long story. I'm just consulting on this case. Rob will fill you in. Why don't we get started, and we can catch up after?"

Sam squeezed his arm. "Of course. But before we do, I want you to meet Alexander Whitfield."

Baldwin shook Xander's hand and Sam watched the two men size each other up. Taylor had met Xander on a weekend trip, but Baldwin hadn't been with her; this was their first face-to-face. Xander was a bit shorter than Baldwin's six foot four, but he looked just as menacing, just as tough. These were two smart, capable, deadly men. She caught their body language, friendly enough, but slightly tense, as if Baldwin was warning Xander not to mess things up. She smiled. It was nice having a pseudo big brother to watch out for her. She knew once they got past the small problem of Baldwin wanting her to work for the FBI, the two men would get along famously—they were of the same mind on many things. And they both had their own version of the rules. Mavericks.

"Call me Xander. It's good to finally put a face to the name. Sam's been talking about you a lot lately."

Baldwin frowned slightly, as if to say *not here,* then smiled. "Taylor told me you were an army ranger. A sharpshooter, too?"

"That's right."

"I looked at your file. It's very impressive. The Silver Star, two Bronze Stars and a Purple Heart? You made quite a name for yourself after that stunt you pulled in Fallujah. It's a bloody miracle you and your men aren't all dead. They were lucky to have you. So are we. I'm glad to have you here."

Xander stiffened slightly, but Sam bumped his shoulder. She saw exactly what Baldwin was doing—giving Xander's bona fides to the other FBI agents. He might not have been law enforcement, but he was one of them, a patriot, a soldier who'd bled for his country. He would be an asset to the case, not a hindrance.

Sam shot Baldwin a grateful glance, and he winked at her. He took a seat and said, "Let's get started. Rob, you want to fill everyone in on the situation?"

They settled around the table. Sam noticed Fletcher was edgy, drumming his fingers, impatient, annoyed at being kept on the leash. He was ready to get out there and find their suspect.

This was big. She could feel it. The tension in the room was overwhelming.

Thurber asked Blake to pass them each a piece of paper. "I need you to sign this. It's a nondisclosure agreement. You know how this works. Everything we discuss in this room is confidential, and if you violate this agreement, you will be prosecuted. Got it?"

Now her interest was really piqued. She'd been asked to sign NDAs before being brought onto a case several times, especially ones she'd worked with the FBI, and the TBI—Tennessee Bureau of Investigations. In every instance, the case ended up being a headline grabber.

Xander signed his and handed it over. So did Fletcher. She glanced at the language. It was pretty standard: you must not share what we're about to tell you under penalty of death, dismemberment and life in prison. She figured she could be safely expected to keep her mouth shut about all this, and signed hers, as well. The quiet agent who'd seen them to the conference room collected the NDAs and left the room.

Thurber sat back in his chair. "All right. First, using the fingerprint cards from Dr. Owens's autopsy, we have positively identified the remains in Lynchburg as our former agent, Douglas Matcliff.

"Seventeen years ago, I was assigned to the Kaylie Rousch case. She was six years old when she went missing from her home in Bethesda. Got off the bus a block from her house like she did every day, and never made it home. I've prepared a full write-up of the case for you to read when we're done here. News clippings, that sort of thing." He handed them each a package of papers.

"Are your notes in this, too?" Fletcher asked.

"Not exactly."

Thurber cast a glance at Baldwin, who shrugged and said, "We try to keep as much off paper as possible. Paper can be used in court, can be acquired through subpoenas. There are certain things we'd rather keep to ourselves. The Rousch case is a good example."

There was a moment of silence while that sank in. Sam watched the three agents. They looked terribly uncomfortable, shifting in their seats like naughty children. She turned to Baldwin. "Why are you here? Really? Is this about—"

He cut her off with a big sigh, a noise she recognized from other cases she'd worked with him, and a small frisson of fear went down her spine. This wasn't about her.

"I'm here because you need a profiler. And I've been on this case for many, many years."

"Are we dealing with a serial killer?" she asked.

"In a manner of speaking, yes."

"Is the man who murdered Savage and Benedict the same one who kidnapped Kaylie Rousch?"

"It's a possibility. There's a complication, though."

"Let me guess," Sam said. "You've seen this M.O. before."

CHAPTER 31

BALDWIN POURED HIMSELF A GLASS OF WATER. "RIGHT AROUND THE TIME KAYLIE Rousch was kidnapped, there was a series of murders. Garrotings. Several people were killed, seemingly at random, with no connections between them. It was a spree that lasted three months.

"We found her body, the body we thought was hers, I should say, on the property of a man named Eric Wright. He lived in a double-wide trailer south of Ryder, Virginia, on about five acres of wooded land. Some hunters found the skeleton. It had been dug up by animals and wasn't complete. There were several important parts missing, specifically the skull, so we weren't able to do any odontological work. But it was clearly the body of a little girl, and the same blood type as Kaylie. The anthropologist who worked with the county made her age as six years old based on the growth plates on the ends of her femurs."

Thurber said, "We're going to have to do some investigating into how, exactly, the lab got the DNA wrong. It is a massive, unacceptable screwup."

Baldwin's voice was hard. "Let's put that aside for now, Rob."

Thurber nodded, gave him a tight smile, then continued. "We went to talk to Eric Wright. He acted dodgy, so we executed a search warrant. In a trunk in his bedroom, we found clothes that matched the description of what Kaylie was wearing when she disappeared, plus her backpack and a child's doll. There was also a garrote, with the blood of one of the known murder victims dried into the dowels. We had our guy. Wright was prosecuted, found guilty of second-degree murder and went to jail for life."

"All right," Sam said, "I'll bite. If he's in jail, how can he be out murdering people?"

Thurber responded angrily, "Because we got the wrong guy. But we didn't know until it was too late. The DNA evidence was sketchy to begin with. Turns out the lab messed up, contaminated the sample—yes, this is the same lab that blew the Kaylie Rousch identification. By the time we discovered there was a problem with the lab, Wright was dead. He died a few months after he was sentenced, shived to death in the prison showers. Wright always claimed his innocence, said he had nothing to do with Kaylie's disappearance or the garrote murders. He was telling the truth. We screwed the pooch, and an innocent man died."

Fletcher had been playing with his pen, absently doodling on his FBI notepad like a bored kid. They each had one to take notes on, though no one seemed to be writing anything down. He looked up from his drawings. "Then how did he get her clothes and backpack?"

"We think they were planted by the real killer to throw us off the trail," Baldwin said. "A man who's been out in the world with impunity, free because another man went down for his crimes."

Fletcher dropped the pen on the table. "So what does this have to do with Savage—sorry—Matcliff and Rachel Stevens?"

"Doug Matcliff and I worked the Kaylie Rousch case," Thurber said. "He's the one who found her personal effects at Wright's house." He shifted in his chair and Sam watched him, trying to decide what this was all about.

Sam shook her head. "You think he planted the evidence? But he was an FBI agent."

"It happens," Baldwin said lightly, and Sam realized her gaff. He'd been involved in a similar situation, had nearly lost his job over it. But his suspect had been guiltier than sin, a child rapist and murderer who had skated on a technicality and killed again. It was different. Very, very different.

Thurber twisted his hands in front of him. "Yes, he was. And he was a good one. But ten years ago, Matcliff went undercover in a new religious movement called Eden, which we suspected of running drugs. After three months, he very suddenly stopped reporting in. He was never heard from again. We assumed either he was found out and killed or he went native."

"Native," Fletcher said. "You mean he got caught up in what he was investigating and joined the cult?"

"Not a cult. At least, that's not the term we use. We prefer new religious movement. NRMs. The vast majority of NRMs are simply new religions led by harmless individuals. They mind their own business, even work with the local authorities so they aren't persecuted for their beliefs. Only a handful are even on our radar, and those are usually because they've applied for some sort of exception to the law that will accommodate their beliefs. The NRMs we worry about are the ones that are clearly apocalyptic and may cause harm to themselves or their members, the ones that are gathering weapons or making threatening gestures and statements to the government or the surrounding areas.

"Eden never had a history of causing trouble, wasn't even a concern, until a couple of hoodlum teenagers accidentally found themselves on the NRM's land and were taken, well, hostage is too strong a word. They were detained for a couple of days. Once the misunderstanding was ironed out, they were dropped off by their car. They reported it, though, and we looked into the group, just in case.

"They were based out in the western part of Fairfax County, self-sustained farming, purely agricultural. A flyover showed some pot plants, and the local police said there'd been a massive uptick in drug-related activity in the area, so we went in and seized everything. They didn't raise too much of a fuss, claimed it wasn't theirs, and when we pulled the property records, sure enough, the crop had been grown on the land abutting theirs, so technically, they hadn't done anything wrong."

"But you got suspicious enough to send an agent in undercover?" Fletcher asked.

"The kids said they saw some paraphernalia, trucks coming and going in the middle of the night, some other things. Since there'd been an increase in drugs in the area and no one knew for sure who the source was, it seemed like the smart thing to do.

"Doug was the one who suggested we look deeper into Eden, and volunteered for the job. Our boss agreed and we moved forward, but there was no way Doug was going to be the UC. He was green as hell, just a few years out of the Academy, and he got turned down in favor of a more experienced agent. He was pissed. At the last minute, that agent had a heart attack, so we had an operation in play with no one to go in. Against our boss's better judgment, she sent Doug undercover into the NRM.

"He was under for about three months when he stopped reporting in. We sent a team, asked some questions, looked around, but Doug wasn't anywhere to be seen. The leader said she'd never known anyone by that name, stonewalled the crap out of our people. We went back to D.C. and got a broad-scoped warrant, but by the time we returned to Eden to do a more thorough search, it was too late. Do you recall Heaven's Gate?"

"The suicide cult," Fletcher said. "Did the folks at Eden do the same thing? Go to meet the comet?"

"Yes." Thurber's face clouded; it was clearly a disturbing memory. "Freakiest thing I've ever seen, right out of a horror movie. Fifteen women and four men, all members of Eden Doug had identified, were found hanging in a barn. Just swinging in the breeze. The only people missing were the head of the cult, surprise, surprise, Doug and a girl he'd mentioned in one of his reports—Lauren. They, and he, never surfaced again, until now." He trailed off, then shook himself as if he'd felt a chill.

"I think I remember hearing about it. I don't recall the name Eden, though, or Curtis Lott," Fletcher said.

"We kept those details out of the media."

Fletcher crossed his arms. "Why in the world would you do that?"

Thurber didn't answer. Instead he said, "Damn, ten years of wondering what the hell happened to Doug, and he's living in Lynchburg, of all places. Why the hell wouldn't he let us know he was okay?"

"Thankfully, he reached out to Sam before his death, so we can start finding some answers," Baldwin said.

"I'd like to hear more about Eden. Is it rare to have a female cult leader?" Sam asked.

Thurber nodded. "Not rare, but certainly not common. Eden was an interesting crew. They were set up to work in a trinity—I don't know if you're familiar with the idea of synarchist rule? Harmony among multiple leaders? Historically, Eden had three leaders, all from the same bloodline. Three generations of women. A young girl, a middle-aged woman and a woman in her seventies."

"Maid, mother and crone?"

"Right. But the older woman was among the dead at the barn. The 'mother' was in her forties at the time, and from the reports Doug sent in, one seriously crazy bitch. I think she decided she wanted the whole thing for herself, killed off dear old Mom and everyone else who might get in her way and reestablished herself somewhere else." He shook his head. "We missed it. Doug never indicated they were headed for any sort of mass suicide. He said the leader was a preacher of sorts, had some funky beliefs about the end of time, but nothing he reported on indicated that the time was nigh."

"Who is their leader?" Sam asked.

"She went by a number of names, but at the time Doug went undercover, she was calling herself Curtis Lott. Some of the clippings in your file are on Eden, their history and such. They were a peaceful group going back to the sixties until all this happened."

Sam sat straighter in her chair. "Her name was Curtis Lott?"

He nodded. "You've heard of her?"

"Yes, but not in the way you might think. Curtis Lott was one of the beneficiaries of Savage's will. And the name Lauren was written on the back of a letter included with the will. She wasn't left anything, and the name was oddly out of place. Let's shoot for the moon here. Are you familiar with the names Anne Carter or Frederick McDonald?"

Thurber nodded. "Anne Carter, absolutely, yes. She was our boss during this time period. She's retired now, lives out in Fauquier County toward Front Royal. McDonald—him I don't know."

"Well, now we're five down with one to go. At least we have an idea of what Savage, sorry, Matcliff, was up to with his will. He was pointing us in the direction of the story. So we'd find these people, and it would all come to light. But why be mysterious about it? Why not just lay it all out? And how did Benedict's killer find out about the will?"

Thurber shook his head. "We don't know. Remember, we didn't know Doug was even alive until this afternoon."

Xander crossed his arms on his chest. "Why did Matcliff leave the FBI hanging, not knowing whether he was alive or dead? Not reporting in, running away from his duty. These don't seem like the actions of a patriot."

"No, they don't," Thurber said. "He walked away from his world, his training, his job. There must be a reason. I think he snapped, and started killing, and realized he liked it. It wouldn't be the first time we've had a military man start killing on American soil."

"I think you're reaching," Xander said evenly. "He's a very convenient scapegoat."

"Then who planted Kaylie Rousch's things at Wright's house? I don't think we're too far out on a limb here thinking Doug was involved."

Baldwin shook his head. "I don't know, Rob. That theory has always felt like a reach."

There was an awkward silence, which Fletcher broke. "So we have a disappearing cult, a missing, now dead FBI agent who might have been a serial killer and a resurrected girl. The will clearly has some clues as to what's been happening to Doug Matcliff over the years, right? I'd say that's something to go on."

Jordan Blake finally spoke up. "All this speculation is great—we need to brainstorm what's happening. But I don't have time to sit here and reminisce. We have another child missing right now, and I vote the rest of this case is shelved until we find her. Rachel Stevens has to be our priority. We owe it to her, and to her parents. We don't need another Kaylie Rousch on our hands."

CHAPTER 32

FLETCHER RAPPED HIS KNUCKLES ON THE TABLE. "I AGREE WITH AGENT BLAKE. THE Rachel Stevens case must be the priority. What do you want us to do, then?"

"You continue to work with Jordan to find the Stevens girl," Baldwin said. "Rob will be recusing himself from this part of the case. He's going to work on identifying the body we've mistakenly identified as Kaylie Rousch. Sam, Xander and I will work on Matcliff and Eden, see if we can't shake things loose from this end."

Sam caught Thurber's eye—he wasn't at all pleased with this turn of events. He hadn't offered to recuse himself. He'd been instructed to. No wonder he was being so pissy.

"You know, Baldwin, if your profile is correct, Rachel Stevens could still be alive. She's only been missing for a day," she said.

Baldwin nodded. "That's why we need to get this profile to the media right away. Since Rachel went missing after Matcliff died, it stands to reason we were wrong, and he's not involved in the cases, after all."

Thurber said, "Hey, now, hold up. Doug went undercover in a psycho NRM and has the DNA of one of the missing girls on his body. Are we sure we want to dismiss him as a suspect? He's certainly involved in this, up to his neck."

"He reached out from the grave to get help solving his murder, which tells me he might have been on the run," Baldwin said. "Maybe we've been approaching this wrong all these years. Maybe he's the innocent one in all of this."

"I don't think so. I think his letter, the will, it's all a confession. Because if he's innocent, why the hell would he go to *her* instead of coming to us?"

Thurber's face was red, and Sam flinched at the tone of his voice. Bitterness, fury, hurt, all bled into the word *her.* She understood, she really did. When someone you trust, who you think is a friend, betrays that trust, it's hard not to have negative feelings.

She tried to calm him down. "Agent Thurber, I'm not sure why I've been brought into this, either. But Doug clearly had a reason for reaching out to me. Maybe he knew I'd take things to you, and you'd know he was trying to help you solve this case. Maybe he thought I'd look at it with a fresh eye."

Thurber crossed his arms on his chest. He looked like an angry kid whose best friend had just kicked a rock at him. "Or maybe he's fucking with us, like he's been doing for the past ten years. He went native in a whacked-out cult, for Christ's sake. How can we take anything he has to say seriously, especially when we have no proof he's the one saying it?"

Thurber's thin veneer had finally cracked, if they'd angered him into using the nonapproved term for Eden. Sam took note. Thurber was more than angry about this—he was bordering on thermonuclear.

"He makes a good point, Sam," Fletcher said. "This guy

had a lot of chances to make things right with the FBI, and instead he stayed quiet for years, then out of the blue went to a country lawyer and made up a bizarre will and spent quite a bit of time following you around. None of this is adding up."

Sam took a breath. They were right. Of course they were right. This was all too weird for words. She looked at Thurber. "Do you have any idea where the cult might be now? Can we go interview them about Doug? And maybe we'll get lucky, and they'll know something about Rachel Stevens."

"NRM," he snapped.

Sam sighed heavily. "Forgive me, Special Agent, but I'm not in the mood to be politically correct right now. Where are they?"

"I have no idea. They haven't been on the radar for years." He looked at his watch. "I need to get to another meeting. Please excuse me. Jordan? You have to prepare the 9:00 p.m. Stevens briefing."

The younger agent rose without saying a word.

"Am I invited to this powwow?" Fletcher asked.

Overtly polite, Thurber said, "Of course. *You're* a part of the task force, Detective. By all means, join Special Agent Blake."

So Thurber's rancor was directed at Sam, and by association, Xander, the civilians on his turf. They were usurping his role in what was becoming a very big, convoluted and soon-to-be media-driven case. Sam mentally set her jaw.

Get used to it, buster. I'm here to see this through to the end.

"Great, I'll be there in a minute. Just need to ask Dr. Baldwin something."

"Fine." Thurber shot Sam a perturbed look as he stalked out the door. Blake followed him. Fletcher gave Sam a smile, and wound his finger around his ear, indicating either Thurber or this case was completely loco. She couldn't disagree.

Fletcher waited until Thurber and Blake were out in the hall, then said to Baldwin, "Yesterday morning I caught a case, and then your people took it over. Oscar Rivera?"

"From the Kenilworth Aquatic Gardens. Yes. What do you want to know?"

"Seems convenient you were here in town while all this shook out. No chance you were already here, working on that case, were you?"

"What makes you think that?" Baldwin asked.

"Awful lot of energy to murder a kid who might be involved in some drug running. It seems more sophisticated than that. Thought you might know more. My boss said your people mentioned it might be a serial."

Baldwin nodded. "Yes, and that's as much as I can tell you right now."

"Ah. Gotcha."

Blake stuck her head in the door. "Hey, Detective, you coming? Chop-chop."

"Let me know if there's anything I can do," Fletcher said. He shook Baldwin's hand, nodded at Sam and Xander and took off.

Once it was just the three of them, Sam said, "Another serial?"

Baldwin nodded. "Someone's been drowning young men across the country. It's not related to this case at all. So let's talk about Matcliff."

"All right. There's more going on than Thurber told us, isn't there?"

"There is. We need to figure out why a man you say is a stranger reached out to you instead of his own agency. Maybe he was worried about being prosecuted, maybe there's something more nefarious at play. But my number-one question right now aligns with Rob's. Why *you?* Why did Douglas Matcliff choose you to get the ball rolling on all of this? Why didn't he just come to us?"

She watched him for a moment. "So you didn't have anything to do with pulling me into this?"

He shook his head. "I swear I didn't. It's a complete coincidence of timing, that's all. Though this is a good example of how you'd work with us, if you chose to come on board."

She shook her head, not trusting her voice. Xander was sitting to her right. He reached over with his left hand and gently touched her arm. She was grateful for it; she'd been feeling very alone for the past half hour.

Baldwin nodded once. "All right. Let's focus on the facts. You didn't recognize the name Timothy Savage. Does Doug Matcliff ring a bell at all?"

"If it did, I would have said something. I can't imagine where I'd cross his path. A marine, an FBI agent? Baldwin, you and your people are the only ones I've worked with from the agency, and I don't know any marines."

"We need to go through all of your files, all your old cases, everything and anything that might give us a clue as to how he knew about you."

She relaxed a bit, seeing he wasn't trying to pull a fast one on her. "That's a good plan. Maybe there's something in Nashville that I just haven't thought of. There's another strange thing I've been wondering about. Everyone who knew Matcliff as Timothy Savage in Lynchburg said he had a son, Henry. Henry is the one listed as the primary heir in the will. We can't find him, but there was a young man hanging around the edges while we were there. He came to the funeral home where I posted the body, and followed us to the cabin in the woods. We need to put our hands on him. He may have at least some of the answers we're looking for."

"We'll add it to the ever-growing list of things we need to do," Baldwin said.

"There's a detective down in Lynchburg named June Davidson. I can't tell you for sure that he's on our side, but he's the only person we've met so far who seems to know anything about Matcliff's recent years. We need to talk to him first." She looked at her watch. It was nearly 8:00 p.m. "Maybe he can tell us how Ellie Scarron is doing."

Sam's stomach growled, loud enough they all heard.

Baldwin laughed. "When's the last time you ate?"

She thought back. Xander supplied the answer. "You had that bag of cashews we grabbed from a Shell station on the drive back up."

"You both must be starving. I'll have something brought in. We don't need you passing out during the interviews."

CHAPTER 33

WHILE THEY WAITED FOR THE FOOD, BALDWIN CALLED JUNE DAVIDSON USING THE speakerphone in the center of the conference table. It looked like a three-sided gray flying saucer. They all stared at the device, waiting. The Lynchburg detective answered after five rings, sounding tired and more than a little annoyed.

"Yeah, this is Davidson."

"Detective, Supervisory Special Agent John Baldwin, FBI. I have Dr. Owens and Sergeant Whitfield with me. We're calling for an update on Mrs. Scarron, and anything else you have on the attack."

Davidson sounded weary. "When did the FBI get involved? What happened to Detective Fletcher?"

Baldwin deflected him nicely. "Detective Fletcher is working on the task force searching for Rachel Stevens. How is Mrs. Scarron?"

"Not good. I'm here at the hospital now. She's not waking up anytime soon. They've put her in an induced coma because of some edema on her brain. She was oxygen deprived for a while before we got there. She'd started to come to, but the swelling began and the docs thought it was safer to knock her out and put in a stent. The only reason she's alive at all is Dr. Owens's quick work. That was pretty impressive, Doc. Sorry you had to rush off like that."

"Duty called," she said lightly. "Did you find anything on the cameras at her house?"

"We did. I have a decent still shot of the guy who broke in and tried to kill her. I can email it. He's a big son of a gun, looks taller than me, buzzed light-colored hair. We don't have an ID, but he was definitely in the house a half an hour before we got there."

"I'll have the photo run through our facial recognition system, see if we can't find a match," Baldwin said.

"Sounds good. So why's the FBI involved with this?"

Sam filled him in as simply as she could, running him through everything that had happened over the past few hours, then broke the news about Savage's background and alias.

"Seriously? He's ex-military, ex-FBI? I wonder if Mac Picker was telling us the truth about the name Timothy Savage not being in their client databases. Maybe he did it under the name Doug Matcliff, and only Benedict knew. I'll have to go over there and have a talk with Mac—it'll have to be in the morning, though. Everyone's buttoned up tight for the night here."

"That's fine. We'll touch base about it then. June, we need you to start from scratch with Matcliff, and his son. Do we have an idea of who this kid's mother is?" Sam asked.

"No. It was common knowledge she was dead. I never saw the need to investigate it further. I will now."

"Great. We haven't found Henry Matcliff, so we're up in the air until we do. Look into their background in Lynchburg. Give us some information so we have an idea of what's been going on down there. Everything and anything you can muster up, property records, physicians, dental work, schooling. You said you thought Henry attended Randolph College—can we get his transcripts?"

"Sure, I'll get on it. I'll have it all for you as soon as I can get it in the morning. By the way, you'd asked about Frederick McDonald. I ran the name through the system, and there is a Frederick McDonald here in town. He's clean, has a couple of minor traffic violations, owns a Mexican food joint out on Highway 29. Nothing strange about him. I gave him a call, told him what's going on. He's never heard of Savage, doesn't have any idea why he'd be on the list. I offered him a protective detail until this gets resolved, but he said no. I'll follow up on the Matcliff angle. Listen, I gotta run, Ellie's coming out of surgery. Have a good night."

He hung up and Xander shook his head. "We'll still want to go down there. I'm not one hundred percent convinced he's telling us everything."

Sam touched his arm. "I think he is, Xander. He's just caught in the middle of a very strange case and doesn't know who to trust. Sort of like us."

A young agent knocked on the door with their food, three bags of Chinese takeout. The smells were heavenly. Sam settled into some fried rice, the hole in her stomach closing with each bite. But while the hunger was being appeased, she couldn't shake the feeling there was something more going on here. Something much bigger.

She waited for the guys to get some food in them before she said, "Baldwin, speaking of people not telling us everything, are you being entirely forthcoming about the history of this case? I feel like we're missing something."

"She's right, you know," Xander said. "Are you going to tell us what's really going on, or let us keep operating in the dark?"

Baldwin swallowed and set his chopsticks across the top of his white cardboard carton. "You always were too insightful for your own good, Sam. What we haven't shared with the media, or anyone else, for that matter, was the content of the note found at Rachel Stevens's house. This is why we're going full bore on this case."

Sam stopped eating, as well. "The note was found at her house? I thought it was found at the scene."

"No, that was a purposeful mislead. We're holding back the real details. It was actually tacked to her bedroom door. It read, and I quote, *You lose one, you replace one.*"

"Jesus," Xander said.

Baldwin tapped the file folder, then took a deep breath. "What I'm about to tell you can't leave this room. It gets worse." He opened the manila folder and laid five clear evidence bags on the table. "We have five notes just like it."

Sam was dumbstruck. "Five more? Five more girls are missing?"

"Unfortunately, yes."

"When? Where? And why haven't we heard anything about them, about their cases?" And then it hit her. The secrecy. The nondisclosure agreement. The stricken faces of Baldwin and Thurber. Her blood pressure spiked.

"Have you been covering this up because you think Doug Matcliff, a former FBI agent, is behind the kidnappings? Because you thought he was your suspect all along? And he's had Kaylie Rousch captive all these years?"

Baldwin put his hands up in defense. "We didn't know where he was, if he was even alive. We weren't covering anything up."

"So why haven't you been shouting this from the rooftops? And why wouldn't Thurber and Blake tell us there are more girls missing? This is rather important, don't you think?"

He didn't answer right away, and she figured she'd hit it right on the nose. They weren't going to admit it, but that's why they were keeping things so quiet. The FBI actually thought the suspect was one of their own.

"They were under my instruction not to share this part of the story," Baldwin said.

"Why?"

"The truth is, Sam, this is all you need to know, and I wasn't sure you wanted to stay involved. Technically, you can walk away right now. You've fulfilled your end of the deal with Matcliff. You did his autopsy, found the only remaining copy of his will. Even saved Ellie Scarron's life. You told me you didn't want to work with me, with the FBI. I respect that. You can go home. We'll put someone on the house to keep you safe until the acute part of the case is through, but…" He trailed off and shrugged.

Jesus. He was right. All her claims, all her posturing that she didn't want to be a part of law enforcement anymore, didn't want to be working on homicides, had gone right out the window the minute she was presented with a juicy case to sink her teeth into.

She should get up and leave. Go home with Xander, go back to her new, quiet, safe life.

She sensed Xander watching her, snuck a look at him from under her lashes. He had a crooked half smile on his face, slightly wistful, as if he knew the decision she was about to make.

Baldwin was sitting silently, his hands folded on top of the file, watching her.

Both of them waiting for her to make a choice.

She took a quick breath in through her nose. "We're staying. And hiding this information from us was ridiculous. I need to know everything if you expect me to help."

Baldwin didn't miss a beat, but his smile was blinding. "Good. I'm glad to have you."

"Just this case, Baldwin. After this, I go back to being a boring old college professor."

He nodded, and the look on his face told her he didn't believe her for a second.

She ignored that. "Let's get back to it, then. Tell me about the missing girls."

"All right. The pattern is very specific. The victimologies are incredibly similar, the handwriting on the notes left at the scenes match, so there's little doubt the same person is behind all the kidnappings. It's been going on since 1998. I think Kaylie Rousch was the first. All six girls—seven now, if we include Rachel—had similar physical characteristics. Strawberry blond hair, light eyes. All were taken when they were between six and ten years old, so we're dealing with a pedophilic mindset. If you think about the way they were, for lack of a better term, *replaced* every few years or so, that tells us the ages of six to twelve are the specific ideation for this suspect."

"I'm not hip on all the lingo here, Baldwin," Xander said. "What do you mean, specific ideation?"

"I mean this particular pedophile likes prepubescent girls between six and twelve years old. Once the child ages and loses the physical characteristics he likes—in other words, enters puberty, which begins changing the body into the more adult female form—she is no longer attractive to the suspect, and he discards her in favor of a child who fits into his specific ideal. With the rate of frequency of these kidnappings, I believe the girls are being replaced, but we haven't found another body since Kaylie. And with her sudden resurrection, I could be wrong. All of them may very well be alive."

"What are the odds?" Xander asked.

"Bleak. But yesterday, they were nil."

"Do you have any idea whose body you found, the child you thought was Kaylie Rousch?" Sam asked.

"We honestly don't know. We're going to have the body exhumed, but that can't happen until next week. We have to get a court order, and the parents' permission, even though it seems that impediment might be gone now."

"Do you think this cult is behind the kidnappings of these other five girls? That Doug Matcliff ran away with them after the mass suicide? And have you found any other bodies?" Xander asked.

"NRM. No more bodies, no. And as of this morning, when I found out about Kaylie Rousch, I have to change everything I think about these cases."

"You're dodging us, Baldwin. Why? You can trust me, you know." Sam gave him a smile, which he returned.

"You're right. I can. That's why we're still having this conversation. Here's the profile I've been working with all these years. The kidnapper was a man acting alone, in his midtwenties to thirties, very smart, very capable, with a steady white-collar job. He's low ranking, not management, but gets good reviews from his bosses, who wonder why, with his smarts, he doesn't try for promotions. He's probably turned down opportunities to move up the ladder if it would mean a physical move. He's not married, has a private place to keep his victims, a basement or the like. He's a loner, one of those men who disappear into the framework of society. He doesn't make waves, doesn't draw attention to himself, but he doesn't set off people's alarm bells, either. The notes indicate he was discarding the girls, even though we haven't found any more bodies. Profiling is an inexact science. I might have that part wrong."

"Does Doug Matcliff fit this profile?"

"Yes and no."

Sam shook her head. "So *if* you've been wrong all this time, and this guy isn't a corporate white shirt, but a part of the NRM, and *if* they were involved, you're saying a whole group of people kept quiet all these years about kidnapped little girls? That seems pretty far-fetched."

"Not as far-fetched as you might think. The power of these

cult leaders defies logic. Look at Jim Jones, and David Koresh. They used mind control and drugs to keep their followers in line. Jones was a con man, through and through. Koresh had a massive God complex, decided he was going to be the chosen one and everyone would do everything he said, at any time. They were both sexual sadists, too, which goes along with this."

"But a female version?" Sam asked.

Baldwin ran his hands through his hair. He looked tired, so tired, and Sam felt bad for pushing him. His job was heavy on the horrible and light on the happy, and she knew he did his absolute best with everything he touched.

When he spoke, his voice was soft. "Sam, you of all people know there isn't anything in the world that surprises me. If it is them, then it seems someone in Eden wanted a very specific type of little girl, and whoever took Kaylie and the other girls fits that profile."

Sam shook her head. "Nothing about this scenario is typical though, is it? I know you said historically there was a series of garrotings surrounding each kidnapping. Where do those murders fit into this?"

"I don't know. They may be totally unrelated. Stranger things have happened."

"You don't believe that," Sam said.

He sighed. "No, I don't. But other people do, and I've had a hard time convincing them otherwise. You know hindsight is twenty-twenty. We can see the pattern more clearly now than before."

"The pattern here seems slightly different, though—Matcliff was strangled, not garroted. And he doesn't seem to have been living with a cult—he was pretty far off the grid."

Baldwin ran his hand through his hair, making it stand up on end, a gesture she recognized as pure frustration. "I'll be honest, we don't know what the link is. Right now it's one hell of a coincidence. We're running the specifics through ViCAP now, and I've extended the search parameters to include the surrounding jurisdictions where the girls went missing. Maybe we screwed up. Maybe there's a more specific pattern than we realized. We've had multiple agencies on these cases across six jurisdictions, and no one's been talking to each other. You know how it is—too many cooks. That's why I'm here now, to coordinate the effort, see the links between all the cases, and work it to the end. With your help, of course."

Sam nodded. "Of course we'll help you. Anything we can do, you know we will." But inside, she had to admit she was a bit surprised. If the FBI's most hotshot profiler was asking for her help, things must be bad. No, that wasn't a fair assessment of the situation; Sam and Baldwin had worked together on many a case in the past several years. He knew he could trust her. That's why he was bringing her in.

A light went on. That's why he wanted her as an official consultant. He trusted her judgment. She wasn't a part of his system. A system that had been keeping the links between six kidnappings quiet until now.

Xander spoke up. "A stupid question. If the kidnappings *are* tied to the cult, could they be using these girls for something? Maybe a sacrifice of some sort?"

Baldwin got up and poured himself a cup of coffee, took a sip, grimaced then downed the cup as if it were a shot of espresso and rejoined them at the table.

"It's not a stupid question at all. Now that we might have a link, it's exactly what I'm afraid of. The notes would certainly lead us to believe that. *You lose one, you replace one.* The particular use of *lose* makes it seem the girls are dead. For years, we thought we had found Kaylie Rousch's body, and the others simply were disposed of more thoroughly. This new DNA evidence throws that theory on its ear. Whether they were kept alive, and still are, or were killed after they grew out of the prepubescent stage, we won't know until we can get our hands on the only one we know is still alive."

"Kaylie Rousch." Sam said. "I assume you've done your magic and put together a geographical profile of the kidnappings?"

Baldwin opened his iPad and showed them a map of the United States with a series of pins spread across it. Beside each red pin was a name and a black circle, another little girl lost. "There's no discernible pattern. The girls have gone missing all over the country. Bethesda, Maryland. El Paso, Texas. Denver, Colorado. Hot Springs, Arkansas. Lexington, Kentucky. We find Kaylie, and Rachel Stevens, and we'll find our answers."

"And you said Eden was a female-oriented group. I don't know if this has anything to do with it, but when I rolled Doug Matcliff during the autopsy, I found an incredibly intricate tattoo on his back. A triskele. Three spokes in a counterclockwise orientation. It looked Celtic to me, actually."

Baldwin pulled a photograph from his file. "Does it look like this?"

Sam glanced at it. "Exactly. This one is smaller, though. His tattoo covered his whole back. It must have taken a long time to finish. The spokes were made up of a ton of different mystical symbols. Moons and stars and inverted circles with lines through them, all kinds of strange stuff."

"This particular triskele is Eden's symbol. We've never figured out the meaning, because we've never been able to talk to anyone about it. I'm hoping Kaylie Rousch can shed some light on things."

"So where do we look for her? Lynchburg?"

"Might be the best place to start, yes. Though I'd like to go by the Rousches and see if perhaps Kaylie showed up there. If she's free and alive, it would stand to reason she would want to see her parents, right?"

"It's a good thought," Sam said.

“That will be our last stop for the night, and we can head to Lynchburg first thing in the morning.”

Sam met Xander’s eye as they gathered their things. He shook his head slightly, almost as if he knew exactly what she was thinking.

There were so many lives at stake, and here they were, stuck sifting through evidence, trying to piece it all together. She wanted to get out there and start looking for Rachel Stevens herself, even though she knew there were hundreds of people with badges searching for her. She couldn’t help imagining the little girl, scared, alone and clearly in grave danger.

She needed to help Baldwin sort through the new information. The more they could discover, the better chance they had of finding the truth.

CHAPTER 34

1989
Washington, D.C.

THEY LEFT THE UNCONSCIOUS GIRL IN THE WEEDS OF THE GARDEN, AND CURTIS Lott took him to a flophouse on Fourteenth Street, and talked to him while a working girl did her thing in the next room. He remembered little of their initial conversation, only that the tall, reddish-blonde woman with bright green eyes was absolutely intoxicating.

It was her scent, he thought, that had stopped his hands from their fateful journey earlier. Honeysuckle and musk and some sort of earthy fragrance he eventually recognized as her natural aroma, as if she were tied directly to the soil they walked upon.

It was nearly dawn when he realized he wanted to bed her more than he wanted to kill her—an evolutionary moment even he recognized.

It was like fireworks going off in his brain. He could master his urges by replacing them with others. Control his homicidal bent through sex.

He put the moves on her then, clumsy adolescent fumblings she endured with a brief smile before she took his hands, set them in his lap and said, "Let me."

In his bloodlust over the past year, he'd forgotten he was still a virgin. Curtis fixed that, carefully showing him the things she wanted him to do to her, explaining with her body and lips what men and women did together in the dark. When they were done, indecently quickly in his mind, he felt a sort of peace he'd never experienced before. This, being inside this woman, was more than sex. It was truth.

"I would do anything for you," he murmured into her hair, knowing it sounded romantic, and meaning it.

"That's good, Adrian, because I have some things I need you to do."

Curtis was twenty-two years older than Adrian, and worldly. She had an air about her, weary, torn, yet joyous and impetuous, that he found mesmerizing. She wouldn't tell him where she came from, only that she'd been put on earth to find him and take him home.

And she did so the next day.

Home was Eden, a small farm in western Fairfax County. The acreage was put to sustainable farming that served a group of people known as the Edenites. There was no electricity, but they did have running water from a pump to maintain the crops. On the drive there, Curtis talked of a happy place where each person had a role, all were considered equals, and how her people, the Edenites, were special. She'd handpicked them all—he was too young, too inexperienced, to realize this meant they'd each been seduced in a small room by this glorious woman before being brought here—that realization came later, when he wasn't cloudy with love.

Adrian drove his beat-up pickup truck through the gates, thrilled to be in the company of the woman sitting in his passenger seat. She was his. He'd claimed her.

When he pulled up in front of the farmhouse, several people came to meet him. They gave him sips of homemade spruce beer, and small corn cakes, an offering from their own hearts to make him welcome. He ate and drank and accepted their gentle touches. Lost in the sea of friendly faces and smiles and polite greetings, he had eyes only for Curtis.

After the Greeting, as it was called, she brought him into the house, into her rooms. There was a small antechamber, the reading room, she called it, which housed her texts, row after row of mystical and spiritual books, unlike anything he'd ever seen before.

The reading room opened into a large square bedroom with two windows on the far wall, sunlight spilling onto an unmade king-sized bed. The room smelled of sweet incense and even sweeter honey. Without saying a word, Curtis shut the door and began removing Adrian's clothing. He was desperate to be with her again, to feel the softness between her thighs, and she was happy to oblige him. He didn't care about the other people around hearing him; he knew no embarrassment when he was with her. And when she cried out, and he knew he'd pleased her, he swelled with pride.

It was known as the Seasoning. In the subsequent years, he'd managed not to kill the men who came after him, who were led into that sweet sanctum with dazed smiles on their faces, who made Curtis cry out in pleasure. But only because by then, Curtis had taught him how to channel himself. His murderous impulses were put to better use in service of the Mother.

After the Seasoning, which lasted a week and a day, he emerged, drunk on love and sex and power, meaning every word of his foolishly romantic statement after their first encounter.

He would do anything for Curtis. And he did.

Anything, and everything.

His first task was to make love with every woman in Eden. This was his first Reasoning, which would be repeated quarterly. Curtis assured him it was not only necessary, but expected. These women were all his. She'd brought him to pleasure them, to give them children. He was a perfect specimen, and they were all thrilled to be with him.

There were fifteen sacrosancts, as the women of childbearing age were known. Fifteen was a sacred number in Eden. The sacrosancts were divided into three sets of five, lived in three small cabins with five small rooms and one large great room in each, and every night for two weeks he fulfilled his duties in each of the bedchambers.

He learned that women were very different. Sizes, shapes, smells, movements; all unique, all precious. His mates ranged in age from twelve to nearly fifty. Some he enjoyed more than others, but he did his duty for all.

At each hearth, he was fed and given sweet homemade wine. He was in fact treated as a king. And he liked it. He liked the attention from these women. He liked the idea of spilling his seed in them, knowing that coupling with him brought them joy. The small whispers in the night told him things he needed to understand about his new life. Eden was a utopia, and he was going to be their greatest asset. If they could have his children—big strong strapping young men—their lives would be blessed by Curtis, and they would bless him in return.

At the end of the Reasoning, sore, tired and happy, he was sent back to Curtis's chamber. She was naked upon the bed, the sun playing off her glorious hair, and she asked him if he was interested in killing anymore.

The question caught him off guard, and it must have shown,

because she told him to be completely honest with her, for she would know if he was lying.

He wanted to lie, to tell her what he thought she wanted to hear. He needed to stay. For the first time in his life he felt as though he belonged somewhere, to someone. He felt loved, and cherished, and desired.

This woman knew what he'd done, and she still wanted him. It was more than a benediction. It was the ultimate forgiveness.

And because she'd been honest with him, he was honest with her.

"Yes, I still want to kill. I won't, for your sake, but I can't tell you honestly that I wouldn't want to. There is something very different here that satisfies part of what I crave."

"Which is what, my Adrian? What do you crave?"

"Feeling the life of a person leave their body."

She was up in a flash, and he thought she meant to slap him, but instead she kissed him and smiled. "You have answered well, Adrian. You will kill again. But you will not do it for yourself. That is wrong. You've spent a year removing people from this earth who have done you no harm, who are innocent. Instead from this moment forward, every kill you make will be in my name. You will do this for me."

"Anything, Curtis. I will do anything for you."

They settled into life on the farm. He was happy. Happier than he'd ever been. They lived a good life. His previous urges were mollified. All he wanted was to retain Curtis's favor, to make her happy, to work hard and have the respect of his fellow Edenites. He was the first to sit when Curtis stood to speak, the first to clap, to allow his eyes to roll back, to accept the Wafer of Life, which gave him insight into Curtis's explanations of the great Mysteries of the Universe.

After a month of excelling, it was time for him to be fully accepted into Eden. Accepting the Mark, as they called it, was a brutal, all day and all night process. His entire back was tattooed with a triskele, the symbols of Eden, as a base. It was an important ceremony. Everyone participated, all the members of Eden spilling their own blood into the ink for the marks they were going to make.

It made them one. They shared all things. The blood of one was the blood of many, and together they were consecrated.

The next day, he was in pain, but happy. All of Eden gathered for a feast to welcome him as a true member of their fold.

He hadn't connected his coupling with the fact that there were no young children or babies in Eden. It was only nine months later, after six of the women he'd been with swelled with new life and gave birth to healthy, squalling children, that he saw any infants. He wondered why there were none before he came, but he soon found out why.

Within a week, all the newborns were gone.

He asked Curtis about this, and was shocked when she flew into a rage. She swore at him, cursed him, punched him, then had three men drag him down the stairs, to the dark, dank cellar below the farmhouse. Things crawled on him, bugs and rats and spiders, but he'd been tied down and he couldn't move to get them off. He was there for three days in his own filth, with no food and only the barest trickle of water from a broken pipe sticking out from the wall, which he could reach if he rolled, straining, to his right.

Curtis would join him once a day and explain his wickedness to him. In those dark moments, when he couldn't see her face or smell her intoxicating scent over the musty earth, he wondered why he was there. What his true purpose was. Why the woman he loved so dearly was hurting him.

This, he learned, was the Great Darkness, meant to strip away the evil within, and it wasn't something he ever wanted to experience again.

People of Eden rarely misbehaved, and he understood why. If they displeased Curtis in any way, from a scorched meal or a weak harvest to a miscarriage or reluctance to engage in the Reasoning, even dressing in a way she found provocative, or speaking to another member when it was not allowed, they were sent into the Great Darkness.

Adrian finally came to understand the Great Darkness had little to do with being left alone for three days in the dark. To be without Curtis's love and favor was painful. She was the most intelligent, gracious, loving person he had ever met. She would do anything for him, allow him transgressions the others were punished for. She kept him above the rest of her flock, exalted, at her side all the time outside of the Reasonings.

And after ten years of living and loving and Reasoning, their numbers growing, their flock content, Curtis announced to the gasps of the crowd it was time for the Reckoning.

This was a dark time in Eden's history, one he didn't like to think about. It went against his nature. But he was bidden to do all of Curtis's work on this earth, and so he obeyed.

It all started with a child named Kaylie.

CHAPTER 35

Bethesda, Maryland

CLIVE AND MAUREEN ROUSCH'S HOUSE WAS TIRED AND WORN, A ONE-STORY redbrick rambler with overgrown shrubs blocking the windows. The sun was gone, but there was still enough light to see the home's disrepair. The driveway was concrete, weeds forcing their way up through multiple cracks, and the lawn was yellow and burnt after a long summer without water. It was a thoroughly depressing scene.

Sam and Xander got out of the car, Baldwin pulled up behind them a second later. Xander took one look at the house and said, "I'll be around. Call if you need me."

Sam and Baldwin made their way to the front door. The porch lights didn't work. There was shattered glass beneath them and no lightbulbs in the sockets. The doorbell was broken, too, the button missing and wires sticking out, so Sam knocked hard, three times, with the side of her fist.

After a moment, the door opened slowly. A bloodshot eye

appeared, then two, then a downturned mouth and wispy gray hair tucked under a faded red bandanna.

"What?"

Baldwin flashed his creds. "Mrs. Rousch? I'm Dr. John Baldwin, FBI. This is Dr. Samantha Owens. We are involved in your daughter's case. There's a new development, and we were hoping we could speak to you."

The face twisted. "New development? Our girl's been dead for a long time. You find who did it?"

"No, ma'am. Can we please come in?"

"No. I don't want you here. You don't got any justice to talk about, go away."

She tried to slam the door, but Baldwin put his foot in the gap. "Mrs. Rousch, we have reason to believe we made a mistake sixteen years ago. We think Kaylie is still alive."

The woman's eyes widened at that bit of news, and the door swung wide open. Sam caught a gust of sandalwood and vodka, smells she immediately associated with the old, unwashed and drunk. Great. Granted, it was late in the evening, but Sam had the distinct impression Mrs. Rousch had been tippling since well before dinner.

"If she's alive, where is she? Why hasn't she come home?"

"We don't know for sure, ma'am. Perhaps we could come in and talk?"

She stepped away from the door and gestured toward the living room. "Want something to drink?"

They both shook their heads. "No, ma'am," Baldwin said.

"I do. You sit. I'll be right back."

The floor was carpeted with white shag so old and dirty it had turned gray, and there was a thick layer of choking dust on all visible surfaces. Newspapers littered the corners, and a bowl partially full of old, dried-out dog food sat forlornly in a corner.

Sam made a mental note to make sure someone came in and tidied up the house before the reporters started banging on the doors and windows. If they found Kaylie, this shouldn't be the homecoming she got after seventeen years away: a drunk mother, a fetid house.

Maureen Rousch came into the living room carrying a tall, clear plastic cup with green bamboo leaves on it. It was filled almost to the brim with clear liquid. With anyone else Sam would assume it was water. From the fumes that drifted out, this clearly was not.

Once the woman was settled on the couch, Baldwin asked, "Is Mr. Rousch home?"

"Yeah. In the bedroom. He had a stroke last year, doesn't get around much anymore."

"Should we go in there to discuss things, then? I'm sure he'll want to hear what's happening."

"He's asleep. He sleeps most of the time. Don't want to disturb him. He doesn't like it."

"All right," he said. "Have you had any contact from your daughter since she disappeared?"

"What, like was I visited from the great beyond? The girl's dead. We buried her. And I don't believe in ghosts. So no, Detective, she hasn't been hanging around."

He ignored the mistake. He knew that to a woman like Mrs. Rousch, who had probably dealt with hundreds of law enforcement types over the years, details like rank and even what agency someone was from were meaningless.

"Nothing unusual happened in the past couple of weeks? Letters, calls?"

"No." She took a slurpy sip of the drink. "She's not my daughter, just so you know. My stepdaughter. I married her daddy when she was just a baby, thought it was going to be nice, like having a family of my own until I had my own babies. I never got pregnant, so things didn't turn out the way I wanted. I wouldn't raise a girl to be such a brat. That child was a nuisance from the first day."

Sam drew back at the woman's tone. "I take it you didn't get along with your stepdaughter?"

"She was a liar. Lied about everything and anything without any sort of remorse. Nothing I did could stop it, neither. Even when she was punished, it didn't seem to make a lick of difference. Always figured she ran off with someone she met online."

Sam was about to explode. This woman's child, whether biological or not, had only been six years old when she went missing. Six. Baldwin put a hand on her knee and she bit her tongue.

"Ma'am, when you say she lied, can you be more specific?"

"I caught her once, taking a cookie from the pack. She wasn't allowed but she did it, anyway, brazen as a hussy. And when I told her I saw her doing it, she looked me straight in the eye and said, no, she didn't. She was always losing her homework, not turning it in, and the teachers would call and complain and I'd ask her why she didn't turn it in and she'd say they didn't give her any homework. But I'd seen her sitting at the dining room table working on it. She was too smart for her own good, skipped a grade and was in a gifted program to boot. She thought she was mighty special."

"But compulsive lying was a regular behavioral problem?" Baldwin asked.

"Girl lied for the sake of lying. I never could understand why. Drove a wedge between me and her daddy, too. He bought every word out of her mouth like it was honey, didn't seem to care she was lying to him, too, stealing money from his wallet, which he blamed on me." She took another drink. "She was a bad girl. I was sorry when she died, but I wasn't surprised. Girls like that, they can't be trusted."

Baldwin nodded, humoring, digging deeper. "I understand completely. Tell me more about her lying. Why did you think she might have met someone on the internet?"

"I see it on the TV all the time, these girls who sign up for dating websites and chat rooms and the men on there pretend to be teenagers to strike up friendships."

"In 1998, did your family own a personal computer?"

"How'm I supposed to remember back to then? That's years ago."

"Personal computers weren't nearly as common then as they are today. And Kaylie was only six, despite being advanced for her age. We don't think she ran away of her own accord, ma'am. We still believe she was taken against her will. Despite the fact that we may have made a mistake about her death, I'm hard-pressed to imagine she arranged this," Baldwin said.

"I don't know about that." She nipped, swallowed, nipped again. "If it wasn't the internet, she probably ran off with some boy she met at school. I never was sure she'd been kidnapped. She never wanted to be here. She probably saw it as an easy way out, and she got famous to boot. If she ain't dead, then I was right. She did arrange for it all."

That was it. Sam couldn't help herself. "She was only six years old. A child. How can you possibly think she orchestrated being kidnapped?"

"Well, she ain't dead, is she? And I told you she was a liar. Those shows always say the kid is usually dead within twenty-four hours. We assumed it was too late from the get-go, even though her daddy insisted on mortgaging us to the hilt to put up a reward, and begged and pleaded for her safe return. None of it worked, so we figured she was dead, just like everyone else did. Then they found the body, and we buried her and grieved and moved on."

She took another, deeper drink of the vodka. She was listing from side to side in her seat. "What are you gonna do with the kid we buried? Do we get our money back? Times are hard since Clive's stroke."

Sam nearly bit through her lip.

Baldwin adopted his most eminently reasonable tone. "Mrs. Rousch, we will need your consent to exhume the body."

"How much is that going to cost?"

"We'll cover it."

"Then it's okay, I guess. You just talk to that funeral home, tell them we want our money back if the kid we buried wasn't ours." She stared off into the gloom of the living room, and her tone softened. "I know it ain't Christian of me to say I didn't like the child. God help me, but there it is. She was wrong in the head, and a liar, and I'm surprised she didn't burn down the house around our ears one night just to pay us back for disciplining her."

Her eyes cleared for a moment and she stopped weaving on the couch. "I know you think I'm just an old drunk, and maybe I am. Maybe I just don't care anymore what people think about me. But I'm telling you the God-to-honest truth. That girl was crooked as a snake, warped inside, even as a youngster. Despite that, her daddy loved her to pieces, and I mourned her loss once. I don't care to repeat the process. I think you should go."

Baldwin stood, and Sam followed. "We'll leave in a moment, ma'am. I'm afraid I will need to speak with Mr. Rousch first."

"Told you, he's asleep. He'll kill me if I let you wake him up."

"Since you say he loved his daughter, I think he'll want to hear about this," Sam said.

Mrs. Rousch stumbled to her feet, swaying alarmingly. "You can't go back there, I said. Now leave!"

Baldwin ignored her and strode down the hall to the bedroom. Sam blocked Mrs. Rousch from following. The woman was drunk but stronger than she looked, and Sam had to force her back onto the couch.

Baldwin returned a moment later, his face pinched. He gestured for Sam to follow him, went out onto the front steps and pulled out his cell phone.

"Where are you going?" Mrs. Rousch yelled. They ignored her.

"What is it?" Sam asked.

"Mr. Rousch is dead. Has been for a while. I don't know if she's just addled in the brain from all the alcohol and actually believes he's sleeping, or if she's been covering it up."

"How long has he been dead?"

"A year, maybe more. He's pretty well mummified. You want to take a look?"

She sighed. No, she didn't, but this was her job, her world. This wasn't her first mummy. It happened more than people thought, a loved one passing away without any fanfare, or even a decent burial, because no one knew exactly what to do. Or they were planning to game the system, collect unemployment benefits or Social Security checks.

She went back inside, ignored a now sobbing, slurring Mrs. Rousch and walked down the hall to the master bedroom.

Clive Rousch was tucked up into the bed, the covers drawn back a bit from where Baldwin had checked on him, the desiccated skin of his face now exposed. His eyes were closed, his mouth open, as if he'd gone to sleep and had never woken up. Not gruesome, not horrible, but sad, so sad.

She snapped on a pair of purple nitrile gloves—old habits die hard; she always had a few pairs tucked into her purse—and did a quick external examination. The skin around his legs and arms flaked onto the sheets as she touched him. His right arm was drawn up, the wrist curled in on itself, an involuntary contracture of the muscles. Left-sided stroke, then. He would have suffered aphasia, language apraxia, paralysis. Baldwin was right. He'd been dead at least a year.

Helpless, paralyzed, unable to communicate, left to die in his bed.

Who was the real liar in this house?

Her heart tripped, and the edges of her vision began to darken.

One Mississippi, two Mississippi, three Mississippi, four.

Pulling off the gloves, she stalked out onto the ramshackle porch, desperate for air. The night was warm and damp. She pulled in three breaths quickly, realized the symptoms of panic had passed as quickly as they'd started.

Baldwin spoke quickly into the phone and Sam stared back inside, swore she could hear Mrs. Rousch crying. She was torn between wanting to leave, to clear out immediately, and going back in to soothe the crazy old woman.

Poor Kaylie. Six years old and on the receiving end of so much hate and mistrust. Sam had wondered why, if she were alive, Kaylie wouldn't have let her parents know. Now she understood, understood completely. She hadn't been wanted, anyway.

It broke Sam's heart to think of that lost little girl being taken from one hell and placed in another.

They had to find Kaylie, and find Rachel Stevens, now.

Xander slid out of the darkness behind the house, came to her side.

"There's something back here you're going to want to see."

CHAPTER 36

THEY HEARD THE BENEVOLENT WAIL OF A SIREN IN THE DISTANCE, AND SAM KNEW the authorities were on their way to take Mr. Rousch to the morgue, and hopefully, take Mrs. Rousch to the hospital. Get her dried out, see if there was permanent brain damage from the years of alcohol abuse or if the old witch was just twisted naturally.

She was still in shock—how could a mother, even a stepmother, be so hateful toward a little girl?

Hopefully Xander had found some answers.

Baldwin retrieved a flashlight from his trunk and gave it to Xander. "Lead on."

They set off around the side of the house, through the backyard, into the woods.

"What's back here?" Sam asked, trampling across what she hoped was just squishy grass and leaves.

"There's a small campsite not far off the trail. Might just be from some homeless, or kids, but the site itself looks old. There's a lean-to shelter and an old blanket, but there's also fresh scuffs in the dirt and a recently dampened fire and the remains of a rabbit. Someone's spent some time back here, very recently."

"Kaylie?"

"Maybe."

The camp was a ten-minute walk. It was as simple as Xander had described. A small stone seat, a worm-eaten lean-to and the remains of a ratty pink blanket. Pink. While the men circled the area, looking for any more signs of life, Sam kicked at the small blanket—it was shredded, had been the home of many mice and insects over the years. Under it, stashed in the corner of the lean-to, was a small, tattered stuffed lion. Sam put on a fresh pair of gloves, picked it up gingerly. It took her a minute, then she realized it was Simba, from the movie *The Lion King.*

Her heart broke all over again. This poor little girl, unloved and unwanted by her evil stepmother, had created a small home for herself out in the woods, with a few treasured comforts. She wondered if Kaylie had cried for her lost stuffed lion when she'd been taken.

Sadly, she probably had bigger issues.

Xander came up beside her. "What's that?"

"Stuffed animal. I think Kaylie must have come out here to get away from that monster of a woman."

"Makes sense. Someone's been here recently, but we can't find anything to indicate where she may have gone. If it's her, that is."

"Who else would it be?"

"Good point. Let's let Baldwin deal with the M.E. and everything. You need rest. You're swaying, you're so tired."

She nodded, stepped closer to him, leaned her head on his shoulder. There was nothing more for her to do here.

Sam was quiet on the ride to Georgetown. Everything about this day had been over-the-top, from Ellie Scarron to the FBI to Maureen Rousch and the small remembrances of a lonely child. She just wanted to crash and sleep.

But she could tell there simply wasn't going to be any decent rest in her foreseeable future, not until this case—no, these cases—was resolved.

The radio blared another warning, the statewide AMBER Alert for Rachel Stevens. Sam listened to the automated voice giving the description of the girl, and was overwhelmed with worry for her. She'd been fighting the visions of Rachel all night. Lost, alone, perhaps being abused, maybe even dead… and what was she doing? Traipsing around after a ghost.

Stop that, Sam. The FBI and D.C. Metro are doing everything they can to find her. That isn't your role here.

All the adrenaline left her. She was dragging. They'd been going hard for two days, and her mind was starting to shut down. Baldwin had instructed them to sleep, that everything would be waiting for them in the morning. She didn't know if she could. She was in that mode of being so tired she was wide awake.

She leaned her head against the window. Thor snuffled his nose into her hair from behind, and she reached up to scratch his muzzle.

Xander was quiet, as well. One of the things she liked most about him was his ability to synthesize a situation. To take in all the variables and make a levelheaded decision about it. He'd make an excellent investigator. She wondered if she should mention that to him, but figured she should stay well away from anything that might be construed as criticism. Their earlier fight was still fresh in her mind, and she didn't want to lay the *you'd be so good at this* thing on him in case his temper was still flared and he took it as her saying he should get off his ass and get a job.

Xander was a unique being. Tempered in steel from his years in the army, when she'd met him, he'd been nothing more than a hermit, living off the grid on top of a mountain, a runaway from life. He was alone by choice, with only Thor for company, hunting the woods for food, growing what he couldn't shoot and kill, playing his piano to the squirrels and deer. Money wasn't important to him. He routed his military pension to his parents in Colorado, only withdrawing cash from the account when it was absolutely necessary.

Meeting Sam had given him purpose again. She knew that, as much as she knew he gave her a reason to get up in the morning, too. It was getting harder for her to imagine a time without him, and she knew that was a good thing. It didn't matter anymore that they hadn't known each other very long. The heart wants what it wants, and you can try to deny it, or give in, let go and acknowledge you sometimes don't have one hundred percent control over your life. Destiny and fate have a say, too.

But today's argument had been much worse than any little squabble they'd had over the past three months. She chalked it up to the pressure-cooker situation they'd been thrust into, but part of her knew it was more than that. Xander had checked out from the world on purpose. Being with Sam was forcing him back into it. And she wondered if that was a good thing.

Saying he'd be good at something that wasn't along the lines of the life he'd chosen was tantamount to saying she wanted to change him, and she honestly didn't. She was perfectly content with his choices. They brought him peace, a peace he'd earned after his service, after what he'd seen.

What she was wondering was how they were going to align his desire to be left alone on top of his mountain with her clear desire to be in the thick of things.

She wasn't ready to deal with the knowledge that being at FBI headquarters, seeing Baldwin, working with him on this case, was bringing back a long-dormant part of her psyche—the part that made her such a good medical examiner in the first place.

Curiosity.

She had it in spades.

She'd been a reluctant participant in anything more complicated than determining whether a person died from cardiac arrest or cerebral hemorrhage for nearly two years. She could tell that was over. Done. She wanted to be involved in this case. Wanted to help solve it.

And wanted, perhaps, to work on some more.

So what did that mean for her and Xander?

She glanced over at him, driving in the now deep darkness through the dimly lit streets of Georgetown, arm casually resting on the steering wheel, a hand over his shoulder massaging Thor's ears. It was going to take some doing to get him to fit seamlessly into this new world she was walking into.

But she loved him enough to make it work.

"Hey," she said softly.

He looked over, face hopeful. He'd caught her tone, heard the unspoken apology.

"I was a bitch this afternoon. I'm so sorry."

He touched her knee with his right hand. "No, you weren't. I can see how intriguing this is for you. You're all lit up inside. Watching you in action today, seeing you save that woman's life—I was a bit in awe, to tell you the truth. And a little jealous. I can see it might steal your attention."

"This is what I'm good at."

"That's clear as glass, sweetheart. I'm not going to stand in your way anymore. Just promise me something."

"What's that?"

"Be careful. I can't lose you, not to something that would have been easily avoidable if I went all caveman on you and forced you to stay home making me pancakes. All right?"

They hit the red light at M Street and Wisconsin Avenue. She smiled, scooted over in the seat, leaned over the gearshift and kissed him. She wasn't gentle about it, either, and she felt him respond. Teasing, she pulled away, back to her own space.

"Light's green," she said.

"I don't care. Come back here."

He kissed her, hard, and she felt it all the way through her body as if she'd been struck by lightning.

The car behind them laid on the horn, three long bursts, and they came up for air, laughing. It felt good. Right. This was how things were supposed to be between them.

She let her hand linger on his thigh. "We're only a few minutes from home. Hurry."

CHAPTER 37

Georgetown

THE HOUSE WAS DARK WHEN XANDER PULLED THE JEEP TO THE CURB. SAM WAITED on the front step while he took Thor for a quick potty break. They joined her quickly, and as she went to unlock the door, Thor suddenly started growling.

Sam could feel Thor's sides quivering, the hair standing on end on his neck. "What is it, boy? What do you hear?"

Thor took two steps toward the front door, completely on alert.

"Pass auf!" Xander said, a term she'd heard him use before. It meant heads-up. All of Xander's commands for Thor were in German, ensuring that a stranger couldn't confuse him with his own orders.

Thor quivered, sniffed the air and barked once. Something was wrong with the house.

Xander pulled Sam back, reached for the doorknob, turned it slowly. It was unlocked. They never left the door unlocked.

Xander's entire demeanor changed. He went operational in a second, so quickly Sam didn't even see him reach for the Glock 17 he had stashed in his ankle holster.

"Stay here," he whispered to her, then spoke to the dog. "Thor. *Voran! Such!*"

She knew the commands—take the lead, search.

He pushed open the front door. Thor burst inside. Xander followed with the gun leveled. They disappeared into the dark and Sam paused, but there was no way she was going to stand on the stoop alone. She stepped just inside the door, heard Thor going wild in the living room, barking his meanest, deepest warnings. A decidedly female shriek rang out.

Xander gave another command that Sam didn't hear, but the dog stopped barking immediately. At least he hadn't set Thor to attack.

Sam rushed into the living room to see a young woman cowering in the corner of the couch. Xander had turned on the small lamp on the secretary against the western wall and it cast a gentle glow over the girl's features. She was wearing a red T-shirt and cargo pants, and had both her hands up as if she'd been caught robbing a bank. Thor had her covered, Xander's gun was pointed at her chest and she was white as a sheet.

"Who the hell are you?" Sam said.

The girl turned a hopeful face in her direction. "Please, ma'am, don't let them hurt me. My name is Kaylie Rousch."

CHAPTER 38

HOW DO I EXPLAIN MYSELF TO THIS WOMAN? SHE IS SO MUCH MORE BEAUTIFUL in person than the photos I've seen. They didn't capture the light in her clear brown eyes, the color of the whiskey Doug would drink occasionally, if he was in a very good mood, or a very bad one. They didn't show the kindness of her face. Even furious with me, she seems gentle, breakable.

Her man isn't. He looks like he wants to tell the dog to rip out my throat, and if the dog disobeys he'll reach over and do it himself without a second thought. He looks dangerous. I don't like him. He is one of them, another Y chromosome, only able to hurt and break, yell and scream. His fists are like rocks, his eyes nearly black, full of rage. What is she doing with him? Doesn't she realize he is a monster?

The woman says, "Xander, put the gun away," and he listens. The dog is still unhappy with me, but after a guttural command, he backs away, too.

The man she called Xander says, "I'm going to search you. Stand up."

I can't let that happen.

I shrink into the corner of the sofa, and the words blurt out in a panic. "No. No way. You can't touch me. Please, ma'am, don't let him hurt me. Don't let him touch me." He takes a step closer and I swear my heart is going to burst from my chest. I can't help myself; a small moan comes from my mouth, from somewhere deep and primal.

I am amazed to see his face soften. He no longer looks like a devil beast, only a man. When he speaks to me this time his voice is gentle, cajoling, eminently reasonable, as if he's talking to a spooked horse.

"Listen to me. People thought you were dead for sixteen years, and your DNA was suddenly found at a murder scene. Several people related to this case are actually dead. And now you've broken into our house. With your permission, Dr. Owens would like to make sure you mean her no harm. Will that be okay?"

A woman's touch doesn't frighten me. Not anymore. I spread my hands wide so they can see I don't carry any weapons and nod.

"Yes. I can live with that. But I am not here to hurt you. Either of you. I need your protection."

At a nod from her man, Samantha crosses the room, asks me to stand. She runs her hands gently down my back to the small space where my too-small T-shirt is tucked into my cargo pants, then down my legs and across my torso. She stops there because it's clear I can't hide a weapon inside these too-tight clothes and she wishes to spare me the humiliation of touching the inside of my thighs.

Of course, that's where I have taped the knife. I honestly don't intend to use it on her. So long as she doesn't give me a reason to.

"She's clean," she says.

No, I'm not. I will never be clean again. But maybe, with her help, I can find a way to become whole.

When she's finished, I bow my head slightly and say thank-you. My voice sounds very small and childish. I haven't heard that tone from myself for a very long time. I thought I was a grown-up. I thought things were going to be okay.

And then Doug was dead and gone, and the cocoon of safety I'd wrapped myself in split wide apart and dumped me wriggling into the mud, caught between chrysalis and butterfly. The world we'd created over the years disappeared, and the gaping maw of reality rushed in, grabbed me by the throat and ripped my heart out.

I can't help myself. I start to cry. It begins gently, just a tear brimming in the corner of my eye, and the woman reaches over and touches me gently on the cheek, and the floodgates open. Before I can stop myself I am sobbing in her arms like a child.

She doesn't shy away, but wraps me in her love and drags me to a seated position on the sofa and holds me while I cry my heart out.

This is perfect. This is what I've always wanted. This simple contact, this loving embrace. I've never felt it before, not like this. It's almost as if an angel lit on this woman's shoulder and brought my real mother with her. I can feel her arms around me. She smells of vanilla and tea and the sweetness of roses, not the vapid emptiness of vodka and cigarettes and hate.

It makes me cry harder. It's not fair, damn it. What happened to me, what happened to Doug, what's going to happen now—none of it is fair.

But life's not fair. Life's a kick in the ass, and you're damn lucky if you make it to the bent and gray stage. There is evil in the world, evil that searches for the innocent to alter them. That is its only purpose, to convert good to evil. And it sends its minions to do its dirty work, and people like Curtis and Adrian heed the call willingly.

Why does it happen? Free will? An evil God overpowering a benevolent one? I don't know.

I don't know.

Samantha hands me a tissue and presses something soft into my hands. I wipe my eyes and look down to see an old stuffed lion, once the prize of my existence, my most favorite toy. My father gave it to me for my birthday the same year I disappeared. Before that I wouldn't go anywhere without it.

"Where did you find this?" I ask her.

"We just came from a visit with your parents. In case you'd gone to see them." Her face clouded. She must have met Maureen. "We found this in your old camp. Did you stay there last night?"

"Yes. But I didn't see Simba. I used to love this thing."

I don't know whether to laugh or cry. I'm reminded of who I was before, who I might have been. It's disconcerting. If I'm not careful, it's going to deviate me from my path.

I'd debated over breaking into my old house last night, but figured I was safer in the camp. I hadn't realized the police were this close on my trail.

I must be more careful.

CHAPTER 39

SAM HELD THE GIRL AND LET HER CRY HERSELF OUT. TO HIS CREDIT, XANDER SIMPLY shrugged and went into the kitchen to put on the kettle. He emerged five minutes later with a teapot, three thick mugs and a bottle of Bunnahabhain.

Kaylie's sobs were slowing into hiccups and breathy gasps. She loosened her hold and collapsed back into the sofa, exhausted.

Xander poured the girl a cup of tea, and held up the bottle of Scotch enticingly. She took a deep breath, wiped her nose with her fingers and nodded. He poured a healthy slug and handed her the mug, then repeated the process for Sam and himself. They all took a polite sip, then Sam cleared her throat. This girl was clearly tough, but also as fragile as a soap bubble. Sam was worried that if she said or did the wrong thing, the girl would simply up and disappear right in front of their eyes. She was careful to keep her voice gentle and soft.

"Kaylie, why did you break into my house?"

She didn't hesitate. "To be safe. I couldn't wait outside on the steps in case he came for me. He found me in the woods, but I managed to get away. I jumped off a cliff. He didn't see that coming."

Sam looked closer. The girl had a bruise across her jaw. She noticed Sam looking and her hands went to the spot, covering it in shame.

"He did that to you?"

She nodded.

"Who's *he?* The man who killed Doug Matcliff?"

"Yes. He is a bad man."

She sounded like a child when she said it, though it was as matter-of-fact as saying the sky was blue and the sun yellow.

"Who is he? Who killed Doug? Who's chasing you? And where have you been all these years? With Doug?" Sam stopped. "Sorry. Sorry. You tell us what you can, at your own pace. As you can see, we have a lot of unanswered questions."

"So you promise I won't get into trouble if I tell you the truth?"

"Not with us. No."

Her face clouded. "I haven't done anything wrong."

"Until you tell us what happened, sweetie, we don't know what to do to help you. Who is the bad man?"

"He is the angel of death." Her eyes grew far away, revisiting a remembered loss, and Sam exchanged a look with Xander, who sighed quietly and took a deep sip of his tea. They were in for a long night.

"The angel of death. Does he have a name?" Sam asked.

Kaylie shuddered. "Adrian. He is her Sacrificiant. He is the one who kidnapped me. And did awful, unspeakable things to me. All because she told him to. But I think he liked it."

"Okay. Good. His name is Adrian. And *she* would be?"

Kaylie took a deep breath and seemed to snap back into reality. Her eyes focused on Sam. She took a gulp of tea.

"I'm sorry," Kaylie said. "I forget that other people might

not know about Eden. Let me explain it as best I can. *She* is Curtis Lott, the Mother of Eden. Eden is a group of people who live an exalted life, close to the land, even closer to God, by simply being in Curtis's presence. Curtis is God's representative on earth. She was chosen from immaculate conception, as all the leaders of Eden are. They spring from their mother's wombs with the knowledge of the universe, and it's their divine duty to share this with the people who can hear the truth.

"Curtis is the fifth Mother of Eden on this earth. There have been many others in many worlds. Their sign, the triskele—you did the autopsy on Doug, I saw you turn him and see the tattoo—is the sacred mark, one given by the grace of God, and all the members of Eden have one. It's a great honor. For each bit of the tattoo, a member of Eden gives their blood to be mixed into the ink and shares a truth they have learned while their section is being done. So you're both marked and enlightened, and it means everyone is one with the other. There is no self-actualization once you've been marked. You are the collective conscience, and you think, do, say, wear and act the way Curtis decrees, because this is what God wants for you. It is a very painful but fulfilling experience, or so I've been told. For me, it was just painful."

"May we see it? Your tattoo?"

Her face grew tight. Then she shrugged, turned and lifted her shirt. Her back was covered in intricate marks. Just like Doug Matcliff's.

Seeing the tattoo in real life, on a living body, knowing about the blood in the ink—Sam was both fascinated and horrified. The triskele seemed to be alive, moving and flowing with Kaylie's every move. It rippled as her muscles contracted under her fair skin. Sam resisted an urge to touch it, to feel it coiling under her fingers like a snake.

"They did all this in a single night?"

Kaylie pulled her shirt down. "Yes. It is their way. There is a second ceremony, and a final piece of the mark put into place, when you *become.* I am missing the centerpiece because Doug got me out before I was made an official sacrosanct. Those are the women of Eden. Women are sacred, and Curtis's purpose on this earth is to see them glorified. But few are worthy of this honor. That's why there were never more than fifteen sacrosancts at a time."

Xander was taking notes so Sam could continue coaxing the story from their surprise guest.

"And Adrian was one of the marked?"

"He was hers. Every leader of Eden has a fiery sword, a man who does their bidding, who fathers the pods, who metes out punishment and rewards. He is to be feared and respected and treated as a god second only to Curtis. She is his only master, but he is our Great Father."

"Pods? Do you mean children?"

Kaylie looked puzzled for a moment. "Yes."

"Oh. Okay. So Adrian is the father of them all?"

"Yes, that's it exactly. He is the Father, and Curtis is the Mother. All things have their opposite—the sun and the moon, the sky and the earth, fire and water, wind and soil. The Father and the Mother are the lifeblood of Eden. Adrian would do anything for Curtis." She shuddered again. "Anything."

"Were there other men in Eden besides Adrian?"

"Yes, but they had no liberties. Adrian was the one who came to the women. The men—there were four or five when I was there—are solely laborers, guards. Despite God's great gift to the women, the divine ability to procreate, there were still a few things the men could be used for. It was a farm, and there are aspects to it that needed brute strength instead of delicacy. Plus, when the women were full of God's gift, they couldn't work in the fields, so the men took care of that, too."

"Where did Doug fit in to all of this?"

She smiled. "Adrian brought him to the fold. He was good

and kind and not like the others. He was special to Curtis, because he knew things from the outside no one had ever heard of. He knew his way around the weapons they had, too."

Xander stopped writing. "What weapons?"

"Guns. Lots of them."

"Handguns, rifles, shotguns?"

"M-4s, AR-15s mostly, though I haven't been there in many years, so they may be using something different now. Curtis couldn't take the chance of something bad happening to Eden. They are a peaceful group in her mind, but there is always room for misinterpretation. After Doug came, the men were also used for the patrols. Real security. Doug taught them the proper way to use the guns, how to load them and care for them, to take them apart and put them together with their eyes closed. He was very valuable to the group. Very valuable. So much so Curtis sometimes talked to him alone. It made Adrian very mad. He was very possessive of Curtis."

"Why did you leave? Why did Doug take you, I should say?"

"Oh." She blushed, a ripe red starting on her throat and rapidly moving upward. "Can he leave?"

Sam motioned with her head to Xander, who said, "It's time to walk Thor, anyway. I'll be back."

When the door closed behind him, Kaylie visibly relaxed. "I had been injured, very badly. I was very small for my age, and the pod tore me apart. I thought they were done with me, and he must have, as well, because he came to the dark place I was left in and took me away. I don't remember much. I was in a great deal of pain. I remember the pod coming, though. You're a mother. You know how much that hurts, that huge thing forcing its way out from between your legs. You were a grown woman when it happened to you. I was still very small."

These words were stated matter-of-factly, no hint of embarrassment. Sam swallowed and said, "I've heard. I've never experienced it, birth, that is. I had a cesarean. Twins. They were early, and the doctors wanted to be sure they would be okay, so they did the operation instead of letting me go into labor."

"Twins! You are doubly blessed."

She bowed her head, and Sam swallowed. "Yes, I was. Very blessed."

"I wonder if I'd had twins if Curtis would have been happier with me. She seemed very disgusted that night. I never understood why."

"How old were you when you had the baby?"

"Pod," she said automatically. "Twelve, thirteen, I think. I'd been there for several years. It took twelve Reasonings to make a pod stay in me."

"Reasonings?"

"The quarterly coupling. It was how the pods were made. The sacrosancts were much better at it than I was. They even claimed to enjoy it. I didn't. At all. It was awful. Adrian was so huge, he's a giant, and his… It was so big. I was never open enough for him. He didn't care, just spread my legs and ripped me right apart. I was so glad it only happened four times a year. It took many weeks to heal."

Sam wanted to kill this Adrian man who raped a young girl so many times she could discuss the awful reality of it almost nonchalantly. "And you and Doug?"

Kaylie jumped back on the couch. "Never! He wouldn't ever do something like that to me. Force me. He was like a father to me, a real one, not a false God like Adrian or a weakling like the man who made me with my mother. She died when I was born, so there was something wrong with her, too. He couldn't make anything with my stepmother, of course. She was so awful and mean I doubt he'd ever want to."

"Were there other girls like you, Kaylie?" Sam asked, carefully.

"Like me? Not that I know of. But I was kept underground most of the time, in the dark, and only summoned for the Reasonings when it was the right time. I didn't get to be with the other people of Eden except for on the special days. I was their special secret. Curtis educated me herself, in private."

"So you don't know if there were other girls that they kidnapped?"

Her eyes grew big and round. "Are there others? Others like me? I thought I heard something once, before I left. They were talking about Elsa, who was one of the older sacrosancts. She hadn't given a pod in quite a while, and so they were going to bring someone new to the sacrosancts."

You lose one, you replace one.

"May I ask, what happened to your...pod?"

Kaylie's eyes grew distant again, her voice desolate. "She went away. Curtis told me she was taken for reincarnation right away because she was so perfect, and they buried the shell in the cornfield. I was too sick to find her then."

Xander came back in the door, Thor moving quietly by his master's side. He raised an eyebrow at Sam, and tapped his wrist. She took the hint.

"Kaylie, I know there is so much more to your story you need to share with me, but I think it's time we call my friends at the FBI. They're going to be very happy to hear you're okay."

"I can't stay here?"

"No, honey, you can't. There are too many people who need to talk to you. I have a very good friend who has been a part of your case since the beginning, and he's going to be overjoyed to talk to you. So let's give him a call, and they'll get you hooked right up."

She nodded, shrinking back into a ball in the corner of the sofa. "If you say it's best, then okay. But I don't want to see my parents. They can't know I'm alive. It's better that way."

Sam wasn't about to let that nasty old hag anywhere near Kaylie. She debated for a moment telling Kaylie about her father's death, then decided to leave it alone. There was enough going on in the poor girl's head without any additional horrors.

"Just my friend at the FBI," Sam said. "We can deal with all that later. Drink your tea, I'll be right back."

"Doug was right about you."

That stopped her. "What?"

"Doug said I could trust you to do the right thing. That you wouldn't let me be victimized. You would know the people who could keep me safe."

"I appreciate that he trusted me with you. Kaylie, did Doug ever say how he knew me? Why he would come to me to investigate his murder?"

"You're a very wise woman. The papers said so. Doug knew you were trustworthy. He knew you lost your pods, that you'd understand why it was so important to help us."

A chill went down Sam's spine. The idea that someone had been watching her from afar, paying attention to her private life, upset her. And that Doug Matcliff had chosen her by reputation alone was even worse. She didn't want to be known. She wanted to work behind the scenes.

She changed the subject.

"Kaylie, do you know Henry Matcliff?"

She smiled, a sweet, gentle look, completely at odds with the situation. "Of course. That's me."

"Excuse me?"

"It was the only way to keep me safe. Doug raised me as a boy. We knew they'd be looking for a man and a girl, a daughter. Me being a son made more sense. I didn't start growing my hair until last year, when I left."

"Left? To go where?"

She just shook her head, eyes downcast. Her lips tightened into a thin line. Sam got the sense she'd said more than she wanted.

Kaylie had shared all she was willing to. For now.

CHAPTER 40

SAM WENT INTO THE KITCHEN WITH HER CELL PHONE AND CALLED BALDWIN. HE answered on the first ring.

"Kaylie Rousch is here in my house."

"I know. Xander called me. I'm already here, waiting outside. Think she's up for company? Xander said she's a little leery of men."

"Yes, but you're going to have to be careful, she's very reticent. In my professional opinion, the girl's suffering from severe PTSD, and God knows what else. She was repeatedly raped, forced into all sorts of things at a very young age. She assured me there was nothing physical between her and Doug Matcliff, but I'm not sure I believe her. And she's mentioned a man named Adrian who seems to be the sledgehammer, for lack of a better term, and this Curtis woman, the cult leader, was—is—clearly mad. Kaylie suggested Adrian is responsible for the current spate of attacks, so there's a partial name ID for you."

"Got it. Did you get anything that might give a clue where Eden is now?"

"Not yet. I didn't want to push her too hard until you were here to guide things."

"Okay. I'm coming to the door now."

"Before you come in, just a heads-up. She's a bizarre mix of child and adult, sane and insane. Her language vacillates between complete frankness and paranoid obfuscation, and she's not all there, if you catch my drift. She's very, very intelligent, though. But the things she's telling me—Baldwin, we have to find this cult and stop them. Now. If they have Rachel Stevens, if they're the ones who have been kidnapping these girls all these years, the poor things are undergoing some horrible treatment. I can't even imagine how Kaylie stayed even partially together. Doug Matcliff must have really helped her."

"I hear you. Ring-a-ding," he said, and her doorbell rang.

She heard Kaylie's high-pitched voice react from the living room, then Xander's deeper voice telling her this was their FBI friend and not to worry.

Sam hoped they were telling Kaylie the truth. There was more going on here, currents running through the house that unsettled her.

She opened the door and Baldwin came in. He'd changed into jeans and a white button-down—the tie gone, the collar open, the sleeves rolled up. He looked casual and friendly, not at all like a cop, and she nodded her approval. Their best approach with Kaylie was going to be the relaxed one. Letting her set the tone, the pace and the rules.

With any luck, after an hour with Baldwin, they'd have every detail they'd need to find Rachel Stevens, and then lock up these horrible people for good.

Sam bolted the front door, then went to the back to double-check it was also secure. Thor was curled up on his plush dog bed, watching her actions with curiosity. Even with her precautions, she wanted him keeping an eye out, so she knelt by him, scratched his ears and said softly, "Thor, *achtung*." Pay attention.

She could have sworn he nodded. She dropped a quick kiss on his snout and went to the living room, satisfied they were covered for the time being.

Baldwin was waiting for her in the hallway. She smiled and gestured for him to let her go first.

Kaylie was staring into the fireplace with a distant look on her face when Sam returned. But she focused and brightened immediately. A friendly face was welcome, clearly.

"Kaylie, this is my friend John Baldwin. I promise you can trust him. He and my very best friend in the world are going to be married. I wouldn't let her near him if I didn't think he was awesome. All right?"

Kaylie looked at Baldwin with open curiosity. Sam wondered what she was thinking. Baldwin was very handsome, which opened many doors, and closed a few, as well. But he radiated intelligence and compassion, and Kaylie visibly relaxed.

"Hello, sir."

"Hello, Kaylie. I have to say, it is wonderful to meet you after all these years. I'm sorry we didn't know you had survived your kidnapping."

"Do you have a gun?" Her eyes were wide, guileless. A child's question.

That startled a little laugh out of him. "I do, but I don't have it on me."

"Good. I don't like guns. I suppose you want to know what happened."

"Why don't we get to know each other a little first? How old are you?"

"Twenty-two."

"Where were you born?"

"Bethesda, Maryland."

"Who are your parents?"

"Clive and Maureen Rousch. Dr. Owens acted strangely about them before. Is my father still alive?"

"Your father, unfortunately, has passed away. But your mother will be happy to know you're okay."

She had that distant look again. "I thought so. He didn't look well when I looked in the window. And Maureen will not be happy when she finds out. Please don't tell her."

"Why not?"

"They both hated me. It was easier for them when I was gone. They didn't have to deal with my constant crying and attention-seeking. I was a bad child, and it was better for them without me."

Baldwin's brow furrowed for a moment. These were words Kaylie had been fed, probably by Curtis Lott, but he kept on. "I have to ask, Kaylie. Can you show me your birthmark?"

"No! That's nasty. You're a nasty, nasty man."

The walls went right back up. She pulled her legs up onto the sofa and curled into a little ball and started to rock, crooning to herself.

Baldwin nodded. "Okay, Kaylie, fair enough. Would you be willing to show Sam?"

"No, no, no, no."

"All right, that's fine. We can come back to that. Stay with me, honey. Do you remember what happened the day you were taken?"

She stopped rocking. "Yes."

He waited for her to continue, then nodded and sat back in his chair, relaxing his arm over the back. Open. Unguarded. Exactly her physical opposite. "Okay, Kaylie. Tell me this. Do you know where you were kept? Before Doug saved you?"

"We were on a farm out in the country. I woke up there and never left until the day Doug took me out, and I was very sick, so I couldn't tell you exactly where we were. Doug said it was northern Virginia."

"Did you move around at all? Did the group move from place to place? Or did they stay in one spot?"

"One spot."

"Did they ever talk about moving to other places?"

"Not to me. But Doug said that they were careful to stay one step ahead of the law. Like we were doing, staying one step ahead of Adrian and Curtis."

"Tell me about them."

"How do you describe the moon and the stars?" She shook her head hard and tapped her palm to the side of her head, almost as if she were trying to dislodge water from her ear after swimming. Her voice was suddenly adult again, lucid, a bit abashed. "I'm sorry. That's something *she* would say. Adrian is very big, very tall and muscular and mean. He had something wrong with him, and Curtis used it against him. She exploits weakness. It's her best tool. 'Learn what the weak points are, my girl, and then you'll always be able to make them do your bidding.' She liked to teach me things about people."

"What was wrong with Adrian?"

"Doug told me his mother dropped him on his head when he was a baby, and she felt so guilty about it she committed suicide. He was left alone a lot. His values became warped. Curtis liked that. She liked giving him presents."

"Presents?"

"People to kill. He liked it. A lot. He told me once, when we were…when he was touching me. He told me how he liked to squeeze the life out of people. He said Curtis had shown him a past life during a ceremony, when he ate the wafer of life with her, and he was descended from a great anaconda snake. He lived in the water and ate things much bigger than he was. He enjoyed it so much. He wanted to squeeze the life out of me, but Curtis said no."

"Did he do everything Curtis asked?"

"Yes."

"Did he ever act on his impulses outside her view?"

She scratched her nose. "Do you mean did he use me outside of the Reasonings? No. He was much too dedicated to her to disobey. But when he did come, he didn't hold back."

"Did anyone else? Use you, I mean."

She shook her head quickly. Too quickly.

Baldwin stepped carefully now. "Is Adrian a threat to us?"

"Yes. He's a threat to everyone he comes in contact with. Whether he plans to kill you, I don't know. He only kills who Curtis tells him to. I am definitely a target." She hesitated a moment. "You are a grave threat to the life they lead. I would not be surprised if you are all targets. Elimination is one of Adrian's favorite pastimes."

Baldwin glanced at Sam, nodded at Xander, who went off to check the doors and weapons for what seemed to be the hundredth time. They'd already done everything they could to make the house secure, but hearing Kaylie's words sent another shiver through Sam. Of course this freak of nature would be after them. They were severely screwing with his world.

Baldwin continued. "All right. You mentioned the wafer of life. What was that?"

Kaylie settled on the couch, more comfortable with this line of questioning. "It's the great truth. It was gifted to Curtis and she was the only one who was allowed to bestow the gift on the people of Eden. Sometimes everyone took a wafer, and they danced all night naked under the stars. Sometimes it was just one person, and he or she would disappear into Curtis's chambers for a week and a day, for a Seasoning. Only the very special were chosen for the Seasonings. Doug did it once. He said he thought she gave him some sort of LSD. It took hours and hours to wear off and he saw all sorts of weird things."

"And did you ever see strangers? Did anyone from the outside ever come to Eden?"

"Not that I saw, though when there were pods, there was a lot of excitement, and then Adrian would go away for a few days."

"Pods?"

"The children born to the women of Eden," Sam said quietly.

Baldwin took a deep breath. "Kaylie, did you ever see any large quantities of drugs moved around the farm?"

"I don't know."

"The reason Doug went to Eden in the first place was that we had charged Curtis with drug possession and distribution. There was a marijuana farm next to the land Eden owned. He went to find out if Curtis was selling drugs. Did you ever hear about this?"

"Drugs? No." Kaylie looked absolutely shocked. She dropped her legs to the floor and sat forward, all shyness forgotten. "I thought you knew. Eden wasn't selling drugs. They were selling pods."

CHAPTER 41

Near Lynchburg, Virginia

ADRIAN DIDN'T WANT TO BE HERE. HE WANTED TO BE IN D.C., AT THE HOUSE OF the doctor, planning how he was going to wrap the wire around her long, delicate stalk of a neck and rip it tight. Feel her kicking, spasmodic and faint, then drop her body on the ground and walk away. He might even get a chance at her man. His size, his strength—yes, he would be a challenge, but Adrian would best him.

And then he'd be left face-to-face with Kaylie, the one who was prophesized to ruin them all.

He could stop it. Stop their ruin, their demise. If Curtis would let him.

But Curtis had other plans. Curtis had been blessed with a great vision. Her fiery sword was sent to eliminate the last connection between them and the girl. Then, and only then, would he be allowed to follow his own rules. Make his own choices. Slip the thin wire around the doctor's neck and make her see God.

He found himself becoming aroused, and forced the thoughts of her away.

He liked the night sounds. The chirp of the crickets and the high-pitched screech of the bats and the slither of the snakes through the soft leaves. He sat cross-legged in the woods and watched the house go to sleep. At 10:00 p.m., the target had turned off the lights downstairs, but it was past midnight now and there was still a lamp burning in the master bedroom.

He was tempted to go ahead, but with everything that was happening, the target could be prepared, waiting for him, and the last thing he needed was a gut full of shotgun pellets before he finished his job.

McDonald wasn't going to be as easy as the others. Adrian wouldn't be surprised if he'd been warned by now, to watch his back, shut things down. Get out of town—he certainly hadn't listened to that warning. Not that Adrian was shocked by this. Fred McDonald wasn't a very smart man. Cunning, yes, but he had always overestimated his own intelligence. And underestimated Adrian's control.

He thought back to the previous day with bitterness. He'd listened to the raging wash of the waterfall and known the girl was gone. Stupid, stupid, stupid, letting her get away from him. Surely she was dead—the cliff was at least one hundred feet high, the water spilling over the edge into what looked like an eddy pool. He'd fought his way down and searched for hours, but the water had washed her away. Washed her clean.

Your sins are gone now, Kaylie. But they are not forgotten. Never forgotten.

It was his fault, and his alone. He'd taken one look at her and just like the first time he'd laid eyes on her, her glowing hair so like that of the woman he loved, he wanted to play, to pull the wings off the proverbial fly. A huge mistake, not his first with the girl. He should have knocked her on the head, gathered her up and carried her back to Eden. Where she belonged.

Where she'd still be if she hadn't escaped with Doug.

Just thinking of him made Adrian's stomach knot. *Traitor.* Stealing their finest for himself. How he'd managed it was beyond Adrian, but he had, snuck her off into the night without a backward glance, not to be heard from again until a month ago, when Adrian saw him driving down the road. What were the odds? Really? He'd followed him to the cabin. He knew where he was, and reported back to Curtis. But not before leaving his old friend a note, hammered into the wood of his bedroom door.

I'm coming for you. Don't make me kill you. Do the right thing.

His first act of betrayal in twenty-five long years.

Curtis had been furious with him when he shared the news. Doug was dead. Kaylie, well, he didn't know. Alive, or dead, he was without her.

Curtis knew there was one way to draw her out. Adrian had completed the task, then headed south again, to finish what he started. Even though he disagreed with Curtis's plan.

He felt that if Kaylie was still alive, she would have gone to the doctor. He'd found the evidence in Doug's cabin. They'd picked this woman, this stranger, to see them to the end.

But Curtis wanted all ties to Eden eliminated instead.

He knew in his core this was a grave mistake, and told her. She threatened him with eternal damnation, and instructed him to do her bidding, then return to Eden.

And in all things, the Great Mother was to be obeyed. So he marched forward, with doubt in his heart.

Adrian wasn't a starry-eyed seventeen-year-old anymore, seduced by the power of physical love and the honeyed words of an insane succubus. He knew exactly what Eden was, exactly who Curtis was and how the group funded itself. He'd helped with the management of those funds after Curtis realized he had a facility for numbers, and he'd grown their meager savings into a little more than ten million dollars over the years.

There was no redemption for Adrian, nor did he particularly want it. He'd done awful things on his own, and worse under Curtis's instruction. Alone, he'd been a monster. Together, the two of them became horror incarnate, creatures more evil, more depraved, than anything he would have become on his own.

And he had reveled in their glory.

Curtis had been searching for Doug and Kaylie for years—violently upset at their betrayal, wanting retribution, but continuing laser-focused on maintaining the health and harmony of the remainder of her flock. Now there would be no rest until she was back in the arms of her great Mother. This time, Curtis must be the one to steal the blood from her veins, to take the strength of the girl into her own body.

So it was written, and so it must be done.

There was one problem. And this was Adrian's fault, his folly, his responsibility. Before Doug died, he had exposed them, which threatened the thing most sacred to Curtis.

Lauren.

Just the thought of her made him smile.

Lauren was Curtis's daughter, and the rightful heir to Eden. Just as Curtis had taken over from Susan, her mother, when she was no longer capable of bearing children, Lauren would inherit the flock from Curtis. Lauren was the only child who was allowed to stay in Eden. She came from Curtis's womb, which had before then been untouched by the joy of an embryo.

Lauren was perfect in all respects, a honey-haired beauty with light, cornflower-blue eyes. The only pod that really mattered.

Lauren was meant to be a mystery to them all. Curtis had managed to become pregnant without lying with Adrian, or any other of the men.

Lauren was the Immaculate. Pure, unsullied. The chosen one. It only happened once in a generation, when the great leader fell pregnant without the sperm of a mate. They were always girl children, and they were always destined to be the heir. It had been happening this way from the beginning.

Despite his deep belief in the covenants of his religion, Adrian, well schooled in biology, knew it was impossible for a female human to become pregnant without sperm.

Though it was great sacrilege, Adrian believed Lauren was not immaculate. As the great father to many of Eden's children, he was aware of his powers of procreation, knew how many bellies he'd caused to swell.

He knew she was his child.

He wasn't allowed to have these thoughts, and was very careful never to give them a voice. But as Lauren grew tall and her hair became the color of wheat and her eyes took on a slightly almond shape, Adrian saw his mother in her face.

And he felt pride, for while the rest of Eden believed Curtis, believed in Lauren's immaculate conception, he knew the truth. And with all that he was, he loved her.

Thinking of Lauren had him off track, as usual. He knew he'd fathered many, many children over the years, but he'd never seen any of them grow past the first few days of infancy.

He shook off the memories, the maudlin excuses. He had screwed up, royally, and he had to find a way to make things right. Over twenty-five years of service, with everything happening the way it was dictated by the stars and the moon and Curtis, had made him complacent, and sloppy. Doug would be his undoing.

His reverie was interrupted. The light in the bedroom went out, drawing his attention back to the house.

His pulse picked up. Two in the morning now, and the night had gone silent with its sleeping. He walked with a hunter's stealth into the backyard, climbed over the fence. McDonald didn't have dogs, the idiot. Dogs were the best deterrent, though Adrian knew many ways to circumvent them. A juicy steak laden with ketamine was his favorite method. He recognized the irony—humans were fair game, but he would do most anything to avoid killing an animal.

But there were no dogs here, no electronic monitoring or well-armed security system, just the peaceful certainty of a man who slept with a Remington shotgun within easy reach that he could handle any and all situations that might arise in the night.

He'd never experienced a nightmare like Adrian, though.

He was across the lawn in five short seconds, walked directly to the back door, used a simple set of lock picks to open it.

He stepped inside, testing the air, smelling, feeling, seeing, tasting, using every one of his predator's senses to ascertain the situation.

He was in the basement. His eyes adjusted to the murky interior, and he started across the room toward the stairs. The house had three floors, and a wide, curving staircase wound to the upper floors.

He'd just put his foot on the first riser when he heard the deep, unearthly metallic clang of a shotgun jacking a shell. His body coiled and his heart nearly stopped.

"I've been waiting for you, you big-assed son of a bitch."

And the man pulled the trigger.

As he fell, Adrian thought of the light that was his great Mother, and the strawberry blonde girl who had set him on the path of the damned.

CHAPTER 42

Washington, D.C.

THEY WERE GOING IN CIRCLES, AND FLETCHER WAS GETTING FRUSTRATED.

Rachel Stevens had been missing for over twenty-four hours and the window to find her safe and unhurt was rapidly closing. The media firestorm was at a fever pitch. Every news station, local and national, had trucks parked across D.C.—at the snatch site, at FBI Headquarters, in the Stevenses' neighborhood—their satellite dishes pushing constant updates into the D.C. night. Blame would be next, aspersions toward law enforcement, most of whom hadn't slept and had barely eaten for the past day as they searched for the child.

At least they hadn't made the connection between Kaylie Rousch and Rachel Stevens yet. That would drive them into a tsunami.

Fletcher was on his way to Bethesda again to talk with Rachel Stevens's parents—the mother was back from her overseas assignment and Fletcher wanted a chance to go at her face-to-face—when he got the call. They had a break in the case, and he needed to get his butt back to the Hoover Building.

Fletcher dodged through the suburbs into the Washington streets, the ever-familiar white marble and snapping American flags, worrying about Sam and the Matcliff case, and about young Rachel Stevens. Worried about the case that wasn't his, the clouded eyes of a young man, staked to a dock to drown. Worried himself right into an upset stomach, stopped and fanned the flames with a Super Big Gulp of Diet Coke. He finally had to dig some antacid tablets out of the glove box to calm things down.

He blamed it on getting older, this worrying, not being able to turn off his emotions as well as he used to. When he was on patrol, and even in the early days in homicide, he was the iceman, able to stomach the most obscene crime scenes imaginable—and in D.C., there were plenty—without a qualm.

But five or so years ago, he'd felt a change. Cases began coming home with him at night, seeping into his dreams, following him on his runs. He'd done the rational thing—too much drinking, too many affairs, a toot here or there, until his wife got fed up and left him, taking his only child with her. His ex was remarried now, and had just had twins with her new husband.

They'd patched things up recently, and that made him happy. He'd gotten himself straight, done his job with his son, refocused his attention on his career. He'd been a man about it all. But the darkness was always with him now, the edge. It wouldn't let him forget how close he'd come to throwing it all away.

Sam Owens was the biggest reminder of them all. She got to him, the way she handled herself, her grace in the face of the abyss. She hadn't let herself be sucked in, and damn it all, he wouldn't, either.

God, what was he going to do when he was homicide lieutenant? He was turning into a full-blown mother hen. Maybe that's why Armstrong had tapped him. He knew things had changed and Fletcher was going to be a little more attentive to those around him.

Traffic was terrible—the Redskins had a preseason game—but he barreled through, his spinning light and wailing siren forcing cars to the side of the street. He finally made it up Pennsylvania Avenue, parked and rushed into the Hoover Building just in time for his second briefing of the day on the missing girl.

Agent Blake met him in the lobby, clearly excited. She hurried him through the check-in process but wouldn't tell him what was going on, just said there was a *development*.

The word hung heavy in the air. He knew the tiniest bit of intelligence could alter the direction of an investigation, and hoped this was good news.

The conference room she took him to this time was on another floor, and it wasn't quiet and calm, but frenetic. There were several screens on the walls—aerial topographic maps, what he thought must be video camera footage from the snatch site. A close-up shot of a footprint in cement and a cigarette butt. A large photograph of Rachel Stevens on her last birthday, the most recent full-frontal shot her parents had. Agents and techs flowed in and out of the room. They were in constant contact with Thurber, who, despite John Baldwin's dictate, was back on the case and parked at the Stevens house.

They sat Fletcher at the table and shoved a stack of photographs in front of him. Blake crossed her arms and said, "Detective Fletcher, do you recognize this man?"

He flipped through them. The photos weren't the highest quality, and he had to squint to make out the man who was circled in red. He was a male Caucasian with a broad face, buzz-cut blond hair and light eyes. He wasn't fully facing the camera, but Fletcher didn't recognize him, said so. Blake plopped another photo down.

"You sure?"

This one was clearer, face-front. It was black-and-white, clearly taken many years earlier. The picture gave a sense of the man's stature—he was big. Really big.

Something tickled the back of Fletcher's brain. "Wait a minute. He does look familiar. I think I questioned this guy years ago. He was loitering around the homeless down by Whitehurst. There'd been some disappearances, and we were watching the area closely. He seemed to be around a lot. Homeless said he was a high school kid who brought them food and blankets, but I thought he was shifty. Is this our suspect? Who is he?"

"Your file says his name is Adrian Zamyatin."

"Another one of the names in Matcliff's will."

"Right you are. He also seems to be a rather prolific serial killer who's managed to stay under the radar for a very, very long time. Detective Davidson sent this—" She set a picture from a home security camera in front of him, time-stamped the previous afternoon. "It's from Ellie Scarron's house. They believe he was her attacker. We ran it through the NGI facial recognition system, and it spit out a match. When we entered his name into our national crimes database, we found your old case file."

"Lucky I took good notes back then."

"No kidding." Jordan swooped her hair back from her face into a ponytail. The formal attitude relaxed. "So we've put everything into ViCAP, right? Nothing pops. Then we started adding in the other geographical areas where the Eden NRM settled over the years. Bam. The computer pegged a very troubling scenario that matches our earlier assumptions. Not only is there a girl missing from each of these towns, but there's a series of unsolved murders in each, as well."

"Nice job. How many are we talking?"

"We've managed to tie twenty together so far, and those are just the cities who've entered their case data into ViCAP. There could be more."

Fletcher let that sink in, whistled softly. "Seems our Adrian Zamyatin gets around. Have you told Dr. Baldwin about this?"

"Oh, yes. He called a bit ago. We've confirmed this man was a part of Eden. An integral part."

"How did you confirm this?"

"Your friend Sam's been entertaining Kaylie Rousch for the past hour."

Fletcher sat back in his chair. "Man, I miss all the fun. When'd she show up?"

And why hadn't Sam called him? Why had she gone straight to John Baldwin, profiler extraordinaire?

Oh, shut up, Fletch. You're being a jealous old hag. There's plenty of room on this case for everyone.

"Apparently she broke into Dr. Owens's house. Mr. Whitfield called Dr. Baldwin. They felt the girl needed a psychological exam as much as questioning."

Figures. He felt his blood pressure rise despite his mental chiding. *Damn it.* That woman was going to get herself killed one of these days, thinking she could handle everything. "She should have called the police."

"The girl's talking, so we're taking advantage of it. Are you ready for this?"

"Nothing you say at this point will surprise me. Lay it on me, sister."

"Wanna bet?"

"A beer."

"You're on. Eden wasn't selling drugs. They're in the baby-making business."

"What?"

Jordan gave him a strained grin. "You should see the look on your face. You owe me a beer. From the briefing Baldwin just gave us, which was only a few minutes long, Adrian Zamyatin was used as a stud, for lack of a better term, getting the women of Eden pregnant, and then they'd sell the children. Called them pods, if you can believe it." Her nose wrinkled, and he couldn't help noticing it made her even cuter, but she clearly found all this disgusting. "There could have been hundreds over the years."

"Who'd they sell them to?"

"We're still working on that."

"This is good news for Rachel Stevens, though, isn't it? She's only ten years old. It's not like she can have a kid."

Blake flushed. "Don't be obtuse, Detective. Just because she can't fulfill whatever bizarre quota system they have doesn't mean they can't start trying."

"Of course. Sorry. Stupid of me."

She yanked her ponytail holder out of her hair, which spilled loose around her neck. She rubbed her forehead. "No, my apologies, Detective. Can I call you Fletcher?"

"Fletch is fine."

"Fletch, then. I'm a bit on edge. As it turns out, you may be right. The Rousch girl described her early days in Eden, and while it wasn't pleasant, the sexual abuse didn't begin right away. She's helping Baldwin with some geographical profiling right now. He's walking her through every detail about where they were so he can see if there's a pattern to their movements over the years, so we can extrapolate where they are now. We're also looking at every recent land purchase in Maryland and Virginia to see if anything with their corporate profile comes up."

"What do you need me to do?"

"Find this man for me." She tapped the picture of Adrian Zamyatin. "He's the key. There used to be a pattern to his kills, four people garroted, then a girl goes missing. It seems all jumbled together now—there were two garrotings and a strangulation, then Rachel went missing. We can't find anything else that fits the pattern. Something's different this time."

"Has anyone looked at his connection to Matcliff? Outside of the cult, I mean?"

She blew out a huge breath, as if deciding how much to say. "We've run into some issues. Too many threads to pull, too little time. We have to focus on finding Rachel before it's too late. Kaylie Rousch is telling stories that would make your hair curl. Five other little girls most likely went through the same thing. I want to be sure nothing happens to this one."

"I get it. But here's my armchair profile, for what it's worth. Matcliff was strangled, not garroted. That screams *personal* to me."

Jordan Blake had nice eyes. They were brown, not too dark, with flecks of green and blue in them when you saw her up close. She was close right now, staring at him while her brain processed what he'd said. "You think this Adrian knew him somehow? Outside of the time they spent in the cult?"

He nodded. "Either that or the Rousch girl isn't telling us the whole truth. Has she been vetted at all? Positively ID'd? Anything she said verified?"

"We're working on it. We'll need DNA to confirm for sure. And hundreds of babies sold is both vague and a lot to track down."

"Have you ever worked a slavery case before?"

"No, I haven't. Have you?" She sat down in the chair next to him, still making that intense eye contact.

"No, but 'selling' equals a commodity. And it's not like this is a common commodity. There's a black market for organs. Why not babies?"

She leaned back in the chair. "Jesus."

"Yeah. My thought exactly. You track who might be buying and selling kids, and we might get a little closer to the truth."

She stared at him for a minute, chewing on her lip. "Where do you suggest we start?"

"Easy. The will. We've figured who several of the beneficiaries are. Anne Carter was Doug's FBI boss. Thurber is his old partner. Curtis Lott—the leader of Eden. Zamyatin—our killer. Arthur Scarron was a beneficiary, but he was already dead, and his wife was nearly killed in his stead, so she must have known something, whether she realizes it or not. Frederick McDonald is the only one left, and we don't know what his connection is yet. Why don't we get someone to ask Miss Rousch who the hell he is? And see if she can't tell us about this Lauren chick while she's at it."

Blake stood up, whipped her hair back into its no-nonsense ponytail. "Do it. Go talk to the girl. You're onto something here, I can feel it. We'll handle Rachel—now that we have a suspect, and a photograph for the media, this is going to move quickly. You go work this angle."

"All right." He stood up, stretched his shoulders to release some of the tension. Blake started walking away, then turned and gave him a blinding grin he felt right to his core.

He responded with a smile of his own. "Hey, Special Agent? Damn fine work."

CHAPTER 43

Georgetown

SAM WATCHED KAYLIE WORKING THE MAP WITH BALDWIN, GIVING HIM AS MUCH information to go on as she could. Doug had been careful over the years to keep an eye on the whereabouts of the cult through the other missing girls, but he hadn't been very forthcoming with Kaylie about anything, thinking the less she knew, the better.

They finally decided to take a break. Baldwin went to call in, and Sam brought Kaylie a warm slice of lemon cake and a cup of tea. Her face lit up at the cake, a child's response to sweets, and she closed her eyes in bliss while she ate it.

Sam waited for the girl to get to the end of her treat. When she'd licked the last of the icing from her fingers, Sam approached her gently. "I have a question about Doug. Several, in fact."

"Mmm-hmm?"

"Why didn't he ever go to the authorities? You guys were

out there in the woods alone for years. All he had to do was call, and they would have come running. Why did he try to brazen it out, all by himself? And if he knew all these things were happening to the girls, the abuse and the rape and the fear, why didn't he pull the plug on it? He knew what happened to you. How could he let that happen to another girl?"

Kaylie set the plate down on the coffee table. Her shoulders hunched in. "Oh. I see. You're blaming him for all of the bad things that happened in Eden."

"No, I'm not. I'm curious why a man with his background—military, FBI, saving you—wouldn't try to save everyone there. He seems like an honorable man. But to know the things that were happening and not report them? It seems very out of character."

Kaylie's face contorted, and tears shone in her eyes. "They abandoned him."

"Who's they?"

"The people he worked for. You don't understand how hard it was for him to do what he did. Adrian was a good friend of Doug's well before he brought him into the fold. And betrayal to Eden is the most terrible thing a person can do. But Doug did it, anyway—for me."

"What do you mean?"

"He was religious about his check-ins. But no one ever responded."

"His check-ins? Kaylie, I'm confused."

Xander came over and sat in the overstuffed chair facing the fireplace. Kaylie gave him a long look, as if she was trying to decide if he was going to attack, and when he did nothing but sit quietly, hands on his knees, she relaxed and nodded.

"Doug didn't tell me everything about it, but he tried to talk to them for a year and no one ever responded. He knew how much trouble he was in. He figured they'd cut him loose. I think he thought about it a lot. Whether enough time had passed, whether he could trust them not to throw him in jail. He needed to wait until I was strong enough to take care of myself and then, when they didn't respond, he decided to go it alone."

"Everything about what?"

"He called it *Sigint.* I didn't know what it meant."

Xander sat up quickly, making her flinch. "Sorry. SIGINT. Signal intelligence. It's a way of capturing messages sent across electronic mediums. Clandestinely. Kaylie, how did he send the messages?"

"A computer."

"Did he leave the cabin to do it?"

"Yes, every time. He'd never compromise our position."

"Did you ever go with him?"

She was watching him cautiously, clearly afraid of him. "Once. He was sick with a fever and wanted to be sure he sent the message correctly."

"What means was he using to send the messages?"

"I don't know. Email, I think. The time I went with him, we drove to Charleston, West Virginia. He told me he always sent his messages from different places so Adrian couldn't track us down. But no one ever responded, so he finally stopped. Is that important?"

Xander gave Sam a quick nod.

"Yes, it is. Kaylie, thank you," Sam said. "I'm going to go tell Baldwin. Do you want to get some rest now? We have a guest bedroom. You can sleep there for a bit. I know you don't want to go into the FBI building, but they're going to insist before long."

"I don't want to go there."

"Why don't you rest now, and we'll talk about it when you get up?"

She stared at Sam for a long moment, then flung herself across the living room, gave her a rib-cracking hug and said, "Okay."

* * *

Sam got Kaylie squared away while Xander told Baldwin what they'd learned. Sam was glad she'd asked about Doug's situation. It just didn't make sense to her that a man so dedicated to the safety of Kaylie Rousch wouldn't at least try to save the rest of the girls.

If he'd known about it, that is.

Xander and Baldwin were deep in discussion when she joined them. Baldwin looked stricken.

"What's the matter?" Sam asked.

"I've just put a call in to the department who would have been overseeing the communications from Doug Matcliff. He could have been using a variety of methods, from dead drops to an internal email system we had back then. If he was sending intelligence and no one was acting on it, no wonder he wasn't willing to come in. He might have thought he'd been cast off, and would be prosecuted. Despite everything, he was FBI and had an obligation to us. He knew that."

"*Would* he have been prosecuted? He'd left his assignment, sure, but wouldn't this be seen as a simple abdication?" Sam asked.

"I don't know what they would have done. We've had undercover agents go sideways before. Usually it's drugs. They're forced to participate so the people don't get suspicious, and the next thing you know, they're hooked. Religious movements can be very persuasive—they prey on the weak, the easily manipulated. It's not unknown, but it's very rare to lose an agent this way."

"It doesn't seem like it was his fault," Sam said.

"You feel sorry for him, don't you?" He wasn't accusing, simply curious. He knew her well enough to know she sometimes became protective of the homicide victims she autopsied, as if she alone could put their ghosts to rest with the right answers.

"I don't know. Maybe. I'm curious about him. Why he

would put himself through all of this. He must have thought the punishment would have outstripped all the chances he was taking."

"From what I've gathered, Matcliff was always a bit high-strung," Baldwin said. "I've got a request in to see his military record, to find out why he mustered out. I will say this, he was much too young and inexperienced to be sent into an undercover operation of this magnitude, and he was compromised quickly. Especially if he knew this Adrian character. Maybe he would have been tossed in jail, who knows? Extenuating circumstances always play a part in these situations. But the word was he stopped communicating, and if that *isn't* true, we've got a bigger problem on our hands."

"Such as?"

He raked his fingers through his hair. "Let's go talk to his old boss, Anne Carter, first. I want to hear from her before I make any judgments. By the way, your friend Fletcher is on his way over here. He needs to talk to Kaylie about Adrian."

"Kaylie's going to get some sleep, and we all need to do the same thing."

"I don't disagree." He looked around the kitchen as if he were seeing it for the first time. "Anne Carter's out in Fauquier County. We can head there first thing in the morning, before we go to Lynchburg. We'll build from there."

"Sounds good. It's nearly 2:00 a.m. now. Let's plan to leave at 8:00?"

"Works for me."

"We've got room if you want to stay here."

He smiled, the first genuine happy look she'd seen since they'd hugged at the Hoover Building hours ago. "I have a room at the Ritz-Carlton. All my stuff's there. And Taylor's probably champing at the bit for a check-in call."

"Two in the morning—more likely she can't sleep, is in the

bonus room playing pool, drinking a beer and watching Red Eye on Fox."

He laughed. "That's true."

"Tell her I love her and I'll talk to her this weekend, okay? And, Baldwin. Thank you. Your help on this is invaluable."

"You got it."

There was a soft knock at the door and Thor gave a little whine. A friendly. Fletcher. Sam saw Baldwin out and let Fletcher in. The two men shook hands sleepily. This case was burning everyone out.

"Fletch, the girl's asleep," Sam said. "We need to wait until morning. I can make you some coffee, or a Scotch, if you want to hang around, but I'm about to fall over."

He smiled. "I don't want to wake her up, but let's just check in case she hasn't fallen asleep yet. You know how it is—adrenaline, worry, all that. There's a big son of a bitch hunting her ass, and she might not be able to sleep."

Sam shrugged. "She's in the guest room. I'll go check."

She mounted the stairs quietly. She imagined Kaylie Rousch hadn't had much rest for a while—underneath the bravado, there were lines of fatigue across her face, and deep black pockets under her eyes.

She opened the guest room door. The light was off, and there was no sound. She crept closer to the bed. She'd just whisper, and if Kaylie answered, great. If not—

An arm grabbed her shoulder and whirled her around, pushing her hard into the wall. The air left her, and as she struggled to breathe, she felt the hardness of a blade at her throat.

She began to struggle. Kaylie whispered harshly, "Stop it, right now. I'll kill you if I have to. I don't want to, so don't force me to be rash."

They were face-to-face in the darkness. Sam stopped thrashing, the air creeping back into her lungs. She nodded. "I didn't mean to scare you. Let me go."

"You're going to help me. Understand? Eden has something of mine, and I want it back."

Sam's years of hostage training kicked in. "Of course. Anything you want. I'm happy to help you. But you have to let me go. Take the knife away from my neck."

Kaylie jabbed harder, and Sam felt blood sliding down her shirt, over her collarbone.

"You aren't making the calls here. Listen carefully. Adrian will come for you. You're dead already. Before that happens, I need my daughter. You have to get my daughter for me. Do you understand?"

Sam nodded. Kaylie relaxed for a moment, and Sam took the chance, her right fist snaking out hard. She connected with Kaylie's chin, and the girl dropped the knife. It clattered on the wood floor. Sam swung her left leg in a strong kick, shoving off and whirling around, but Kaylie anticipated the move and blocked it, then grabbed Sam's leg and slammed her back against the wall. Sam punched her again, and they toppled, landing with a crash.

Sam started to shout for Xander, but Kaylie punched her in the stomach, hard, and she doubled over in pain. When she caught her breath and managed to stand and flip on the light switch, Kaylie was gone.

She slid down the wall, all the adrenaline leaving her in a rush. A moment later, Fletcher burst into the room. He took one look at her and turned white.

"You're bleeding. What the hell happened?" He pressed a handkerchief against her throat.

"Kaylie happened."

"Whitfield! Get up here."

But Xander was already dashing up the stairs, taking them two at a time. Her neck was starting to hurt. She was sure it was only a minor cut, but it stung. And she felt as if she were going to throw up.

A daughter. Kaylie had a daughter. She was caught in the cult. And Sam was a dead woman.

Xander dropped to his knees beside her as Fletcher rushed off, gun drawn.

"Are you okay? What happened?"

"I'm all right." She was, though her hands were shaking. "She jumped me, stuck the knife in my throat then said she wanted my help. Hell of a way to get me to cooperate."

"Where did she go?"

"Out the window, I guess. It's a pretty big drop to the ground, but she was rather desperate."

Xander helped her stand. She pulled the white cotton away from her neck. "Is it bad?"

He peered at her, lips in a tight line. "You won't need stitches. Let's get you bandaged up. Is your hand okay?"

She looked down to see her knuckles were abraded. "I'll be fine. I'll put some ice on it."

Fletcher came back. "My people are on their way. She won't get far." He saw her sucking on her knuckles. "You beat the crap out of her?"

"I wouldn't say that. She got in the last punch."

He gave her a proud smile. "But you clearly connected with a few. What's this?"

She glanced where he pointed. The bed was made, and the small stuffed lion was sitting in the middle of the spread. Kaylie had never gone to bed.

Fletcher picked up the stuffed lion. There was a piece of crumpled paper underneath. It looked to be a page torn from a book; the edges were ragged and the stock was much heavier than a notebook. He handed it to Sam. She read the words, made in a childish scrawl across the page, then handed it to Xander, who read it aloud.

"Dear Dr. Owens, I'm sorry. Thank you for being kind to me. I know you're going to be able to find my daughter."

CHAPTER 44

XANDER DABBED AT SAM'S WOUND WITH SOME BETADINE, THEN PUT ON A BUTTERFLY bandage. He was too gentle. She had to use her fingers to push it down to adhere to her skin, and her stomach turned at the pain.

"You okay?" Xander asked, his eyes dark with anger.

"Yeah. I'll live."

Fletcher examined Kaylie's egress. "The window lock is busted," he said. "She managed to get it open, then cut her way out through the screen. Dropped right out onto the roof, down the pear tree then over the fence onto the street. I can't believe we didn't hear her."

"I can't believe Thor didn't warn us," Xander said. "Thor! *Komm!*"

Fletcher was still wide-eyed, anger written across his face. He asked Xander, "Where'd she find the knife?"

"She had it on her, I think. When Baldwin asked to see her birthmark, she freaked out. It's on the inner part of her thigh. She probably had the knife strapped there the whole time. Jesus, how did I miss it?"

Sam touched his shoulder. "Because I'm the one who patted her down, and I certainly didn't put my hands between her thighs."

He nodded, a short jerk. He was clearly furious with himself. She gave him a smile. "I'm okay, really."

"You're being awfully calm about this. She could have killed you," Fletcher said.

"Apparently Adrian is coming to take care of that for her." She told them the rest, trying hard to keep the fear out of her voice. When she got to the part about the daughter, the idea hit Sam like a bolt of lightning.

"Was Rachel Stevens adopted?" she asked.

Fletcher tossed his hands in the air. "There's been no mention of it. There are pictures of Claire Stevens holding an infant on the mantel in their house, I know that."

"Someone needs to check. The pictures of Rachel I've seen bear more than a passing resemblance. The timing is right. Rachel just turned ten. Kaylie said she had her child when she was twelve or thirteen, and she's twenty-two now. If she's telling the truth about them selling babies, it's possible that Rachel is her daughter. And they're using her to draw Kaylie back to the cult."

"More than possible, damn it," Fletcher said. "I'll make sure someone investigates whether Rachel is adopted or not. That information would have helped before now." He flipped the paper over in his hands, looked at the note again.

"Hold on. Give me that back." Sam snatched the note from his hand and turned it over. She realized the paper Kaylie had written on was from one of the encyclopedias she had on the bookshelf, a remnant left over from her life in Nashville. When she was pregnant with the twins, she and Simon had purchased a set of Encyclopedia Britannica in the hopes of giving Matthew and Madeline an actual paper snapshot of the world, rather than allowing them to rely solely on the internet.

Of course, they'd never grown old enough to read, much less study.

She felt her heart start its familiar anguished tattoo, and sternly told it, *Not now.* She shut her eyes and took a deep breath through her nose, then opened her eyes and spread the crumpled paper out against her hand.

Amazing. It worked. Her heartbeat was normal. She was beginning to think she actually had this under control. Either that or she needed to take up boxing.

She looked closely at the paper. Kaylie had ripped a page from the V volume—specifically, the map of northern Virginia. Sam ran her finger along the page, went over to the bedside lamp to get the most light on it she could. There was something... she held it to the light and saw a pinhole in the paper.

"I will be damned. She's left us a way to find Rachel."

"How?" Fletcher asked.

Sam brought it to him, held the paper up to the overhead light so he could see it. "There's a hole, right here, out near Great Falls. That must be where they are. That must be where Eden is keeping Rachel."

"Or she stabbed the pen through the page writing her little love note. Come on, Sam. That's a reach."

"So you're telling me she just chose this page at random? The book was on the bottom shelf. If she just needed a piece of paper, why didn't she use the pad next to the bed, or get one from my office down the hall? No, she chose this page purposefully."

"Great Falls wasn't on any of the maps she showed Baldwin," Xander said.

Sam looked at him, saw the worry and exhaustion etched across his face. "This means something, Xander. I'm sure of it."

He was quiet for a moment, then nodded. "All right. Fletch, can we get a topographical map of this area, and a list of property owners?"

Fletcher already had his cell phone out and was dialing. "I'm on it. Right after I put out a BOLO on Kaylie. What was she wearing? Describe her to me."

Sam conjured a mental image of the girl. "Light green cargo pants, red T-shirt with Munich on it in white letters, brown military-style combat boots. Her hair is shoulder length, strawberry blond, obviously, and she had it in a ponytail. She's tan, from being outside, but freckled, too. My build, but maybe an inch or two taller than me."

Xander said, "I make her at five-eight and one-twenty soaking wet."

Sam gave him a smile. Leave it to Xander to have the specifics.

"She didn't steal anything, did she?" Fletcher asked.

"No. Surely not," Sam said.

"Better check," he said. And then into the phone, "Jordan, hey. We need a BOLO on Kaylie Rousch. She just attacked Dr. Owens. Label her armed and dangerous. Last seen in Georgetown, wearing—"

Sam walked down the hall to her bedroom. She hoped Kaylie hadn't stolen from them.

She was wrong.

Her bedroom was a shambles, the closet open and clothes strewn everywhere.

She called, "Fletch! Hold up. She might not be wearing the same clothes."

God, what an idiot she was thinking this stranger could be trusted. Maybe she wasn't even Kaylie Rousch; they hadn't done a DNA test at the door, just took her at her word. How dumb of them. She'd already broken into the house. Why not devolve into stealing from them, as well?

Thor followed her into the room, his nails clicking gently on the hardwood. "Some guard dog you are," she said, and she could have sworn he hung his head in shame. "Oh, no, don't you do that. *Komm!*" He came to her immediately and she bent to scratch his ears. He licked at the bandage on her throat.

"*Braver Hund!* I love you. But your daddy's going to hit the roof in two seconds. Be prepared."

Xander stopped in the doorway, his eyes narrowed, then entered the room. Fletcher was right on his heels, his cell phone to his ear.

"What'd she take? What's missing?"

"I don't know yet. Is it okay to start looking?"

"Jordan, hold on a sec, she trashed Sam's bedroom, too," Fletcher said. He took three shots of the room with his phone's camera, just in case they were needed for evidence. "Okay, Sam, go ahead. See what she took."

She started with her jewelry box, carelessly left unlocked on the dresser. She didn't have a lot of jewelry. As a doctor she always had her hands in gloves, so rarely wore rings. That's why Xander's ring was so perfect: tiny and thin, it wouldn't catch on things and she could always leave it on. She touched it once in thanks.

And bless all that was holy, she'd put her wedding set in her safe-deposit box after she'd moved to D.C., knowing having them in the house would make her life hell. They'd been safe away from Kaylie's sticky paws.

She combed through the box, saw nothing overtly out of place. Her TAG Heuer watch had been lying on the bathroom sink. It was gone, along with the cash from her wallet.

She waved it at Fletcher. "There was three hundred dollars in here. And she took the watch my father gave me for my high school graduation."

"Fast money. She can hock the watch, and clearly the cash was a necessity. Nothing else missing?"

"I love that watch, Fletch. She better not hock it. There are some clothes gone, too. She snagged some tops and pants. There are hangers empty that I know had stuff on them, but with the pile here in the middle of the floor, it will take me a while to figure out which ones. I hate to admit it, but I'm not the best at keeping my closet in perfect order."

Fletcher gave her a half grin. "I am completely and irrefutably disillusioned by that fact, Dr. Owens." He spoke to Jordan. "Rousch is funded and mobile. Get them on it now!" He hung up and looked around the room. "This is a lot of disorder for such a short time frame. What she took was easily reachable, right?"

"Yes. Out in the open. My wallet was at the top of my bag and the watch was on the bathroom counter. Grab some clothes to change into on the road, and she's on the move."

Fletcher spun around in a circle. "So why make such a huge mess? Do you think she was looking for something specific?"

"Like what?"

"I don't know, Sam. Something Doug Matcliff might have sent you? Did anything come in that letter he mailed to the office?"

"No. Just the letter. Benedict gave me the key, but that was to the safe at Matcliff's cabin, where we found all the pictures of me and the copy of the will."

"Well, he'd been stalking you for a while. Maybe she thought he left something else for you."

A chill ran down her spine. "Jesus, this gets better and better. What can we do to help, Fletch?"

He looked at his watch. "God, it's 2:30 a.m. Honestly, there's nothing more you can do right now. Get some sleep. We'll pick this up in the morning."

"I can't sleep knowing she's out there."

"Every cop on overnight patrol will be watching for her. I'll ask someone to park it here, in case she decides to come back."

"That's not necessary," Xander said, but Fletcher held up a hand.

"Yeah, it is," Fletcher said. "Damn, man, she sliced Sam's

neck and snuck out right under your nose. She's been off the grid and off the radar for at least ten of the last seventeen years. Matcliff clearly educated her. You have to assume she has every bit of training you have. He was a marine, a cop and an FBI agent."

Xander openly bristled. "Oh, bullshit on that. I was a ranger. Our training is highly superior to those powder puffs." But he smiled, and Fletcher laughed.

"Good." He nodded toward Sam. "Make her sleep. Knock her on the head if you have to. I'll call in a few hours, give you an update."

"We're meant to interview Anne Carter, Matcliff's old boss, and then go to Lynchburg," Sam said.

"Well, with any luck, it won't be necessary and we'll have it all wrapped by then. See ya."

Xander walked him out. Sam stood staring at the mess in her room, knowing she'd never get to sleep until she cleaned it up.

No good deed went unpunished, that was for sure.

She started pulling the clothes from the floor in piles. Xander joined her, and they got everything sorted out quickly.

"Fletcher's right, you need to get some rest," Xander said.

"I know. I can probably talk myself into popping a quarter tab of Ambien. Do you want one?"

"No way."

His vehemence stung her. "I thought I'd offer."

"One of us needs our wits about us."

She realized he was mad at her. She crossed her arms on her chest. "What did I do? Why are you upset with me?"

His dark eyes were troubled. He shook his head and touched her cheek, gently. Unwound her arms. Pulled her into his. "I'm not mad at you. We were both stupid to let her stay here. We should have let Baldwin haul her ass into the FBI. Now not only is she gone, but she's hurt you, and stolen from you, and trashed our house."

Sam merely nodded. "I hurt her, too. What did you do with that key, by the way?"

"The one to Matcliff's safe? I have it right here." He pulled the small silver key out of his pocket. "You think this is what she was after?"

"Maybe. What if the safe at Matcliff's place isn't the only thing it opens? What if there's another lock that fits that key?"

He turned it over and over in his hand. "It's entirely possible."

"Maybe Doug Matcliff hasn't given us the whole story. Not yet."

"Maybe not. But we're going in circles, and you need to get some rest. Come on. I'll tuck you in."

She was foggy and uncertain, and so tired. Her neck was throbbing, as were her knuckles. Her stomach felt raw where Kaylie had landed the final punch. A few hours of sleep might be just the trick. She took two ibuprofen tablets, then broke an Ambien into pieces, popped one in her mouth and let him put her to bed.

Xander made her get under the covers and kissed her lightly on the forehead. He started to leave and she asked, "Where are you going? You need sleep, too."

"Thought I'd mess around on the computer for a while, see if I can relax."

In other words, he was going to keep watch. The man was a machine.

"Xander?"

He came back and sat on the edge of the bed. She reached up and pushed his hair off his forehead gently.

"We have to find them," she said. "We have to find Kaylie and Rachel."

"I know. I'm going to do a little snooping, see if I can't turn up a few leads of our own. Sleep a bit, okay?"

"Only if you promise you will, too."

"Cross my heart." He kissed her again, then shut off the light, whistled for Thor and pulled the door.

She tossed and turned for a few minutes, waiting for the edge of sleep to come, to soften her mind, her worry. Five minutes later she was still staring at the ceiling. She got out of bed, went to the window of her bedroom and looked out through the blinds. The night seemed very dark, and she heard a rumble of thunder. She touched the bandage on her neck.

Kaylie Rousch was out there. So was Rachel Stevens, and a violent, remorseless killer. She felt eyes on her, and pulled the cord on the blinds. Breathed deep, and lay back down.

It was all going to break tomorrow. She could feel it.

CHAPTER 45

THERE IS A STORM COMING. THE WIND IS PICKING UP, THE MOON BLOTTED OUT BY the thickening clouds. There is the tiniest hint of coolness in the breeze, and the sudden change in temperature makes me shiver.

I stand on an anonymous Georgetown corner, waiting for the cop who pulled up with a screech in front of Dr. Owens's house twenty minutes ago to drive away. When another patrol car arrives and it is clear this one has settled in for the night, I know there is no return to the succor of her living room and lemon cake, warm arms and motherly embraces. I start up N Street, the heels of her boots clicking on the pavement. I had half hoped she wouldn't have called the cops, that she would recognize the desperation of a lost little girl.

Oh, well. The woman can fight. She'd nearly had me; it was pure luck I was able to take her down. She doesn't stand a chance with Adrian, though.

I have given her what she needs, her and that brute of a boyfriend. If she's as smart as Doug said, and he has half a brain, they'll figure it out.

The rain begins to fall, a soft spatter, making steam rise off the still-hot streets. I draw the cardigan closer. I like her clothes; they are soft, expensive and smell good. Like money and happiness. I know she has had a hard time over the past few years, but this is a woman who has only used her brain to survive until now, not her body, not her soul. Despite her frenzied rally, she is soft, like her clothes. And comfortable. Too comfortable.

All I want is a head start. If I can find my daughter, and eliminate the unholy alliance that tore me from her, I will do so. It ends now. No more hiding in the forest, pretending the world is all right.

I will save Rachel, or die trying.

CHAPTER 46

Capitol Hill
Near the Longworth Office Building

JORDAN BLAKE CALLED FLETCHER AS HE PULLED AWAY FROM SAM'S HOUSE. SHE told him to head home. It was too late to rattle any more cages tonight—the key to the puzzle was off on walkabout, and without further authorization to check out the spot on the map Rousch had left behind, their hands were tied. And they all needed rest. They'd be useless without at least a few hours of sleep.

He had to cross the Key Bridge to circle down the George Washington Parkway toward his place on the Hill. He was tempted to exit right onto the Parkway, drive out to Great Falls and see what was there. See whether it was simply a pinprick on a map, or something more. But common sense prevailed. Jordan was right. Rest. Recharge. Up and at 'em tomorrow. Maybe a few hours of sleep would help him see things clearly. Because right now this whole case and its various facets made zero sense to him. And the thought of Sam with a knife to her throat made him want to tear Kaylie Rousch limb from limb.

So when he pulled up to his house on Capitol Hill, he was surprised to see Jordan Blake sitting on his doorstep. She had a pizza and a six-pack on her lap, and a document box by her side.

He parked and joined her. "I thought I was supposed to be resting."

"You rest, I'll talk."

He pointed at the box. "What's all this?"

"Two years' worth of SIGINT. If Matcliff really was checking in, we should be able to find evidence of it in these files."

He raised an eyebrow, walked up the stairs and unlocked his front door. He reached for the brown cardboard box, hefted it into his free arm. It was heavy.

"Place is a mess," he said.

"I'd expect nothing less."

He shrugged and opened the door. "After you."

Once they were both inside, she double-checked the door was locked and leaned up against it. She looked around the room for a minute, didn't seem inclined to run screaming into the street. Still, he didn't let his guard down, especially when she started to talk.

"Listen. What I'm about to share with you—we're totally off book. This might cost me my job. I can trust you, right?"

He paused a second, then set the box down gingerly on his coffee table, sending a prayer of thanks to whatever god was responsible for inciting the random cleaning spree he'd done last week. At least there was room on the table for the box—if this had been last Saturday night, it would have been covered two feet deep in back issues of *The Washington Post* and the corners of the rooms would be full of random crap. He tried to remember when he'd last changed the sheets, and chided himself—she wasn't going to be seeing his bedroom, so it hardly mattered.

He tapped the lid of the box. "I take it you're not supposed to have this stuff?"

"Nope. Thurber made it very clear I was on ViCAP matches to the information Baldwin pulled out of Rousch tonight, before she took off on you. Slipped right out from under your protective little thumb, eh, Detective?" She grinned. She was too damn cute for her own good.

"Focus, Special Agent. My thumbs aren't little. Now, ViCAP?"

"Right. There's a definite link between the garrotings and the sightings of Eden. We're running a property check. Seems they owned land in all the same places where our girls went missing, so I'm fairly confident this is our group."

"So why are you here with this?"

"When I got home tonight, this box was on my porch, with a note that said 'Keep it to yourself.' I opened it, saw the SIGINT traffic, knew exactly what it was, figured you're outside the Bureau, might be willing to lend a hand."

"Who left it for you?"

"It wasn't Thurber, that's for sure. He's acting weird. I think it was Baldwin. He was completely shaken up by the news Matcliff was still calling in."

"What about Rachel? Any sign of her?"

"They're working the map Kaylie Rousch left. It's our best lead yet. Problem is, there's nothing out there. Not that they've found, at least. Big push in the morning, search teams, aerial, the whole works. We all need some sleep in case we get into trouble out there."

"I see. So instead of sleeping like everyone else, we're going to go through reams of paper looking for…what, exactly?"

"I don't know yet." She plopped down on his couch and popped open a beer. "You ready for an all-nighter? We find the good stuff, maybe I get a promotion."

He sighed and shook his head, reached out for a beer. "You so owe me."

She opened the box and pulled out the file on top, gave him a little smile. "Matcliff's jacket. Want to read over my shoulder?"

"Naw, you read it to me. It'll be faster if you pick out the important stuff."

"Suit yourself." She flipped the first page. "Douglas Carl Matcliff the Third, born 1969, Fairfax County Hospital, mother Mary, father, obviously also Douglas, attended Langley High School, graduated 1987. Enlisted in the marines right out of school, looks like more to get a piece of the G.I. Bill than anything else. Served his three years, got an honorable discharge then matriculated from George Mason University with a degree in Economics in 1996. He applied to Fairfax County Police Academy, was accepted first round. We picked him up in 2003, put him through the Academy at Quantico, and he was assigned to Headquarters under Supervisory Special Agent Anne Carter." She stopped, took a sip of her beer.

"Plum assignment, working with Anne Carter. She was a mover and shaker, smart, attractive, articulate, able to lead and a solid investigator, one of the ones the brass keep their eyes on."

"Like you?"

She smiled wide, which made her dimples show. "You're too kind. Doug caught her eye while he was at the Academy, and he attached himself to her, knowing full well as her star rose, so would his. And they were both rising. When all this went down, Anne was about to be moved to the New York Field Office as an ASAC in the Criminal Investigative Division up there. That's the big leaping-off point, New York CID."

"Until Eden made everything go south."

She flipped a page. "Not exactly true. It didn't stop Anne. She was on record saying it was a bad idea to send Doug undercover, knowing he wasn't ready, but she was overruled. It was her boss who got yanked and sent out to run one of the

Midwest field offices, and Anne went on to New York without a blemish."

"Interesting. So tell me, how could an upstanding guy like Matcliff, with all his training from the marines, the Fairfax County Police and the FBI, get roped into a religious cult? Did he have a record of being a spiritual guy?"

She looked at the file. "Episcopal, nonpracticing. Nope."

"Do you think it's possible he was kept against his will?"

"I don't know. I don't think so. He clearly got out the first chance he had."

"What was his MOS in the marines?"

"MOS?"

"Military Occupation Specialty. It's what they do. Like Xander—you met him earlier—was an infantry guy. Eleven Bang Bang, they called his group. But he was also a sniper. Rangers are known for multiple skills."

"Oh. Let's see. Matcliff was Field 0621—a radio operator."

"Which answers nothing. Okay. Consider the Spanish Inquisition over for now. Let's start looking at these captures, see if we can find his check-ins."

They split the box in two, worked for an hour, devouring the pizza, highlighting anything that looked interesting. There were pages and pages of old SIGINT electronic traffic, and Fletcher hadn't seen anything that seemed remotely tied to Doug Matcliff, Eden or Kaylie Rousch.

Jordan tossed her glasses onto the stack of papers, stretched and yawned. "This isn't getting us anywhere. This is the old email database system. They shut it down several years ago. Our newer versions are much more comprehensive, and easier to scan."

Fletcher went to sip his beer, realized it was empty. He reached for another, and Jordan handed him the opener. He cracked the lid. "There's a reason this box was left for you. We just need to figure out what it is. There's probably a codex we're missing, something that will translate this stuff."

She looked at him as if he'd said the most brilliant thing in the world.

"What?"

"Fletch, you're absolutely right. We need to find the patterns in the communications, and use a key to unlock it."

"And here I was, just tossing it out there."

"No, you're onto something. So where do we find the key? Is it in the names, the dates, the addresses?"

He looked down at the paper he was holding. It was an email sent in to the FBI's old private email system. "The FBI uses code names for cases, right?"

"Absolutely. Just like the military. Ensures privacy, a sense of pride in the mission, all that good stuff. Why?"

"What was the code name for Matcliff's cult infiltration?"

"Operation Hierarchy."

He looked up from the paper. "Seriously?"

"Hey, I didn't name it."

"What was Matcliff's code name?"

She flipped through the file. "Saxon."

Fletcher grinned. "At least that makes sense. He went to Langley High School. Their mascot is a Saxon."

"A Saxon?"

"Yeah, the Anglo-Saxons, for the Scottish heritage of the area. Dude looks like a Viking to me, with the yellow hair and a crazy helmet, but who the hell knows. That's irrelevant. Let's look for communications that might have *Saxon* in them."

Once they knew what to look for, the information they needed became clear. Matcliff had been sent into Eden in November 2004, when the cult would have been settling down for the winter. In an agrarian society, when there isn't much to do outside, everything becomes internal, and Eden didn't seem to be any different. The days followed a familiar pattern—

religious study, led by the "Mother," morning, noon and night, what they called feasts every Sunday, where the whole group ate together, and preparation for what he referred to as a Reasoning, which sounded like more lessons from their leader.

Matcliff messaged dutifully every Tuesday night at 10:00 p.m. for the three months he was under. At first they were simple, straightforward communications. Nothing new to report, Eden operating on a routine schedule, names of the followers, some unimportant details. They all finished with "I can't find anything wrong. Give me more time. Geddon."

They didn't know what *Geddon* meant. They set it aside to look at later.

In February 2005, there was a sudden shift in the pattern of the messages. He skipped two Tuesdays, then filed from a new IP address. Fletcher read it aloud. "Eden on the move. Will travel with them. Must go, more later. Geddon."

And that was it. The messages stopped entirely.

He flipped through the pages again, thinking he'd missed something. No, it all stopped. There was nothing more from Doug Matcliff.

"No further communications from Saxon after February 2005."

Jordan was staring at a piece of paper, eyes narrowed.

"What is it?"

"I think I found where it picks up again. It's months later. He's using the code name Savage instead of Saxon, but it's clearly him. How did they miss this?"

"He set up shop in Lynchburg under the name Timothy Savage. It fits. Let me see."

She hesitated.

"Jordan, what is it?"

With a sigh, she handed the pages over. "Confirmation of something we expected. God, why didn't he just pick up the phone and call in?"

Fletcher read through the pages one by one, each word filling him with absolute horror.

"Jordan, Matcliff claims there was another girl like Kaylie brought into the cult. He's giving instruction on how to get her out. Her name was—"

She sat back on the sofa and crossed her legs. "Names, Fletch. Names. Emily Harper, Ella Reynolds, Nicole Wells, Kelly Rodriguez and Olivia Mills."

Fletcher looked up. "What did you say?"

"Emily Harper would have been the one he's talking about, I suppose."

"And the other names?"

"The other girls who resemble Kaylie Rousch and who disappeared over the past fifteen years."

"You mean to tell me you have more girls missing? Why wasn't this part of the briefing?"

"Because Thurber didn't clear any of you to be told about it."

"Well, shit, sister, you better start talking, because I don't work on cases without all the facts, and I don't appreciate being kept in the dark."

He leaned back and crossed his arms. *What the hell? Five more girls?*

"Don't get angry with me. I'm here, aren't I? And telling you the whole story, against orders. Rob and I had a big fight about this earlier. He's worried about the way it looks."

"He's right to worry. But I don't give a crap about how it *looks.* Facts. Now. Or I'm out."

She looked down, bit her lip and told him everything.

The more he heard, the more he knew there weren't going to be any happy endings to this story.

CHAPTER 47

Near Lynchburg, Virginia

ADRIAN STRUGGLED THROUGH THE WOODS. HE KNEW HE WAS LEAVING A TRAIL, bending the shrubs, blood leaking onto the green moss, but it didn't matter. He needed to get back to the car and get the hell out of Dodge.

The darkness in Fred McDonald's basement had saved him. When the gun went off, Adrian hit the floor and rolled backward toward the open door to the yard. The man's aim had been slightly off. If he'd pointed the shotgun to the left even ten degrees, he would have taken Adrian down, permanently. But the pellets had missed his vital organs, spraying across the left side of his body, causing crippling pain, but not stealing his life.

Adrian got to his feet and charged McDonald, put his arms around the man's ample body and squeezed, hard. He fought back, slamming the stock of the shotgun into Adrian's knee. There was no time to play. Adrian had to end it immediately or risk losing his own life. He couldn't afford to let the man go for a moment.

McDonald's neck was meaty, corpulent, and when it was clear strangulation was going to take too long, Adrian simply put his hands on either side of McDonald's ears and wrenched the man's head hard to the right.

There was an unholy crack, then the smell of ammonia and shit filled the air. Adrian dropped McDonald to the floor and rushed out of the basement.

The bastard had been waiting for him. He'd shot him.

Adrian saw spots in front of his eyes, and knew he didn't have much time.

He rested against a tree, smelled the blood seeping from his side. He must return to Eden. He needed Curtis's healing power, and the power of his sacrosancts. They would be able to pick the pellets from his side and nurse him back to health.

While he rested, catching his breath, he thought about his old friend Doug. The man who'd betrayed him, who faked his love and duty, who'd stolen Adrian's plaything. The younger girls were his to do with as he saw fit, and while he understood the necessity of the Reasoning, he didn't particularly enjoy his job with them. He was all about the chase, the challenge, finding the right look then ripping them from their lives to please his mistress, who wanted girls in her own image to be Eden's daughters.

Curtis's love was more important than any tenet in the Book, or what little morality he'd been taught. When he brought the unclean ones to her, he was rewarded with a week of freedom, freedom to roam, to fulfill his base urges, to steal life from the unsuspecting.

He'd lived for those moments.

Things were going so well.

And then his old friend, the one they'd made the bargain

with, the one they'd promised to leave alone, had to torpedo their lives and ruin everything.

He would kill him all over again if he could, wrap his arms around his neck and squeeze until his limbs splayed out like a spider pinned to a board, his arms pummeling Adrian's chest, heels against his thighs, as the life left him.

How far the mighty had fallen.

He pushed off the tree, worked his way through the woods, back to his car. He gave it a quick look and it appeared undisturbed. He fumbled with the keys, realized he was lightheaded. He got the door open and sat heavily.

He needed to go now, or he'd be too weak to make the two-hour drive.

Two hours to the love of his people, the gentle hands of his mistress, and then they'd make their plan.

He pulled out onto Highway 29 too fast, the tires scrabbling in the scree until they gained purchase on the pavement, and drove north, letting his mind wander where it would.

It was a week before Christmas, 2001. Adrian had spent a week waiting every night at the Tombs, a bar he knew Doug liked to frequent back in the day. He'd kept an eye on his old friend since he'd returned to northern Virginia after his stint in the military. He'd gone to college, and landed a job with the Fairfax County Police. Through all of that, Doug was predictable. He returned to his old haunts on a regular basis, almost as if he were looking for something. Or someone.

Curtis had decided she needed Doug, and it was Adrian's duty to bring him into the fold.

Doug walked through the doors at eleven, already drunk, a blonde wearing a postage-stamp-sized dress on his arm. He'd grown over the years, filled out, was broad and tall and handsome. Not as big as Adrian, of course; few were. But the marines and the police had done a good job of turning Doug from a boy to a man. The way Curtis had done for Adrian.

He let his old friend get a beer, dance a bit and stick his tongue down the blonde's throat a few times before he approached. He went slowly and gently; he knew his size alarmed people. That and the look of reckless fury simmering in his eyes. He had become the fiery sword in the years since they parted. He had the power now.

Doug saw him coming. His eyes opened wide, then he was in his old friend's arms, slapping him on the back.

"Where the hell have you been all these years? You dropped out of school and no one heard from you."

"Around. How are you, Doug?"

"Good, good. This is..." He paused and the girl supplied her name, which Adrian didn't hear. He was too focused on Doug. On how he was going to recruit him. He didn't want to bring Doug in kicking and screaming. He wanted him to see the joy and beauty Eden had to offer, and want to be a part of them.

Adrian leaned in, shouted in Doug's ear, "Let's get out of here. It's too loud to think."

"Sure, okay. Let me get rid of this chick. I'll meet you outside in ten."

It had been a night to remember. Drunk on beer and life and happiness at seeing his old friend, Doug was willing to talk honestly and openly about things Adrian never thought he would. Like his time overseas, about how he became disillusioned with the political agenda, saw where they were headed, right into another big war, and decided to come home and finish college. He thought being a cop would satisfy him. But there was something still missing from his life.

And when Adrian told him about Eden, about the love and acceptance and journey he'd been on, Doug was genuinely happy for him. He hadn't wanted to come home with Adrian, but said maybe another time.

He certainly seemed open to the idea of being a part of Adrian's world.

Adrian knew how much Curtis needed Doug. To watch out for them. To cover their backs. They needed someone on the outside to run the operation. He had a flask in his pocket, which contained a fine single-barrel bourbon. And a little something extra.

The kick that pushed him right over the edge. After swigging from the flask a few times, Doug was intoxicated enough to admit what was really the matter with him.

What he was looking for. Who he was looking for.

He was sloppy with it, the admission. And Adrian realized this was the opportunity he'd been waiting for.

They found themselves alone in a gorgeous park, the night breeze scented with the last bit of summer jasmine and honeysuckle. They walked along the path into the darkness, and talked about loneliness, and when Doug stumbled, Adrian reached for his old friend, brought him into his arms and bent his head to his lips. Doug only resisted for a moment.

Adrian's head jerked suddenly and he realized he'd almost driven off the road. Lost in the memory of that night, he'd started to drift to sleep. It was a happy memory, though it had turned ugly down the road, when Doug hadn't wanted to be their man, and Adrian was forced to show him the pictures he'd taken that night.

The photos were brutal, intimate and clearly showed Doug in the most compromising positions. When he saw them, he got right in line. He couldn't afford for his life to be ruined, for his secret to get out. The police would drum him off the force if they knew. So Doug kept his head down, and worked hard to make the big leap into the FBI, the perfect place to cover all their asses.

Doug was a part of Eden, whether he wanted it or not.

What they weren't prepared for was Doug being sent into Eden to investigate them. He sat down with Adrian and Curtis that first night and explained what was happening, how they were going to work it all out.

Adrian and Curtis had their first true disagreement over Doug's plans. Adrian was all for taking his old friend into the woods and permanently removing him from their lives. Curtis, levelheaded Curtis, knew she needed to keep Doug around, and vetoed Adrian's proposal.

Adrian had been right all along when he said they couldn't trust Doug anymore.

He flipped on the radio, knowing the music would help keep him awake. But his favorite station wasn't playing music. They were talking about a missing girl, and a ghost, resurrected from his past.

Kaylie Rousch was alive and on the run.

He slammed his fists into the steering wheel and screamed. He let the anger course through him, felt his control slide back into place.

Ten years ago, Doug had spent three months misleading them. He orchestrated the move to Texas, helped them with everything—everything!—and then he'd betrayed everyone by running away with the girl once she'd dropped her pod.

His brother, his lover, his friend—had betrayed them all for an inconsequential girl.

And now Doug was dead, the girl was alive and Adrian had to make this all right. He just wanted his old life back. The old rhythms, instilled by Curtis, based on centuries of belief and structure. The balance and harmony he'd grown accustomed to.

And the only way to do that was to find and silence the only person left who knew everything. He had to rid the world of Kaylie Rousch, and all the people she'd been casually touching since she came out of hiding. Her poison must be stopped.

And he knew just where to find her now. He knew she would be waiting for him. It was time for their decades-long dance to end, with her in the ground, where she belonged.

SUNDAY

"What would your good do if evil didn't exist, and what would the earth look like if all the shadows disappeared?"

—Mikhail Bulgakov

"Evil is the bane of the world, sayeth our Lord, the one truth we cannot escape. From the matter given by the stars on the day of our great birth to the dust it becomes as our bones rot in the ground, evil will be eradicated by love of the Mother. Do not fear your dark thoughts, my children. My love ensures that you will not succumb."

—Curtis Lott

CHAPTER 48

Capitol Hill
Near the Longworth Office Building

FLETCHER WOKE TO THE SMELL OF COFFEE AND BACON. CERTAIN HE WAS DREAMING, or had simply caught a whiff of brunch from Bullfeathers, a nearby restaurant, he rolled over and tried to go back to sleep. Instead he fell off the couch onto the living-room floor with a thud.

It all came rushing back—the very late night, the beer, the horrible revelations. The fruitless search in the files for more information about where Eden was holding the missing girls, his gallant offer of his bed to the young FBI agent, who, to his everlasting shock, had said yes, because she wasn't about to drive home after three beers.

He glanced down—yes, he was fully clothed. He gathered himself up from the floor and cracked his neck. He wasn't dreaming. Someone was in his kitchen, cooking.

A feminine voice called out, "Rise and shine."

He wandered into the kitchen, yawning.

"What, no kiss?" She had on the same clothes from the night before, black pants and red silk top, but was missing the jacket, and her bra.

His eyes must have gotten wide, because Jordan started to laugh. "You really need to lighten up, Detective."

"You're in a good mood. Are you like the battery on my iPhone, just plug her in and she charges up in an hour?"

"No, I'm younger than you, and don't need as much sleep."

"Ouch." But he smiled and so did she. Jesus, she was flirting with him. And he was flirting right back. *Head in the game, Fletch.* She was adorable, and smart, and driven in a way he totally respected, and he'd like to get to know her better. But they had a child to find, and he needed to keep that front and center.

He realized something else was becoming front and center, and turned, busying himself in the refrigerator until he was decent again. He laughed at himself. Dirty old man.

"I hope you're hungry," Jordan said, setting cutlery and a juice glass on the table.

"To what do I owe the honor?"

"I was starving, and unlike many a bachelor, you actually have food in your fridge. It didn't seem fair to run out on you after you were kind enough to give up your bed last night. And I might have found something you'll want to see."

"What's that?"

"Eat first. Then we'll look."

"Look first, then eat."

"Oh, you're no fun." But she turned the heat off and grabbed a sheaf of papers from the counter next to her.

"We've been looking at this all wrong. Matcliff was given a new code name."

"Saxon to Savage. Right. Why?"

"Your guess is as good as mine."

"Who gave him the new code name?"

"I'm betting it was someone who knew him."

"Thurber?"

"Explains why he's been so freaky about all this."

"So Thurber lied when he said he didn't know the name Timothy Savage," Fletcher said.

She went back to the stove, flipped the eggs onto a plate, added the bacon and thrust it at him. "I wouldn't characterize it as a lie, exactly. A bending of the truth. I think Rob might feel responsible, which is why he's throwing up roadblocks and being such a jerk about this. It's out of character. He's always been a good, levelheaded guy. Of course, I'm newly partnered with him, so I don't know everything about him. We're still in the honeymoon phase."

"He's an honest sort, though, right?"

"Until an hour ago, I would have said yes. Now I don't know."

She scooped eggs and bacon onto her own plate and joined him at the table. "Once the code name shifts, it's a cat and mouse game. I think they were trying to get him to come in, and he wasn't willing to take the chance. Before it all shuts down, he gives the location of the cult in 2006, near El Paso, Texas. So we can tie them physically to Emily Harper's disappearance. It's enough to get a warrant, assuming we've found where they are now."

"Did he happen to say what they were doing with the girls?"

"No. Nothing new there."

"Good work, Special Agent."

They ate in silence for a few minutes. Fletcher tried to wrap his head around it, knew they were still missing something. Why in the world would the FBI shut down their own channel into the cult? Especially when their agent had presumably gone missing within that same organization—after telling them there were more girls being brought in?

Every time they found an answer, two more questions cropped up.

Fletcher heard a noise, paused with his fork halfway to his mouth. Jordan heard it, too. Her eyes met his. They both jumped to their feet and inched to the back door. Fletcher was still wearing his backup gun. He pulled it from his ankle holster and muttered, "You loaded?"

Her Glock was out, already pointed at the noise. "I'm an FBI agent, Detective, not a Girl Scout. Of course I am."

He resisted the urge to laugh, signaled the count—one, two, three—then threw open the door to his meager little deck.

"Don't shoot, don't shoot!"

He dropped his weapon. Lisa Schumann, *The Washington Post* reporter he'd blown off a couple of days ago, was hanging over the railing of his deck, preparing to drop down to the alley below.

He grabbed her arm and hauled her back over the edge. She landed in a heap at his feet.

"Ow! Gee, thanks for nothing, Detective. That hurt."

"Talk. Right now. Or I swear to God I'll shoot you. What the hell are you doing out here?"

Her chin rose an inch. She had guts; he'd give her that.

"What do you think I'm doing? I'm trying to drum up a lead on the Rachel Stevens case."

"By spying on me?"

She looked down and didn't answer.

"Not acceptable. Get the hell out of here. And don't even think about making a sympathy play. I'm calling your boss, and he's going to have your head. You're lucky I'm not taking it to him."

Jordan's phone rang. She holstered her Glock and went inside.

"But, Detective—or should I call you Lieutenant now?"

His stomach hitched. "How do you know about that?"

A coy little smile. "I do have sources, despite what you

think. And my sources tell me Kaylie Rousch is back from the dead. True?"

"Go away, Lisa."

"If you won't give me anything, maybe you'll listen. Twenty years ago, around the same time Kaylie Rousch disappeared, another little girl went missing. She was the daughter of one of the homeless from down under Whitehurst Freeway. No one ever did anything about it because she was a black girl in an orphanage, and no one cared enough to look for her."

He shook his head. "You are so off base. If we'd known about it, we would have investigated it. What sort of cops do you think we are?"

"The kind the homeless didn't trust enough to tell you the truth, I suppose. Her name was Jennifer Harvey. That's who you dug up when you thought you'd found Kaylie Rousch."

Fletcher sighed. "Where did you find this?"

"I've been working on an enterprise piece about the inequalities in criminal investigations and the media exposure. White Girl Syndrome. I talked to a lot of people down in Anacostia. They all mentioned this little girl who'd disappeared and no one ever did anything about it. Kaylie Rousch disappeared, and every media outlet spent weeks on the coverage. Jennifer Harvey goes missing, and no one even knows her name. It's a shame."

"Well, I thank you for the tip, and I'll certainly follow it up. Now leave."

"That's it? Come on, Lieutenant. Don't you want to know who did it?"

"You think you know who did?"

"I'll show you mine if you show me yours."

Fletcher gritted his teeth together. Jordan looked out the window, ran two fingers in a circle. Wrap it up, her look said.

"Lisa, you are trying my patience. If you have information on a criminal case, spill it, right now. I won't give you speculation in return, but I will tell the brass you gave us the lead, and will keep you in the loop on the investigation. Deal?"

She smiled widely. "Deal. Look for a guy named Big Tommy. He ran heroin out of Anacostia. Word is Jennifer was one of his corner runners, and she got caught up in a dispute between him and another dealer. That's all I've got so far."

It was solid information. He knew all about Big Tommy, a ruthless son of a bitch who'd been in and out of prison for years. He had a sheet a mile long; Fletcher wouldn't be terribly surprised to see murder added to the list.

"All right. Quid pro quo. Kaylie Rousch is alive, and we are endeavoring to find her right now. There is a BOLO out for her."

"I know she's alive, dummy. It's all over the news. Is it a BOLO, or an arrest warrant? I heard she was armed and dangerous."

"We just want to talk to her. Last known was Georgetown, 2:30 a.m. She stole some clothes, money and jewelry from—never mind, that's not relevant. But if a redhead comes into a pawnshop today with a TAG Heuer watch, you let me know."

She pulled herself up to the railing and said, "Thanks."

He leveled a finger at her. "Lisa. Hear me well. I ever catch you out here again, and you're finished. You got me?"

She nodded, then gave him a sly grin. "Your FBI agent friend is smoking hot. You should tap that."

He slammed the back door a little harder than necessary to drown out her laugh.

Jordan had straightened up all the papers, was putting the dishes into the dishwasher.

"Leave those, I'll clean up later. You ready to head out?"

"Yes. That reporter, she's quite resourceful."

"She's a gigantic pain in my ass is what she is. Always lurking around trying to drum up a story. I can't believe she was foolish enough to peep in my windows. We arrest people for that shit."

He grabbed his cell phone to call the *Post.*

"Don't turn her in," Jordan said. "She's just trying to make a living. Use her instead."

"She's not someone I trust."

"She'll be more help if she's out there digging things up."

"I can't believe you're defending her. "

She tossed a dish towel onto the counter, put her hands on her hips. "I'm not. But I want every eye out for this little girl, even unscrupulous reporters. Unfortunately there's no news out of headquarters. Let's go talk to Rachel's parents. It's time we got the whole story on her background, don't you think?"

CHAPTER 49

Georgetown

SAM WOKE AT 6:30 A.M., THE SUN STREAMING IN THE WINDOW. XANDER HAD never come to bed.

She tiptoed downstairs, saw him asleep on the couch, shirtless, an arm thrown over his head, blocking the sun's rays. Thor slept next to him, though he raised his head hopefully when he saw her. His people stirring meant food, and a walk.

Sam used a hand signal and he came willingly. She snapped on his leash and started for the door.

"What do you think you're doing?"

She jumped at Xander's voice, turned around to see him standing in the foyer behind her, the top button of his jeans open, hair wild and tousled.

"I was going to walk Thor."

"Negative. Take him out back."

Crap. Xander had gone operational on her, never a good sign. She crossed to the back doors and let Thor out into the yard.

The pool took up almost all the grassy space, but there was a spot for him. She brought him back inside and locked the door, knowing if she didn't Xander would instruct her to, anyway.

"Are you hungry?"

He gave her an amused look.

"Right. When are you ever not hungry? Let me put something together and you can tell me what you found."

"What makes you think I found something?"

"Xander, love, you look like you have a flagpole glued to your back. I suppose telling you to relax would be a moot suggestion?"

"Coffee. Then we'll talk."

He went into the kitchen to put together one of his infamous pots of coffee. It made her laugh. For all his attempts to be a laid-back mountain man, he was an absolute coffee snob. Before they'd gotten together, he ran his fly-fishing guide service out of a small coffee shop an hour down the mountain from his cabin. He swore it was one of the few places he could get a decent cup. He claimed it was army life that did it to him; being stationed all over the world, he'd been able to sample some of the best brews out there. She thought it might have been his upbringing, his commune-living parents who'd instilled a love of all things natural in him. Whatever it was, it was a skill and preference she benefitted from. She loved a good cup of coffee.

Minutes later, hot joe in hand, leftover blueberry popovers in front of them, Thor fed and watered, they sat at the kitchen table and he filled her in.

"I found the definitive link between Doug Matcliff and the man named Adrian Zamyatin. They went to high school together at Langley. Adrian's mother died soon after he was born, and his father worked for a grocery chain as a long-haul trucker. He was rarely home, and Adrian was left to do what he would.

"Doug's family were polar opposites—both his parents were

lawyers. They divorced in 1993, just before Doug started high school."

"So you're saying these two weren't just familiar with each other—they were friends?"

"Good friends. The online photos from their classes at Langley show them to be inseparable." He took a sip of coffee, broke off a piece of the pastry. He waited while she processed that information.

"How'd you find the photos?"

"Facebook. There are several groups from their high school on there. I faked a profile and joined a few. They've done a nice job uploading the old yearbooks to the sites. People like to chat. I asked a few discreet questions, got an earful."

He had a little smile on his face. There was more, but he wasn't going to just give it to her.

"It's early and I'm foggy, hon. What?"

"Guess who handled his parents' divorce?"

"I have no idea."

"Think of a lawyer's name you might have heard in the past couple of days."

She thought. There was too much leftover Ambien; nothing was clicking for her. "Mac Picker?"

"Bingo."

She let that wash over her, felt her pulse pick up. "So Benedict, Picker, Green, Thompson handles divorces. What else do they do?"

"Adoption has a legal component."

She watched him take a self-satisfied swig of his coffee.

"They were the ones handling the adoptions of the babies born in Eden."

"Yep."

It all made sense. Before she could say anything else, her phone rang. She didn't recognize the number. It was still obscenely early. This had to be news.

"This is Sam."

"Dr. Owens, this is Lisa Schumann, from *The Washington Post*. I have a couple of questions about the Stevens kidnapping. Can you—"

"No comment."

"Dr. Owens, please. Hear me out. I understand Kaylie Rousch came to visit you last night. Don't you find that odd? Why would a girl who everyone thought was dead show up on your doorstep, very much alive?"

Damn it. One of the cops talked. "No comment. Seriously. You can direct your inquiries to the authorities. Good day, Ms. Schumann."

She was about to disconnect when the girl yelled, "Wait! I know where Kaylie Rousch is now."

Sam put the phone back to her ear. "What did you say?"

"I know where Kaylie Rousch is. I'll tell you if you hear me out."

"You'll tell me now, or I'll have D.C. Metro on your ass before you can blink."

Schumann had the audacity to laugh. "I can take care of myself. I have more friends at Metro than you do. Is it true, then? Did Kaylie Rousch resurrect and show up on your doorstep?"

Sam shook her head. No, she wasn't going to fall for this. "I'm sorry, Ms. Schumann. No comment."

She hung up the phone, and immediately called Fletcher.

He answered on the first ring, sounding slightly more awake than she felt at the moment.

"What's shaking? Any news?"

"A reporter from *The Washington Post* just called me, told me she knows where Kaylie Rousch is and wanted a quote about Rachel."

She heard him cursing a blue streak, then a female voice in the background.

He had company. And it wasn't Andrea Bianco.

"I'm sorry. I didn't mean to interrupt," Sam said.

She hated herself for the chilliness of her tone. It wasn't fair, and it didn't matter. He was her friend, nothing more. Thankfully, he didn't seem to notice.

"You're not interrupting. Jordan and I spent the whole night going through the signal intelligence from Matcliff."

She felt like an idiot. Jordan Blake. So he'd been working. *Get a grip, Sam.*

Fletcher yawned. "Sorry. This case is going to kill me. So where is Kaylie Rousch, according to Ms. Schumann? Who's a pain in my ass, by the way. That girl is a climber. We need to be careful around her."

"So I gathered. I said no comment and hung up on her."

"Good girl. She's just fishing. Glad you didn't take the bait. She almost got her head shot off here a minute ago, sneaking around my backyard. Caught her looking in my windows, nearly booted her ass, bullet included, clear to the Potomac."

"What if she knows something?"

His voice hardened. "If she does, and she's trying to protect her story, she'll regret it. I'll call her, tell her to stop bugging you. Listen, we went through about a million pieces of paper last night, and came up with a few things."

He filled her in. She told him their suspicions about Mac Picker. They both sat in silence, processing their individual information.

"I think we can agree Doug Matcliff wasn't an innocent in all of this," Sam finally said. "He knew exactly what was happening with Eden. Chances are, he set them up with Picker early on. He knew the name, knew the work they did. He's complicit in this up to his eyeballs, and that law firm needs to be taken down. My question is, why now? He's been on the run, hiding from the cult and from the FBI, for ten years. Why blow his cover now?"

"Maybe Matcliff had enough, and was trying to do the right thing."

"Maybe. But I don't know, Fletcher. He may have started as the go-between, moving the babies out and delivering them to Lynchburg, assuming we can confirm that the adoption paperwork came out of Picker's firm. But at some point, Kaylie's well-being became more important to him, and he took her from the cult and went off-grid. These are the actions of a man in love, don't you think?"

"Go on."

She played with her empty coffee cup. "He was in love with Kaylie, and would do anything to keep her safe. Then ten years later, out of the blue, he suddenly puts together a will, then winds up dead. It doesn't make sense."

"I agree, it doesn't. But we know he was a duplicitous bastard. From what we gathered, going through this intelligence, his check-ins were intended to mislead the FBI into looking in all the wrong places for Eden."

"He certainly managed to make Kaylie believe he'd been cut loose by the FBI, that they were on their own. Isolating her, making her all the more dependent on him."

"Classic abuse scenario."

"It is, isn't it?" Another thought struck her. "Fletch, remember what Davidson said Arthur Scarron did? He was some sort of doctor before he began to run his family's oil company. Davidson said he thought it was plastic surgery or O.B. Regardless of his specialty, he's certainly trained in obstetrics. We all have the basic knowledge of each field. Perhaps he was involved here, too. Any chance Ellie Scarron is awake?"

"Not that I've heard, but you're right. It's time to go dig deeper into the names on that will."

"What about Rachel Stevens? Any word on her?"

"Jordan's people are looking for the spot Kaylie pointed out on the map, and the minute they find something, I'll let you know. We're headed to the Stevens's now to find out if Rachel is really their kid. If she's not, I'll find out who handled the adoption. You're going to Anne Carter's place?"

"Yes. Baldwin should be here shortly."

"Then I suggest you grill the crap out of the woman, get her to share all her dirty little secrets."

CHAPTER 50

Bethesda, Maryland

THE SUN WAS CRAWLING STEADILY OUT OF THE HORIZON WHEN FLETCHER AND Jordan rolled up to the Stevens house. The overnight team gave them bleary looks, clearly disappointed they weren't being relieved.

Claire and Kevin Stevens were sitting in the kitchen, also bleary-eyed, and their joint looks of hope morphing into despair were hard to take. Claire vaguely waved her hand at the coffeepot. Fletcher poured coffee for everyone, then joined them at the table.

"Any news at all?" Claire asked in a whisper.

Jordan touched her arm lightly. "We're doing everything we can, Mrs. Stevens. Trust me. I know this is incredibly difficult, but right now we need some information. Can you tell us a little more about Rachel?"

"Of course. What do you want to know?"

"I'm sorry for being blunt, but is she your biological child?"

Claire Stevens had ivory skin. It was astounding to imagine she could get any paler, but she blanched so violently Fletcher reached out to steady her in case she fainted. "I take it that's a no?"

Kevin Stevens's face turned a mottled red. "I can't believe you're asking this now. She's our daughter, and she's missing. Nothing else matters."

His wife's mouth was working silently, as if she was trying and failing to find the appropriate words. She finally straightened her slim shoulders and spoke quietly. "How did you find out? It was a closed adoption. We were assured no one would ever know Rachel wasn't ours."

Fletcher looked at Jordan, and she leaned forward a little bit. "We believe we've found Rachel's biological mother."

The look of hope returned to Claire's face. "Oh, thank the Lord. Did she steal her? Are we dealing with a custodial battle then? We can get our lawyers involved. We are her legal parents. Her mother abandoned her when she was a day old, and when she didn't come back to claim her within thirty days, we were told we were in the clear. There's no legal recourse for her to take Rachel back."

"Let's back up a minute, ma'am," Fletcher said. "Tell us who helped you with the adoption."

"No. Who is this woman? I want to know. I want to know who's taken my daughter."

Fletcher's voice was gentle and steady. "Mrs. Stevens, please, calm down. We don't believe Rachel's biological mother is the person who took your daughter. But we do believe that her name is Kaylie Rousch, and she was a missing child, just like Rachel is now."

"I don't understand what you're saying."

But Kevin had leaned back in his chair, a look of wariness on his face. "Kaylie Rousch is the little girl—she's a woman now—who's been all over the news this morning. She was dead, they found her body. Now we find out they made some terrible mistake and she's come back to life. You're telling us this woman was Rachel's biological host?"

"Yes, sir, that's what we think." Fletch sat back in the chair. *Biological host?* God, what an expression.

"But according to the news, the Rousch girl was stashed away in a cult for years, right?" Stevens asked.

Jordan nodded, took a sip of the coffee. "Yes, she was. We need to know how the adoption worked. Who facilitated it for you?"

Claire had recovered her composure. She was still pale, but there was some life in her eyes. "We had a lawyer. He helped us find the firm who did the private adoption. They were out of Lynchburg, Virginia. I only know that because I ran a background trace on our lawyer's phone and saw all the calls he made when he was billing us were to a firm down there. We were never given their name, and to be honest, I never wanted it. What we were doing wasn't against the law, not at all. They said it wasn't going to take much time to get us a child, and we were thrilled when they were true to their word."

"And you never dug any deeper? You checked out your own lawyer but not the firm he was working with?"

"That's right. Our lawyer was taking our money regardless of whether we got a child. I wanted to be sure he was legitimate. And he was—he checked out. After that, I let it drop."

"What's his name?"

"Barry Evans, but he passed away a few years ago. He was based here in D.C., but he was diagnosed with pancreatic cancer soon after Rachel came home to us. He sold his practice, shut everything down to try and fight the disease. Sadly, it didn't work out for him," Stevens said.

"That's good information, Mr. Stevens, but still, I need both names. Do you know who was your lawyer working with?"

Kevin Stevens looked at his wife, who nodded. "His name was Rolph Benedict."

* * *

Fletcher called Sam as they left the Stevens house, told her what they'd learned, promised to keep her filled in. Confirming Rachel was adopted, and knowing that Rolph Benedict had brokered the deal, brought many things into focus. They now had proof Mac Picker's firm was involved in baby-brokering. Claire Stevens even admitted they'd paid a hundred thousand dollars for Rachel.

It was a lot of money, but not if you didn't want any trace of the fact that you weren't the biological parents of a child. Rachel's birth certificate listed Claire and Kevin Stevens as her biological mother and father. There were no adoption records at all, no paperwork. Even the money trail had been erased. A child bought with no one the wiser.

Fletcher wondered how many more were out there.

He stared out the window as Jordan drove back into the city. The day was going to be a scorcher, followed by wicked thunderstorms in the late afternoon and early evening. Stormy weather would hamper their search. He wanted to find Rachel before then.

They had all the threads. Now it was time to weave them into some semblance of a fabric everyone could understand. If they could do that, they'd find Rachel Stevens and Kaylie Rousch. And destroy Eden.

CHAPTER 51

Fauquier County, Virginia

BALDWIN ARRIVED AT THE UNHOLY HOUR OF 7:00 A.M. XANDER HAD BEGGED OFF, said he wanted to spend some time on the computer seeing what he could find about Eden and its followers. She knew he was going to do some deeper sleuthing, in places the FBI couldn't legally go. With any luck, they'd all get some answers soon.

He came to the door as Sam was leaving, kissed her, gave her a pat on the bottom and sent her on her way. All she was missing was a lunch box.

She was somewhat refreshed after a few hours of sleep, a hot shower and half a pot of extremely strong Turkish coffee. The bandage on her neck itched. She'd checked the wound and thought it was going to heal fine, possibly without a scar. Her hands hurt, and her shoulders were sore from the struggle with Kaylie, but other than that, she felt good. Jazzed. Everything was coming together, and she was certain they were on the right track at last.

She kept an eye out, knowing Adrian or even Kaylie might be lurking nearby. But the birds were chirping and people flowed up and down the Georgetown streets without a care. She didn't get the sense either of them were nearby.

That's the point, isn't it, Sam? He's a prolific serial killer—he knows how to make himself invisible.

Bravery banished, she hopped into Baldwin's vehicle and triggered the door locks.

He glanced at her but didn't say anything. Once they were over the Key Bridge and driving west on the George Washington Parkway, Sam told Baldwin everything Xander and Fletcher had discovered, and asked him what he hoped to accomplish talking to Anne Carter.

"That's a good question. I don't know, exactly. We're missing something. She was in charge of the operation, had access to all the files, all the intel. It's been ten years. There's a whole new round of leadership in place. More than that, I'm not convinced the files we have are accurate. You know we don't like to commit everything to paper. An agent going rogue is what we fear the most. I'm hoping Carter left something out, something important, that might help us."

"Any news on Rachel?"

His lips tightened. "No. The search resumed at first light. There have been hundreds of tips, and we're chasing them all down, but none has been the one we need. Like Fletch said, Agent Blake is putting together a team to go into the area specified in Kaylie's note. The BOLO on her got us exactly squat. She's quite good at blending in."

"I think you were right. Matcliff had years to teach her military survival tactics. The question is, where do you think she'd headed?"

"Same place we are, when we find out where it is. Eden."

"You know that's where Rachel has to be. Shouldn't we be helping them?"

"I'm happy to let Jordan's team handle the operational stuff. They can't go in without authorization, and that's going to take a while. We'll catch up to them. I have a hunch we're going to find something useful out here. We'll talk to Carter, and then we'll head back and see if they're ready to saddle up. What's Xander really doing?"

She smiled. "You're quick. Most people think he just lazes about by the pool and jogs with the dog."

"He's much too intelligent to waste his time doing nothing. I figure he's been working all the angles this whole time."

"You're right. He has been. So I'll be honest with you. If he's not on the computer digging, he's probably on the road behind us, heading out to Great Falls with Thor."

Baldwin shot her a glance. "Should I let the team know there's a friendly in the woods?"

"You can, but they won't see him. He's like the wind out there. If he finds something worth our time, he'll call in."

"You sure about that?"

She watched the Potomac slip by the highway, the water on its incessant southerly march. "I know him well enough to know we can't put him back into the chain of command and expect him to listen to orders. I will tell you this—he must think highly of you to let me off on my own without an argument. He's been ridiculously overprotective of late, and he wasn't exactly thrilled at your offer to have me join the Bureau."

"Well, when we see him again, I'll tell him I'm honored. You ready to talk about my offer again?"

She grinned at him. "Nope."

Half an hour later, Baldwin's GPS unit, a device he called Lola—because what Lola wants, Lola gets—told them their exit was ahead.

Anne Carter lived on forty acres of prime horse country in Fauquier County. Once they exited the highway, it was a bucolic drive—emerald fields and black fences supplemented by stacked field stones; muscular black and brown horses let out to graze. Gold Cup, the biannual steeplechase event, was coming up in a couple of months, and Sam wondered how many of these beauties would be running.

The country morning wasn't as unbearably hot as it had been in the city, and Sam was enjoying watching the horses scamper about, playing in the fields. They were in Civil War country, the rolling verdant hills still masked with the slightest haze of early morning fog, and despite the clear sense of health and happiness around them, Sam couldn't help feeling the shadow of those lives lost.

Carter's drive was flanked with stone pillars and a twin row of poplars, evenly spaced on either side of the drive to create a multidimensional picture as they drove toward the house. The circular drive held two Range Rovers and a convertible BMW similar to Sam's own, and had plenty of room for more. The cars surrounded a small fountain with a bronze statue of nymphs dancing in the spray.

Carter's home was breathtaking, a slice of old Virginia. The house was set right in the wave of a hill; three stories of fieldstone with black shutters and a black roof, four chimneys pointing up to the sky. There was an arbor visible behind the house, rows and rows of grapes running away from the expansive backyard.

Sam thought she wouldn't mind having a working vineyard on a century-old horse farm. She wouldn't mind it a bit.

Anne Carter met them at the front door wearing a riding habit, the knee-high boots worn and muddied from an early morning ride. Her hair was short and white, eyes as bright blue as Sam had ever seen, her eyebrows still dark despite the white hair, which was slicked back under a headband so it wouldn't interfere with her helmet. Her lips had a hint of red lipstick.

Everything about her, from her house to her barns to her

clothing, was no-nonsense and elegant, a lethal combination. Even her accent was as cultured and Southern as the environs.

"Come in, come in. Let me get you something to drink. It's so beastly hot out there. I can't wait for fall. Just a few more weeks and there will be a bit of relief."

She ushered them into a casual wood-paneled den and made sure they were comfortably seated before handing out tall, cold glasses of tart lemonade.

Baldwin introduced himself and Sam.

Once Carter settled across from them, she said, "I just can't believe what I've been hearing. The news this morning is full of excitement. Kaylie Rousch is alive, and Doug Matcliff was, too? We'd given up on him. I was so torn up when I heard the news. That he was out there alone, thinking we hadn't been in place to help him? It's such a shame. Such a damn shame. And with all this hoopla, I hope this means you're on the right track to find the Stevens girl?"

"About that," Baldwin said. "I don't mean to jump right in—"

"Oh, by all means. We don't have all day. You're on a case. I don't miss it, that's for sure. The pressure, the horror, the intensity day in and day out. I loved what I did, but I was also happy to retire, to buy this farm with my husband and live out here in the quiet where the worst things we have to worry about are whether the grapes are ripe or the horses lame."

Realizing they were waiting patiently for her to finish, she said, "I am so sorry. Forgive an old woman her ramblings. Please, do go on."

Old woman. She couldn't be a day over sixty, and Sam could tell immediately she was as sharp as a tack. So why the artifice?

Baldwin merely nodded. "It's no problem, ma'am. Doug Matcliff wrote to Dr. Owens, and told her he was going to be murdered, and then, of course, he was. We've located, and now lost again, Kaylie Rousch. She's the one who indicated

Matcliff had been checking in regularly to no avail for at least a year after they escaped the NRM."

"Oh, call it by its rightful name, Dr. Baldwin. Eden is a cult, and always was. That woman, Curtis Lott, was as bad as Jim Jones as far as I'm concerned. Letting all those people kill themselves in that barn. She will surely burn in hell for her actions."

"I understand you've been involved in investigating cults before. You were on the task force that went into Jones's Guyana compound after the mass suicide, correct?"

Her eyes grew distant. "Yes, I was. What a scene that was. Jones was the worst sort of fraudster, a drug-addled predator preaching peace, love and harmony among the races, all the while bleeding his followers dry, getting them high and raping their children. We had a chance to take him out once but couldn't get authorization. Think how many people could have been saved if someone had been willing to make the hard choice."

"Was that what happened with Eden? No one was willing to make the hard choice?"

She took a sip of her lemonade. "*I* made the hard choice. But we were too late. Doug must have warned them, briefed them on how it would go down when we came in, that they'd have a window to get everyone dead before we returned with the warrant. They had to be ready to move at a moment's notice, and the skills to evade us could only have come from insider knowledge."

Her tone was bitter, and the faraway gaze was gone, replaced by the anger of a predator who'd missed its prey.

"So you're saying when Doug went native, he went in all the way?" Sam asked.

"Yes. So you can imagine, hearing after all these years that he actually got out and took the Rousch girl with him is confusing, to say the least. If he was so disillusioned, why not come back to us?"

"He was afraid of being prosecuted," Baldwin said.

"Yes, yes, that's the party line, I'm sure. It wouldn't have happened. We would have spent time and money to see him deprogrammed, and he would have been a hero for finding that little girl. He wouldn't have been an agent anymore, but he wouldn't have to stay on the run, either."

Sam couldn't help herself. "What do you really think happened with Doug? You had serious clout. You could have protected him. Surely he knew that."

She took another sip of lemonade. Pointedly avoiding Sam's question, she held up a finger and shook her head.

"I assume you got the parents' permission to exhume the body of the one we messed up on?" she said to Baldwin.

Baldwin nodded. "We have a tentative ID—Jennifer Harvey. Lived in an orphanage in Anacostia, may have gotten caught in the cross fire in a drug deal. We're following up, and Kaylie's stepmother is willing to cooperate if reparations are made. She's a piece of work. We found the father dead in the bedroom. He'd been there for months, if not longer. There's a team liaising with the local homicide office to make sure there was no foul play, but the woman was clearly addled. She hated Kaylie. That much was clear. Said she was a compulsive liar."

Anne leaned forward in her seat. "Did she, now? How very interesting."

CHAPTER 52

SAM WAS FASCINATED BY ANNE CARTER'S SUDDEN CHANGE IN DEMEANOR. IT WAS as if she'd seen an answer to a question Sam and Baldwin hadn't asked yet. She began muttering to herself, quietly, under her breath, like a simmering kettle ready to boil.

Sam leaned back on the sofa. "Why do you say that, ma'am?"

The blue eyes lasered onto Sam. "First, Dr. Owens, tell me, what information did Kaylie Rousch give you about the cult?"

"That they were selling babies. The women were routinely raped in something they called the Reasoning, and the resulting babies were sold off."

"Is she telling the truth?"

Baldwin set his glass on a marble coaster with a clink. "We're looking into it. A trafficking operation of this scale, totally off the record, would take quite a few people to pull off. There would have to be a funnel organization, so to speak, to get the babies to the market, and the money back to the cult. That's a lot of people along the chain to stay silent. We've never seen anything like it."

Carter's eyes narrowed, and she clasped her hands in her lap tightly. "Dr. Owens, you asked what I think happened. Doug could have put the ball in motion for them, then got scared and run. He had a business background, studied economics. We were going to help him get his MBA. He had a strong head for business, and a promising future. It was one of the reasons I brought him along."

"Trafficking is a big charge to level. Did you feel betrayed by his actions?" Sam asked.

"Betrayed?" She huffed out a short laugh. "I'm a grown-up, Dr. Owens. This is a sad reality we sometimes have to acknowledge—people do stupid things for stupid reasons. I suppose Curtis Lott made it worth his while to leave our fold and enter hers."

"But he ran away, then spent a year sending in reports asking for help."

"Was he asking for help? Or was he sending us on a wild-goose chase?"

"That's part of why we're here, Anne," Baldwin said. "The SIGINT from Matcliff indicates he wanted help extracting another girl from the cult."

She looked pained. "If only that were the case. Those girls are dead, Dr. Baldwin. You know that."

"I don't know that, not at all. It wouldn't be unheard of for us to find them alive."

"Now who's kidding whom? You really think the Eden cult would keep them alive, all these years? Use them for this 'Reasoning,' sell their babies? It's preposterous. They are victims, like Kaylie was. She just got lucky, made an impression on Doug somehow, and he got her out. The rest are gone. We searched for them high and low. Each one, each case, thousands of man-hours."

"Yet you were promoted and sent to New York. You weren't

on those cases anymore. Right?" Sam couldn't help prodding the woman; she was holding back on them.

The sharp cheekbones got even more pronounced when Anne Carter pursed her lips. "It's entirely possible Doug Matcliff was behind all of this, you know. We found all sorts of things on his computer when we searched his home."

"Like what?"

"Child pornography, for starters."

"Could the files have been planted?"

Carter sighed, clearly running out of patience. "Dr. Baldwin, you of all people know there are aspects to this case that defy logic. We were tipped off to Eric Wright and the trailer that held Kaylie's things, but it was a setup. I wasn't entirely convinced the photos were Doug's, but when you look at the situation *en totale,* what else were we to think? He went down the rabbit hole and chose not to come out. I always thought he was the one who set up Wright. He knew exactly which buttons to press, and we fell for it."

"That's very possible. And yet, after everything, he chose to come out of the rabbit hole, and not come back to you. Maybe he was afraid you'd given up on him," Baldwin said.

Or framed him, Sam thought, but bit her tongue. She wasn't sure she liked Anne Carter. She had to remind herself the woman had been a star in the upper echelons of the FBI, and you don't get there without being one hell of a good politician in addition to being a good cop. And pragmatic. Anne Carter was nothing if not pragmatic.

Carter waved a hand, dismissing the thought. "So long as he hadn't killed anyone, I would have welcomed him back with open arms and made everything nasty go away. He was a good man, even if he did some stupid things. But if it's true the other girls were in the cult, he wouldn't have risked signal intelligence, which was why, after several months of nonactivity, the channel was closed."

Baldwin couldn't hide the shock in his voice. "You were the one who closed the SIGINT channel? Your only connection to a missing agent?"

"I didn't close it. My successor did. When I found out about it, and looked into the SIGINT, I couldn't disagree with the decision. The last several messages we received were out of sequence, didn't use the appropriate language and codes. Then they stopped completely."

She paused a moment. "I may not have made the same decision if it was mine to make, but I understand what happened. A new system was being put into place. Attempts were made to utilize the channel, but there were no responses. We were dealing with a compromised agent, and we all thought he was dead. After a year of silence, the channel was shut down to protect the Bureau from outside infiltration."

She ran a long finger along the side of the lemonade glass. "Dr. Baldwin, you're a lifer with us. You know that mistakes get made. Looking at the situation now, in hindsight, it's easy to see that was a very bad choice. At the time, it seemed...logical."

Logical. "And that protected quite a few people, didn't it?" Sam blurted out.

Carter stood and stalked around the room. "You didn't know Doug. He was smart, and dedicated to making me believe he wanted to be on my team. Enough that I fell for his lies, too. I always believed if he was alive and knew there were more girls at risk, he would have come to me directly and told me. He may have gotten his own signals crossed, so to speak, but I always thought his moral compass was sound. If he was aware of something terribly untoward going on at Eden, he would have told us. I believed he would come in if it meant saving lives. I was wrong about him. A mistake I'll have to live with for the rest of my days."

"But he did continue sending in information, instead of coming in to you. We're going through his SIGINT now, looking for what he had to say," Baldwin said.

She stiffened a bit, but gracefully covered the movement with a small back stretch. "I was told this morning the new SIGINT traces—with an unauthorized code name, at that—were misleading at best. They were misdirections, lies, and we would have wasted a great deal of time and energy chasing down false leads."

She sat across from Baldwin. "Knowing he's been alive all these years infuriates me. If he wasn't dead, I'd see him prosecuted to the fullest extent of the law. But there is nothing more to be done here. Mistakes were made, and my part in this case is finished. Now, are we through? I have another horse that needs a bit of a frolic."

Baldwin was angry. Sam could see the muscles in his shoulders were tensed. She didn't blame him.

"A shame, isn't it, that your pride and ambition took precedence over retrieving an asset," he said.

Carter's eyes flashed, and her lips thinned into a grim line. "You forget yourself, Dr. Baldwin. I still have friends at the FBI."

He grinned at her, feral and quick. "As do I, Anne. As do I. Just a few more questions, and then we'll leave you to your frolic. Do you know anyone named Frederick McDonald?"

She started to say something, then stopped and watched Baldwin closely. "What do you know about Frederick McDonald?"

"He was one of the beneficiaries named in Doug Matcliff's will. We believe the will was solely designed to lead us through this story to all the players. So far, we've identified each one—and they're all either dead or close to it. Who is he?"

She leaned back in her seat, the soft old leather easing with a small squeak. "McDonald was a bagman for the Dixie Mafia. He got out, supposedly, though do they ever get out? He set himself up a nice little operation in Asheville, North Carolina, running moonshine out of the mountains, of all things. We turned him, and he was a very helpful informant over the years."

"What did he inform about?"

"Dixie business. Drug running, mostly. Supply chains. He helped us wrap up several elaborate operations, and he was rewarded for his troubles with a clean slate. I've often wondered what happened to him. He seemed like an intelligent man, happy to have a chance to start his life over."

"He's dead now. Someone broke into his house and turned his head the wrong way around last night."

She didn't look terribly surprised. "That is a shame. Clearly he didn't keep himself on the straight and narrow, after all. But I haven't heard his name for many years. And I'm afraid I have nothing more of use for you." She stood, signaling the end of the interview. Smiled at them both graciously, let a bit of Southern pleasantness back into her steely tone. "If you find out anything more, or need more help, please don't hesitate. This case seems quite complex. There's nothing I'd like more than to hear those little girls are actually alive after all this time. But I'm not going to hold out hope."

The interview was over. Baldwin stood, as well. "Anne, Adrian Zamyatin is systematically eliminating everyone on Matcliff's list. Your name is on it, front and center. I have a couple of agents on their way out here to watch your back until this is all finished."

She opened her mouth to protest, then sighed. "That will be fine. Thank you."

She walked them out, and waved as they climbed into Baldwin's car. Sam watched her smile disappear when she thought she was out of sight.

"Pride goeth before a fall, eh?" Sam said.

"You know it. Man, they really screwed up on this one."

"She could have been more forthcoming. She knew more than she said. At this point, what does telling the truth matter?"

"Anne is making sure her ass is covered in case this all blows up and she's called to testify. She gambled and lost the chess match with her boy wonder. It stands to reason there will be fallout."

"She's lost more than that, if those girls really are dead. I can't believe she'd play games with their lives."

Baldwin gave her a shrewd look. "Lesson one. Not everything in the FBI is what it seems."

They headed down the winding drive, back onto the main road toward the highway, both lost in their own thoughts.

"You didn't tell me about Frederick McDonald. That he was killed," Sam said finally.

"Sorry. June Davidson called early this morning. McDonald tripped his silent alarm last night, which called the police to his house, but it was too late when they arrived. He was dead, and there was a trail of blood out of his basement into the woods. A shotgun by his side had been discharged, so we believe he took a shot at someone, and hit him, before he was taken down. Lab down there's pulling samples and sending them to us."

He pulled the car onto Interstate 66 and headed east.

"This doesn't feel like a serial killer on a spree, does it? Someone is cleaning house. First Doug is killed, which he knew was coming, then everyone who was involved with him in this scheme, peripherally or otherwise, gets taken out," Sam said.

"You're probably right. The question is, who's running the show?"

"Curtis Lott?"

He nodded. "Until we locate the cult, and find Adrian Zamyatin, we're at a loss there, too. We need to be able to take Curtis Lott into custody and talk to her, find out the true story. See if the girls are still alive. If this is a massive supply chain of babies into a black market, we're going to be arresting a lot of people."

"Supply chain." Sam tapped her fingers on the dashboard. "Anne Carter said Frederick McDonald was in charge of the drug running for the Dixie Mafia. If he knew how to move product from importer to distributor, he might know how to move something more esoteric. Like babies."

"It's very possible."

"Someone will be given immunity to rat out everyone working on this. Baldwin, you can't let them do that. Everyone involved is culpable here. They all need to be punished."

"I know, Sam. I know. But our witnesses are being knocked off before we can get to them."

Sam was quiet for a moment. "Do you think Adrian is going to go after Anne Carter? Or will he be coming for us instead, thinking we're keeping Kaylie from him?"

He rubbed his hand through his hair, spiking it up, and looked downright miserable. "I honestly don't know."

CHAPTER 53

Washington, D.C.

THERE WERE MEDIA VANS LURKING AROUND FBI HEADQUARTERS. FLETCHER wondered what the press knew about Kaylie Rousch and Doug Matcliff, but didn't let it get in the way. Lisa Schumann had a scoop, and the rest of the D.C. media machine was churning, as well.

Thankfully they all hadn't been peeping in his windows last night. A female FBI agent spending the night at a D.C. homicide cop's place? All sorts of misunderstandings might ensue. Then again, this was D.C. What was shocking and inappropriate in some places was de rigueur for this town.

Jordan drove under the building, parked and got Fletcher checked in and into the elevator, but she was clearly lost in thought. When they hit her floor, she crooked a finger and said, "Come on. I have an idea."

"About what?"

"How to find Eden. And, hopefully, Kaylie Rousch."

She pulled him into her office, closed the door. "It was in the SIGINT from Matcliff. Something about beginnings and endings circling back."

"All right. What does that mean to you?"

"I'm not sure. But there was something else. Remember he used the word *Geddon* several times?"

"Yeah. So what's Geddon?"

"That's what I want to find out. Maybe it's a person, not a word."

She put a red thumb drive into the slot on her computer and booted it up. "We have two networks. One's public. That's the green side. One's secure, totally private, for classified information, interagency stuff. That's the red side. We're going in the red side, so don't try to check your Facebook, okay?"

"Ha-ha. You're going to see if there's a mention of Geddon in the files?"

"You're a smart cookie, Fletch. That's exactly what I'm doing."

She pulled up a database and typed the name into her search field. The computer cooked for a second, then started spitting out a list of files. Jordan leaned in closer to the screen, touched the tip of her finger to the list.

"Oh, wow. Bingo," she said.

"What is it?"

"Geddon is a holding company owned by…come on, you guess."

"I have no idea."

"Oh, Fletch. You're no fun. Arthur Scarron's family trust."

"Ah. So what does it do?"

"Manages all the properties the Scarron family owns."

So that's why Scarron was named in Matcliff's will. "Okay, now let me guess. The property holdings match the places where girls went missing?"

"Exactamundo. And there's a nice little parcel of land out

in Great Falls. Matches the latitude and longitude of the mark on the map Kaylie Rousch left for us."

Thurber knocked on her door and came in, looking exhausted. "You eat? Someone left some pizza in the conference room."

"I never say no to cold pizza. First, though, I've got something. And don't get pissed, but I filled Fletcher in on the other girls. He couldn't operate without that knowledge. I made a judgment call."

Rob narrowed his eyes at her. "We'll discuss that later. Show me what you have."

She laid it all out for him. "It's early, but this is it. I can feel it. Matcliff did tell us the truth, after all. Everything matches, including the site in Great Falls. Rachel Stevens must be out there. And the rest of Eden, too."

Thurber made her show him each step, then nodded and cracked what would be called a smile if he had the energy to make it meet his eyes.

"Hell of a catch, Jordan. I'll take it to the brass, see if we can't add this to the warrant. It might speed things up. When we saw Kaylie Rousch's tip, we went ahead and mapped the property. It's a good fit for the type of land Eden liked to settle. Unplugged and out of the way."

"That's good. When do we go in?" Fletcher asked.

"Soon as the paperwork's ready. Everyone is gearing up. We reconvene in thirty. Good work, Jordan. You too, Detective. Go get some coffee, or that leftover pizza, clear your brains."

"Will do."

Thurber left and Jordan gave Fletcher a dazzling smile. "That went better than I expected. We've got her. I know Rachel's out there. We're going to find her, and she's going to be okay. I can just feel it. Let's go take a look at the maps in the conference room. I'm sure there's something there with specifics so we can start thinking about where on the property they might be holding her."

They walked down to the empty conference room and started combing the maps staked to the corkboards.

The FBI had been busy since Fletcher had left the night before. Thurber hadn't been kidding when he said they were moving on the Rousch girl's tip.

Some of the maps he could interpret himself. Others had shapes he didn't recognize.

Jordan was standing in front of a green-tinged aerial shot with small gray markings on it. "Oh, look at this. They are patrolling the borders of the land." She used a white grease pencil to sketch out a perimeter for his eyes to follow.

His mind made sense of things. "The gray blobs are people?"

"Yep."

Fletcher cracked open a Diet Coke and handed it to Jordan. She set down the pencil, took the chilly can absently with her left hand. She grabbed a slice of cold pepperoni pizza with her right.

"See this, right here?" She used the can to point to a spot on the map. Her mouth was full, the words a bit garbled, but he got the gist.

She swallowed. "I think this is our entry point. The satellite imagery shows no guards in this area for the past several hours. We have a shot if we move quickly. We can come in overland, through the woods, get a surrender and retrieve the girl."

"You mean you and I can slip in the back while the rest are engaged up front?"

"That's right." She took a sip of soda. "We'll be able to go straight to the house through the field. They're not going to be watching the back when all the attention is on their front gate."

"Don't underestimate Curtis Lott. I think this woman will have that house guarded six ways to Sunday. I can't imagine we're going to have a shot at getting close without taking a few of her people out."

"We'll coordinate with our hostage rescue team. HRT will throw some flash bangs in there, gas them, knock them out. Then we'll be safe to take Rachel."

"What about the rest of the cult?"

"They're down and get arrested. After we get the girl, the rest isn't my problem."

She set the can down and turned toward him. "What do you think?"

"I think you're crazy. But I like it. Here."

She had a crumb on her lip. He brushed it off with the pad of his thumb. She didn't move. Her eyes were locked on his, and he realized he had the most insane urge to kiss her.

She knew it, too. She smiled when he furrowed his brow and dropped his gaze.

"I won't hit you if you kiss me, you know."

His head shot up. "What?"

"You heard me," she said, then leaned in and touched his lips with hers.

A shock of desire flooded his body, and without thinking he gathered her in his arms and deepened the kiss. She fit against him well, and her arms immediately snaked around his neck so they were pressed together, every exquisite inch from knees to lips. She was strong and soft and smelled like lilacs.

One of her hands dropped to his hip and he realized he was getting dizzy. They shouldn't be doing this. Someone might walk in.

Don't think, Fletch. Just go with it.

Her back was long and smooth and he ached to feel her skin. Carefully, he pulled her shirt out of her pants so he could run his knuckles along her rib cage. She sighed and relaxed into him, accepting, allowing, and he had to stop himself from bending her backward over the conference table, stripping off her pants and forgetting everything for a while.

Breath coming in short gasps, he said, "No chance you locked that door, did you?"

She laughed quietly. Her hands went to the front of his shirt. She laid her palms on his flat stomach. "Where's the fun in that?"

He kissed her again, ran his hands down her back and around to the front. "Why the hell do you wear pants all the time?"

"Because I wanted to see how long it would take for you to try to get into them."

That was it. He was lost. "I think I have a crush on you, Special Agent Jordan Blake."

They heard noises in the hall and broke apart, giggling like schoolkids.

He'd pulled her hair out of its ponytail holder. It was mussed around her face, and her cheeks were flushed. Very fetching. He watched her search for the small rubber band, and it was all he could do not to walk over to her, unbutton her shirt and take things further.

"You are thinking dirty thoughts," she said, smiling. She looked down, around her feet. "Where the hell is that thing?"

He also glanced down, trying to remember. He'd pulled it out of her hair and tossed it…to the right. He followed the remembered trajectory and spotted it on an empty chair. He handed it to her sheepishly and she kissed him again, quick and hard.

"That was fun. We should do it again sometime," she said.

"I have the next five minutes free."

She laughed, a throaty sound that got him going all over again, but they heard voices, coming closer this time, and quick, heavy footsteps. Jordan was suddenly in motion, tucking and straightening. By the time Thurber walked in, they were calmly eating cold pizza and sipping on their flat Diet Cokes, and Jordan was pointing at the map again.

God, he was in so far over his head.

Thurber tossed a sheet of paper at them. "We got the warrant. HRT is already suited up. They'll meet us out there. We need to stake out the land. We roll in fifteen. Be ready. You hit the spot?"

Fletcher looked down so Jordan wouldn't catch his eye and start laughing and blow this whole thing.

"Yeah, I've got it," she said. "There's a tunnel on the easement to the property we should be able to sneak through. They might have guards on the other side, but as of the last satellite pass, it was devoid of living beings. If they are there, we can take them out without a problem. Then it's a clear shot into the farmhouse."

"Good. Suit up and get downstairs. Get Detective Fletcher a vest, too."

"Are you inviting me along?"

Thurber's face was like granite. "You worked this case, didn't you? Yeah, you're in. Now get your shit together and let's roll. Brass is putting together the ROE right now."

He stalked out of the room.

"ROE?" Fletcher asked.

"Rules of engagement. How we approach, what the shooters are allow to do. Self-defense, shoot to kill, whatever they decree is what we all have to stick to."

"They'll try negotiating first, right?"

"Absolutely. Which is why you and I are going to get out there and find Rachel Stevens. You trained for SWAT by any chance?"

"Yeah, but it's been a few years."

"Our HRTs are built on a similar premise. They're badasses. They deploy all over the world at a moment's notice to save our citizens. They're the best at what they do. We'll follow their lead."

"We need to call Sam and Baldwin."

She had her phone out already. "On it."

She'd slipped back into straitlaced FBI agent mode. Not that he blamed her. But he was definitely interested to see where this might lead. He hadn't been all that perturbed when Andi told him she was lighting out for New York and they could play things by ear. He realized if Jordan said the same thing, he'd be pretty pissed. *Interesting.*

He listened to her talking to Baldwin and Sam, liked the sound of her voice when she got all bossy—a lot. Shook his head and grinned to himself.

Fletcher, you are such an idiot.

CHAPTER 54

Interstate 66
Northern Virginia

THEY WERE NEARING THE EXIT SOUTH TO LYNCHBURG WHEN BALDWIN'S CELL RANG.

"It's Jordan." He put it on speaker. "What's up?"

"Kaylie Rousch's map was right on the money, and Doug Matcliff left a bread crumb trail in his SIGINT no one bothered to follow. We looked at the property records in Great Falls. They're in the name of a trust, run through a shell company. The forensic accountants are on it, tearing apart the details. So far, they've been able to tie several holdings in several states to this shell company. Want to guess where?"

"Virginia, Texas, Colorado, Arkansas and Kentucky."

"You got it. All of which are held by...drumroll please...the Scarron Family Trust."

"Well, I'll be damned. What sort of warrant did you get?"

"Broad scope. Covers everything. We aren't taking any chances. Exigent circumstances, too, since we think Rachel

Stevens might be there. They're pulling together the ROE right now. We won't get any pushback. In the meantime, we have some excellent satellite shots from early this morning. There are several people wandering around the area, looks like guards. Armed guards."

"This is all good news."

"Yep. There's more. There's a small outbuilding, and thermal imaging shows at least fifteen people there. The main house has a couple of people in it, too, and more bodies in other outbuildings."

"So we're up to twenty, twenty-two? What are the guards armed with?"

"Don't know. But this isn't exactly a normal setup for a parcel of undeveloped land."

"Any confirmation or sighting of Rachel Stevens?"

"Negative. But we've got convergence on three levels, and I've got a gut feeling she's in there, just waiting for us to bust in and save her. Do you want in? We're rolling now."

"On my way. And, Jordan, you need to be mindful of the situation. This woman hasn't hesitated to eliminate her followers before. We don't want another Ruby Ridge."

"Trust me, none of us do."

Baldwin hung up and put his foot on the gas. "Now might be a good time to call Xander."

Sam already had her phone out. Xander didn't answer. She left him a quick message. "FBI confirmed the land out in Great Falls is owned by a shell holding company. They're pretty convinced this is the spot. Be careful. You're about to have a mass convergence, including FBI HRT. Call me."

She hung up, fiddled with the phone. "Baldwin, what if this isn't what we think it is?"

"What do you mean?"

"Something Kaylie's mother said has been bothering me.

That she was a compulsive liar. Anne Carter reacted to that information, too."

He glanced over at her. "Go on."

"Honestly, Maureen Rousch is a miserable excuse for a human being, but what did she have to gain by telling us this? She certainly wasn't interested in currying favor. And Kaylie has shown herself to be less than honest."

"You think we're running into a setup?"

She chewed on a fingernail for a second, thinking. "Kaylie was abused, abandoned, raped. She spent the past decade on the run with a disgruntled ex-cult member who has an ax to grind against the FBI. She showed up at a very convenient moment, dumped a lot of fascinating information on us that we'd be sure to immediately follow up on, including claiming Rachel Stevens was her child. Then she attacked me, stole my clothes and money and disappeared. What if she's not what she says? Or who she says?"

"Then we need to be especially careful going forward."

"I still don't understand why Doug Matcliff chose me, of all people, to drag into this."

"We may never know the answer to that, Sam. But thank goodness he did, because without you, we wouldn't be aware of any of this. It might have been years, or never, until we put it all together. We all owe you one."

Xander called as they raced into D.C., Baldwin speeding across the George Washington Bridge, the flasher spinning on his dash.

The connection wasn't great and she didn't catch the first few words. Then he came into range.

"...tell them to be very cautious. These people have serious ammunition. I made five guards with AK-47s, AR-15s, sidearms and grenades on the western front. Assume there are more around the periphery."

"Where are you now, Xander?"

"Three clicks south of their compound. They have it locked down completely. You're going to have to fight your way in."

"We can't do that," Baldwin said. "We have to try to negotiate with them. We can't just go in there blasting."

"They don't look like the negotiating type, Baldwin. I'm looking for a way to breach the perimeter. I'll call you back if I find anything."

"Xander, pull out. We've got this. I can't have you getting hurt," Baldwin said.

Xander laughed. "I'll worry about my own skin. There's a lot of land to protect. I'm sure there are going to be a few ingress routes they can't cover. I only count twenty people, but they're all heavily armed. I'll be in touch."

"Stand down, Sergeant," Baldwin shouted, but it was too late; he was already gone. "Damn. Does he do that often?"

Sam nodded. "Ignore the orders of those in charge to do it his own way? That would be a yes."

Baldwin pulled into the garage below the Hoover Building. "Get him back on the phone and tell him to get his ass out of there. We can't move against them effectively if we have a civilian in the mix."

Sam shook her head. "He's an asset, and he won't stand down. You know that. So use him. He knows what he's doing and he's got the eyes of an eagle. You get him tied in to the strike team and he'll get your people in and out without them getting killed. This is what he does best, Baldwin. Trust me."

He tapped his hand on the steering wheel. "I suppose you're going to want to come along for the ride, too?"

"Of course. You may need me."

She didn't mention she was only good at working on the dead. She hoped there wouldn't be a need for her particular skills.

* * *

As they suited up, June Davidson called with more information.

Baldwin put him on the speaker.

"Two things. Ellie Scarron woke up an hour ago. You aren't going to believe the story she just told me."

"Let me guess," Sam said. "Her husband was funding an illegal adoption ring, run out of the law offices of our friend Mac Picker."

Davidson was clearly caught off guard. "How'd you figure that out?"

"It's a long story. But we think Kaylie Rousch is Rachel Stevens's mother, and she, along with a number of other women who were a part of the new religious movement the FBI's been tracking called Eden, were being impregnated and forced to give up their babies."

"And they've been running this out of Lynchburg? Under my nose? Son of a bitch!"

"It looks that way," Baldwin said. "We don't know how deep this goes, Detective, so watch your back. Our forensic accountants are gathering everything they can from the law firm's databases, so do not, under any circumstances, tell anyone what we suspect. Our paramount issue is finding the NRM and recovering Rachel Stevens alive. Then we'll go around the back end and mop up the rest. Are we clear?"

"So what am I supposed to do down here, just twiddle my thumbs while y'all rush in and save the day?"

"No. I want you to start taking apart Scarron's life, and see where and if it matches up with Doug Matcliff."

"Hold up a minute. Ellie Scarron already told me her husband was a saint. He put infertile women in contact with the law offices so they could work a private adoption. He even funded part of the operation. But when the firm started getting more and more kids, they reached out to him to start finding more adoptive mothers, and he started asking questions. She's fully convinced he was murdered."

Sam was surprised. "So Scarron was the good guy in all of this, just trying to help women? You think he was legitimate?"

"I don't know. But it bears looking into. He died here in Lynchburg. I'm going to reopen the case as a homicide, throw some resources to it, see what we can dig up. Don't worry, I'll do it quietly. It looked like a heart attack, and he was cremated, so there's no chance of repeating the autopsy, but perhaps they still have the samples and slides."

"Cremated? Where?"

"Hoyle's. Where else."

She hated to hear that. She liked Regina Hoyle. It was too early to assume she'd been on the wrong end of this, but even the thought made Sam's stomach curdle. "Do we need to be looking at them, too, June?" Sam asked.

"Yep. Don't worry, I'll get everything cooking down here. So, the second thing, I'm pretty sure the man who killed Frederick McDonald is long gone. There was a blood trail from the house to a spot that had a surveillance camera. A Nissan Pathfinder with a Virginia license plate was parked there overnight. Looks like even though the killer was wounded, he made it back to his car and got out of Dodge."

"That's a good catch, Detective," Baldwin said.

"Yeah, well, McDonald refused our protection, but we were on the lookout for anything suspicious near his house. Don't tell anyone this, but one of my patrol guys saw the truck earlier in the night and thought it looked out of place, so he took down the plate and put a GPS tracker under the wheel well. The signal stopped emitting an hour ago near Great Falls, Virginia. Turned off like it had been damaged, or discovered. So you might consider watching your backs, too."

"Roger that, Detective. We'll be in touch." Baldwin looked at Sam. "This just gets better and better, doesn't it?"

CHAPTER 55

Near Great Falls, Virginia

EDEN'S NEW HEADQUARTERS WAS ON THE FRINGE OF CIVILIZATION. THERE WERE well-populated areas less than fifteen minutes to the west, south and east. To the north, across the Potomac River into Maryland, was an upscale country club community. They were surrounded by normalcy, harmony, life. But back in the woods where their little farm was secreted, time had been arrested. The land was completely undeveloped, pristine. There were no power lines running into the compound, no sewer or water, either. They were living off the land, land purchased and owned by Arthur Scarron's trust.

The entrance to the compound was on a dirt track deep in the woods, its access blocked by a silver three-bar gate. And though there was no power, there was a camera pointed toward the road, and a small metal arm reaching from the ground with a box on top. Either this was meant to be a deterrent, or they were running everything off generators.

Pull up to the gate, get seen by the cameras, speak into the box and presto, the gate would open and Eden would accept you into their land. It all looked so simple, Sam thought.

Except things weren't going to be nearly that easy.

Operation Angel Fire, as this incursion had been named, was well under way. Sam sat on the hood of Baldwin's car, safely out of the way, watching the melee. There were federal agents everywhere, helicopters flying in and out, assault vehicles rolling up the road. The FBI wasn't exactly being subtle. She thought that was risky. A magnificent show of force might make Curtis Lott and her people come out of their compound unharmed, bringing Rachel Stevens with them. Or it could drive them into a mass suicide, as the Edenites had done before.

The head of the HRT was a thick-necked man named Brian Cole. Ten minutes earlier, he and his crew had flown in on an MH-6 Little Bird, the men bristling with weapons, M-4s cradled in their arms, Colt 1911 .45s strapped to their thighs. There was also a gorgeous German shepherd named Dry, sitting patiently by his handler's feet, tongue lolling out of his mouth to combat the heat.

Sam expected the HRT to be aggressive and mouthy, but she was totally wrong. Cole was quite mellow, giving instructions in a calm voice. There were smiles and clear respect from his men. On his command, his team separated themselves into two units. A sniper/observation team stalked off into the woods, weapons up, to get the lay of the land. An assault team began making their preparations, laying out extensive maps and satellite imagery, drawing on the paper with grease pencils. To Sam, their markings looked more like an SEC football play than a deadly assault.

Rob Thurber and Jordan Blake were off to one side, deep in discussion. Fletcher was standing by Jordan. Sam couldn't help noticing Fletch glance at the FBI agent every so often, even when she wasn't speaking. There was a clear attraction between them, though Sam could see Jordan was doing her best to remain neutral. *Interesting.*

Unlike her less than charitable thoughts this morning, she realized Jordan would be really good for Fletcher. Smart, pretty, clearly a hotshot at the FBI. Sam thought she was a better match for him than the incredibly intense and sometimes overbearing Andrea Bianco.

Baldwin walked up, his body armor in place. Sam was wearing a bulletproof vest, too, and was chafing in the heat.

"You okay? Any word from Xander?" he asked.

"Nothing yet." She tried to keep her tone light, but she was very worried.

"He's fine, I'm sure. Like you said, he knows what he's doing. Everyone here is aware that he's in the field, and what he looks like, so don't worry. The rules of engagement have been laid out, and they are very tight and very specific. This is a rescue mission, and everyone is under strict orders not to shoot at anything unless in extreme self-defense. With any luck, we'll be able to get in and out without any bloodshed."

"Any sightings of our friend in the Pathfinder?"

He shook his head. "Maybe he bolted. The truck was found several miles away. It's possible he found himself another ride and left the area."

"No way. From everything we know, Adrian Zamyatin isn't the kind to run from a fight. These people are his home, his world. He'll be back, if he hasn't already managed to get in. He could be waiting for us."

"Or he could be lying dead on the side of the road somewhere. You heard Davidson. He'd been shot badly enough to leave a trail of blood to the car. There's a good chance he had to stop for medical help."

Sam watched the second HRT unit start moving into the woods, the dog, Dry, going first. Thurber went with them, Jordan and Fletcher following at a respectful distance.

"What's their plan?" she asked.

"Thurber's going in as the hostage negotiator. He knows the most about this group. He's even had contact with Curtis Lott before. They're going to have a chat with her, get her to surrender herself and her people, then start searching for Rachel."

"Where the hell is Kaylie Rousch?"

Baldwin looked around as if she might appear. "No idea."

Sam drummed her fingers on the hood of the car. "So what am I supposed to do out here? Sit around and wait?"

"Yep. And keep trying to connect with Xander." He press checked his Glock out of sheer habit, made sure he had a bullet in the chamber, then holstered the weapon. "I'm going in with them. You sit tight, and keep out of harm's way."

Being left behind annoyed her more than she could express. Her face must have shown her thoughts, because Baldwin thrust a radio into her hands. "You can listen. But they'd have my ass if I let you come into the extraction zone. You're not FBI. Not yet, anyway. You shouldn't be here at all. So don't fight me on this, okay?"

"Sure. I'll just sit here like a good little girl, wait for the menfolk to do the hard work."

"Sam. We're trying to keep you safe."

"I know." She sighed. "Doesn't mean I have to like it."

He patted her on the knee and jogged off into the woods after the rest of them.

She wasn't alone. There were plenty of people milling about, support staff doing the procedural end of things—setting up tables and cameras, checking radios. She was safe enough. But damn it, she wanted to be where the action was.

It would take the team an hour to hike in and get into position, barring unforeseen problems. Xander was out here somewhere, with Thor at his side. Safe, she was sure, but it had been hours since he last checked in. Granted, there weren't any cell towers out here. Though surely he'd heard the *thwap, thwap,*

thwap of the Little Bird chopper when it came into range, and knew the cavalry had arrived.

She waited for ten minutes or so, realized she needed to go to the bathroom. At least she was in the woods. She could find herself a quiet tree.

She slid off the hood of Baldwin's car, leaving the radio behind so she'd have some privacy. Twenty yards into the woods, she unbuckled her jeans and laughed to herself. Before Xander, she would have held it until she found a bathroom. Preferably with marble fixtures. She'd learned living in the woods did have its advantages.

"Fancy meeting you here."

The voice came from behind her, and Sam froze. She pulled her jeans up and turned slowly. Kaylie Rousch was leaning against a tree, wearing one of Sam's good cashmere T-shirts, and the knee-high cognac riding boots she'd bought on a trip to New York two summers earlier.

Kaylie didn't look like a scared little girl on the run anymore. She looked very much in control of the situation, and Sam knew she was at a disadvantage.

"You little bitch," Sam said. "You could have killed me last night. After everything I did for you, you shove a knife in my throat and steal from me?"

She couldn't help it, her fists clenched and she took a step forward.

Kaylie danced backward. "Ooh, someone's testy today. It wasn't stealing, Doc. Borrowing. The first time my daughter sees me, I can't look like a beggar who's been camping in the woods. You understand."

"I want my watch back."

Kaylie brushed her left hand past her hair, smoothing the edges, and Sam saw the weapon in her right hand. She thought it was a Glock .40, but she didn't have Xander's talent for recognizing every gun on sight. It was definitely a semiautomatic. Not good.

She stopped her advance, went for casual. "Where'd you get the gun?"

"Oh, there's always someone willing to make a trade in this world. Only cost me a hundred bucks for the gun and two magazines of ammo. I'm telling you, these D.C. boys know how to make it worth your while. I didn't even have to throw in your precious watch."

Kaylie unclasped the TAG Heuer watch from her wrist and tossed it to Sam, laughing.

A chill went down Sam's spine. She caught the watch and put it on. Just having the stainless-steel and gold links around her wrist made her feel safer. She knew she needed to distract the girl, make her put the weapon down. Sam might be able to wrestle it away from her, but she was hesitant to get into hand-to-hand combat. Kaylie seemed different today. Much less fragile.

"What's your plan, Kaylie? There are fifty FBI agents roaming these woods, all well armed and better trained than you."

She smiled. "Oh, I know. I need them. They're a perfect diversion."

"What do you mean?"

"Come on, Dr. Owens. You have to admit, you're a bit predictable. I give you one crumb about my daughter, and look at what you can do. Bravo, madam. You've laid it all out on a platter for me. The FBI gets everyone all riled up and looking forward, and I go in the back. Doug explained to me how their incursions work. I know where everyone is right now."

"You're crazy if you think this is going to work, Kaylie."

The girl's face darkened, and she leaped forward so quickly Sam barely had time to put an arm up in defense. Kaylie grabbed her hair and yanked her head back, setting the barrel of the gun against Sam's throat. Sam froze.

Kaylie spoke through gritted teeth. "Don't ever call me crazy. Now. It would be very nice if you'd come with me, Dr. Owens."

Sam shook her head, felt the hard metal biting into her skin. "Not going to happen, Kaylie. Let's go back to the clearing, let them know you're here and safe. Let the professionals do their job."

"You don't get it, do you?" She pressed the gun harder, pushing against the knife wound, making Sam suck in her breath in pain. Shit. Sam needed to manage the situation, keep Kaylie from doing something stupid. Like killing her.

"Curtis will kill Rachel before she lets her be taken by the FBI," Kaylie said. "She hasn't ever hesitated to sacrifice the sacrosancts before. She won't start now."

Sam was reminded of Thurber's description of the barn, and the people of Eden hanging from its rafters.

"You think she's going to let *you* have her instead?"

"Yes, I do." She lessened the pressure of the gun slightly, but her hand was still caught up in Sam's hair. Her voice was calm, assured. "Curtis took Rachel to get me to come back. An eye for an eye. That's what Curtis believes in. The only way this goes down is if I sacrifice myself for Rachel. So I need you to come along with me and help with the exchange."

She pushed Sam away, but kept the weapon pointed at her. "I know you're going to help me. You're a good person, Dr. Owens. You'll do the right thing."

Sam wasn't having any of this. Kaylie was as twisted as Curtis Lott. She needed to keep her talking, keep her from trying to storm the compound, with Sam in tow. That was an assured death for them both.

"If you think I'm going to let you threaten me into helping you, you're out of your mind. They'll kill us."

"It has to be this way! The minute Adrian figures out what's happening, he'll slit the throats of everyone in Eden with that nasty garrote of his. Rachel won't be given any mercy."

Kaylie gestured toward the woods with the gun. "Now, start walking, Dr. Owens. And don't you dare scream for help. Or I swear to all that's holy I will shoot you dead and leave your body in these woods for the wolves to find."

Sam began to walk.

CHAPTER 56

AS THEY WENT DEEPER AND DEEPER INTO THE FOREST, KAYLIE WAS SILENT. SAM focused on scrambling through the brambles and over the fallen logs, chiding herself for being so stupid.

She should have told someone she was leaving to go to the bathroom. No one would miss her. No one would even know she was gone until Baldwin and Fletcher came back. They all had their own roles to play. They weren't watching out for her.

Sam tried to gauge where they were headed. It seemed as if they were walking away from the entrance gate, not toward it. The trees surrounded them. It was cooler under their branches. Flies and gnats lit upon her, making a meal out of her exposed arms and neck.

She debated the different ways she could disarm Kaylie, and when to make her move. She decided to see where they were headed first, to be sure she didn't screw up and get hurt, or killed, in the middle of nowhere. They'd need to follow the vultures to find her, and Xander would be furious with her.

Kaylie hadn't taken Sam's phone away from her. She hoped to

find a chance to send a text or dial 911, but she'd need seclusion to do it, if she could even get service deep in the woods. No, she'd be better off catching the girl off guard and overpowering her. Sam could do it—she had a great deal of training—but again, she wanted to wait until they were someplace easily accessible to the teams in the field.

As if she knew the mental space was sufficient for Sam to plot an escape, Kaylie started to talk.

"What is it like, doing an autopsy?"

Play along, Sam. You'll get your chance.

"Messy," she said.

"Is there blood? I always figured once a body was dead and gone, there wasn't any more blood pumping through the heart."

"The human body contains about five liters of blood. Unless there's an incidence of exsanguination, small or large, that blood stays in the body. So yes, there's quite a bit of blood."

"Was there a lot of blood in Doug when you cut him open?"

"No more than the usual," Sam said. "Why?"

"What did he look like inside? He was very health-conscious."

"His body showed that."

"What about cancer? Did he have cancer?"

The sun was shifting in the sky; Sam saw the dappling on the leaves moving farther down the trees. Great. They were heading into late-afternoon now. How long had they been gone?

"I didn't see anything that indicated cancer. But there are many different kinds. It's possible. We'd have to run tests on his blood to know for sure."

"But there was nothing that looked like cancer to you? No tumors, no lesions?"

"No. Why are you asking?"

Kaylie bit her lip and didn't respond right away. "Why did you decide to become a pathologist?" she asked, finally. "That's the right word, yes?"

Sam clambered over a log. "Yes, that's right. I found the inner workings of the body of interest."

"That's all? 'Of interest?' Come on, Doc. We have a ways to go. Tell me the truth. Why do you do it? Why do you cut people open and peer into their bodies? It seems like a grave invasion of privacy to me."

What's with this line of questioning? "I do it to give peace to the ones who need it. So many people are killed, so many are hurt, or die alone. Without me, there are no answers. I give the body a last moment to explain itself, to share what happened, and why. Then the loved ones will know, and are able to mourn their dead and move on with their lives. It is very satisfying."

"That makes sense. Doug taught me a lot about anatomy, what went where. He thought it might be useful if something happened to us."

"He was right, it is useful. What else did Doug teach you?"

Sam glanced over her shoulder. Kaylie waved the pistol to indicate she was to keep moving.

"Kaylie, can we stop? I'm thirsty. I hear water."

"No. Keep walking. You'll be fine. Doug taught me a lot of things. He was kind to me. He read to me. He showed me how to grow things. How to manage money, how to stay off the grid. How to be my own person. How to heal from all the horrible things that happened to me. The things Curtis did to me, and Adrian." She went silent. "Doug was a good man. He loved me, and I loved him. I have no one to tell my truths to anymore."

"Tell *me*, Kaylie. Tell *me* about Eden. Tell *me* what happened to you."

"I already did tell you."

"I don't think you've told me everything. Why did Doug decide to take you away from Eden? Why you, and no one else? He could have saved everyone. He could have stopped

Curtis and her awful operation in its tracks. Why did he disappear with you?"

"Because he loved me."

"He loved you so much he decided to get himself killed and expose you. Why, Kaylie? Why now? Why me? He could have gone straight to the FBI and shut it all down. Instead he's playing some sort of sick game from the grave, dragging all of us into this situation. People could die today. Can you comprehend that? The FBI isn't playing around. Your daughter is in that compound, and she could be killed. Help me understand."

"He was ill. It was eating him alive. It was time."

Her voice was atonal, eerie.

"Time for what?"

"Time for the Reckoning. He wanted it to stop. He ate the wafer of life, and it told him this was the time to stop the Reckoning."

"You're not making sense, Kaylie. What's the Reckoning?"

"When a child is brought into the fold. For Adrian. And when the Reckoning is finished, Adrian is sent to the Great Sacrifice."

"Which is?"

"He is allowed."

"Allowed what?"

"I cannot say. When we accept the mark we have the blood of Eden in our veins. It is sacrilege to speak of the Great Sacrifice. It is the one thing we are not allowed to know of."

"You're not a part of Eden anymore, Kaylie."

The girl shuddered. "I know that. I am one of the lost, forever damned. I will never be able to stop wandering. Eden cast me out, the world cast me out, even Doug left me. I am unclean. I am doomed."

"That's not true. You are a victim, and you didn't do anything wrong."

"You don't understand." Her voice went up an octave, tears

threatening. "I will never be normal. I will never be able to have a normal life. I am cursed, and I will forever be marked as the cursed one. That's why Doug took me away. Curtis foretold that I was the Cursed One. She saw it, knew I would be the end to Eden. There is nothing that can be done to change that. Doug set me on this path, and I must follow through."

"What do you have to do?"

"Expose them. Betray them. Save my daughter." Her words were spitting out, rabid and scared. Sam realized she was treading the edge; she flipped from sanity to insanity at a moment's notice. And she fought so, so hard to keep it together.

Sam kept her voice calm and smooth. "You aren't betraying them. You're going to set them free."

"Only Curtis sets them free. I am shedding light. It is forbidden. I will burn for my actions." She was crying, and finally, finally, the gun dropped down by her side.

Sam was about to reach for it when a shadow overcame them, blocking the light of the sun, and a deep, angry male voice rang through the trees.

"Yes, you will, Kaylie. You will burn for your sins."

CHAPTER 57

FLETCHER HEARD A HIGH-PITCHED SCREAM. HE STOPPED MOVING, WHISTLED LOW to make Jordan and Thurber stop, too. Listened for it again. Heard nothing.

Then there was a crashing sound—something was coming at them, fast and hard, through the woods. He raised his weapon, pointed it toward the noise. The ROE ran through his mind—*only shoot in self-defense, only shoot in self-defense.* It was damn unnerving standing there facing whatever was coming toward them. His finger slid to the trigger.

Sam burst through the woods, running hard, like something was chasing her.

He eased his finger back, realized he'd been holding his breath. He was grateful he'd been trained not to react until there was an immediate threat. "Sam, over here."

She heard his voice, altered course, leaped over a tree trunk and ran to him. Her eyes were wide and she was out of breath, sweating in the late-afternoon miasma.

"Kaylie's back there, with a huge man. It must be Adrian."

A dog's bark broke through the air. Her head whipped around toward the sound. "Oh, God, that's Thor!"

"You sure?"

Her face was white. "Yes, absolutely. He's attacking. We have to go back there. Xander must be with him. Thor wouldn't attack without direction."

"Negative," Thurber said. "We have to stay here. This is our position."

Sam shot him a look. "You stay. I'm going back."

She turned and began running toward the sound of Thor's bark. Fletcher was right on her heels, and so was Jordan. It only took them a few minutes to get back to where Thor was barking.

The dog had cornered Adrian and Kaylie. Sam was right, the guy was huge. He was holding Kaylie in a firm embrace with a Glock .40 tight against her temple.

Fletcher took a shot at him, but Adrian ducked away, taking shelter behind a tree. The sudden movement got him off balance, and he tripped. Kaylie grunted in pain as they crashed to the ground together.

Fletcher started forward, but Jordan hissed at him, "Don't shoot, damn it. The ROE says self-defense only."

"He's trying to kill her, or us!"

Sam saw Xander standing fifteen feet away, his back against a tree trunk, cradling an arm Sam immediately realized was broken. But he was alive and not bleeding. Sam sent thanks heavenward, then crept to his side. She managed to get there without drawing any attention to herself. "What happened?"

"Son of a bitch got me with a tree branch across the body. Snapped my arm. Then he turned and ran. Thor went after him."

"Let me see." She ran her fingers along his forearm, making him wince and gasp. "It's a clean break, but both the radius and ulna are broken."

"No kidding. Clean enough I can't hold my weapon. I've been tracking him for miles. He parked out on the main road and hiked in. I'd circled around but he must have heard me."

"Relax for me, hon. Let me have your arm. There you go." She poked around a bit more, ignoring his grimace. "It needs to be set temporarily, but we have to get you to a medic. You're going to need some surgical help getting it back together permanently." Sam ripped off the sleeve of his good arm and fashioned a sling, then found a sturdy flat piece of tree branch. They heard Fletcher and Jordan screaming at each other, then the rotors of a helicopter coming closer.

"Hang on, okay? Quit fidgeting. I need to reduce this, and I don't have an X-ray to work with. Talk to me. Where was Adrian headed?"

"There's a tunnel up ahead about a hundred yards. It's the ingress to the compound. I saw where he was going, thought I'd cross over quickly and tell the Feebs. My cell is worthless. I have no signal. I was almost to the opening in the woods when he clocked me."

She lengthened his arm, getting the bones in proper alignment. "Ready?" she said, and before he could tense up, she pulled, hard. He inhaled sharply but didn't cry out. She ran her fingers along the break. Perfect. The bones were back in the right spot.

"Okay, tough guy, that will do it for now." She braced his arm with the wood, tied a couple of strips of his shirtsleeve around his forearm, then slid it in the sling. "Okay?"

He was pale but kissed her, quickly on the mouth. "I'll be fine. But you need to take this."

He handed her the M-4.

She hefted it into her arms. It was heavy, lethal. She didn't like guns, but living with Xander, she knew how to handle them. He'd insisted she be fully competent with every weapon he owned, and they'd spent many an afternoon on the mountain doing target practice.

She cleared it, as he'd taught her, then flicked the selector to Safe. Xander reached over and set it to a three-round burst. "Just in case," he said. She hated it but nodded. She had no intention of pulling the trigger, but as he always told her, if she had the gun in her hands, she needed to be prepared to use it. This wasn't for fun, or target practice. This was very real.

Fletcher and Jordan were shooting again, but the huge man and Kaylie had disappeared. Xander whistled hard and long and Thor stopped barking. Sam heard him running back to them.

Xander reached cross-handed for his pistol, pulled it out of its nylon webbing.

"What are you doing? You can't get in that fight. You're hurt."

"Wanna bet?"

Thor came skidding toward them.

"Thor, *blieb!*" Xander said.

Thor sat at her feet, looking confused.

"Don't you dare," she started, but he was gone, slipping through the trees. Bloody fool. Leaving her with a hot weapon and an even hotter dog? Maybe she would use the gun. On him.

She smelled something odd and realized the HRT were tossing tear gas canisters. They must be very close to the compound. She wasn't going to stand here in the trees, out of harm's way, while everyone she loved was throwing themselves into the fight.

"Thor, *voraus!* Let's go."

He didn't need to be told twice. He wanted to follow his master into battle, as he'd been trained to do. Together they traced Xander's path. They found him five minutes later, standing with Jordan and Fletcher.

"What's happening?" Sam asked.

If Xander was Medusa, Sam would be solid stone beneath his furious gaze. "I told you to stay there, damn it."

Jordan tapped her headset. "Shut up!" She listened for a moment. "HRT stormed the breach. No one responded to the call for negotiations, but someone set fire to one of the outbuildings. We had no recourse, we had to go in. There are casualties. They're looking for Rachel now. It's not looking good. How the hell did that huge guy disappear?"

"There's a tunnel, ingress into the property. We need to get there now," Xander said.

"Give me coordinates, I'll radio the team—"

"No time. Follow me."

"Stand down," Jordan yelled. But Xander was already moving away quickly.

"Damn it," she said.

Fletcher shook his head. "Yeah, he does that. Come on."

Sam started to follow. Fletcher took one look at her, holding Xander's M-4 at the ready, and fought not to smile. "You all set there, G.I. Jane?"

"Don't even think about it, Fletch. Let's go."

The tunnel, as Xander called it, was more of a drainage culvert, only large enough for them to go through one at a time. The land they were on was close to the Potomac, and the culverts were in place in case of flooding. It would effectively drain excess water away from the fields. It was dark and nasty, slimy with mold and moss. A trickle of water ran down the center, a remnant of last night's rain. The damp, cool marshiness seeped through the leather of her boots, and Sam shivered as they crossed through the tunnel.

She was third in line. Xander and Fletcher were in front. Jordan was behind. Thor padded along without difficulty. After five minutes of walking, Xander held up his hand, and Fletcher took the lead position. They were at the entrance to Eden's land. She heard the two men murmuring to each other, deciding who was going to go where. Suddenly Xander was next to her. He motioned for Jordan to come in front. She nodded and passed them.

Xander whispered in Sam's ear. "They're going first. I don't see anyone here. Adrian must have taken Kaylie into the compound. We'll follow when Fletch signals. They don't need us getting hurt. Technically, we aren't allowed to be here."

"You're already hurt," she said, but leaned close to him.

"I'm okay. You did a good job patching me up. Fletch said HRT is combing the site, looking for survivors. Someone set the barn on fire with people inside it."

"Jesus. They are vicious, aren't they?"

"Next time I tell you to park your ass, you—"

Fletcher whistled twice, low and sharp.

Xander cut off the diatribe, gave her a little push. "Go."

She went in front of him. He had a hand on her shoulder, and they broke out of the tunnel into the beginnings of twilight. She had no idea they'd been in the woods so long.

There was smoke drifting toward them. Fletcher was crouched down, weapon raised. Jordan was next to him with a scope to her eye, talking on her comms unit.

Sam heard her say, "Roger that." She stood and signaled for them to come closer.

"HRT reports four guards down, fifteen hurt in the barn fire, some critical, and no one can find Curtis Lott or Rachel Stevens."

"What about Adrian and Kaylie?" Sam asked.

"Negative. No sightings."

"They must be on this side of the compound," Fletcher said. "Maybe there are more tunnels."

"You're right," Sam said. "When Kaylie was telling us about Eden, she said she'd been kept in the dark. She thought it was underground, because the floor was dirt. And they'd take her to another room, also underground, for her 'Reasonings.' We need to be looking for more tunnels."

Jordan hit her comms unit and relayed that information. A minute later, she was given the go-ahead to begin a ground search.

"We're a go." She pulled a map of the compound out of her vest and laid it on the ground. "HRT cleared the farmhouse and the barn and all the surrounding areas. They're starting in the farmhouse basement. We are right here." She pointed to a spot two clicks away from the farmhouse. "Let's fan out and start looking for an entrance."

"Thor can find it," Xander said. He gave the dog a series of commands, and Thor started off, nose to the ground.

"He's a smart dog," Jordan said.

"I trained him from a pup. He's the best."

In just a few minutes Thor uttered a sharp bark. Xander joined him at what looked like a wall of thick, impassable brush. But the air felt cool, cooler than the surrounding forest, and Sam knew they'd found it.

"In there," Xander said quietly.

The brush was thick, but not impenetrable, and they were suddenly in a cool, dark cavern. A natural cave. It wasn't much more open than the culvert. They stopped, let their eyes adjust. Sam realized there was a fluttering motion up ahead, and the darkness wasn't quite as deep. A torch. They were definitely in the right place.

Jordan backed out for a moment, relayed their position then rejoined them. She nodded at Fletcher then took the lead, weapon up, moving carefully toward the flickering light.

CHAPTER 58

ADRIAN WASN'T FEELING WELL. HE'D LOST MORE BLOOD THAN HE'D REALIZED. THE stupid pellets must have nicked an artery in his stomach. He'd knocked the vile, unclean woman on the head, and carrying her weight coupled with the injury made the going slow.

His only thoughts were of home. The quiet solitude of his chamber; the blood of the sacrosancts making him whole. Part of his mind was in revolt, screaming at him to run, to hide, to escape, but he couldn't leave Curtis behind. He was bound to her, bound to Eden, as tightly as if she'd yoked a golden rope around his neck that became a permanent part of his skin, tying him to her slender hands.

When she'd received the copy of Doug's will, the greatest betrayal of all, and understood that the operation was in jeopardy, her first and only thought had been the welfare of her people. She had to keep Eden safe. Adrian had been sent to clean up the mess, to retrieve the lost one's pod and come home.

Now he was torn asunder, bloodied and weak, barely able to stand. But still triumphantly dragging their nemesis into the void. He had no doubt the FBI were behind him. The only thing to do was push on, forward, ever forward, and fulfill Kaylie's destiny. She was to be the Greatest Sacrifice, and Doug had stolen her from their grasp, throwing the universe out of balance.

The sun needs the moon; the tides, the shore. The trinity of Eden had been disturbed for too many years, and now he was going to bring harmony back to their world.

He stumbled into the opening, eyes momentarily blinded by the light of his sun. Curtis was lying on the altar, dressed in flowing white garments, her hair a blaze of red against the cool gray stone.

He dropped the sullied one onto the floor and rushed to his maiden. Wiped the hair back from her face. Realized she was bound, hand and foot, tied onto the sacrificial space. Between her legs was the child Rachel, eyes closed, skin pale as wax, her head resting on Curtis's womb.

"My love, what have they done to you?"

Curtis looked at him, saw deep into his mind, as she always had. "You have done this. Remember this always. I am the light and the resurrection. Never forget me, Adrian. I will be your salvation."

He kissed her, heard her words, momentous whispers, growing louder and stronger, and smelled the fire, coming closer, burning his lips and hands and hair, her fire, her lovely, deathly fire, consuming him.

"You have done well, my love," she whispered, and the men came. They flooded into the chamber from both sides, shouting.

"You take the right side, I've got left, I've got left."

"Lock down that south spot. Kill his egress."

He spread his arms wide and faced them, shielding Curtis with his body.

"He's moving. Stop him."

"Firing, firing, firing."

The bullets seared into Adrian's flesh, a burning pain so intense he screamed in agony, and he knew there would be no recovering from this.

Curtis was watching him with eyes wide, her arms still bound, as he fell to the floor, first on his knees, then onto his side, knocking the breath out of him. Blood seeped from several wounds. Their eyes locked, and he ceased to know the passage of time. He was safe within her mental embrace.

Her sunlight spilled into the chasm, lighting the air on fire, and as his vision began to dim, the glamour fell away from the woman he loved. He saw the truth. Her skin was gray and wrinkled, the elasticity of youth forever gone. The lovely strawberry blond color he'd so loved, the one he'd sought to recreate over and over, from the first girl he took, little Kaylie Rousch, to the last, Rachel Stevens; the color that made the little girls look like the daughters he and Curtis would have had, was dulled to a buttery patina, heavily laced with gray. Her lips drew down toward her chin, not in pain, but in age.

She was old and wrinkled and no longer the carefree, brave woman who had kissed him after watching him try to kill a girl and forgiven him afterward. But she was and always would be beautiful to him. She gave him his soul, his freedom, kept him from becoming a raving lunatic. Gave him boundaries, and cared for him. Gave him a home and love and guidance. She'd led them to where they would be. Shared her beliefs, the one true way. Her death would be the harbinger of the apocalypse, which was the reason they needed to keep her alive, through the sacrosancts.

The light began to fade, he couldn't see her face clearly. An FBI agent, the big dark-haired one who'd shot him, lifted the child from her very womb and cradled her in his arms. Another tended to Curtis, unbound her hands and feet, helped her to a seated position then to stand. She looked toward the door, turned away from him and did not look back. As she walked away, each step took a piece of his heart with her.

He saw Lauren then, his blue-eyed girl. Her inner sun glowed, a fire that could never be dampened, and she blessed him with the nod of her head, and her lips formed a single word. *Father.*

No matter what happened to them, their daughter would live on.

The flash of prescience gone, another man came to him, the detective. He kicked the gun from his hands, knelt and pressed his fingers into Adrian's neck.

"Sam, come here, hurry."

Then she was touching him, pressing on his chest hard, over and over, her lips against his, her sweet breath pushing air into him, air his body would not accept.

His last caress. He used her air, spoke the words he needed to be forever shriven.

"I did not kill Doug. He was my friend. My only true friend."

Eyes staring, Adrian's head slumped to the side. The pain disappeared, blackness enveloped him and despite the woman's frantic attempts, his chest ceased to rise again.

CHAPTER 59

XANDER TOUCHED SAM'S SHOULDER WITH HIS GOOD HAND. "HE'S GONE," HE SAID.

She heard Jordan mutter, "Good riddance." But she wanted to cry. Feeling a life slip away under your own hands, watching that light dim, made her ache with bitter sorrow, even if the soul she'd failed to save was black with evil.

She stood, wiped her lips with the back of a bloody hand, wondered how long she'd been working on him. She should have left him to die in the dirt, but some part of her had been drawn to try to save him, even if it was simply for other people to see justice.

"Where's Rachel?" she asked.

"Jordan's people have her. She's okay."

"Thank God." She turned and saw the woman then, standing between Fletcher and Baldwin, felt a coolness slip over her.

Curtis Lott was in her early sixties, tall and slim, with the deepest strawberry blond hair Sam had ever seen. Her eyes were like the sky, deep blue and unfathomable. She watched Sam with her head slightly cocked to the side.

"Thank you." Her voice was soft, gentle. "You have saved us all."

Sam knew she was speaking to the FBI agents, but the woman's voice seemed to echo in her mind, as though she was speaking directly to Sam.

Baldwin slapped handcuffs on the woman's wrists. She didn't fight him, just stood there serenely, as if she had all the time in the world.

A young woman appeared in the mouth of the cave.

"Mother!"

She started to run to Curtis and Sam saw the resemblance between them. They had the same eyes, though the girl's were blue, not green; the same tilt of the head. Their hair was different, too. The girl's was a light blond. Sam glanced down at the dead man at her feet. Just like his.

Jordan caught the girl and whirled her around, toward the cavern wall, her forearm in the girl's back so she wasn't a threat.

"It is well, my child," Curtis Lott said. "Do not fight them, Lauren. These are the brave souls who have saved us."

She stopped fighting, and Jordan released her. Lauren's face was streaked with tears, but she was still beautiful, delicate in the ways her mother had aged away from. She nodded to each of them in turn, her eyes touching them in benediction, her white robes making her look like an angel.

"Thank God for you. You have removed the beast from this earth. Adrian has been terrorizing us for years. He moved us around, kept us locked in dungeons and basements. He kept Mother and me prisoner. We've been locked away for so long. The things he did to us—" She broke off, went to her mother's side, put her arm around her waist.

Curtis leaned her head on her daughter's shoulder. She addressed the wall of FBI agents still on alert, still holding their weapons up. "Is the girl still alive? She told me her name was Rachel."

Baldwin looked skeptical. "Yes, she is. So is Kaylie Rousch."

Sam looked immediately for Kaylie, realized one of the men must have taken her out of the cave.

Curtis smiled beatifically. "Kaylie is alive? She made it out? He told us she was dead. That he found her body rotting in the woods, along with Doug. Oh, we must give thanks. Lauren, will you lead us?" They both bowed their heads, but Baldwin interrupted.

"Now isn't the time. You're under arrest, Ms. Lott. You're going to be transported to FBI headquarters, where you will be interrogated, and then charged."

She nodded and smiled, spoke as if he'd complimented her cooking instead of signed her death warrant. "I understand. There is much we need to discuss. We will have time to thank the great Mother later. She knows all our thoughts."

Curtis stumbled a little bit as Baldwin led her from the cavern as if her legs had been numbed from the bounds. Sam could have sworn she saw Curtis nod at her daughter. Lauren stayed back a few feet, following slowly.

Sam turned to Xander. "I'm confused. What just happened? Why didn't they arrest Lauren, too?"

"While you were working on Adrian, Curtis Lott told Baldwin and Jordan that she and Lauren have essentially been held hostage for years. There are a lot of questions to be answered."

"Do you believe her? It contradicts everything Kaylie told us."

He watched them disappear into the darkness, adjusted his arm in the sling. "No, I don't. But she might have a shot at convincing a jury." He pulled her to him with his good arm. "It's over, Sam. It's over."

They emerged from the cave to see the flames licking at the remains of the farmhouse. There was a group trying to extinguish the fire. Others were running a hose from the well, pumping water onto the surrounding trees so they wouldn't catch and light the entire forest.

Fletcher joined them, and together they watched the wall of flames.

Thor pressed against her legs, cautious of the fire. It smelled much different than the one in their fireplace at home, or Xander's fire pit; he knew it wasn't safe.

"Where's Rachel? And what happened to Kaylie?" Sam asked. "Do they have her in custody?"

"Rachel's with the EMTs. She's been drugged, probably from the get-go, so she's not going to be a good witness. She's in and out of it, but she's going to be okay. Nothing appears to have happened to her, nothing physical at least. We'll have to wait for the drugs to wear off to find out the whole truth. Kaylie's being transported, too. She took a pretty hard knock to the head when Adrian hit her. She's got a bad concussion. But, Sam, I have good news. We found the other girls. They're all alive. All five of them," Fletcher said.

A huge breath of relief left her. "Thank God. Who set the fire?"

"You know how those flash bangs are. They catch things on fire. Whoever was in the farmhouse and the barn was shooting the hell out of the HRT forward advance. They had to put a stop to it. They lobbed a few in, but whatever was in there caught, and whoosh, the whole thing went up."

"Where are the casualties?"

"Being evacuated. Only two women were in dire straits. The rest were rounded up and are being treated. The four guards are being transported to the morgue once the scene has been secured."

"So we have witnesses. Good. Is Jordan okay?"

They looked over to see Jordan gesticulating wildly as she argued with Thurber about something. "Yeah, she's good. She's a hell of a shot. She took Adrian right in the neck, dropped him.

I think this is probably the first time she's fired her weapon on a scene. She'll be okay."

Baldwin joined them.

"What the hell just happened down there?" Sam asked. "Curtis Lott was claiming she was the victim, not the perpetrator?"

"That's what she's saying. And that's what the rest of her flock are saying, too. They're acting like they haven't seen her in years."

There was a knot of people about a hundred yards away. Sam could just make out flowing white robes as Curtis was led to a car, arms behind her back, head held high.

"Are they brainwashed? Or did Adrian really run this place, after all?"

Baldwin had been running his hands through his hair. It was sticking up in all directions. "Honestly, I don't care. We found Rachel Stevens, and she's in one piece. We found the other missing girls. The rest is going to take a while to sort through." He smiled. "You did wonderfully, Sam. You, too, Xander. Though I need your weapon."

Xander handed it over. "I shot four center mass. You'll get that back to me?"

"Assuming it all matches up, yes, but it might be a while. There's so much brass down there it's going to take ages to sort. For right now, Sam, let's get you and Xander out of here. We'll take it from here. Go get Xander fixed up. I'll touch base with you tomorrow. We're going to need full, official statements. But good job, both of you."

He hugged Sam, shook Xander's good hand, and Fletcher's, then strode back into the fray, shouting orders.

"I'll take you out," Fletcher said. "It's a straight shot up the drive. Jordan said there were a bunch of ambulances waiting up there."

"I am not going anywhere in an ambulance," Xander said.

He was smeared in smoke and dirt and blood. Sam knew she must be a sight, too.

"At least let them look you over. You are going to need a decent orthopedic surgeon for that break," Sam said.

"What, you think some EMTs are better docs than you? It's fine. I can feel it knitting already."

But she knew she'd won, and he wouldn't make too much of a fuss. He looked as though he hurt, and they could help with that.

They started the walk up the long drive. People in FBI jackets were still pouring in to help with the wounded and put out the fire.

Sam had a moment of sheer exhaustion. Her feet dragged like they were encased in mud. She didn't know if she could walk all the way back. She just wanted to sink down into the ground and sleep.

Xander noticed, put his good arm around her waist. The M-4 bumped her in the back. She hadn't shot a single bullet, and was very thankful she hadn't been forced into firing at Adrian. Xander and Baldwin and Fletcher and Jordan had taken care of it for her.

She leaned her head on Xander's shoulder, grateful for the support. He gave her a little kiss on the forehead.

Fletcher turned and put his hands on his hips. "What are you guys doing? We don't have time for a make-out session."

Thor began to growl, and the forest suddenly came alive.

Fletcher pivoted and raised his weapon, shouting in surprise, and Thor leaped at him. His teeth sank into Fletcher's sleeve and he went down under one hundred pounds of dog. Xander pushed Sam to the ground, whipped the M-4 over his good shoulder and got his finger on the trigger. Both he and Fletcher returned fire. A figure in white fell to the ground from a spot in the trees, blond hair sailing behind her, and the shooting stopped as suddenly as it had begun.

It was Lauren. Lauren had somehow evaded the FBI agents and fired at them.

Sam crawled onto her knees, saw blood.

But it wasn't coming from Xander. It was Fletcher.

He was staring down at his chest, his mouth open in shock. He was on his back, Thor on top of him, teeth still latched onto Fletcher's sleeve.

Xander called Thor, but he didn't move.

Sam scrambled over to Fletcher. The bullet had entered his neck and exited out the back, but nicked the carotid artery. Blood seeped from the wound at an alarming rate, staining the leaves and dirt with blood.

Xander grabbed Fletcher's radio and starting screaming, "Officer down, Officer down," while Sam put pressure on the wound.

She thought Thor was shot, he was so limp and heavy, but she realized Fletcher had the dog locked in his arm. She moved his hand. "It's okay. I've got you. You can let him go now. You're going to be fine. Fletch, stay with me, come on, that's good, stay with me."

He relaxed his grip on the dog, and Thor stumbled to his feet. His snout had a graze, a small channel of red. Sam realized the trajectory of the bullet, coming down from the trees, would have been a head shot for Fletcher if Thor hadn't knocked him down.

"Braver Hund!" she said, touching his snout. "You're going to be fine. Now let me work." Thor trotted to Xander while Sam assessed the full extent of Fletcher's injury.

"Shit."

Xander leaned over her. "What do you need, what do you need?"

"An operating room," she said. "Sutures, and a thrombin bandage to help stop the bleeding. It's just a nick, but it needs to be sutured immediately."

Fletcher was groaning. She touched him on the shoulder and smiled down at him. "Come on, Fletch, 'tis but a flesh wound. You're going to be fine."

But her eyes didn't look as calm as her voice sounded, and his were rolling in pain. He tried to talk, but she shook her head. "Shh. It's okay. I'm going to fix you right up. Might hurt a bit. Be ready."

Xander handed her the emergency medic kit he always carried. She ripped it open with her teeth, pulled out what she needed. She swiped Betadine over Fletcher's neck, then used a scalpel to open the wound in his neck so she could ligate the hole in the artery. Fletcher grunted, and tried to roll away from the pain. "Hold him down," she shouted at Xander, who moved to the other side of Fletcher's head and put his knees on Fletcher's opposite shoulder.

There were people coming toward them, shouting, and she heard the rotors of the Little Bird drawing closer, but she ignored it all and swept the thin sutures through and in and out until the blood stopped pulsing from his neck. She tied it off, slapped the thrombin field dressing on.

Fletcher had gone limp beneath her hands. She freaked for a moment, felt for his pulse, realized he'd conveniently passed out. She didn't blame him. She felt a bit like passing out herself.

One of the medics knelt beside her, grilled her about what she'd done, said, "Well done," when he heard. They trundled Fletcher onto a portable stretcher and carried him off to the helicopter, which took off into the air so fast it made her dizzy. Leaves and dirt and branches rained all over them, then settled as the helicopter rose farther into the sky.

Sam sat down hard, legs crossed in front of her. She wiped her hands on her jeans. Xander dropped in the dirt beside her. They were both breathing hard. Thor cuddled between them, licked Xander on the nose.

She buried her hands in his thick fur and laid her head on his flank.

"Braver Hund," she whispered. *"Braver Hund."*

And the shadows grew close, and rain began to fall.

MONDAY

"In faith there is enough light for those who want to believe and enough shadows to blind those who don't."

—Blaise Pascal

"Faith in the Mother is the only true path. Those who do not believe will not be chosen to move on, will not see my love in heaven."

—Curtis Lott

CHAPTER 60

Fairfax County Hospital

LAST MONTH, IT HAD BEEN FLETCHER VISITING XANDER IN THE HOSPITAL. NOW the tables were turned, and Sam and Xander waited outside Fletcher's room. She heard him arguing with the doctor, and it made her heart leap with happiness.

Xander saw her smile, squeezed her hand with his left. His other arm was in a right-angled splint cast that went over his elbow. He'd ended up not needing the plate and screws she expected. Even Thor had gotten a few stitches. He was at the vet, relaxing after a quick knockout to sew his snout back up.

Everyone around her was so battered and bruised, it didn't seem fair that she was unscathed.

The media were having an absolute field day, though they were being supportive of the FBI's actions because Rachel Stevens had been found alive, unharmed, along with five other women of varying ages who had gone missing over the years. Every television station was running footage of the scene in front of the Stevens home, where Rachel had been restored to her parents. The national media were scrambling to get reporters in all the cities to speak to the parents of the girls who'd gone missing over the years.

The faces of those missing girls were being kept from the public while their families were told in private of their recovery. Three couldn't wait to get home, but two had refused to go and insisted on staying with Eden.

The final count was five dead, all men. Four were guards protecting the perimeter, and the fifth was Adrian, down in the cave. Two women were still in critical condition with third- and fourth-degree burns, and thirteen more of various ages and injury had been treated and released.

Lauren had been hurt badly. Fletcher's bullet caught her in the shoulder and she'd landed awkwardly when she fell from the tree, breaking both legs. She was being held in the prison ward of the hospital. She'd shot a police officer, and was going to be in jail for a long time.

Curtis Lott was telling all sorts of tales, magnanimously praising the FBI for their actions in freeing her people from the tyrannical clutches of the madman, Adrian. She claimed she was a peaceful preacher, only doing what was best for her flock.

Eventually a jury would decide her fate. After a night of interviews, she'd made her first appearance in federal court, and a bail hearing had been scheduled in three days' time. Sam truly hoped she'd be kept behind bars. She couldn't imagine this woman walking free, out on bail, but anything could happen.

Curtis Lott was a sudden anticelebrity, the object of scorn and derision and fascination across every news outlet in the country.

What was even more worrisome, while Xander was getting X-rayed and casted the previous night, Sam had gone to visit Kaylie, only to be told she'd checked herself out against doctor's orders and was nowhere to be found.

Sam didn't know if they would ever have all the answers

she wanted. June Davidson was working on tracing every detail surrounding Doug Matcliff's life in Lynchburg, but there were holes in his story, holes so big and deep it seemed unlikely they'd ever get the whole truth.

They needed time to unravel everything, to put all the pieces together, to have it all make sense. She knew one thing—she was going to be on her guard until Kaylie resurfaced.

The doctor huffed out of the room, followed by Fletcher, wearing clean clothes. She wondered for a minute how, then saw Jordan bringing up the rear, a hospital bag in her hand.

She saw Sam and waved. "Talk to him. He refuses to stay, refuses a wheelchair. Maybe he'll listen to you."

Fletcher turned and saw Sam and Xander sitting in the chairs outside his room. He went to Sam, pulled her to her feet and kissed her on the lips. "Thank you."

"For what?"

"You saved my life." He slapped Xander on his good shoulder. "I'd hug you, too, if it wouldn't hurt us both. Where's Thor? I need to kiss that dog, too."

"Jordan's right, Fletch. You're clearly out of your mind. You need to stay," Sam said. But she was grinning. He was okay. She'd saved him.

"We're not done. This case isn't finished. We need to get the rest wrapped before things fall apart. Let's roll."

He took two steps and his legs buckled. He started to go down. Sam and Jordan caught him, got him into the chair Sam had been sitting in. He was pale but began to laugh.

Sam touched the bandage on his neck. It was much bigger than her own. "Slow down there, cowboy."

"Okay, maybe I need that wheelchair, after all."

Jordan shook her head and went to get the nurse.

"You should stay another day, Fletch. Maybe I didn't stitch you up tight enough. Your blood pressure could drop. You could throw a clot. It's better for you to stay in bed, rest."

"You did it all right and you know it. I trust you more than these yahoos. Nurse showed up in the middle of the night, woke me up and said it was time for my enema. She had the wrong freaking room. I just want out."

"Okay. We'll get you out. What did you mean, the case isn't finished?"

"June Davidson called me. He hasn't called you yet?"

Sam shook her head.

"You can stop fretting about why Doug Matcliff contacted you. It was Rolph Benedict. He sent the letter. He was under instructions to put the game into play if Doug ended up dead. I don't think he knew he would be a target, as well."

"Fletch, you aren't talking sense. Slow down, breathe and explain."

"All right. Davidson got into Benedict's computer. Mac Picker wasn't lying. He didn't have Savage's, or Matcliff's, will on the firm's computers."

"So Doug Matcliff didn't make a will?" Sam asked.

"He did, but Benedict did it for him. Privately. According to Benedict's notes, Matcliff was sick. Leukemia. He didn't have long, and he must have decided it was time to set things right."

"So who killed him?"

"It must have been Adrian. There was a note in Matcliff's file. It said, 'I'm coming for you. Don't make me kill you. Do the right thing.'"

Sam shook her head. "Adrian whispered something to me as he died. He said he didn't kill Doug."

"I don't know what to believe. We'll have to keep on it, try to solve the case."

"But Doug knew he was going to be killed. He must have assumed Adrian was coming for him."

"Someone certainly was."

"Did Benedict's notes say why he picked me, Fletch? Why not just go to the police, or the FBI?"

"Davidson said there was a copy of the article *Washingtonian* did after the subway murders in Benedict's files. Your name was featured prominently. He admired and trusted you."

"He didn't even know me," she said.

But Xander nodded. "He knew your character. Sometimes that's all a man needs to make a judgment. And look. You did the right thing by Matcliff, like he knew you would."

Jordan came back with the wheelchair, and a harried brunette nurse.

"You!" Fletcher said in mock horror.

The nurse blushed. "I said I was sorry."

They all laughed, and followed Fletcher and the nurse out into the pickup area. They got him situated in the front seat of Jordan's car.

"I'm taking you home," Jordan said.

Fletcher shook his head, wincing a little as his bandages pulled. "I'm hungry. They haven't fed me anything but Jell-O. Sam, Xander, meet us at the Hawk 'n' Dove. I want a burger."

"I want a nap," Jordan said. "And I think you should have one, too."

He smiled at her. "Food first. We need to decide the best way to take Mac Picker's law firm down for good."

Sam followed Jordan out of the hospital grounds, breathing a sigh of relief.

Xander put his good hand on her leg. "You okay?"

Sam picked up her phone, which she'd left in the car to charge. "I want to talk to Davidson myself."

Davidson answered on the first ring.

"Dr. Owens. Good to hear from you. I left you a message earlier. Sorry if I was cryptic."

"I didn't get the message, June, I'm sorry. What was it?"

"Did Fletcher tell you about what I found on Benedict's computer?"

"Yes. He said Benedict targeted me directly because of the *Washingtonian* article."

"Yes, that's right. We've been combing his house, his computer, his accounts. We've found a letter in Benedict's things, addressed to you, marked private. He mailed it to himself from D.C. the night you met. Do you want me to send it to you?"

"Read it to me, would you?"

"Sure."

She put the phone on speaker so Xander could hear, as well.

"Dear Dr. Owens,

If you're reading this letter, I certainly hope you'll forgive me. And if you have no idea what I'm about, allow me to explain. There is an illicit adoption ring being run out of the law offices where I work. All the partners are involved, and the Hoyles, as well. They house the children when they arrive in Lynchburg. When I was diagnosed with Parkinson's I knew it was time to leave trial law. I signed on as partner with Mac Picker, an old friend. One of the aspects of the firm was private adoptions. After the horrors I've seen, I was pleased to work on something loving, and happy.

The Stevenses were my first adoption. There were many more since, all of which I've documented at great length in my private files. I can't tell you exactly when I became suspicious of the vast number of adoptions, but it was a few years after I joined the firm. I eventually began asking questions, and when no good answers were forthcoming, I did some digging myself.

Before I could figure it all out, Doug Matcliff came to me. He knew I was a partner in the firm. He also knew I was bound by attorney-client privilege not to share his story.

I must, in good conscience, break my vows and do just that.

Matcliff claimed he was dying, and wanted to come clean about his role in the adoption scheme. He wanted it to end, but didn't know how. I don't know if I believe he was sick. I do believe he was a man haunted, who was making some very serious decisions about his future.

And then he was dead, and I grew concerned for my own well-being.

I am writing this down in case something happens to me before I have a chance to set things right for Douglas, and with the firm. I hope it is enough to bring an end to the atrocities we've committed. We are both guilty. I hope, with this letter, we can at last be shriven.

Yours,

Rolph Benedict, Esquire"

Davidson stopped talking. Sam went silent for a moment. "Wow."

"Exactly. There's a lot of information here in his files, but I don't know whether it's going to hold up in court. We'll try. I'm having the State's Attorney General open an investigation to see if what he says is true. If there's enough evidence, we'll take it to the grand jury, get Mac Picker, his partners, Stacey Thompson and Tony Green, and everyone else involved indicted."

"It's true. And you may have to fight off the feds for jurisdiction."

"I'm aware. Right now all we have is Benedict's word. We're going to need proof. Lots and lots of proof."

"I hear you. I'll get back to you, June. How's Ellie Scarron?"

"She's going to make it, thanks to you."

"Good to hear. Thank you, June. We'll be in touch."

She hung up, looked at Xander.

"At least now we know," he said.

"Yes," she said. "Now we know. He's right, we need proof. The word of a dead man who clearly was compromised by his disease will get them in the door, but Mac Picker's smart. He won't have this stuff lying around the office. We need another play. We need someone to talk."

"I doubt Curtis Lott and Lauren will be willing to provide it. They've already said all they have to say until their trials."

She smiled at him. "I think I have a better idea."

CHAPTER 61

Lynchburg, Virginia

FLETCHER DROVE SAM TO THE LYNCHBURG LAW OFFICES OF BENEDICT, PICKER, Green and Thompson, a look of concern etched on his face.

"You think I'm crazy for doing this, don't you?"

"Yep. It could backfire. They know you've been hanging out with the cops. They aren't stupid. On the contrary, these people are so incredibly smart, they'll make you immediately if you don't handle this perfectly. If they see even a hint that you're lying, they'll kill you. You need to be convincing. More than convincing."

"I understand your concern. I really do. But, Fletcher, you have to trust me. I have a lot of experience being this particular woman. Firsthand knowledge. I spent two years being her. People looked at me like I was addled in the brain because of what happened. Who knows, maybe they were right to think I was screwed up."

"You *were* screwed up."

She shot him a glance.

"Sorry. And I'm sorry for this, too. I gotta ask, sunshine, and don't take this the wrong way, but three days ago you were shaking like a leaf on the floor of Matcliff's cabin, rattled to the core because some stranger had singled you out. Are you absolutely sure you can do this?"

Sam was quiet for a minute. She allowed herself a moment to think back to the episode at the cabin. It seemed as if more than three days had passed. It felt like a lifetime.

Something had changed in her. The pervasive panic was gone. She didn't feel it anymore, lurking around the edges of her mind like a stalking lion, ready to clamp its jaws around her thin, delicate leg, twist her down to the earth and rip out her throat.

She'd spent two years in a fog, barely able to function, to breathe, to think of her family without shutting down, forcing her hands under piping-hot water in punishment. Suddenly the need to punish herself was gone, and its absence was extraordinary.

She touched them then in her mind—Simon, his geeky glasses and floppy hair and crooked grin, the man she'd loved since they were teenagers; Madeline and Matthew, twins who'd shared her womb; the faceless little stranger taken from her by force. Four reasons for living, four senseless deaths.

She waited for the urge to overtake her, but it didn't.

This must be what they meant when they talked about acceptance. And hope.

She took a deep breath. "You want to know the worst part of losing Simon and the kids? Aside from their permanent absence, I mean? The pity. People pitied me. And damn it, I didn't want that. I didn't want their pity, their shoulders to cry on, their casseroles and whispers. I lost my world, and they just looked at me like I was the girl in the after-school special, incapable and sad and not myself. I didn't become a different person, but everyone treated me differently. This is one of the big reasons I moved to D.C. You, and Xander, and Nocek—you don't pity me. You understand what I've been through without making me feel bad about it. And I love all of you for it. But I am strong and capable and sick to death of these shackles. I refuse to feel guilty anymore for being happy. I'm going to go by the beat of my own drummer, and to hell with what people think."

The voice in her head stood up and took a bow.

Fletcher's face broke into a huge grin, making the bandage on his neck shift. "Well said, sister." He held up a hand and high-fived her, making her laugh.

"You seem awfully happy, my friend."

"That's because as of this morning I've officially been promoted. Improves my outlook on life."

"To lieutenant? Congratulations. But I thought you wanted out?"

"I did. I don't know what possessed me to say yes, but I did, and so it's happening."

"What's Jordan think?"

"She's really happy for me."

"I'm happy for you, too, Fletch." She put her hand on his arm, hoped he understood she was talking about more than his promotion. "Let's get this over with."

Fletcher spoke into his comms unit, checked off everyone listening. They were all set. He raised an eyebrow. "You ready?"

Sam adjusted the small wireless microphone they'd taped between her breasts, making sure there was no way anyone would suspect it was there, then gave him a sly smile. "Don't worry. I was the lead in every school play we had. I've got this."

Mac Picker ushered her into his office with a look of sheer confusion. She liked that he was off-balance. It had been a perplexing few days for him, certainly, but Sam hoped this little charade would be the key to getting the proof they needed to take Curtis Lott and Mac Picker down for good.

Picker offered her coffee, which she accepted. Having a cup, a prop, would give her hands something to do so they wouldn't shake.

As cocky as she'd been in the car with Fletcher, she was feeling a few nerves now. This was it, this was their chance, and she couldn't afford to blow it.

Coffee doctored, she took a sip, then set it in its fine bone china saucer. Picker took the hint.

"What can I do for you, Dr. Owens?"

She smiled, tremulous. "For starters, can you call me Sam? I'm not here in an official capacity. Actually no one knows I'm here, and I'd like to keep it that way."

"Oh?"

"Yes. You see…well, this is going to sound crazy, but I was hoping you could help me."

Picker's face softened a touch, and he gave her an avuncular smile. "Help you how, my dear?"

She cast her eyes downward. *Careful, girl, careful.* "This is very hard for me. I have a request of a very personal nature." She looked up, knowing there were tears shining in her eyes. "Very personal. I'd like to state up front this conversation is so far off the record, I will deny ever having it if it comes to light."

Now she had his attention. He leaned forward in his old leather chair, the springs creaking under his weight. "If you retain me as your lawyer, everything we discuss here will remain under attorney-client privilege. Would you like to take that step?"

She nodded. "I think that's a very good idea. It would protect you. Especially considering what I'm about to ask."

"I see. All right, then. Let me just grab an attorney-client privilege form. Once you sign it we can talk freely. It will protect both you and me in the event there are questions later about our conversation."

He walked to his credenza and thumbed through a file, pulling out a single sheet of paper and bringing it to her. He was careful not to touch her as he handed her the paper. She glanced at it quickly—it wouldn't do to look too interested in what it said—then signed her name. He signed, as well, then slid the form to the corner of his desk and sat expectantly in his chair.

"What can I do for you, Sam?"

She blurted out the words. "I want to have a baby."

He didn't react, didn't move.

"I'm sorry. That didn't come out right." She took a deep breath. "I'm unable to have children anymore. I was married, and had twins, and was pregnant again when..." This time she did swallow hard, then stood and pulled the front of her shirt up. The scar was four inches long, sliced diagonally across her stomach below her belly button. She knew it was dramatic, the edges silver, the twist at the end leaving absolutely no question as to the nature of the wound.

"I was held captive by a deranged man, and he made sure I lost my baby. And that I wouldn't ever be able to have one again."

Picker sucked in a breath. "Dear God in heaven. I am so sorry."

There was no reason for him to know that the stabbing hadn't caused the miscarriage; it was the stress of being held against her will, the stress of being captured and nearly eviscerated by a madman. That according to her doctor, there was no reason why she couldn't conceive again, should she so choose.

"Since I can't have a child of my own, I'd like to look into adoption. With all the things that have gone on since Rolph Benedict's murder, I'll understand if you say no. But I overheard one of the detectives on the case when he was talking about you facilitating private adoptions. I certainly don't want to go through an agency or anything like that. And when I say private, I mean private. I don't want anyone to know the child is for me, and I want the mother to sign away her rights to any sort of future contact." She gave him a meaningful look. "I don't intend for my child to know I am not his or her mother."

He actually looked relieved. "Oh, Sam, I am sorry. We don't engage in private adoptions anymore. There are so many legal issues these days with adoptees searching out their biological parents, the lawsuits were becoming more trouble than they were worth."

She shook her head.

"Forgive me for being forward, Mr. Picker. And if you're not interested, of course, you can tell me right now, and I'll leave and you won't hear from me again. But when I say private, I mean I want this adoption totally off the books. Your name, and your firm's, wouldn't be anywhere near it. It would just be an exchange of funds, cash, from me to you. You get paid, and I get the child I so long for. Everyone's happy."

"Don't you have a husband? A boyfriend? Wouldn't he like to know about this?"

"This is only for me, Mr. Picker. No one else. The way I see it, it's simply no one's business. Hypothetically speaking, how much are we talking here? How much would a baby cost me? Fifty thousand dollars? A hundred thousand? I have plenty of funds, Mr. Picker. Mac. Can I call you Mac?"

She could have sworn his face lit up when she mentioned funds, but he was a careful old codger; he wasn't biting. Not out loud, at least.

"Sam. I understand your predicament, I surely do. Who could blame you, after losing your own babies? Of course you'd want one of your own. There are many firms who do this sort of thing. I can put you in touch with a couple, very reputable, very professional about all this. I'm afraid this simply isn't our bailiwick at Picker, Green and Thompson."

The missing "Benedict" hung between them like a shiny ringing gong. The firm certainly hadn't wasted any time getting Rolph's name off the masthead.

"Never? You can't do a favor for a friend?"

"I'm sorry. No."

She cocked her head to one side. "Are we negotiating?"

He shook his head, the avuncular and sympathetic smile gone. "There's nothing to negotiate. I don't do this sort of thing. It's not proper. I'm very sorry, Dr. Owens. Sam. I'm not the right lawyer for you, and we're not the right firm for you."

"If we could just talk a bit more about this, Mr. Picker."

His voice was cold and distant. "I'm afraid I have another meeting. I think it's time for you to leave now."

Damn it. She'd lost him. Something she'd said must have tipped him off.

He stood, and bent over his desk, pulling a yellow Post-it note from behind the phone. "Good day to you, ma'am. I hope your drive back to D.C. is pleasant."

He wrote something on the Post-it, then folded it and reached a hand out to shake. She stood, as well, and accepted his hand.

He pressed the paper into her palm, then dropped his hand as if burned. He grinned at her then, and showed her to the door.

She couldn't wait to get out of the office. She stepped down the wide graceful stairs to the sidewalk, wiped the sweat from her brow. The mike was sticking to her skin in a most unpleasant way. He must have suspected he was being taped, was very careful not to say anything that could implicate him or the firm. But he was greedy. She'd seen it in his eyes. He wanted the cash. Maybe he was going to use it to sneak away; maybe he was playing her. Who knew? They'd have to be very careful going forward.

She waited until she heard the door close behind her to check the note he'd given her. She unfolded the small square of yellow paper and felt her heart leap.

$250k, cash, today by 5. Drop at Hoyle's.

They had him.

TUESDAY

"Keep your face always toward the sunshine—and shadows will fall behind you."

—Walt Whitman

"Freedom is at hand, sayeth the Mother. Accept this dying breath as your final benediction and know, at last, you are free."

—Curtis Lott

CHAPTER 62

Georgetown University School of Medicine
Washington, D.C.

THE FIRST MEETING OF SAM'S FORENSIC GROSS ANATOMY CLASS WAS OVER. Unlike other med school anatomy classes, this program was in place to study those who'd died violent deaths. It was specifically designed for doctors who wanted to be forensic pathologists. Who wanted to use science to right wrongs.

The room smelled faintly of formaldehyde and the meat of open bodies, the sweat of anxiety and denatured alcohol. She dismissed the students with a smile. They'd done so well. Not a fainter in the group. She remembered her first gross anatomy class, her knees knocking in fear, the surreal experience of the bodies lying inert on the tables, the unshakable feeling they might all rise from their metal graves and march out of the room to a deeper unknown.

The students left, chattering in excitement, and she packed her own things, happy to know she'd done a good job.

The craziness of the weekend would never truly fade away, but she was determined to let it go. She'd done the best she could, and that was all anyone could ever ask of her.

She ran back to her office to drop off her things, and was surprised to find her T.A., Stephanie, today with deep red streaks in her black hair in honor of the first day of bloodletting, in deep conversation with John Baldwin.

Sam gave Baldwin a quick hug, watched Stephanie wilt. Then the girl smiled at her boss and walked out, leaving them alone.

"I thought you went back to Nashville."

"I've got a flight in a couple of hours. I wanted to say goodbye properly. Can I buy you a quick lunch?"

"Sure."

They walked to the Tombs, a Georgetown favorite, which was already thrumming with life at noon, the students who didn't have afternoon classes tilting their pint glasses in happy abandon. Sam ordered a Lagavulin and fried calamari. Baldwin got Guinness and a bowl of chili.

"So. Have you decided you miss this life enough to join us?" he asked.

The server returned with their drinks. Sam swirled the amber Scotch around the glass. "I don't miss it," she said.

"You're lying, and we both know it. You should have seen yourself out there in the woods. The whole place was burning down and you're scheming, then saving lives at the drop of a hat. The most experienced medics would have had a hard time with Fletcher's injury. You did it without a thought."

"I was thinking, Baldwin, trust me." *More than you want to know.*

"I know you think you want to teach, be quiet, stay out of the fray, but it's in your blood, Sam. Just like it's in mine, in Xander's and Fletcher's. In all of us. We'll make it work for you, however you need."

"You aren't going to give this up, are you?"

He grinned at her. "Nope."

She watched his deep green eyes, and nodded. Raised her Scotch, tapped his pint glass. Gave him a smile. "All right. I'm in."

Xander and Thor were waiting for her at home, sitting out by the pool. Xander couldn't get in the water all the way to swim, but could dangle his legs on the edge. It would be a few weeks until he could get back into his normal groove, and she knew it was already driving him mad.

Thor barked once in hello. The cut on his nose was healing well. The vet had done a wonderful job.

She kicked off her shoes and sat next to Xander. "Baldwin took me to lunch."

"Did you give him an answer?"

She ran her hand in the water, watching the ripples. Like her life, everything she did rippled out and affected the people around her. "I said yes."

He hugged her with his good arm. "I figured so."

"Are you sure you're cool with this? It's going to mean changes."

"Hon, your drive, your passion, your commitment to helping others is one of the reasons I fell in love with you. Hell, you got me down off my mountain and inserted back into the real world. I wanted my life to start again because of you. I want you all for myself, but I know that's not going to happen. You're going to be great."

"I'll continue teaching. That would be my primary job. D.C. would be home base. Baldwin said I could pick the cases, and I'd only be called in for special situations."

"This is good. You can still teach, still drive me mad, still do whatever you want."

He ruffled her hair off the back of her neck. Air flowed over her shoulder blades, cooling her. She was ready for summer to end. For the next phase of her life to begin. She kissed his cheek. “Thank you for understanding.”

“I do. More than you know. Now. While we’re discussing big, life-changing events, I have something else I’d like to run by you.”

She ran her finger along the edge of the ring he’d given her, and smiled at him. “Do you, now?”

EPILOGUE

I SUPPOSE YOU REALIZE THE TRUTH BY NOW. I WAS THE ONE WHO KILLED DOUG.

I know you hate me. I hate myself. I never should have listened to him. Never agreed to his stupid plan, the one he cooked up with that crazy old lawyer.

You're asking yourself how I could do that to the man who saved my life. Who brought me out of the darkest recess of the world into the light. You want to know how I could kill a man I claim to love. And why I would cry for him when I was finished choking the life out of him.

I had no choice. In the end, Doug betrayed me. He'd conceived a plan to end his own life, because of his guilt, or his sickness, or whatever it was. In so doing, he brought every nasty, seedy, horrible moment of mine to light. I had put the past behind me. I had no desire to relive it. Yet now I have. Every wound reopened, every decision rethought.

Now I know he was lying when he told me he had been to the doctor and was riddled with cancer. That he had only weeks to live, and those numbered days would be incredibly painful. He told me that he would die by his own hand were it not the gravest sin, and if I could take that sin from him, he would be forever grateful.

When I refused, he reminded me of the horrible favor he'd done for me all those years ago, the night I'd been ripped apart from childbirth, tossed bleeding and exhausted into the darkness, left with a bottle of water and an empty womb, my blood leaking onto the dirt floor. He'd found me there, and spirited me away. Treated the infection that almost killed me, nursed me back to health, gave me a chance at a better life.

He reminded me he *chose* to do that, to break with Eden, and his life. That he'd compromised everything he believed in, spent all those years hiding me, keeping me safe from Adrian and Curtis. That he'd educated me and loved me like a father, a brother, a lover, and if I loved him at all I would do this for him.

When I still refused, he flew into a fury and attacked me. He said words I still do not comprehend about the night I was given to the Reasoning, the Reasoning that started the life in my womb. That the man Adrian was not the one who'd been there in my blindfolded darkness, but it was Doug, my surrogate father, my best friend and teacher, who'd held me down and raped me for hours. He was full of rage, his eyes wild and fiery, and he put his hand around my neck and forced me to listen to his confession, and in those brief moments of cataclysmic shock, I realized what he said was true.

He knew exactly what touching me in violence would do. The bastard did it on purpose so I'd follow his instructions. Between his threatening touch and his awful, painful truth, I had no choice but to fight him off.

Before I knew what had truly happened, he was dead on the floor, my hands locked in a death grip around his neck. When I came back from the dark place, realized what I'd done, I sobbed, tried to bring him back to life. When it didn't work, and I began to comprehend the enormity of my situation, what

I'd done, I cleaned him, wiped the blood from his face with the dishtowel I'd somehow wrapped around his neck and followed through with the rest of his ridiculous plan to bring these hateful shadows into the light.

I will always be haunted by the knowledge that at the end, when I began to put pressure on his throat, he did not resist me. He wanted his death to be at my hands.

And now I have what some people like to call closure, what he'd always wanted for me. All I ever wanted was to be with my daughter, but I'd never admitted that to him, or even myself. I spent years pretending to be something I was not. Doug kept me at home, dressed me as a boy, educated me himself. When I went out in the world, I kept to myself, made no friends and continued the charade, because I loved him for saving me.

Always on my mind, though, was the child I will never see again.

They are good people, her adoptive parents. Kind. They love her. Though they still don't seem to realize that locked doors are no match for a true mother's love.

I am happy she loves them, and they her. She probably won't remember me when she's grown, or if she does, she'll have a foggy recollection of a strange woman who held her close and whispered *I love you* a thousand times over the course of a starlit night.

Rachel's bedroom is pink and full of soft things. She sleeps like a lightning bolt, arms and legs spread away from her body at odd angles, the sleep of a child well loved, and safe. I spent the dark hours of that night tracing her limbs under the sheet, looking at the tiny similarities between us—she has my nails, longbedded and elegant, and my nose and eyelashes and freckles. She has parts of him, too, the broad forehead and cornflower-blue eyes, and while I should hate him for what he did, I smile to see them.

I have forgiven him. I know now why he did what he did,

and how his actions, though horrible, saved me from a far worse fate. I am grateful his blood flows through her veins and not the filthy, tainted blood of the killer who should have been her father.

That night, watching my daughter sleep, her rosebud mouth puckered as if she just learned to stop sucking her thumb but it hadn't forgotten the motion, I knew exactly what must be done. She is so beautiful. So perfect. So clean. I cannot allow anyone else to be sullied.

I am not clean. I am not good. I am a depraved, broken human being who has no right to live. I want things to be all right, to go back to the way they're supposed to be. If only I had lived in a world where my parents loved me, walked me to the bus stop and met me there when school let out. Parents who made more of an effort to find me when I went missing, and were happy when I was rescued, all these years later.

If wishes were horses, right? Or something like that.

Here is the truth, if you are brave enough to hear it.

There is darkness in the world, a heavy hatred of all that is good and right. You might call it evil, or immorality, or simple a callous disregard for humanity. Some people choose this path through the shadows, their breath hot and frantic on the wind. Their poison spreads, infecting others who also embark on the dark journey.

Curtis is one of these people. Mother to us all, she was bereft of any maternal qualities. She allowed unspeakable things to happen to me. She used me as her personal broodmare. She forced drugs into me and made me listen to her endless ramblings about the mystic cosmos and our place in it. She marked my soul, and my skin, made me her drudge, tortured and humiliated me, then built me up, fed me golden stories and washed my hair and feet like I was a supplicant.

She is a demon, come to earth to punish the wicked.

And because of her, I am so very wicked.

Yet Curtis taught me perseverance, and strength. How to survive, to stay sane in the face of darkness. That the absence of light did not make the person, that only the long wait for a shadow to find you, to cross from the afterlife and attach itself with painful stitches to your soul, makes you whole again. This is the greatest lesson a mother can give to her children. How not to be completely broken by a situation.

Curtis taught me to accept myself, all my faults. To greet my darkness like an old friend rather than an enemy. She saw something in me I'd never known existed in my soul—power. The power to right wrongs, to change things.

My power scared her, made her trap me like an animal, keep me in a cage. She kept me in the darkness until it fed on my blood and gave me back the strength I'd lost.

Adrian was weak compared to me. All he could do was give in to his urges.

Curtis, in all her bizarre, unfathomable glory, taught me how to channel mine. She made me in her own image, yet she was so very wrong.

I am the light, and she is the darkness.

I am the good, and she is the evil.

By blood born, and by blood taken, we move through this life in a fog, briefly touching those around us, imparting wisdom or love, pain or sorrow, or even a mother's gentle kiss.

We are born alone, and we die alone.

I stand in the darkness of Curtis's chamber and watch her sleep. When I move toward her with the blade raised, my breath catches in my throat. I know that I am doing the only thing that is good and right in this world.

Vengeance is mine.

The blade falls.

* * * * *

ACKNOWLEDGMENTS

WHEN SHADOWS FALL wouldn't be in your hands today without the support of the following people:

Scott Miller—who is more than a wonder agent. He is a friend, a confidant and a trusted member of the *familia*. Thanks for always happily handling the drama lama from Nashville.

Stephanie Hoover—who is more than the assistant to agent extraordinaire, and a joy to work with.

Nicole Brebner—who saw what the story could be and helped me find the way home.

Laura Benedict—who is my sanity, my daily dose of reality and a brilliant first reader, and always knows exactly how to fix that f-ing plot hole.

Sherrie Saint—who did a ton of research legwork for this book and believed in it from the very first Starbucks pitch.

Paige Crutcher—who teaches me yoga, and so much more, especially for pointing me in the direction of The Farm.

Catherine Coulter—who helped me cook up the cult idea.

Karen Evans—who helps us both when we get off track.

Jennifer Brooks—who reads, edits, cheers and otherwise makes these books what they are.

Del Tinsley—who is my other mother.

Jeff Abbott—who continually steers me toward the correct path.

Erica Spindler—who taught me the real meaning of gratitude attitude.

Alex Kava—who gives such sage advice.

Deb Carlin—who is always such a joy.

Sandra Thomas—who is the harbinger of the scalpel, and helps Sam come alive in the autopsy suite.

Andy Levy—who read a terrible first draft and told me he loved it, despite its flaws.

Joan Huston—who is my grammar goddess extraordinaire (how's THAT for a promotion?).

Nicole Brebner—who saw what the story could be and helped me find the way home.

Miranda Indrigo—who cheered me on from near and far.

Susan Swinwood—who helped shepherd this baby into being. All the amazing folks at Mira Books—who support the dickens out of me.

Rachel Stevens—who agreed to be murdered (sorry you're not dead, but only dented about the middle bits).

Anna Benjamin—who touches my heart daily.

Blake Leyers—who helps me be all kinds of girly.

Deanna Raybourn—who is my favorite cheerleader and eighty-year-old Englishwoman (cream tea, dear?).

Chuck Beard—who owns East Side Story, an incredible bookseller as well as a dear friend.

My Nashville Literary Libations Peeps—who manage to meet up every fourth Thursday whether I can make it or not (Ha!).

All the awesome booksellers and librarians who get my work into the hands of my readers.

My readers—who listen to me wail on Facebook, share their love (and hate) of the books and always keep me honest.

And finally,

My mom—who really did ask every day if the words were any good, and probably drove me to peaks of insanity making sure they were all wonderful. Thanks for making sure they all count.

My dad—who is a first reader, an extraordinary man and an unflagging cheerleader for all my words, even the ones that suck.

Randy—who deserves more than thanks, more than words on the page, who cooked and cleaned and read this book three times and managed my world while I tried to make a very close deadline. You have the keeping of more than the words, darling—you have my heart.